Clare Morrall

Clare Morrall's first novel, *Astonishing Splashes of Colour*, was published by Tindal Street Press in 2003 and was shortlisted for the Booker Prize. Born in Exeter, she now lives in Birmingham where she works as a music teacher, and has two grown-up children. *Natural Flights of the Human Mind* is her second novel.

'Solid, satisfying and skilfully plotted, with a cast of wholly believable characters. As the tension mounts *Natural Flights* really takes off. At its helm, Morrall comes into her own; steering a shuddering, febrile last chapter into an elegant denouement.'
Zoe Paxton, *The Times*

'Clare Morrall's debut was the surprise contender for 2004's Booker Prize. Its follow-up proves she's no flash in the pan. With quiet control and a deliciously unsentimental wit, she tells the story of two peculiar characters. Their misadventures are accompanied by outside events that move towards an unexpected and oddly touching climax.'
Tina Jackson, *Metro*

'An engaging mystery about solitude, guilt and eccentricity.'
Justine Jordan, *Guardian*

'Morrall delicately balances all the strands of the story, playing on the possibilities, teasing the reader with half-understood knowledge, before bringing them to a moving climax. Poignant without being sentimental, it's also surprisingly funny, and never less than believable . . . a wonderful, warm and worthy follow-up'
Cathy Winston, *Birmingham Post*

'Warm, witty and a testament to the human spirit'
Australian

'Wry and engaging'
Vogue

'Absorbing . . . The humdrum incidentals of the average British experience – supermarket doughnuts, Penguin biscuits, scotch eggs and dahlias – form the ordinary backdrop against which hefty human emotions are played out. They are all the more powerful for their context. She is particularly good at grief.'
Lucy Atkins, *Sunday Times*

Clare Morrall

Natural Flights of the
Human Mind

SCEPTRE

Published in association with Tindal Street Press

Copyright © 2006 by Clare Morrall

First published in Great Britain in 2006 by Hodder and Stoughton
A division of Hodder Headline

Published in association with Tindal Street Press

The right of Clare Morrall to be identified as the Author
of the Work has been asserted by her in accordance with
the Copyright, Designs and Patents Act 1988

A Sceptre paperback

1

A CIP catalogue record for this title is available from the British Library

ISBN 0 340 89651 5

Typeset in Sabon by Hewer Text UK Ltd, Edinburgh
Printed and bound by Mackays of Chatham Ltd, Chatham, Kent

Hodder Headline's policy is to use papers that are natural, renewable
and recyclable products and made from wood grown in sustainable forests.
The logging and manufacturing processes are expected to conform to
the environmental regulations of the country of origin.

Hodder and Stoughton Ltd
A division of Hodder Headline
338 Euston Road
London NW1 3BH

For Emma Hargrave
with thanks

The natural flights of the human mind are not from pleasure to pleasure but from hope to hope.

Samuel Johnson, The Rambler no. 2

Chapter 1

He dreams of skulls. Seventy-eight of them – factors 1, 2, 3, 13 and 78. While the rest of the world conjures up sheep, he counts skulls, hoping that the number is smaller, that someone made a mistake, that the missing ones are really alive somewhere in the world after all. Once or twice, he only manages to reach sixty-eight, but he can't turn away and be satisfied. He has to count again and bring himself to the same degree of culpability as before. Sometimes there are more than seventy-eight and he feels the sweat in his bed, the heat of his fear, and wakes up abruptly.

He knows there are seventy-eight. Why does his mind play tricks on him? Why does he count at all when he knows the answer before he begins?

He lies completely still and waits for the physical manifestations of his fear to ease. If he doesn't move, the heat will go, the sweat will dry and it will be just him, Peter Straker, no skulls, alone in his lighthouse in Devon, living with the shriek of the gulls and the frenetic howl of the wind.

———

Once a week, Straker goes shopping. He starts his day by going down to one of the three keepers' cottages and boiling up a saucepan of water, then washes meticulously. Cleanliness is important to him – it's the last barrier between the uncertainty of his precarious existence and barbarity. He selects a white shirt, a silk tie – pale blue with jagged dark blue patterns down it – and the navy pin-striped suit that he's worn once a week for twenty-four years. He takes it to the dry cleaner's on the first Wednesday of every month. He can't find a matching pair of socks, so he puts on one brown and one green. Then he pulls on his yellow oilskins and boots.

As he walks down the stairs, he passes Suleiman and Magnificent. They usually sit on a windowsill, almost on top of each other, their long Siamese faces turning together to watch him pass. They spend most of their time on this windowsill, dozing comfortably, sitting up every now and again to watch the gulls soaring outside, their ears twitching as they remember their younger glory days, a time when they were more interested in chasing birds than keeping warm.

Straker stops to stroke them and they push their heads towards him. Under my chin, says Suleiman. Top of my head, says Magnificent. They know they have to purr loudly to shut out the seagulls and the sea and the wind. When he stops stroking them and starts to descend, they watch him with a resigned disappointment, but he can't stay there for ever. He has other things to do.

He carries on down, and opens the door to the cliff-head, stopping, as always, to fight for a breath, and calculate the energy required to stay upright. The short blades of grass have surrendered to the constant gales, tugged mercilessly to one side, their shiny blades rippling in the occasional sunshine. He leans in the opposite direction to the wind, not bothering to lock the door behind him. There's nothing of value in the lighthouse, and people don't come out here, miles from human habitation. They do occasionally pause in the middle of coach-trips, which incorporate all the local sights (the cottage where the Beatles once stayed when they were first famous, Beckingham Manor, Hillingham Gardens with a funfair for all the family), but the road runs a mile from here, and there aren't any guided tours round the lighthouse. No souvenir shop, no cream teas. On a fine day, they might get out and walk a bit closer, cameras to their faces, inappropriately using the flash. When it's a tour for pensioners, they often wave like children, but Straker doesn't wave back. He pretends they're not there.

'Why can't you just leave me alone?' The voice of Felicity, eighteen years old. Slightly high-pitched, and vulnerable, the trace of a Black Country accent still there, behind her elocution lessons.

'Because I have to know.'

'Know what?'

'You can't stop him.' Maggie. Older, confident, motherly. She was there at the beginning, a voice without a background. Once she'd arrived, she invaded all my dreams and stayed. 'He does it to all of us.'

'Well, I have to know you. You have to be real.'

Felicity: 'You keep waking me up. I was dreaming about marshmallows. It's all too long ago.'

'Rubbish. Twenty-four years is nothing. You haven't even started.'

'Go away, Maggie. Stop taking over my conversations.'

'I will never go away, Straker. Depend on it.'

'I know.'

Thirty yards from the front door, the cliff ends abruptly and there's a precipice of a hundred feet. Straker likes to stand close to the edge, rocking in the wind, testing his balance, feeling his centre of gravity. He sees it as a daily test. Is he still here? What roots him to one spot? Can the wind catch him out? He waits for the moment, the final battle, but it never comes. He remains hovering above the precipice, never quite certain why he continues to survive. The waves roar through the rocks below, pounding against the cliff, challenging the wind to a contest of sound. Raging, shrieking, howling, buffeting. There's no clear winner, just a meeting of currents below the cliff, thirty-foot-high waves regularly crashing against each other, the spray nearly reaching him. Since he's been here, ten feet of the cliff have fallen. That averages out at half a foot per year. But it doesn't work like that. The closer it gets to the lighthouse, the quicker it goes. The elements will win in the end.

He once met a young man up here who wanted to commit suicide. Most potential suicides go to the next headland where the new lighthouse is automated, so there's no one to watch them, but there hasn't been a very high success rate. It's tricky calculating the energy required to push yourself over the edge. You tend to get blown off-course by the wind, and end up further back than where you started.

This young man collided with Straker as he came out of the door of the lighthouse. The stranger had his head down (gelled black hair parted in the middle) and his arms wrapped tightly round his quilted anorak, which nevertheless ballooned out like a crimson bubble.

He jumped when he saw Straker. 'Get away from me,' he shouted.

Straker stepped back into the doorway, shocked by his presence. Who was he? Where had he come from? Nobody ever walked out here.

But the young man stopped unexpectedly and lifted his head. 'It's no good,' he said. 'I can't go on.'

He didn't go on. He stood against the wind, desperate, his eyes bloodshot and red-rimmed. He looked about fifteen. Straker didn't know what to do, so he said nothing and watched him.

'I loved her. I really, really loved her. She said – university – house – lots of children—'

Straker listened to him, although he lost some of the words in the wind and didn't think he could ask him to repeat anything. He could feel the girlfriend's betrayal, the hopelessness of it all.

4

'She gave it back to me, *Great Expectations* – really, really expensive – hard-backed – lovely smell – What am I supposed to do with it now?'

He produced it from an inside pocket and held it for a while, fingering the cover, unable to turn the pages in the wind.

They stood there together, the wind pulling at their hair, rocking them, changing direction unexpectedly so that they nearly fell over, while they looked at *Great Expectations*. Tears were pouring out of the young man's eyes, but they were swept away before they could run down his cheeks.

I should do something, thought Straker, but he didn't know what. There wasn't a telephone in the lighthouse. The best he could do was leap on to his bicycle and pedal to the village, five miles away. It would all be a bit late.

Suddenly, in a brief lull, the young man leaned back and looked as if he were going to race to the edge. Straker reached out an arm to stop him, but the young man pushed him aside and ran. At the last minute, he veered to one side and threw the book through the air instead, over the side of the cliff. A perfectly judged moment when the wind was at its weakest. He must have been a cricket player. A powerful right arm.

Straker walked to the edge of the cliff to join him and they looked down. The waves were having a good day, colliding and merging, the spray almost reaching the top. There was no sign of *Great Expectations*.

The young man grabbed Straker by the hand. 'Thanks,' he shouted. 'You've been a real help.'

Then he sprinted back along the cliff towards the road.

Straker wondered if he would be allowed to subtract him from the seventy-eight. Seventy-seven. A good number, only four factors, 1, 7, 11 and 77. Much more satisfying.

———

The lighthouse is not functional. In 1970, Trinity House decommissioned it and the keepers left. Their three cottages lie abandoned at its base, the walls crumbling, all traces of the original human habitation blown away into the wind. There's a smaller lighthouse now, built on the next headland, full of switches and control panels, run by electricity and solar power. But what about power cuts, what if the sun fails to appear, the ships' radar breaks down? What then? One day the experts will regret this. They'll search out the old keepers in their retirement homes, and try to lure them back with money. But they will be too old, their knowledge slipping out of their Alzheimer brains.

Straker's lighthouse is little more than a folly, a rocket pointing defiantly at the stars, waiting for take-off, destined for great things, but unfairly abandoned. Part of the flotsam and jetsam stranded on the high-tide mark, in the right place at the wrong time. Straker understands its redundancy. *I and the lighthouse. The lighthouse and me.*

Straker keeps his bicycle in the old lounge of a keeper's cottage. It's dry and he can mend the punctures here, oil the brakes, pump the tyres. He slept in this room, on the bare floor, twenty-four years ago when he first came. There was a bed in another room – 'It's fully furnished,' his father had said, before driving away – but he couldn't make it to the bedroom. He lay there for ten days, shaking with cold, feverish nightmares, pain and fear, only moving to drink water out of the dirty tap in the kitchen. When he finally went out, looked at the lighthouse and ate some of the food his father had left him, the fear wouldn't go away. It was like contemplating a blank cavernous opening that he had to enter, knowing there was no choice. The bridges behind him were smouldering ashes.

Finally, he discovered, the only way for him was into the lighthouse and up. He could find a counterfeit safety there that would hold him together. He watched the sea and the sky from the outside balcony, where the keepers used to clean the light, and taught himself to breathe again. Eventually, he carried furniture up into the service room, below the light. One at a time, a chair, a mattress, a table, very slowly, round the corkscrew steps, thinking of the old keepers bringing up their daily supplies of oil. Every few minutes, the furniture stuck, but he worried away at it, an inch at a time, leaning it over, forcing it two steps up, one step back until he reached the right floor.

Much later, once he'd learned to numb the fear with numbers, he took up an electric fire, then the cooker. He has them arranged neatly in a circle on the floor round the central column on two floors. The cats arrived, one day, unannounced, and he waited for a week, expecting them to melt into the wind as naturally as they had come. When they didn't, he cut a cat-flap into the lighthouse door.

This morning is unusually calm. A May blue sky, a thin mist drifting in muslin swathes above the water. Straker stands for a while on the edge of the precipice and watches the water lapping and curling against the base of the cliff, still active, still destructive, but less wild than usual.

He could cycle all the way to the village, pulling his cart behind him for the shopping. But it's a long way, much of it on an uneven path. On a good day, he prefers to go by a more direct route. He cycles only half a mile along the headland. Then, as the land becomes lower and more sheltered from the wind, he stops and gets off his bicycle. He leaves it chained to a rusty iron railing that was put up years ago to prevent people falling over the side of the cliff. Most of it has been wrenched away by the wind and the storms, twisted into sad, abandoned shapes, overwhelmed by creeping ivy, but it's strong enough to secure a chain. He then climbs down the side of the cliff, making steps from the roots of trees that jut out of the crumbling sandstone.

His dinghy is anchored as far back into the cliffs as possible, and only floats in the highest tides. Today he crunches through the shingle, over the dried seaweed, which pops and crackles in protest, avoiding the patches of tar that regularly appear. Nobody comes here. It's a tiny secluded beach on a bay that is nearly always calm, sheltered from the weather by two headlands.

Straker drags the dinghy across the shingle, through the low-tide mud and into the sea. The boat rocks gently, water gurgling and slapping against its sides, and he steadies it with his hands before climbing in. He sits down, balances himself and puts the oars in the rowlocks. It's only a short row on a good day. He's fit and strong, and runs up and down the lighthouse steps ten times every morning. He's fifty-three, and as strong now as he was at eighteen. His father had been a scrapyard millionaire, who had expected his sons to shift cars from the age of fourteen.

'You'll go far, Pete,' his father used to say. 'You'll always find work with muscles like that.'

He went further than his father anticipated. He'd had no idea.

On a low tide, he can do fifteen minutes, forty-five seconds. He sets the stopwatch, and goes, straining to beat his last efforts. On a high tide, twenty-five minutes, thirty-two seconds. The records are complicated and need careful calculation. Stage of the tide, time of day, weight of the shopping. He writes it down when he reaches the other side, but waits till he's back in the lighthouse to work it all out. If he's within two per cent of his personal best, he gives the cats gourmet tins of fish (52p each) and cooks himself some salmon. (Two fillets – £3.45. Unsalted.)

Felicity: 'How did you find me?'

'I struggled. It takes for ever. Letters, more letters, no replies. Old newspapers, records of birth certificates, marriages, deaths. I've written to your father.'

8

'That's a waste of time. My mother was the one who did everything. Took me to ballet lessons, made me wear a brace, told me what to eat. He wasn't there.'

'I know, but he's a link.'

'I haven't seen him since I was five. He never even sent us any money.'

'Fathers. Are any of them any use?'

'Don't be pretentious, Straker. What do you know about it?'

'Quite a lot, actually, Maggie.'

'Some of us were good fathers.' Alan's voice. 'Whose fault was it that we couldn't go on being good?'

'I know.'

Felicity: 'What do you want from me?'

I ache for her nearly adulthood, her lost potential. For her photograph in the Sun. *Pretty face, long legs, stuffed bird on her shoulder.*

———

Straker moors at the side of the pier, running his rope through a rusty iron loop. It's not really a pier, more a breakwater to shelter the harbour from storms, but he's heard the villagers call it a pier, so he accepts their judgement.

He strips off the oilskins and leaves them in the boat, then climbs the metal ladder.

There are two boys on the other side catching crabs in fishing nets. Straker looks into their bucket. Several small crabs are scrambling over each other at the bottom, crawling up the sides and falling back into the water.

'Look at this,' says one, pulling up a crab with a diameter of two inches.

The other stops to look. 'Great,' he says. 'We could eat that for dinner.'

The boys are not very old, but Straker can't guess their age exactly. He's not much good at children. On holiday, he supposes. They wear baggy shorts to their knees and T-shirts with writing on them: *Listen to the dolphins.* Shouldn't they listen to the crabs?

He looks at their heads, bent together over the bucket. One is ginger, curls falling naturally inside other curls, nestling cosily round his ears, creeping easily down the hollow at the back of his neck. The other is light brown, shaggy and probably uncombed, the brown of his hair mingling with the brown of his skin.

Brothers? he wonders. They're absorbed in their crabs, peering into the bucket. One puts in a finger and pulls it out hurriedly with a yelp. They giggle together.

No. Not brothers.

They look up and see him watching them, and their faces close. They turn away quickly, their easy chatter freezing into nervous silence. Straker walks away from them and hears their urgent whispers start once they think he's out of earshot. He wonders what they say about him.

Three old men sit outside the boathouse sucking at their pipes. They're nearly always here, and have been for the last twenty-four years. They were ancient when Straker first came, their beards grizzled with grey, faces weathered all year round, eyes creased into permanent slits as they look companionably out to sea. They're like full-grown gnomes placed where they can be seen by passing tourists. He keeps waiting for the paint to peel.

One of them pulls out his pipe when he sees Straker. 'Morning, Mr Straker,' he says, and puts the pipe back in. The others grunt. Straker nods in reply and walks round them into the boathouse. He doesn't understand how they know his name. He's never told them and doesn't know theirs.

In the gloom of the boathouse, lit by a few random holes in the corrugated iron of the roof, he finds his Sainsbury's trolley. It's parked against the back wall, next to a pile of fishing-nets and behind a sailing dinghy that has never been moved in all the time he's been here. It lies on its side, barnacles crusted on its bottom, crumpled, off-white sails mingling with the dust. Sometimes, on a good day, he considers making a claim for it, rowing it home, cleaning the sails, varnishing the hull, but he'll never do it. It wouldn't fit into his routine.

He pushes the trolley up the hill to the village, preferring to walk in the road rather than on the cobbled pavement. If a car comes, he stops and stands aside, then continues. He recognises the people he passes, and they recognise him, but they don't speak. Just a nod, a hint of a smile. An agreed status quo. Don't rock the boat, or try to take on passengers. The boat would be too heavy, and he'd probably ground it on his shingle beach. It would be much harder to anticipate when to step out into the water and start to pull it in. He's never tried it – never wanted to.

He parks the trolley outside the post office. Mrs Langwell (name outside above the door) nods and smiles as she cashes his cheque.

'Nice and early, Mr Straker. Plenty of time for shopping.'

He avoids looking into her eyes.

'You have some post.' She hands him a letter. 'Some interesting ones there.'

Does she steam them open, then reseal them? How does she know if they're interesting? She's older than him, brown and crinkled all over, tiny and shrivelled. He's seen her on the rocks by the pier, lying in the sun whenever she's not working – a sun-worshipper. Straker can't imagine her doing anything else – eating or washing or cleaning her flat above the post office.

'See you next week, Mr Straker.'

He dislikes the fact that she knows his name when he's never spoken to her. He gets some stamps from the machine, posts the letters he's brought with him and picks up his shopping trolley. A mile's walk along the main road out of the village until he reaches Sainsbury's. He likes supermarkets, pushing his trolley up and down the aisles, examining everything, willing to give almost anything a trial. Chicken nuggets, sweet and sour stir-fries, tins of stewed apple, mango slices, bamboo shoots, Monster Munch (pickled-onion flavour). He spends time with the soaps and deodorants, smelling them all, deciding between washing powder, liquid, capsules. There's an ancient freezer in the keeper's cottage and he likes to keep it full. Library books have taught him how the old lighthouse keepers managed, bread-making being part of their essential training. He has no desire to recapture that world. He's satisfied with supermarkets, freezers and microwaves.

He pays the checkout girl and pushes his trolley down to the village. Nothing to hold him here. Straight back to the lighthouse and Suleiman and Magnificent. One of the letters in his trolley has a gold label with the name and address of the sender. Mr Jack Tilly, Worthing. He's cautiously pleased.

He passes a house that's been steadily dying in the time he's been here. It's a tiny cottage, very old, with crumbling cob walls, which looks idyllic, but probably isn't. The windows are far too small – the rooms must be dark and dingy. He's watched it deteriorate, once a week, since he arrived here. An elderly couple lived there for a short time, but they've gone now.

Today, as he passes it, he sees that something has changed. Somebody has trampled a path to the cottage door. The three-foot grass that is turning to hay has been pushed aside and the peeling front door is ajar.

He stops and looks, moving just inside the open gate so that cars sweeping round the corner don't take him or his trolley with them.

Tiles have started to slip down recently and several have fallen and shattered on the ground. But now there's a ladder against the side of the house, and a small figure on the roof. He edges closer to the house until he can identify it as a woman. She's moving slowly and nervously, pulling at the tiles, shifting them round and trying to fasten them. She's small and slightly plump, with dazzling yellow hair that glitters in the sunshine. She's wearing a ridiculously brief pink top, which shows a layer of unsightly flesh, and shorts, which are a frayed and faded khaki. Her arms and legs are whiter than those of anyone who lives in the village.

She needs sun-block. She should be careful. He moves closer to the house.

At that moment, she sees him. She stops what she's doing and glares in his direction. 'Who are you?'

Does it matter? She wouldn't want to know.

'What do you want?'

Nothing. He's only looking.

'Speak, man, for goodness' sake. What's the matter with you?'

He shakes his head, turning to push the trolley back to the gate. He's only entered out of curiosity, with no intention of trespassing.

'Wait!' she shouts.

He stops. Why? She won't want to talk to him.

But she's climbing down the ladder rapidly, and running over, until she stops about ten yards away from him. She's about forty, older than he'd thought. Her stomach bulges over the top of her shorts, she's dirty, streaks of grime down her face, and her blonde hair isn't so yellow when it doesn't catch the sun. She's not an attractive woman.

'Well?' she says.

He spreads his hands. Nothing to say.

A dark flush spreads up her face, and he watches her with interest. He's not familiar with anger.

'Speak to me.'

No.

'OK. I'll speak to you. I'm Imogen Doody. Don't laugh. It's not my fault. You can call me Doody. Everyone else does.'

He's not laughing. He never laughs.

'So who are you?'

Peter Straker. Failed human being.

'Why don't you speak? Answer me. What's your name?'

Ah, a teacher. Useless at everything except telling people what to do. He turns away. He's not interested in teachers.

She leaps after him. 'Stop! Why don't you speak to me?' He walks faster, but she chases him down the path, and shrieks just as he reaches the gate. He nearly doesn't turn round, wishing that she could be more dignified, and when he does look back, he can't see her. Surprised, wondering where she's gone, he edges towards the house again and finds her lying face down in the long grass. She's caught her foot in the root system of some very elderly, very bent hawthorn bushes, and is scrabbling around with her hands trying to find something to hold on to. Her yellow hair is on end and her pink top even shorter when she's upside down. She reminds him of a hen, free-range, scratching its feet among the dirt and grain of a farmyard.

He looks at her, feels a strange sensation somewhere deep inside him. A trembling, helpless feeling that he can't control. His shoulders are shaking, his chest is moving. He realises that he's laughing.

Chapter 2

The letter came one Saturday at the end of April, when Imogen Doody was retrieving balls from the canteen roof. This was part of her job as caretaker, and the whole process represented an ongoing battle between her and the entire male population of the school. She knew they threw them up on purpose, but she had to remain one step ahead. Once she had the balls in her possession, she could confiscate them for a fortnight. It was a hot day, even hotter on the roof, so she was anxious to get down as soon as possible.

She could see the postman walking up the path from the main school building. Patrick Saunders, an odd man – the children called him Postman Pat. He ambled and stopped to talk to anyone who was interested, which meant his delivery times were unreliable. She remained where she was on the edge of the flat roof, not wanting to be seen, unwilling to talk to him. From her high position, she could see that he was nearly bald, and there were clusters of dark freckles on his head, brown against the unconvincing wisps of his pale hair. She didn't like this glimpse of his frailty. It made her feel sorry for him, and she knew she wouldn't be able to express that sympathy.

He rang twice, and kept shifting his bag from one shoulder to the other while he waited. Doody resented this. Why should she have to worry about his aching back? He chose to be a postman.

She threw down a ball – orange, soggy, in need of new air – and he jumped. He squinted up at her through the fingers of his free hand, and she was pleased that he couldn't see her properly.

'Why are you ringing the bell?'

He waved a letter at her. 'I've got this.'

'You can put letters through the letter-box. Get it? Letters – letter-boxes.'

He shrugged and turned away. 'Please yourself. It's registered post.'

'Hang on,' she called, and came down the ladder. He was waiting for her at the bottom.

'It's not addressed to you.'

Doody scowled at him. She put her hands into her pockets and pulled out a handful of small balls, multi-coloured and very bouncy. She dropped them, and they scattered in all directions. Their bouncing continued until they settled cheerfully into drains, corners, dips in the Tarmac, delighted with their miraculous escape. 'So you ring the doorbell twice to give me a letter that you're not going to give me?'

'It's your address, but it says Imogen Hayes.'

She tried to take it from him, but he moved it out of her reach. 'That's me. How many Imogens do you know?'

'So why's the name different? Is it your undercover name?' He looked pleased with himself.

'Yes,' she says. 'I'm a Latvian sleeper. Waiting to be activated. Perhaps that's what you've got there. My orders.' Anything would be more interesting than the reality of her present life. She reached for the letter, but he moved it away again.

Anger was brewing inside her, bubbling away ominously, but she wanted the letter, so she made herself speak in a calm manner. 'It's my maiden name. I was Imogen Hayes a long time ago. Now I'm Imogen Doody. Mrs Doody to you.'

He gave in. He was looking very uncomfortable, with beads of sweat on his top lip, his feet shuffling. She snatched the letter out of his hand and he didn't resist. 'You have to sign for it.'

She took his pen and signed the electronic screen he put in front of her. Should she offer him a cold drink?

If he'd done his job properly, he wouldn't have been standing so long in the hot sun.

'Thanks!' she shouted at his retreating back.

He didn't turn round. He let himself out of the gate and plodded heavily past the blue iron railings of the school. He was stubborn, but too pedestrian for a real argument.

Doody was pleased to have had the last word, and the fact that it had been a gracious word made her feel even better. She decided to make herself a glass of lemonade before opening the letter.

Doody sat opposite Piers Sackville of Sackville, Sackville and Waterman, and wondered how solicitors made so much money. The room smelt new, the carpet not yet flattened by passing feet, the gleam of the desk unchallenged by the sharp edges of stray paperclips or unprotected coffee cups.

'Oliver d'Arby was your godfather, I believe?'

'I wouldn't be sitting here if he wasn't.'

He remained distantly polite. 'I'm relieved that my letter reached the right person.' There was something phoney about him. Pretend interest, counterfeit sympathy.

'I never knew him. He was a waste of time. Didn't write, didn't visit, didn't send any presents.' She could remember her hollow jealousy when Celia and Jonathan received presents through the post and she didn't. As usual they were winning while she came last. After all this time, it still produced a dull, metallic bitterness that she could literally taste on her tongue. 'He forgot about me.'

'Apparently not. He's left everything to you in his will. A cottage, all surrounding property.'

The bitter taste fled. Her head started to whirl and hum with snatches of thoughts. A faulty CD jumping tracks. Cottage –

property – me? She tried to speak but, unbelievably, no words came out.

'I can see that this is a surprise to you.' His professional face slipped slightly, so that he almost looked gentle, but she wasn't fooled. The man was an expert – he was paid to be nice.

What did she know about Oliver d'Arby? Her parents had only ever been mentioned him in passing. He had worked for the Inland Revenue and played the cello. It was the cello they remembered and described to her. How he had played it at the wedding, how he changed when he was playing, how they forgot about his tax-collecting. 'But why did he leave it to me? I've never spoken to him.'

The solicitor smiled, openly and genuinely, and she was confused, unsure if she should believe in him or not. 'Perhaps he had no one else to leave it to.'

'Don't you know? Aren't solicitors supposed to advise people?'

He looked down at the will. 'Normally, I might well have done, but unfortunately, this was long before my time. It's dated the sixth of July 1966.'

'I was only five years old then. Why would anyone leave all his worldly possessions to a child who'd just started infant school?'

He had some pages of typed notes, which he examined for a few seconds, turning the pages quickly. Nobody reads that fast. He cleared his throat. 'It would seem that you're not the only one never to have seen him again. He disappeared about twenty-five years ago.'

'Twenty-five years? It's taken that long to get round to telling me?'

'The fact that someone has disappeared doesn't mean we can assume he's dead. The information has only recently come to our attention, and there are procedures to follow.'

'So how did the information reach you?'

Piers Sackville coughed and almost looked embarrassed. 'I'm afraid I don't know. Someone must have informed us.'

Doody stared at him. 'You mean there's a secret – a big secret – and I'm not allowed to know?'

He looked indignant. 'No, of course not. Someone else in the office must have the information. I'll talk to one of my colleagues.'

'Not a Mr Sackville, by any chance?'

'How did you guess?'

He was gaining confidence. She could feel him altering the pace of the conversation, adjusting to her, and she didn't like it. She wanted to reach over, grab the will and his notes, tear them up in front of his pseudo-kind face and watch his reaction. Then she would know what he was really thinking. Her fingers were itching, her breathing accelerating. 'So when do you decide a missing person is a dead person? Do you try to trace him?'

'It's complex. We've had to make announcements, write letters, get a court ruling. However, I should point out that he was born in 1904. It's rare for people to live beyond a hundred.'

'Some do.'

'Indeed. And let's hope that both of us here will be in that fortunate position. But it's not common, I'm afraid.'

'I suppose it only matters if he leaves property behind. Nobody's going to care otherwise, are they?'

He nodded, quite openly, with no hint of embarrassment. 'Quite.'

Why does a non-existent man with no relatives make a will? Where does a seventy-five-year-old, cello-playing tax inspector go? On holiday and forget to return? Walking the streets? But what about the cello? Does he carry it around with him? Every park bench, every shop entrance would have to be twice as big for a man with a cello. Perhaps he had had a second home somewhere, with a wife half his age and four children.

They'd all be getting old themselves by now, wondering why there wasn't a cottage to inherit. Or did he go abroad and get kidnapped? Bad luck if there's no one to pay the ransom. Perhaps he's died in a plane crash, or a bomb in London, a body that can't be identified.

'It's amazing that more people don't disappear like that.' Carelessly, slipping away by mistake.

Piers Sackville laughed this time, out loud, and Doody felt pleased with herself. He was beginning to notice that he was talking to a real human being. 'I expect they do. We just don't get involved.'

'No.' She resented the fact that she now knew two people who'd disappeared. Which way round did it work? She made connections with people who disappeared, or people who were going to disappear were drawn to her? 'I'd be careful if I were you, Mr Sackville. People I know often disappear. It could be you next.'

'Well, let's hope not, Mrs Doody. I still harbour ambitions of reaching that elusive hundred.'

'So what happens now?'

'You sign a few papers for me, and then I give you the key.'

'Mother?'

'Imogen. How are you?'

'Fine. I want to know about Oliver d'Arby.' She didn't want to discuss why she hadn't phoned recently.

'Who? Oh, yes, your godfather. Goodness, I haven't thought of him in ages.'

Hardly surprising. She didn't think of anyone except herself and the characters in *Coronation Street*. 'Were you very friendly with him?'

'Of course we were, he often came round. He was a pilot, you know.'

'No, he wasn't. He was a tax-man.'

She hesitated, clearly confused. 'Oh, yes, I'd forgotten that. But he did fly planes – those little old-fashioned ones that people have as a hobby. He took us to an airfield once, long before you were born. Didn't take us up, though – far too precarious. I wouldn't have felt safe.'

A thrill of pleasure swept through Doody. Oliver d'Arby was a pilot, a Biggles character, a genuine link to her childhood. He assumed a new image in her mind, one that she felt she could identify with. A young man in flying goggles, taxiing out on to a grass airfield, raising a hand to her as he passed. The roar of the engine, the blue sky—

'Imogen? Are you still there?'

'Yes, yes.' Doody pushed back her excitement to a place where she could examine it later. 'Why was he my god-father?'

'Because we asked him.'

She didn't normally say 'we'. The subject of Doody's father was meticulously bypassed, driven round at high speed. But it wasn't easy discussing their life together during Doody's childhood without a passing reference to him. 'Why did you ask him? He was much older than you – nearly sixty. Wasn't he an odd choice?'

'I don't know. It was all so long ago, Imogen.'

There was no point in pushing her – she'd never produce any information. Doody imagined her sitting in the tiny hall of her flat, wondering if she'd have the energy to water her African violets, counting her pills in her mind, making sure she wouldn't forget to take any.

'Did you know he disappeared?'

'Disappeared? What do you mean?'

'Twenty-five years ago, he just vanished. Nobody knows what happened to him.'

'How mysterious.'

Doody wondered if her mother had secretly kept in touch with him all this time and knew exactly where he was. But she couldn't imagine why anyone as interesting as Oliver d'Arby would willingly maintain contact with her mother.

'How did you know him? Where did you meet?'

'Oh, I can remember that. He was a friend of my father's – your grandfather. They were in the services together – I told you he was a pilot, didn't I?'

'Yes.'

'Well, I think they were in the war – it must have been the First World War, I suppose, a very long time ago.'

Doody made some calculations. Oliver d'Arby must have been ten at the beginning of the First World War, and her grandfather would have been even younger. 'I don't think so,' she said.

'You must stop doubting everything I say, Imogen. It's not an attractive quality.'

'But it can't be right—' She stopped. It didn't matter. At least she now knew where Oliver d'Arby had come from. She might never understand his real connection with her mother or father. 'And he played the cello.'

'Did he?'

'Well you're the one who told me that.'

'Then he must have done, I suppose, if you say so.'

Doody felt herself getting angry. This was the way all conversations went with her mother. The logic became slippery and facts shifted and abandoned their shape, so that she lost her sense of direction and everything became her fault.

'I've been having trouble with my eyes,' her mother said.

'Have you had them tested?'

'No, but I'm thinking about it.'

'You probably need new glasses.'

'It's not easy, living on my own—'

'Did you like Oliver d'Arby?'

'Oh, yes, he was a lovely man.'

'Was he married? Did he have a family?'

'No – it was all rather sad. His wife died of some illness –

22

pneumonia, I think – before we met him, so he didn't have any children. That was why he was so pleased to be asked to be a godfather. But then he didn't keep in touch. We never saw him again after the christening.'

Doody's fault, then. 'Did you find out why not?'

'Not exactly, but I think it brought it all back, seeing the children he could never have. I distinctly saw something in his face when we went back to the house, as if he wanted to cry but couldn't.'

Doody paused and tried to imagine her mother being compassionate, perceptive, caring. But it was a false picture. Her mother was just constructing the image that she felt would impress Doody most. Then Doody realised that the whole business of Oliver d'Arby not having children would have been out of date when she was born. He was too old – he must have gone through all that anguish long before. She decided that she wouldn't tell her mother about the cottage – not yet.

Immediately after the telephone conversation, Doody collected together all her notebooks, pencils, sharpeners and rubbers. She arranged herself on the settee, leaning against one arm, cushions comfortably at her back and her legs stretched out in front of her. She picked up a new, unused exercise book and a pencil.

'Chapter One', she wrote – and stopped.

She couldn't think of a title. The previous one didn't have a title either, but that wasn't important, because she'd already decided to abandon it. There were now six unfinished novels sitting upstairs under her bed, and she had no great desire to go back to them. She wanted to start afresh, to experience the surge of adventure and promise that came with a new idea. This was going to be the good one, the one that would go on to the end.

Her mind felt open, exhilarated by the discovery that Oliver d'Arby was worth knowing, a benefactor she would have approved of. She imagined meeting him, a thin, grizzled, ancient man, whose mind went backwards to the flying.

'Did you fly a Camel?' she would ask.

'Sopwith Camels? Goodness, no. You couldn't get hold of them after the war. We flew whatever was available.'

What was it like? She wanted to ask.

She wrote down a sentence: 'The little two-winged Gipsy Moth came out of the sun, a tiny speck in the massive sky—'

She looked out of the window at the darkening sky, heavy with rain, and thought of Biggles, who had accompanied her through her childhood, a fictional friend who always came back. He didn't die, or disappear. She still half dreamed that he would turn up one day, fly low over the school, land on the playing-field, ready to rescue her from her tedious, lost life.

'Come on!' he'd shout.

She would race across the field, in full view of all the children, leap on to a wing and lie flat, and they'd take off together, with an unknown enemy firing pistol shots at them. Escaping.

Sometimes he would resemble her husband, Harry.

She sighed and looked back down at the page.

Suddenly, Detective Inspector Mandleson, better known to his friends as Mandles, heard a change in the familiar sound of the engine—

Mandles had lived in Doody's imagination for years. After Harry had left, she had felt the need to withdraw from reality. She had crept back to her childhood fantasy life, crawled into the hidden labyrinths of her mind, searching for comfort, and rediscovered Biggles. She transformed him into Mandles, recognising a need for her own hero.

The needle on the altimeter was spinning madly out of control, and the Gipsy Moth revolved round and round on an invisible pivot, heading directly for the drink—

It started to rain, big heavy drops splashing against her window.

Doody drove down from Bristol on the next Saturday to see the house. In her mind, she told her father that she'd become a woman of property, but she didn't think he'd heard her. He was too dead for that kind of news. He wouldn't believe her, anyway.

The cottage gate was on a corner of the village road, with only a narrow strip of cobbled pavement outside, where cars dashed past blindly. She liked this. It was not a place where people would stand and watch.

She opened the gate and waded through the long grass, pushing aside poppies, dandelions and forget-me-nots. Huge red petals flopped down from the poppies, leaving the centres black and quivering.

This belonged to her. She owned land, a house, a space. She wasn't worried about the garden. She didn't even care if the house was falling down. Now that she was here, she could feel that it was hers – it entered her body, creeping along her veins, taking root in her mind.

It was very strange to enter a house that had been empty for so long. The furniture was still there, waiting, unaware that it had been abandoned. To a sofa in a corner where the sun can't reach, one year or twenty-five years is all the same. The house wasn't like the *Mary-Celeste*, abandoned unexpectedly, a meal left half eaten on the table. Oliver d'Arby must have planned his departure. There was no washing-up waiting for attention, no grease marks on the cooker. Everything was tidy. Neat and ordered, like a holiday home. One night he must have decided to go, so he packed a suitcase. Then the next day he got up, had breakfast, made the bed, put out the dustbin and went. There were still clothes in the bedroom, suits hanging in the wardrobe, jumpers in drawers.

But there was no underwear, no socks. So he knew he would be away for some time.

The furniture would have to go. She couldn't live in the shadow of Oliver d'Arby even if he did play the cello, even though he was her benefactor and might still be alive. But she didn't want to get rid of it yet. She would like to spend some time here first, guiltily finding out about him, painting a picture of him in her head, conscious that she had had no interest in him until she had known about the will. There was a bureau full of papers, letters, bills. She wanted to go through it, but needed some time for that.

She could do anything here, and nobody would know where she was. A place where she could go if she wanted to disappear for a while. No children, no headmaster, no bunches of keys. She had a picture in her mind. A house in the woods. A gingerbread cottage. Smoke curling out of the chimney.

She needed some expert advice because she'd never renovated a house before. Her brother, Jonathan, was the man for this.

Back at the school during the week, she phoned him. 'Jonathan. How do you fix tiles on a roof?'

'Find a reliable builder.'

'I'm not going to pay someone. I haven't got any money.'

'I thought you worked all week.'

'Don't be ridiculous. I live on that money. I can't afford to pay someone else's wages too.'

'Buy a book, then.'

'No. You tell me.'

There was a pause and she suspected he was silently yawning. 'Imogen—'

'What?'

'Are you sure this is wise?'

'Don't patronise me. I'm very capable. I'm a caretaker, you know, and I can do things.'

'Fixing a few dripping taps and mopping up a leaky radiator doesn't qualify you to rebuild an old ruin.'

How did he know what condition the cottage was in? Had he opened her letter and gone down there to inspect it?

'Jonathan, stop trying to lecture me. I need your advice.'

'You'll need tools.'

'I already have tools. Well, I can borrow them from school.'

'You need to get a good DIY book. Honestly. If you see it illustrated you can work it out.'

'I'm not wasting money on a book.'

'The first thing you need is a ladder.'

'Why didn't I think of that?'

Actually, his advice was good. She borrowed a book from the library, but didn't tell him. He would have many years of usefulness ahead of him before she'd finished.

On the next Saturday, Doody drove down with a ladder on a roof-rack and tools on her back seat, and parked in the road round the corner.

There was no one there. She was fenced in, or hedged in, and didn't have to speak to anyone. No children to shout at, nobody to give her helpful advice. She was alone under the clear blue sky and the hot sun.

First, she went into the loft to look at the rafters. She needed to know their condition before she examined the tiles outside. She now knew about purlins, wall plates, ties, etc., and she could see it didn't look good. Some of the beams were damp and rotten.

She went back outside again and consulted the book. It was not helpful. She read each bit several times, but it didn't explain properly. It seemed to think she knew things already. It described what a roof looked like, how it was constructed, but it didn't tell her how to mend it. She gave up on the book and went to stand in the garden where she could examine the roof. There were several gaps between the tiles. It might be possible to replace them, which would do for a start. If she could stop the rain coming in, the beams might dry out inside.

She stripped off as many clothes as she could, made her

ladder secure and crawled on to the roof. She wanted to know exactly how many tiles were missing, and she needed a sample tile, so she could find the right ones in B&Q. She felt strangely powerful, under control. An aeroplane droned overhead and bees were buzzing round an enormous white lilac tree that was hanging over the front of the house. She could smell honey-suckle, even up here. After a while, she stopped counting tiles, and sat still, ready to fall asleep in the warmth of the sun. She could see the lighthouse, shimmering in the haze of heat, and the sea beyond, calm and tempting, the horizon blurring into the sky.

She looked down and saw a man standing inside her gate with a shopping trolley. For a few terrible seconds, she was seized by panic. It was Oliver d'Arby come to reclaim his house. She shouldn't be here, sitting on his roof.

But this man did not fly Sopwith Camels or play the cello. It was obvious, even from a distance. He was tall with an untidy beard, wearing a suit and tie and boots. He had a huge nose. He was very ugly, but not a hundred years old.

'Who are you?' she shouted.

He looked at her but didn't answer.

––––––––

Doody first discovered serious anger at the age of eighteen, when it hit her like a surge of electricity and shocked her with its life-giving intensity. It had changed the nature of her existence, woken her up, made her think better. Now she has learned how to let it grow from a tiny pinpoint of light to a full-grown open fire, greedily hunting around for more fuel to burn. From the first moment when the spark ignites, a fierce excitement takes root inside her because she can feel some-thing.

She knows that she irritates people by automatically taking the opposite view from them, but she's waiting for the moment of self-belief, the rush of adrenaline that tells her she's right and they're wrong, that she's indestructible. She doesn't drink and she's never taken drugs because she can't see the point. They give an artificial high. Why bother when you can have the real thing?

———

This man is not predictable. When she trips over the roots in the grass and falls over, he comes back. She knows he's there, even though she can't look up, because she can hear him breathing. But nothing happens. She remains stuck and he doesn't do anything to help her. She wriggles herself into an awkward kneeling position, scrabbling around in the long grass at the roots of the hawthorn, but there's nothing without thorns that she can hold on to. When she finally manages to find a position from which to see him, she realises that he's laughing. Shaking uncontrollably, gulping for air, tears rolling down his cheeks.

'Very funny,' she says. 'How long is it going to be before you decide to help me? Five minutes? Half an hour? All day?'

But he keeps on laughing, twitching and jerking with the effort, completely unable to control himself.

'Moron,' she says. 'Idiot, fool, imbecile.'

The trouble is, she needs his help. Her foot is caught upside down and her leg is awkwardly twisted. She can't get into a comfortable position so that she can reach her foot and pull it out.

'Haven't you ever heard of being helpful?' she yells at him, desperate to break up his hysterical laughter. 'Didn't you do the Good Samaritan when you were at school?'

He ignores her.

'What's the purpose of you?' she shouts. 'You're ugly, you trespass on other people's property, you steal shopping trolleys, and you're incredibly stupid.'

Everything she says makes him laugh more. She's not used to people laughing at her anger. It makes her feel insignificant.

She stops shouting at him and settles herself back on the ground. She lies on her stomach, relaxes, ignores him, and contemplates the situation.

It's like waiting with children. If they're not listening, and you want them to stop what they're doing, you just shut off and do nothing. Eventually they become conscious of the silence and give up.

So she lies still in the long grass and waits. The idiot eventually stops the hysteria, and his breathing becomes more regular. The roots of the hawthorn are in the shade, but she can see the sun a yard away and smell the heat of it coming closer. She hears the bees, a bird trilling – but she can't identify it because she's no good at birds. She's never bothered about them before, never listened, never given them a thought. So now she finds she's hearing a silence that is new to her. There's quietness, calmness. A car drives up the road past the cottage, but she doesn't mind that. It shows her the extent of her stillness.

She can't hear him at all, so she moves her head round to see if he's gone.

He's sitting down close by, unmoving like her, and she realises that they're sharing the same silence. They're hearing things together: the crack of the hawthorn as it settles slightly into itself, preparing for the full sun; the crawling of a caterpillar past her arm; the rustle of the grass as it eases upright again, reasserting itself after being disturbed by their feet.

'Well?' she says at last. 'Any chance of helping me?'

He's unwilling, she can tell, but he moves towards her, and spends a few seconds examining the situation. Then she feels his hand on her leg. She jumps when he first touches her, but the hand stays there. Slowly, gently, he begins to untangle her. She waits and lets him finish. She likes the sensation of his calm hands on her leg.

He lets go.

She waits for a second and then tries to move her leg. It's free, so she rolls over, away from the roots, and struggles to get to her feet.

He stands up and watches, but seeing her difficulty, leans forward to help. She tries to pull herself up on a branch of the hawthorn, but there are too many thorns, so she grabs his arm instead. He doesn't react. He is solid and motionless beside her. She holds the foot still at first, then lowers it to the ground and puts some weight on it.

'Ouch!' She lifts it up again hurriedly.

The idiot man kneels down. He moves his hand along her foot, pressing as he goes.

'There!' she shrieks. 'Ah!' She tries to jerk it away, but he's holding it too firmly, and she has to balance herself on his shoulder. 'Let go!' But her anger won't come back. She looks for it and it's not there any more. 'I must have twisted my ankle,' she says, sounding pathetic. 'Can you help me back to the house?'

He nods, and they stumble together through the long grass. They would be more successful if he put an arm round her for support, but he's not offering this service and she's not asking.

The ladder is still up against the wall, tools strewn around at the base. He attempts to take her through the front door.

'No,' she says. 'There's no point in going in. It's all dead. Been like that for years.'

He helps her to sit down again on the grass and lowers himself next to her. She's conscious that he's looking at her. Perhaps he's dangerous. She is being helped by a man who could be a lunatic. Nobody knows she's here. She'd be yet another disappeared person, buried under the hawthorn bushes, in the long grass.

She turns to examine his face, and he doesn't appear to be dangerous. He doesn't even seem stupid. There's a scar on his left cheek, stretching from the corner of his eye, down to the chin, lost in the grey and black grizzle of his beard. His eyes, however, are remarkable. They're bluer than she's ever seen in real life. Frank Sinatra, Steve McQueen blue. As soon as she looks directly at him, he averts his gaze, but she's seen his expression, his intelligence. If he's a lunatic, he's a clever one.

He gets up and starts collecting the tools into a neat pile. She has a very good idea.

'Listen,' she says, 'you couldn't do me a favour, could you? I need to get a tile down from the roof so I can buy some new ones. I want a sample.'

He pauses and glances at her. She can see the sweat on his forehead, the thoughts passing across his face, the quick turning away when he meets her eyes. He looks ridiculous in his navy suit and wellington boots.

'It might be better if you took your boots off,' she says. 'It's awfully hot, and you might slip.'

He doesn't take his boots off. He climbs the ladder cautiously and, after fiddling for a while near the eaves, brings down a tile. Then he puts the tools just inside the front door. He pulls the ladder down and starts to fold it up.

'Hang on,' she says. 'Maybe I haven't finished.'

He stops, shrugs, then puts the ladder into the house as well.

'Thanks a million. My ankle could be all right now, for all you know.'

He has a puzzled expression on his face. She can feel herself becoming irritated again. Why does he have to be so silent?

'Say something,' she says. 'It's not fair, me making all the conversation. I don't mind if you want to shout a bit. We could shout at each other, see who's the loudest.'

He avoids her eyes.

She sighs. 'Please yourself.'

He's completely still. She's seen a street performer who paints himself grey and stands motionless long enough to give the impression that he's a statue. Then, after a time, he twitches once, or winks, moves his head. People stop in amazement until a crowd gathers, waiting for his next movement. They always give him money before leaving.

'You could earn a living with your skills,' she says. She tries moving her foot again and it still hurts. 'I can't walk,' she says. 'I'll have to ring for a taxi to take me to the station. I don't suppose you drive?'

He doesn't shake his head, but he's not offering.

'No, of course not. That would be too good to be true. Could you fetch my bag? It's just inside the door – by the hall table.'

He fetches the bag and hands it to her. He'd make a good butler.

She digs out her mobile from the bottom of the bag. 'I don't suppose you know the number of a local taxi firm?'

He shakes his head.

'No, I thought not.'

She rings directory enquiries, then arranges for a taxi to pick her up at the gate.

The man watches her, then goes back to the house and pulls the door shut. He takes the key out and hands it to her.

'Can you help me down to the road?' she asks.

They stumble awkwardly back to the gate, with Doody leaning heavily on his arm. He's not very good at it, because he lurches around too much and they have to keep stopping to recover their balance.

'Great,' she says, when they get there.

His shopping trolley is still waiting for him.

'I hope you don't have anything frozen in there.'

But he does. She can see the fish fingers and the frozen chicken breasts. 'Oh,' she says. 'You'd better send me a bill.'

He seems perplexed and walks off, pushing his trolley along the side of the road, avoiding the cobbles. Just like that, without a backward glance.

She watches him in amazement. Is he just going to walk away? 'Hey!' she shouts.

He stops, but doesn't turn round.

'Thanks!' she shouts. 'All right? I appreciated the help.' He makes her feel guilty.

He starts walking again, away from her.

'If it wasn't for you, I wouldn't have needed the help!' She feels better.

A taxi drives up from the other direction and stops at the gate.

Chapter 3

43 Westside Close,
Blenheim Rd,
Birmingham.

19/5/04

Dear Mr Straker,

I was surprised to receive your letter out of the blue as it were. My poor Felicity (Fliss, as I liked to call her) has been dead for nearly 25 years and not a day goes by without me thinking of her. We was very close. There was a train crash. You might remember it was a London to Birmingham train. 78 dead but only one close to my heart.

She was a lovely girl. I don't know if someone like you in your profession as it were would remember seeing her photo in the Sun and the Mirror and the Evening Mail. Maybe they didn't put her photo in The Times which you probably read. Anyway she was going to be the model for Parrot, I think they call it The Face, but they only had a few pictures from the photoshoot and they used them all for a bit then found another girl. You might remember her, Lucy Something and she was in all the pictures after Fliss. Black girl.

Anyway, I expect you know Fliss (Felicity) and I lived apart, but she wrote to me all the time and we was like real mates. Her Mum (Rita) died of cancer and Fliss nursed her on her deathbed, like the good girl she was, but I'm her next of kin, there isn't anyone else.

Of course it grieves my heart to accept a legacy that was meant for my darling Fliss (Felicity) but I think she'd like it

that way. We was very close. She told me about her American
cousins lots of times.

Anyway you can contact me at the address above.
Yours Truly
Jack Tilly

$78 = 1 + 2 + 3 + 4 + 5 + 6 + 7 + 8 + 9 + 10 + 11 + 12$. A beautiful number. As if Straker had planned it. Each one an individual, each number irreplaceable. You can't take any one of them away, because forgetting would be as great a crime as killing.

At first, they were only numbers. Nameless, anonymous, hammering through his mind, inanimate as nails, kept at bay with other numbers. Twelve years ago, they changed, or he changed. He kept dreaming about them, a crowd of strangers, a turmoil of spinning legs and arms, faces without features. He wanted to know their names, and then the numbers became a list. A silent roll-call that echoed through his mind all day and night. Two years ago, he changed again. He wanted to know who they were.

He's found plenty of excuses to contact them. He's writing a book; he runs a firm that investigates unclaimed inheritance; he's a journalist researching an article.

Now when they come into his dreams, chattering, arguing, being ordinary, his mind becomes full of them all, bursting with their problems. They are rich and alive, their thoughts pouring out of them, frantic in their desire not to get lost. Sometimes he can't cope. His brain isn't big enough, his shoulders not broad enough. He wants to live their lives for them, carrying on where they left off. But he can't do it. He hasn't the strength or the ability.

The voices stay with him long after he wakes up. He carries them round with him like a tape recorder that switches itself back on when he's not looking, so their conversations echo through his mind at unexpected moments.

––––––––––

Sangita: 'Rob Willow was doing a concert in Birmingham. I had to go.' Her voice is gentle, diffident.

I have a photograph sent by her mother. Young and sweet, a darker, more demure version of Felicity, in a pink sari with a single gold chain round her neck. A long black plait. 'Who was Rob Willow?'

'Rob Willow? Who was he? You don't know?'

'I don't know anything.'

'Well said, Straker.'

'Thank you, Maggie.'

Sangita: 'Rob Willow was gorgeous, the most handsome man in the world.'

'What did you want from him?'

'Want?' Her voice crumples, uncertain. 'I don't know. I just wanted to be near him.'

So she didn't know him. She was just a fan.

'What happened to him?' Her voice is shy, hesitant. 'Does he still perform?'

'I have no idea.' I don't read newspapers, watch the television, listen to the radio. How would I know if he's still around?

She's crying, softly but desperately.

'But he wasn't real. He was just a distant figure you imagined you knew.'

The weeping gets stronger, more desperate.

'Shut up, Straker. You're just making it worse.'

Maggie, who, as always, knows the right thing to do.

When he wakes, it's with a painful jolt, as if he's gone down a step that's steeper than he expected. He lies, panicking, for a long time, his heart beating aggressively, Sangita's face in front of his eyes. He doesn't want to see her once he's awake, but she's so real that he finds himself looking for her in the curved walls of the lighthouse. Surely he can still see an echo of her pink sari, hidden behind the table, a flick of the fat black plait swinging out of sight up the stairs to the light room.

He's so exhausted he can't move. He's only pretending to be alive. All his energy is used up by the seventy-eight. And his investigations of the last two years take him back to a dangerous time. They're opening up the scars, tearing through hidden tissues that were pretending to be healed.

He should never have started. They were all safely stored away, wrapped up, concealed in a drawer. A mass of bodies, victims, a collective tragedy. Why had he let them out? But if he had left them there, he would never have known Maggie. There would be no one to argue with him, nag him, make him think.

It was the poster that changed everything. He was going to Sainsbury's one day, and there was Felicity on the advertising board outside the car park. Four times larger than life, tattered rags of material substituting for clothes, her eyes luminous and innocent. The multi-coloured parrot on her shoulder blended with the green and purple wisps of hair on her almost shaved head.

'FELICITY TILLY,' it said. 'THE TRAGIC FASHION OF 1979.'

The poster was advertising a television programme about changing fashions, but it was some time before that became clear. What he saw was Felicity Tilly, alive, looking directly at him, accusing him. He forgot the shopping. He abandoned his routines without being aware of it. He returned, over and over again, spending most of the week on the opposite pavement, staring at her, unable to reconcile her vitality, her aliveness, with his special knowledge about her death. He wanted to know her, understand who she had been, what she thought.

When they replaced the poster with another about yoghurts, he was bereft.

So it had started there. He opened up files for all of the seventy-eight and found he was hungry, starving, desperate to know them, speak to them, longing to bring them back to life.

He keeps thinking about Miss Doody, the way everything is absorbed by her anger. It comes and goes, like a lightbulb. On, off, on. Does she do the switching consciously? Does she like it?

He's managed to avoid people for years. Why should she come along like that and force him to pay attention to her? She's not one of the seventy-eight. There isn't room in his mind for anyone else. So why has she begun to edge her way in?

She frightens him. He needs to find a way of switching that light off, so he can eliminate her from his mind, go back to where he was, leave her as she was before he met her.

On Sunday, the day after her accident, he should be working on his garden for the whole day. The carrots are coming through nicely, he needs to thin out the new lettuces, and there is plenty of weeding to do, but instead, he finds himself preparing to go into the village again. He stands in front of the only mirror in the keeper's cottage and examines his Aran jumper and black trousers, although the mirror is small and he can't see his face without bending his knees – which he seldom does.

A strange plan is forming in his mind, but he can't think about it too closely without a thread of panic worming its way into his stomach.

He goes to the edge of the headland before leaving. The wind is fresher than yesterday. Foam touches the tips of the waves as they race cheerfully towards him, leaping over each other, recklessly hurling themselves against the cliff. There's so much energy here, the will to go on indefinitely. How easy it all looks, so inevitable and perpetual. Most things that are left alone for long enough will crumble and decay, like the lighthouse, so why is everything around him so alive, so furious? The wind, the sea, the grass, Imogen Doody?

He turns away and fetches his bicycle. From a distance he can see two coaches stopping for the view, and he hesitates before mounting it. Will they see him and laugh? Will he appear in their photographs of Beckingham lighthouse as a dot, a smudge, an insignificant blur? The more he thinks about it, the less likely it seems that he would appear at all. A non-person lost in the landscape of sea and sky and lighthouse. Just as he would like it.

When he reaches the pier again, there's no sign of the boys who were fishing for crabs yesterday. The sailing people have come down to catch the rising tide, and he has to moor quickly to get out of the way. They launch themselves with dedication. People who don't see him, who look past him because he doesn't count. Their faces are brown and healthy from sailing and living. They wear life-jackets, yellow, blue, orange, and the wind whips through their hair as they rush to get their dinghies into the water. With every gust, the cord on the flag at the end of the pier cracks against its pole. There's going to be a race. Two men are standing by the flagpole waiting to fire the starting gun. There's a distant crack and Straker senses the panic of the last few boats to get launched.

'Come on, Tara. Get in and I'll shove off.'

'What about Sam?'

'Leave her. We can't wait any longer. It's just you and me.'

Straker doesn't look at them, just lets their voices wash past him like a current, until they are drops of water in the wind. When he first came here, it was mainly fishermen sailing out on the tide, returning hours later, their motors chugging tiredly and weakly. They were part of the pattern of the weather. Now they have been replaced by these confident, brightly coloured young people who appear to be having fun.

He goes to the back of the boathouse, ignores his shopping trolley and crouches down beside the old dinghy. He examines the crumpled plastic sails, separating them from the tangle of ropes, smoothing them out so that he can see their shape. He produces a Stanley knife from his pocket and starts cutting them away from the ropes, listening intently. His ears strain with the effort, as he half expects someone to come striding in with authority, ready to accuse him of stealing.

Nothing happens. The three old men outside have their backs to him, watching the race. If they know he's here, they make no acknowledgement.

He cuts through the last rope and sits back for a few seconds to ease his hand. Outside, the folded sails of the unused boats pulled up into the harbour clatter urgently in the brisk wind, their tarpaulins tugging against their restraints.

There are two sails, and he takes them both. They're cumbersome and difficult to fold, but he manages to cram them into the shopping trolley. The three men won't hear him, because their ears are deadened by the wind. The sailing club has a new clubhouse, further round on the coast, and he has seen the recreational sailors meeting there, happy with their bar, their retired admirals, their trophies in a glass case. They don't waste time thinking about this dilapidated old boat-house with a corrugated iron roof that leaks, where heaps of red sandstone crumble down from the cliff at the back. Would he have been one of the sailors once, if things had gone differently?

He walks up the road to the village and stops at the corner of Miss Doody's house. It looks the same as yesterday. The path through the long grass to the front door is still visible, and the area round the hawthorn bushes where she had her accident looks well flattened. There's no sign that she's returned today, but there wouldn't be. A twisted ankle needs rest, and she'll be restricted for a while, unable to get on a bus, or climb ladders.

He pushes the trolley through the gate and shuts it behind him, standing still and listening for sounds that might tell him he's doing something wrong. Nothing changes. The dandelions and rosebay willowherb rustle in the wind and a branch from the lilac tree taps gently against an upstairs window. He looks up at the roof and tries to estimate its size. It's not enormous. The two sails together may not be quite big enough, but they'll certainly make a difference.

He takes a deep breath. He laughed here for the first time in years. Something crept inside him and ran its fingers over his nerve ends, played them like a harp so they became suddenly alive. Something strong and powerful.

Of course it all went away afterwards, but now, standing inside the gate, he has a hint of it again, like an unfamiliar smell, new and dangerous. He stands looking up at the roof for so long that his neck starts to ache.

———————

He remembers a time, long ago, at a fair with his father. They stood together looking up at a big dipper, huge and brilliantly lit, painted in vivid, exciting colours. The boats were rocking gently as people boarded them, and they moved up slowly, higher and higher, waiting for the moment when the fun would begin.

'Look at them, Pete,' said his dad. 'That's where we're going. Right to the top.'

They stood side by side, Pete's left shoulder touching his dad's right wrist. He was a huge man. Gulliver in Lilliput. Physically big, mentally big, and ambitiously big.

Pete had no ambition to be up in the sky then. That would come to him later. What he did see was their two shadows, stretching out before them in the late-afternoon sun. His father's was so long that you couldn't see the end and his own appeared tiny beside it. He thought that he would never be as tall as him, that however much he exercised, ran, ate, he would never catch up. As his shadow stretched, his father's would always reach further. But he felt safe next to him. Nobody was as big as his dad, and nobody ever would be.

'Come on, Pete. Let's have a ride.'

Pete was terrified, but pretended not to be. The man taking

42

the money put him up against a chart on a wall, and said, 'Sorry, mate, he's too small. Can't do it. Too dangerous.'

'I'll pay double,' said his dad. 'More.' He waved a five-pound note at him.

'Sorry,' said the man. 'I'd lose my job.'

His dad was furious and Pete pretended he was furious too, to please him. He was secretly relieved.

In the end, they gave up and went to the shooting gallery instead, where they shot ducks and won a goldfish in a plastic bag. But his father was still annoyed and gave him all the good reasons why they shouldn't have been turned away.

He was like that, his dad. He wouldn't leave anything alone.

Straker uses the lilac tree to climb on to the roof. The ladder is just inside the front door, and it would take ten seconds to break the lock, but he decides not to do this. Miss Doody will feel safer if the door's still locked when she comes back.

There are two separate ridges – the long one that travels the length of the cottage and a smaller one at right angles that comes out over the front door. He's not sure how he's going to fix the sails. He's brought a hammer and nails, but the wood doesn't look sound enough to accept them. It may be possible to anchor down the edges with something heavy, so he goes back down and looks around for any stones or rocks he could use. He shuffles his feet through the long grass round the side of the cottage and almost bumps into an old, gently collapsing outhouse. It's barely visible, smothered by a web of ivy and periwinkles that have spread up, round and through it, until it's just part of a group of overgrown trees. The roof must have caved in many years ago, and crumbling bricks are scattered haphazardly around in the undergrowth. Delighted with his find, he carries several to the base of the lilac tree.

He starts work immediately, hauling up the sails and spreading them across the top of the ridge. He nails where he can, and goes up and down for bricks to make them secure. His knees creak alarmingly, but he likes the rhythm of climbing, making an easy route for himself through the lilac. He may be slowly disintegrating as he grows older, but he's more viable than the outhouse.

He's crawling across the roof, holding one end of a sail and trying to pull it smooth, when he hears music. He stops immediately and listens, but there's no sound except the wind. He moves again, and the music comes back, like something you glimpse out of the corner of your eye. He stops and starts several times, puzzled that he can't always hear it. It takes another five minutes before he realises that he's making the music. He's whistling as he works.

He feels useful and capable, and finds himself calculating what to do next. He could go to the B&Q store, next to Sainsbury's, and get extra polythene for the small ridge. He could buy some new beams, balance them on the trolley, put them in before she returns.

As he climbs down the lilac for the last time, he hears the church clock striking and counts the chimes. Two o'clock. Where did the morning go? The weeds are growing frenetically in his absence. He shouldn't have neglected them this morning – he'll never catch up. The number seventy-eight has been missing for four hours. He's rushed past it, ignored it, forgotten it. But they're still there, waiting for him – 1 + 2 + 3 . . .

Standing near the gate, he looks up at the roof. The sails are ruffling gently in the wind, but apparently secure. He starts to worry about Imogen Doody again, a jittery fear creeping through him. Will she be pleased, or will she be annoyed at his interference? Should he have done it? Has he implied that she's incapable of doing it herself?

Should he take it down again? He walks back to the house, comes away again, unable to think. Cars are rushing past the gate on the corner, and there seem to be hundreds of them, the entire population of Hillingham wanting to spy on him. Can they see him? Will they tell her it was him?

He picks up his rope and hammer and nails, and retreats. He doesn't want to be seen, for people to make a connection between him and her roof.

As he hovers, he goes over the events of the previous day in his mind. Was it really his fault that she fell? What did he do? He stood at the gate for a few minutes. Nothing more. But even now, he can feel the urgency of her shouting, and worries again about the roof. Her presence is so powerful, so electric, that she can make him nervous without even being there.

He decides he shouldn't be there. It's not his property. He pushes the trolley to the gate, opens it and leaves quickly, before he can be seen. There's a group of smartly dressed women approaching from the village, their mouths moving up and down passionately, all talking at the same time. He looks at the ground and lets them divide and flow round him. He's completely invisible. All is well.

––––––––––

Maggie: 'Why didn't you find out about Felicity earlier? All those pictures in the newspapers, the magazines. I'd have done her first.'

'I didn't know until I saw that poster two years ago. It was the first time I'd seen her.'

'Are you serious?'

'I don't look at newspapers. They're too violent.'

'Are you really the best person to make judgements about violence?'

'Leave me alone, Maggie.'

'Absolutely not, Straker.'

'Do you know what happened to my mother?' Felicity is growing stronger in my mind, coming in without any nervousness. More real. She can join the others who are queuing up to have their say.

45

'Well, I think she died.'

'I know that. She had cancer, and I shouldn't have gone to the audition. The nurse wasn't very pleased with me, but Mum said I should go. She'd spent years working for it. Did she know about the crash?'

'How could I know that?'

'You could find out for me.'

'How? Who would know?'

Maggie in her gentle mode, the motherly voice, the caring grandmother: 'Some things you never find out, Felicity.'

'What a waste of time.' Felicity's voice is losing its naïvety, becoming high-pitched, almost strident. 'My mum never told me she was ill until she went into hospital. She made all those sacrifices for me. I need to know. You owe it to me to find out.'

'I've only just started. I expect in time I'll get some idea—'

Maggie, sharp and hard again: 'Don't flatter yourself, Straker. You can't play at being a miracle-worker. Your miracles will have negative equity.'

'I know.'

———

The rain wakes him as it dashes against the window, hard and angry in the dark. Suleiman and Magnificent are lying at the end of his mattress, curled up inside one another, not yet disturbed by the storm.

The tiny room is suddenly and briefly lit, frozen by a flash into a photograph in time. Then vast claps of thunder burst out above them, rolling loosely around the sky, powerful and uncontained. The cats wake with a jump and howl in harmony with each other, their heads up, their tails straight and upright with terror.

He gets out of bed and pulls waterproofs over his pyjamas. He buttons the jacket, puts on boots and a sou'-wester, then climbs up to the light room. Outside, the world is disintegrating. He fights to open the door on to the outside balcony, pushing against the wind. He reaches for the handrail, and edges his way out, testing his strength, determined to take part in this battle of wills. The rain is a solid sheet, buffeted by wind, sometimes vertical, sometimes parallel. The waves, heaving, crashing monsters, hurl themselves against the cliff and rise up towards him, finally dashing against the lighthouse in an unassuageable rage.

He steadies himself against the wind, braces his legs, and fights to stay there. The wind pins him against the lens and he's unable to move.

'Come and get me!' he shouts. 'Now's your chance. Pick me up, throw me over the cliff.'

His voice makes no sound. It doesn't exist in this chaotic world. He remains stationary and powerless.

'Here I am. You want a sacrifice? I'm your sacrifice. I'm available. Forget everyone else and come for me!'

The wind screams, the rain pours past him and the waves leap into darkness. He's invisible. He stands there for a long time, until he's frozen and drenched and deafened. The thunder moves on and he can see the lightning out at sea – a beacon to guide ships on to the rocks. The new lighthouse flashes with minute precision at the correct intervals. Smug, secure in its superiority.

He and his lighthouse are nothing. Washed up, abandoned, useless.

He pushes his way back inside and undresses. The cats have moved up the bed in his absence, found the warmth that he left and snuggled down under the blankets. He removes them one at a time. Suleiman comes easily and he puts him into the cat basket at the foot of his bed. He purrs briefly and vaguely. Magnificent is more unwilling. He snaps at Straker as he tries to pick him up, so he taps his head firmly and lifts him. Then he crawls into bed. The cats leave the basket and climb back onto the end of the mattress. He feels them on his legs and looks up. Their eyes light up indignantly with every flash of lightning.

He shuts his eyes. The wind and rain continue to hurl themselves against the side of the lighthouse.

You could go quietly mad in a lighthouse when your only companions are cats.

———————

A thin, reedy voice burrows deep into my head, half waking me, but not quite. It's one of the children, crying.

Maggie is here, ready before me. 'Now, now. There's no need for tears. We can't change anything.' When she tries, she projects an extraordinary warmth, and it hurts me – actually makes a physical pain in my chest – that I can't be the recipient of any of it.

I try to speak, but my throat has seized up in my sleep, and no sound comes out.

'Tell me what the matter is, Wayne.'

Did my mother talk to me like that?

'I can't find my mummy. She's gone away and I want her to come back.'

'No, no, no. Your mummy never left you. You left her and she just went on without you. But she misses you.'

The wailing eases and stops. 'Why?'

Maggie pauses. 'Why anything, Wayne? It just is.' Maggie, the great philosopher, the oracle, the source of all wisdom.

'Straker!' she says sharply. 'I know you're listening. What do you think I should say to Wayne?'

I don't know. I don't know.

'Come on, don't you have anything to say?'

The pain in my chest is growing. I can't stop it. I can't speak. It presses against me, pushing, suffocating.

———————

The next morning is breezy but quiet. The violence and the rage have been hidden away, swept under the table, and he's presented with a false serenity. Hypocrite, he thinks, looking at the smug, shining sea.

How many times has he gone up there in a storm and offered himself to the elements? He can't understand why he's constantly rejected. He wants to jump, to leap out into this cauldron of energy and fly through the air for a few seconds. The thought of this brief flight has sustained him for years. He could loose himself from the tight grasp of the seventy-eight, soar freely into a silence in his head before he surrenders and joins them. To expect a little helping hand from the weather doesn't seem unreasonable, but he survives every time.

He takes his breakfast of two stale doughnuts up to the light room and goes out on the balcony to eat, squeezing his legs against the iron railings. It's impossible to reconcile the sea of today with the sea of last night. Despite all the time he's been watching, it can still surprise him.

Suleiman follows him on to the balcony and stretches out in a patch of sun, purring to himself. He looks at Straker affectionately, narrowing his eyes, half asleep before he's finished washing. Straker puts out his hand to rub his ears and the cat pushes his head up against him.

Magnificent never comes up here, but Straker knows exactly where he is. Further back on the headland, he'll be sitting on a grassy mound, silent, alert, watching. Waiting for the first twitch of a mouse's tail. Magnificent is the great survivor. Part of him will be hunting and sustaining himself long after Straker's generation goes.

Straker enjoys the solid texture of the doughnuts, the way the jam oozes as stickily as when it is fresh. Something about it reminds him of his childhood. Every time he takes a first bite, he's eight again, watching his mother's face as the sugar coats his chin and the jam spurts out on to his cheeks. He buys fourteen every Saturday and they usually last all week. If mould appears, he throws them away, but that only happens in summer. The cold preserves them through the winter.

He sits down on the floor next to Suleiman and shuts his eyes, feeling the sun against his eyelids, making calculations.

He spends a few minutes every day memorising the tide tables so that he can carry them around in his head. He needs the structure in advance so that he can organise his thoughts into compartments – a way to force time to pass. He started this process long ago, once he had recognised that he would have to go on living. The routine of the calculations, the predictability, was soothing. He began to like the tides and the moons, the position of the sun, the hours of daylight, the shape of the day. There are charts on his walls – hours, days of the week, months, years. His mind walks down orderly pathways where the edges are laid out – neat, predictable, reliable. The hedges alongside are clipped and immaculate; the angle to each new path is precise, ninety perfect degrees. He likes right angles. The square of the hypotenuse equals the sum of the squares of the two opposite sides. He has a feel for Pythagoras, convinced that their minds are similar. But Pythagoras was ready to take risks, leap into the dark, think the unknown.

Not Straker. He never strays, never thinks the unknown. His mind never moves beyond seventy-eight.

His day is mapped out before him. He has a timetable that he makes out every week, and he sticks to it rigidly. Parcels of time, manageable periods, attainable tasks. Breakfast; working on the garden of the keeper's cottage, growing food that he often never eats; doing his laundry – a little every day – and hanging it out to flap in the wind behind the keeper's cottage; rowing across to Hillingham; shopping; going to the library; writing letters.

Today he's going to break out of his routine again so that he can check on Miss Doody's roof. It makes him nervous, but he needs to know that the sails are still in place after the storm. He won't stop. He'll just pause at the gate, then go away again. When he returns he'll revert to the timetable and write some letters, in an attempt to find more information on the schoolchildren. The list of names doesn't give him enough information. He has to know them. They cannot remain as a block of anonymous children. They were real too, just as much as Maggie, Felicity—

As he goes downstairs and opens the door, Magnificent slips past with a friendly chirrup and runs up the stairs to the food bowls. Straker walks to the edge of the cliff and examines it. There are clear signs of another fall, the edges sharp and irregular, the sandstone bright and exposed.

Returning to the lighthouse, he counts his strides. His instincts were correct. A further two feet of the cliff have disappeared.

Chapter 4

Alan Fisher sat neatly on the train, his back to the engine, pretending to read the *Telegraph*. His feet were placed together, exactly parallel with the side of the train, and he'd folded the newspaper into a manageable size so that he wouldn't disturb his fellow-passengers. He tried not to think about his job. The job that he might not have in a few months' time.

'Targets, Alan,' the men in London had said to him. 'You must have attainable goals that are beyond your present expectations.'

'We do have targets,' said Alan. 'And we reach them.'

Paul Wilson, the marketing manager, was younger than Alan, and reminded him of a schoolboy he had employed last Christmas to stock the shelves. Fair, floppy hair, glasses and a very slight lisp. But somehow he had a threatening presence, even though he talked in a calm, friendly voice, which was never raised. 'We're in a competitive market, Alan. If we don't fight, we get taken over. It's sink or swim in this game.'

Alan sighed without making a sound. He hated the language, the words that meant nothing. It was just a game to these people. He had staff who had stayed with him since he first took over the store. They liked working for him. They felt secure.

He looked out of the train window to where he could see headlights on a distant motorway, and rows of illuminated houses where families would be meeting up, eating together, talking. He turned back to his newspaper and avoided looking at the girl opposite.

She was very pretty, her long arms dropping gracefully down to her lap, but her purple skirt was far too short. He could just catch sight of the black lace edging her knickers. She wriggled slightly, trying to readjust the skirt, but it was not flexible enough and he glanced away quickly.

'Excuse me.'

He raised his eyes and she was looking straight at him.

'Do they have a buffet on the train?'

'I don't know,' he said.

'They do a lovely fruit cake,' she said, in an immaculate BBC accent. 'I saw it on the train to London. It's yellow, packed with cherries and sultanas.'

He smiled. 'Perhaps you should go and get some.'

'Yes,' she said, but she didn't move. His eyes slid on to her legs, which were too thin, he thought.

He was hungry. He wanted to be home, away from this sharp, hard world where he didn't belong.

'Hello,' he would call out, as he came through the front door.

Nobody would answer, but it wouldn't matter because he knew where they were. Stuart would be upstairs doing his homework. Perhaps later, after supper, Alan would go up and they could worry away at maths problems together. He liked that. He would sit on Stuart's bed and ignore the posters of Hot Gossip on the wall, understanding his need to impress his friends.

Stuart was taller than both of his parents, calm, with grey eyes, and comfortable with everyone. He was perpetually easy, a skilled rugby player, and somehow in control of his life.

They often struggled on his maths together. 'How about the 180 degrees on a straight line?' said Alan.

'No,' said Stuart. 'It's not a straight line.'

'Good point,' said Alan. He realised that, of course, but he loved to see his son working things out, untangling the threads and straightening them back into clear, logical lines.

Kieran would not hear him come in. He would be out in the back garden, absorbed by his latest project – building a run for his rabbit – and would only come in for supper if someone went to fetch him. More than once, Alan had stood unnoticed behind him, watching. He wanted to step forward, take the pliers or the hammer, and make his progress easier, but he knew he couldn't do this, that his son had to find his own way, however tortuous it might be.

Kieran was small for his age and wore glasses. He looked clever and bookish, but he wasn't. He never seemed to make the right connections in any part of his life. Reading, maths, friendships. They all slipped away from his grasp, leaving him lost, bewildered, confused. Alan pictured him now, the curly hair that resisted any kind of control, the shirt that never stayed tucked into his trousers, the quick, nervous movements of his fingers as he fiddled with a piece of wire.

Eventually, Alan would speak: 'Hi, Kieran. I'm back.'

And Kieran would turn round, smile at him, his eyes crinkling. 'Great, Dad. What's for supper?' Alan couldn't bear to think of him becoming a teenager.

The girl opposite Alan on the train kept opening her briefcase and reading something inside, her lips moving silently. He thought she could be really pretty if she made more effort – softer clothes, calmer makeup and better hair. Whatever had made her shave away most of her hair and dye it purple and green? It looked very odd. Guiltily he realised that she probably had cancer. The chemotherapy did that to hair, he remembered, and maybe the colour was a protest.

She met his gaze again and smiled, her large eyes luminous and beautiful. 'I've just got a contract,' she said.

'Really?'

She must have been waiting for an invitation to talk. 'It's for a cosmetics company. My mum always wanted me to be The Face. Modelling tights wasn't good enough for her. "Go for the top," she said. It's with *Parrot*.' She looked at him as if she expected him to know the name.

'*Parrot*?' he said.

She nodded. 'Yes. Do you know it? I've just done a photoshoot. I had to put grey on my cheeks to highlight the cheekbones and green mascara. They made me stand in a sandpit with a parrot on my shoulder, and there was a wind machine to make my clothes all wild.'

'Goodness,' he said.

She smiled again and looked out of the window, folding her hands neatly on her lap.

———

'Look, Alan,' said Paul, 'cards on the table. You have six months to improve your profits.'

'And then what?' said Alan, knowing what he was going to say.

'Then we have to review your position.' Paul smiled, opened his hands wide. 'But we both know there isn't going to be a problem, don't we?'

Alan would have liked to resign there, on the spot, and walk out of this world of profit-margins, share-holders, management jargon. But he had a family.

'One other thing, Alan.'

Alan held his breath.

'You're going to have to hot things up for your staff. Set them individual targets. You need to isolate those who are slacking, marginalise them. Give them the message that they have to deliver the goods or leave.'

Alan had never given anyone the sack in his life. 'I have good staff,' he said. 'Loyal, hard-working—'

'But not hard-working enough. You could be more efficient with less staff, and that's where I want you to start. You need to lose ten per cent.'

Lose? How do you lose people? Drop them into the big

freezer at the back of the shop and put the lid down? Send them out on the motorway for a non-existent delivery? He tried not to say this because he knew he would have to try. He couldn't afford to be sacked. He and Harriet had been talking about schools this morning.

Harriet had finally put it into words: 'Kieran is not going to get into the grammar school.' She bent her head over her morning cornflakes and refused to look him in the eye.

The top of her head is beautiful, he thought. He knew its shape: the low smooth forehead, the unusual bump at the back, the way the strands of hair fell away from the centre parting, light brown and turning gently grey.

'He won't survive in Trinity Road comprehensive,' she said, still not looking at him.

'No.' He sipped his coffee. He thought of Kieran's enthusiasms. Building impossible edifices for his pets, kicking a football around in the back garden, longing to be in a team, believing he could get there if he practised hard enough.

'We have to look for a private school,' she said.

It was inevitable. He couldn't send his cheerful, untidy, vulnerable son to a place where older boys beat up younger boys when they wouldn't hand over their bus passes or dinner money. He had seen them come out of school, smoking openly, aggressive with anyone who gave them more than a passing glance: 'Who d'you think you're looking at?'

He sat on the train, opposite the girl with the long, classic neck and perfect teeth, and rehearsed his speech to his staff. Targets, incentives, the least efficient ten per cent out in a month's time. Orders from above. Everything inside him reacted against it, but there was no choice. He had to pay for Kieran's education.

Harriet would not have started to cook supper, he knew. She always waited for him. 'You're so much better at it than me,' she would say, with a smile.

He loved to come in and find her sitting in the living room, knitting in her lap, a book open on the side-table, Barry Manilow playing on the record player. He would kiss the top of her head, that centre parting. 'How are you today?' he would say.

'A bit tired.' She would move the wheelchair past him and head for the kitchen.

'It's all right,' he would say. 'I'll do supper.'

He was tired, but he knew that she would be more tired. Supper wouldn't take long. Half an hour for the potatoes and carrots, twenty minutes to grill the lamb cutlets. He was pleased that she always waited for him to come home, that they still sat down together every evening for a family meal.

He checked his watch. Ten past seven. Only another twelve minutes on the train.

Chapter 5

'Jonathan. It's Imogen. Listen. You know the roof?'

'What roof?'

Voices in the background are arguing about how to cook pasta. 'I'm talking about the cottage.'

'I've got friends here, Imogen.'

He's always got friends there. They hang around in the kitchen and cook together – arguing most of the time. 'Right. Well, I brought a tile home with me, so I could get some more, but it's not the same.'

'The same as what?'

'The same as the tiles in B&Q. Any idea where I can get old ones?'

Murmuring in the background – 'The oil needs to be hotter.'

Doody leans forward tensely, putting pressure on her swollen ankle. Reacting to the pain, she eases back into the sofa and places her foot on the chair opposite. 'Jonathan, are you still there?'

'Yes, yes.' She can hear the effort he makes to talk to her. He'd rather go back to his cooking, but it's impossible to find a good time to talk to him.

'You must know the right place to go.'

'I've no idea. I haven't got much experience with these things.'

If only he wouldn't sound so pathetic. 'Rubbish. You've got all the tools. You built your own kitchen, for goodness' sake, and you were right about the book.' He probably paid someone to do the kitchen and didn't tell her.

'It's not the same as doing a roof.'

'Come on, Jonathan, help me.' She hates begging, but she needs his advice. He's the only man she knows well enough to ask. She could ask Philip Hollyhead, the headmaster at her school, but she can already hear his response: 'Fixing roofs, now, Doody? Is there no end to your talents?'

Which means that he sees her as a little woman, a caretaker with no intellect, who wouldn't even contemplate writing a book. People with powerful brains don't do practical things. They pay someone else to do them while they make money. Philip likes to believe he knows her. He hasn't even got to the front door.

'You're going to have to get someone to do it,' says Jonathan.

'No. I want to do it myself.'

'It doesn't sound as if you can. Where are you going to find antique tiles?'

'They're not antique. They're just old.' Maybe he's right and they're worth a fortune. How does she find out?

'Whatever. Meanwhile, I imagine the only solution is to remove all the existing tiles and start again.'

'There has to be a better way.'

'Not that I can think of. I keep telling you, I'm not an expert. You need someone who knows about these things.'

She imagines his friends round the kitchen table, chopping mushrooms and carrots together. They probably have whisky in front of them, their lap-tops open so that they can fiddle with finances between courses. Jonathan doesn't like wasting time.

'It would cost a fortune to buy new tiles.'

'Yes. You should get some quotes, but don't take the cheapest. Ask for qualifications, experience, references.'

She's heard this before. If a job's worth doing, it should be done well, says Jonathan. Never mind the expense. 'Don't be ridiculous,' she says. 'I can't afford to pay someone.'

'Look,' says Jonathan, and the tone of his voice indicates

that his eyes are being drawn back to the garlic sauce on the hob, 'if you really want to do this, I'll help with the cost.'

'It doesn't matter,' she says. 'I'll sell it. I could do with the money.'

'OK,' he says. 'Let me know if you change your mind.'

She puts the phone down hard and catches her nail under the receiver. She sucks it miserably. She knows Jonathan. He starts by offering her money. By next week he'll have reduced it by half. By the following week it will be an offer to lend her a fraction of what she needs. He means to be generous, but his lifelong association with money makes it impossible for him to share.

When Jonathan was six and Imogen was fourteen, he first revealed his fascination with finance. He sat next to her at their father's funeral and whispered in her ear, 'What happens to Daddy's money?'

'What money?' Imogen was watching her mother sitting unmovingly in front of her, wondering why she didn't cry. Surely everyone cried at funerals. Especially if they were married to the corpse. Why did she sit so still, her face so composed, so controlled in the heather tweed suit that she always wore on smart occasions?

'He must have made a will.'

Imogen looked down at his earnest little face. He was wearing the short grey trousers and maroon blazer of his school uniform and a tiny maroon and gold striped tie. Even when he was six, it was easy to see where he was going. He was very serious. He wasn't interested in having fun.

She shrugged. 'I don't know. I suppose he has.'

She thought they should all be dressed in black. Her mother should have a black veil over her face and break into tears as she threw a clod of earth on to the coffin. They should stand around the grave on a bleak November day to remember their father. Rooks should be circling in the bare branches of the trees, cawing bleakly in the bitter wind.

'He might have left everything to me. I'm the only son.'

'Ssh.' People were turning slightly towards them, sympathetic, but unwilling to tolerate much whispering.

'He told me he wanted me to take over from him. The man of the family. I'll need the money.'

'Don't be silly. Mummy will have the money.'

He looked so sweet sitting there, his eyebrows crushed as he worried about money, his solemn eyes framed by his first pair of glasses. He had amused people then because he looked like a miniature man. They had always wanted to hug him. Nobody had wanted to hug Imogen.

There wasn't a grave. Daddy was cremated and Mummy never shed a tear. She even asked people not to send flowers. 'Such a waste,' she said. 'Send the money to a charity.'

It might have been better if someone had recognised that they were in need of charity.

'I've already made my will,' said Jonathan later, following Imogen with a plate of chocolate biscuits as she carried cups of tea to the people who came back to the house. He kept eating them himself when he thought nobody was looking. Everyone was out in the garden, talking cheerfully among the lavender, the yellow roses and the box hedges. It was June and a very hot day. Every now and again bursts of laughter broke out, and they all seemed to be having a good time. Imogen couldn't understand it. She'd always thought that funerals were meant to be sad.

'Go away,' she said crossly.

'I won't put you in my will.'

'You haven't got anything to leave.'

'That's what you think.'

A tall man with dark crinkly hair and hazel eyes bent towards them. 'Best to make an early start on your financial affairs,' he said. Hugh Mandleson, a colleague of her father. His voice was deep and solemn.

Imogen could feel a deep flush creeping up her face and she stared intently at his feet – large, in laced tan-leather shoes. She had not been able to look at him directly since she had heard her parents discussing the fact that he used to be a pilot before he became a solicitor. A real live hero, a man who flew aeroplanes, who knew how it felt to fly.

'That's what I've been telling Imogen,' said Jonathan, in his usual clear, confident tone.

'Terrific,' said Hugh Mandleson, and wandered off to talk to someone else. Imogen watched his long back and despised herself for not being able to talk to him.

Celia came up to them. 'Mummy wants you in the kitchen,' she said to Imogen. Her clever green eyes looked out from under her fringe. She was wearing her ash-blonde hair down and it was long and completely straight. She disappeared every fifteen minutes to comb it. Imogen hated that hair. She wanted to creep through the house at night and cut it off while Celia was asleep. For a time, this was her favourite daydream.

She was pleased to go and leave Jonathan and Celia together. They would enjoy plotting about money. They had a lot in common.

The only recollection she has now of Jonathan being truly happy is when he was winning at Monopoly. He glowed. He made no concessions, no easy terms if you landed on Mayfair with a hotel, or if someone wanted to buy Bond Street from him. He asked outrageous prices, so no one except him ever had complete sets for houses. He was born to be a money-maker.

————

Doody knows that she can't afford to keep the cottage.

It doesn't matter. Six months ago she didn't have it, and in six months' time she won't have it again. She'll just return to where she was. When her ankle's better, she'll go down and find an estate agent. The land must be worth something. The cottage is too neglected anyway, and probably needs to be knocked down. Why would she want something that's going to drain her limited money supply? What's the point?

She hobbles around the house irritably, frustrated by her limitations. She's been to the hospital and had her foot X-rayed, but it's not broken, just sprained. It still hurts, though, and she left the car in Hillingham, so she can't go out much. Normally at half-term she goes round the second-hand bookshops, looking for first editions. She's wasting all her free time—

She's concerned about the car. Did she lock it securely? There'll be vandals in Hillingham – people aren't more honest because they live in the country. She spends time with her Biggles collection, taking the books out and dusting them, holding them, reading random sections. It's so much easier to like an unreal person than a real one. There's no mess. You can be sure that he won't just disappear when you're not looking.

She concentrates on her writing. By now, Mandles has crashed into the sea and swum to a deserted beach, somewhere on the Devon coast. He is limping badly, having sprained his ankle in the wreckage.

The sun was at its zenith, a brilliant, pulsating orb of suffocating heat—

Outside, it's grey and windy, thick clouds lowering over the school, the poplar trees on the edge of the playground twisting furiously in the gale. She worries about the rain coming into her cottage through the holes in the roof.

Every now and again, tiny traces of doubt tiptoe into her mind. Should she be doing something more useful with her time? But she loves the way her mind works when she writes – clearly, logically – and that she can organise everything. People do what she wants them to do. It gives her a control that she has never managed to master in her own life, however hard she tries, or angry she gets. Surely writing children's books is a legitimate occupation.

Philip Hollyhead, the headmaster, eventually comes to see her. He hovers on the doorstep. 'Just came to see how you are, Doody.'

Instant caring. It's taken him nearly a week to walk the hundred yards from his house to hers. 'Come in,' she says, and hobbles into the kitchen ahead of him. 'I'll make you some tea.'

'It's not necessary.' He talks to her with a detached indifference, as if she doesn't matter.

'What's that got to do with it? Just sit down.'

He sits down. She should have been a teacher. She likes telling people what to do – especially if they obey – and Philip is usually compliant because he's used to it. His wife, Doris the Lion Tamer, gives orders all the time, and he slips easily into a nonchalant resignation to her demands. It infuriates Doody and makes her more determined to annoy him.

'So, how's the leg?'

'It hurts,' she says. 'That's why I'm limping.'

He pauses, but she won't say any more if he doesn't ask.

He looks uncomfortable at the kitchen table. He rarely comes into her house, and she knows how much he would like to examine the evidence of her existence, but she won't let him. She watches him steadily, and he's nervous about letting his eyes wander while he is being watched. He's about fifty-five, and probably contemplating an early retirement. His hair is receding towards its own retirement, and the strands left at the back are an unrealistic solid brown. He probably gives it a rinse once a week, somehow avoiding dyeing the bald bits.

'I've inherited a cottage,' Doody says, as she plugs in the kettle.

He looks pleased to have something to talk about. 'What good news. Where is it?'

'In Devon, on the coast, near the village of Hillingham. I expect you know it.'

He doesn't, of course, but she likes to make him feel

ignorant. 'How exciting. Will you move down there?' He lays his hands in front of him on the table and examines his fingernails. She can see that he's wondering if she'll give up her job.

'No,' she says. 'I'll sell it.'

'Oh.'

They've worked together for the last seven years, since Philip took over as headmaster. He's been there longer than his predecessors, and Doody knows him better than she did any of the others, but he is no good at conversation. He treats her as if she's not his intellectual equal. She's tempted to prove him wrong, but it's more fun to let him believe she's stupid. That way, she keeps the element of surprise, the excitement of knowing she can shock him at any time.

'How many sugars, Philip?'

'None for me,' he says, with a faint grimace. 'Doris never allows it.'

He once asked Doody to call him 'Headmaster' or 'Mr Hollyhead' in front of the children. 'It's a matter of respect,' he said. 'For the children's benefit.'

'All right, Philip. I'll think about it.' Now she makes a point of calling him Philip wherever they are.

She hops to the kettle as it boils and pours the water into the teapot. 'It was nice of you to come and see me.'

'It's always a pleasure to see you, Imogen.'

'You'll have to take the teapot to the table. I'll probably spill it.'

'Yes, of course.' He gets to his feet immediately. 'How did you hurt your leg, did you say?'

'I fell off the roof.' It sounds better than getting caught in hawthorn. She hasn't told him the details yet. He hasn't seemed interested.

'Oh,' he says, and she knows he isn't listening.

She pours his cup of tea and pushes it over to him.

'I was wondering,' he says, after a pause, 'are you going to be able to mow the field in the next few weeks? The children like playing out on the grass now the weather's better. Should I find someone else to do it?'

'No, I'll be fine soon.' She fiddles with the spoon in the sugar bowl, scooping up the sugar and letting it all fall out. She wants to distract him. 'Is that Charlie Miller out there?' she says, peering past him with a worried expression.

He turns in alarm. Doody lifts the spoon of sugar to his cup, hesitates, then pours it in. 'Oh, no, sorry. It's a magpie on the roof.'

He turns back and regards her suspiciously. 'There's not much resemblance between Charlie Miller and a magpie.'

'A trick of light,' she says, watching him sip tea.

'Could you keep your cottage for weekends or holidays?'

'No,' she says. 'It's too much trouble.'

'This is a very good cup of tea, Doody,' he says.

———

She dreams of Oliver d'Arby. She walks through the front door of the cottage and out into the back garden where he's playing the cello. The deep dark tones reach inside her and stir up something in a long-forgotten secret place. She becomes aware of tears sliding down her cheeks, dripping off her chin. She's incensed that he should make her cry, and rushes up behind him.

'Stop it!' she shouts. 'Stop it!'

He stops abruptly in the middle of the tune and turns to face her. He's tall and thin with a grey and black grizzled beard and a long scar from the corner of his eye to his chin.

She wakes up and decides that, as soon as she can walk properly, she'll go down to Hillingham and find an estate agent. It won't matter if she doesn't make much money from the sale. Every penny is welcome. She's only a school caretaker.

———

The doctor told her not to put any pressure on the foot, but after three weeks of boredom, she finds she can limp adequately. The hospital has lent her some crutches, which she only needs for longer stretches. She catches the train and takes a taxi. More money dripping away.

When she goes in through the gate (her gate, not Oliver d'Arby's), she sees the flattened pathway to the house, the hawthorn bush where she fell, the tangle of wild and tamed flowers, and feels again the sense of ownership that she felt before. She's never owned a house, never had possessions. Everything has been borrowed, scrounged, donated. Markets, Salvation Army, Oxfam.

Then she looks up at the roof. She rubs her eyes and looks again. Somebody has been up there. Two large sheets of off-white plastic have been draped over the main part, either nailed down or held in place by bricks and stones.

For a while, she can't work it out. Were they there last time and she didn't notice? But she went up on the roof, crawled along it looking for gaps. Someone else has been up there. He hasn't even done a good job. One edge has come away completely from the side and is flapping noisily in the wind.

She knows who it is. How dare he come here without her? It's her house. She's the one to save it, not him.

The woman in the post office smiles at her as she goes up to the counter. She's small and suntanned and wrinkled, like a sultana. The place is empty. Just Doody standing at the counter with nothing to buy.

'I want to find a man,' she starts.

The woman keeps smiling. 'Oh, I don't think we can help you here. Aren't there agencies for that sort of thing?'

Doody stares at her. Is she deaf, stupid or making some kind of joke? 'I want his name.'

'Whose name?' The woman fiddles with some forms and looks genuinely perplexed.

'The man. Very tall and thin, with messy hair and a beard. Looks like he's out of an old black-and-white horror film.'

Someone comes into the post office and stands behind her, so that she finds herself part of a queue. There's immediate pressure on her to hurry up.

'Hello, Mrs Whittaker,' says the post-mistress. 'Lovely weather – just right for June.'

'Bit windy for me,' says the woman. Doody refuses to acknowledge her, or take part in this conversation. She was here first.

'He has a scar,' she says, her voice shaking with the effort of staying calm, 'and he's not chatty.'

'That'll be Mr Straker,' says the voice behind her, comfortable and knowledgeable. Doody turns to look at her. She's elderly, her curly grey hair pinned back with an array of grips. She peers at Doody over the top of her glasses. 'Who are you?'

Doody concentrates on being pleasant until she's got the information she wants. 'Straker,' she says. 'Where does he live?'

'He lives in the lighthouse.'

'You won't get anything out of him,' says the woman behind the counter. 'He never talks.'

'Never? That's impossible.'

'Well, he manages it.' She looks very smug.

Doody ignores her and turns back to Mrs Whittaker. 'He's the lighthouse keeper?'

'Oh, no. There's a new lighthouse on the next headland. Mr Straker just lives in the old one.'

Doody pauses to think about this. He lives in a lighthouse. He has a scar and he doesn't talk. Is he real? 'How do I get to the lighthouse?'

'It's a long way. You can take a number twenty bus to the

beginning of the path and then walk about a mile across the cliff.'

'Could I take a taxi to get closer?'

Mrs Whittaker shakes her head and a grip falls out. 'There's no road. You'd never get a taxi driver to do it.'

'I wouldn't go out there on your own,' says the post-mistress.

'Why not?' Doody remembers her fears about this man on the day she hurt her ankle. Was she right to have worried?

'I'm told he's killed someone. That's why he doesn't talk.' Her voice deepens and drops to barely above a whisper.

Doody experiences a great desire to argue with her. She laughs and talks more loudly. 'Rubbish. I've already met him. He's perfectly normal.' Not true, but she refuses to acknowledge the nagging worry she can feel at the base of her stomach.

Mrs Whittaker puts her hand on Doody's arm gently. 'Just be careful, my dear, that's all. If even half of what they say about him is true, you would be unwise to put yourself at risk.'

Her touch is hot and clammy, and Doody steps back with distaste, anxious to break the contact. She compares it to Straker's cool, competent hands untangling her ankle three weeks ago, and knows which she wants to trust. 'So why isn't he in prison, then?'

Mrs Whittaker raises her eyebrows a fraction. 'Maybe he has been.'

Doody smiles brightly. 'Don't worry. I'll ask him who he's killed. That'll show I'm on to him.'

'He won't tell you,' says the post-mistress.

'How do you know? He might talk to me.' Doody makes a silent promise to herself. She will somehow make him talk – about anything – just to prove she can do it.

'No,' says Mrs Whittaker, shaking her head. 'He won't talk.'

'I'll let you know,' says Doody, and limps out of the post office.

So she has to walk a mile. No problem. She has crutches. The ankle's getting better.

————————

Half-way to the lighthouse, she regrets her decision. Her shoulders ache from the crutches, the bad foot throbs, the good foot is developing blisters and there's a fierce wind that seems determined to prevent her moving forward.

She pauses to think. Should she go back? But she's half-way there and still fired up by her decision to confront him. She can rest when she reaches the lighthouse. She refuses to give up. There's an added incentive now that she's talked to the smug, elderly natives of Hillingham. She'll get him to talk even if they can't manage it.

Of course, he might murder her instead. Beneath her public performance, there's a jittery awareness that he is more sinister than she's acknowledged. But he's had his chance to kill her off and didn't take it. On the contrary, he helped her. Surely that should count for something. Unless he has some secret plot that he has yet to reveal and intends her to come out to the lighthouse alone. Is that why he put those sheets on her roof?

She dismisses the theory almost immediately. He is too stupid. A murderer would be clever and calculating.

Anyway, she would know if she was being manipulated.

This walk to the lighthouse is like running a marathon. Ambitious and exhausting, but as you approach the finish, you find a fresh energy, a second wind, a rush of adrenaline to give the final push. The closer she gets, the more excited she becomes. She wonders if he might be out, but persuades herself that it's unlikely.

————————

She stands at the bottom of the lighthouse and peers up. It is old and neglected, long dark patches emerging through the paint at the bottom, and streaks of rust dripping down from the window-frames over the red and white stripes. The light at the top has a neat, circular green roof, topped by a perfect half-sphere that makes it look like a mosque. There are green railings on the edges of the balcony that surrounds the light. They're all rusting too.

A cat rubs against her leg and nearly pushes her over. She struggles to remain upright. 'Hey, show some manners.'

The door opens unexpectedly and there he is, exactly as he looked last time, same beard, same blue eyes, same wellington boots.

'You!' she shouts at him.

He takes a step backwards with an appalled expression.

'I know your name. Straker. Remember me? I'm the one who owns a cottage. The one with the roof.'

He stares at her and says nothing.

'Who said you could go up on my roof? Did I ask you to? Did I give you permission? Is it your roof or mine?' She feels better. The tiredness and the aching have gone. 'If I'd wanted you to go on my roof,' she points her finger at him and waves it wildly in the rhythm of her words, 'I'd have asked you. What gives you the right to—'

The door closes in front of her, squeaking in protest. She can't believe what she's seeing. 'Open the door again!' she shouts. 'How dare you do this to me?'

The door remains closed. She tries knocking on it with her fists. 'Open the door. I was talking to you.'

She can't make an impression. The wood is too thick and it absorbs the energy of her arms, so the blows don't make a satisfying enough sound, and it hurts her hands.

'Open the door!' she shrieks. She picks up some stones and hurls them against it, one at a time, but the sound is still too small. They bounce back and fall ineffectually to the ground.

After a few minutes, she walks a distance away and sits down on the grass facing the sea, her back to the lighthouse. It's very windy.

She's trying hard not to cry.

Chapter 6

Straker is not interested in the rows of televisions in the window of Curry's or the newspaper headlines where they line the shelves at the entrance to Sainsbury's. What he needs to know is all in the past. The facts will never change, the lives can't go on, so he's desperate to find out about them and make them real. The voices in his dreams must have something to say. If he can just hang on to them, they can go on existing, be living people and not just figures in grainy newspaper pictures. Every time he receives an answer to a letter, it's like a new mark on someone's portrait. A crease in the dress, a shaft of sunlight on a cheekbone, a glint in the eye behind the glasses. He knows Felicity's father is not telling the truth, but there's something there – maybe a trace of truth in his lies.

There was once, a long time ago, a history teacher called Mr Hardcastle, who'd believed in him. 'Apply to university, Peter,' he'd said, his penetrating eyes peering out over his red, porous nose. 'You're good at drawing the truth from historical documents. Do something useful.'

Mr Hardcastle had appeared in Straker's mind recently, while he was walking out of the village towards the library. Thirty minutes' walk there, an hour's research, thirty minutes back. He stopped as if the teacher was there in front of him, tall, skeletal, drooping over his pile of exercise books. His look was one of such reproach that Straker felt he was being cut open with a scalpel. He could feel the flesh above his heart being parted, folded outwards, exposed to the passing breeze. He struggled to breathe, to speak to Mr Hardcastle, but nothing came out.

'Go to university, Peter.'

If only, if only—

Seventy-eight people would still be alive.

Unless they'd had another accident instead. This thought eases the sharp pain slightly. One person might have walked under a bus the next day. Another could have died of a heart-attack within six months. He had just speeded the whole thing up. Got rid of them in one easy step.

He doesn't know Doody's at the door. He's listening to the wind when he comes downstairs. It rattles the window of his sleep room, usually randomly but today it seems more orga-nised. Gusts are coming at regular intervals, cannon balls fired at the lighthouse. Somewhere out to sea there's an intelligence, someone who wants to destroy him, and knows how to wear down his resistance.

He's timed the bangs – 15 seconds apart. 78 bangs would take 1170 seconds – 19 minutes, 30 seconds. He has been sitting on his mattress and counting. The nearer he gets to 78, the more alarming it becomes. A roll-call in his head, a funeral bell tolling into the wind. He'll go to 50, he decides, and then stop counting. But 50 comes and goes. 60, 70, 77. He leaps up in panic and runs down the stairs, his feet clattering on the concrete steps, the number 78 chasing behind him.

'You!' she says, as he opens the door.

He looks at her in confusion, waiting for the number to catch him up and explode over his head. What does she mean? He isn't the seventy-eighth. Is she the seventy-eighth – alive after all? Has the number gone down to seventy-seven and nobody's bothered to tell him?

She's too close and he steps back, but she moves forward and fills the space. She's wearing a brilliant peacock-blue blouse that hangs loosely over her stomach, flapping in the wind, and patterned leggings that end half-way down her legs, making them look unnaturally thin. She's waving a finger, pointing at him, but he doesn't understand. It's not the seventy-eight that frightens him, not the words she's saying or the stabbing finger. It's the anger.

He's seen people like this before. Twenty-four years ago, on the first day of the inquest. He'd returned to his own house after a few suffocating weeks with his parents, but for the first time in his adult life, he missed his father's confident presence. Straker came out of his house, and was confronted by a bewildering crowd of people and their anger. He knew they were there because he'd seen them from the window, but he wasn't prepared for the noise. There were journalists with cameras, calling out questions, and a group of policemen attempting to hold back the people so that he could get into the waiting car, but the women were the most frightening.

'Murderer!' they screamed.

'String him up!'

He heard the words, but couldn't take in any of them.

There was a woman at the front with a little boy in a pushchair. He was wrapped in an all-in-one blue suit, with the hood up, fastened firmly round his chubby face. He was sucking a dummy and gazing out serenely, unmoved by the commotion around him.

His mother had shoulder-length ginger hair, thick with tangled ringlets. She might have been huge, or it might only have been her mouth. Perhaps she was pretty when she was at home feeding her baby, perhaps the father of her child loved her. But now her lipsticked mouth was open and cavernous, forming all sorts of words that children shouldn't hear. And her eyes were wild and rolling. There were other women there, but she dominated the scene.

'Get in!' yelled the solicitor from the car. A policeman

grabbed Pete by the head and pushed him on to the back seat.

The door closed. They were safe, shielded from the anger. The car edged its way through the crowd, which parted reluctantly to let it through.

Journalists ran alongside for a while, their cameras flashing optimistically.

The last face Pete saw was that of the ginger-haired woman, her eyes bulging with anger, her scarlet mouth spitting at him. He could just see the boy in the pushchair, who had gone to sleep. He's started to worry about that child recently. Was he deaf? What chance did he have with a mother like that?

Streaks of red poured down one window.

'Blood!' said Pete. 'Where's it come from?'

'Tomatoes,' said his solicitor. 'They're throwing tomatoes.' He sounded quietly proud, as if this was the high point of his career.

———

Miss Doody's hair is blonde, dyed, presumably, and there are no ringlets, just straight, dangling, unevenly cut chunks. But there's something about her face, the pointing finger, that makes Straker remember. There's a terror building up inside him, pulsing down his legs, along his arms, into his fingertips, his toes, the tips of his ears. The scar on his face is throbbing. He sees her angry face without hearing the words. She seems to be repeating the word 'roof'.

He shuts the door.

Standing on the other side, he shivers into the emptiness, temporarily paralysed by fear. He starts to count. Backwards from seventy-eight. He stops shaking. Numbers going down, bodies decreasing, people being resurrected, into the twenties, below twenty, single figures—

After a time, she stops shouting and starts throwing things at the door. Whatever she's using, it doesn't make much impression. Then that stops too. There's a silence. The cat-flap rattles and Suleiman climbs through, looking annoyed, ruffled. He stares at Straker, as if it were his fault, then races past him, up the stairs.

Straker waits for a long time, aching into the emptiness. He remembers the other silence in the garden, under the hawthorn, which he shared with her. Is it happening again? Him inside, her out? No. Today, they're so far apart they're at opposite ends of the world.

Gradually, as his numbers go into minus figures, sensation returns to his legs, so he climbs the stairs, putting a greater distance between him and her, right up to the light room, and the balcony. The expanse of the sea opens up before him, empty and vast, blending with the horizon so they become part of each other with no defining line. The rhythm of the waves racing towards him, the inevitability of their progress, soothes him. He stands there for a long time and clears his mind.

His original instincts were correct. She's furious that he attempted to help. It seems obvious now. He should have known that she's not someone who needs help and anything he offers is inevitably going to be wrong. Tomorrow he'll go back and remove the sails.

————

Wayne is crying again.

'Stop whingeing,' says Katie. 'You're always crying.'

'Poor little thing,' says Felicity, and her voice has become softer, childish again.

Wayne: 'I want my mummy.'

Katie: 'We all want our mummies. You're only saying that because you want some sympathy.'

How old are these children?

'Nine years old, all of them. You should know that.' Maggie knows everything. 'Thirty-three children. A whole third-year class from Piccadilly Street Junior. You wiped them out.'

Alan is there too. 'It's the best age. Close to you, not ready to be a teenager.'

Maggie: *'How do you run a school with a whole class missing? Have you thought about that? A third of the year not there. Does it affect their budget? What do they do with an empty classroom and the spare teacher? How do they work out the numbers when they all go up to senior school?'*

'Please, Maggie. Give me a break.'

Silence.

Her silences are more confusing than her accusations.

––––––––––

He follows the progress of a wave as it rolls in towards the rocks, but something distracts him. Lowering his gaze, he can see Miss Doody, sitting on the cliff with her back to the lighthouse. Her legs are sticking out in front of her awkwardly, like two pieces of string, ending in sandals with ridiculously high heels. There are two crutches on the grass beside her.

Instinctively, he steps back. Has she seen him? He stands with his back against the light for some time, then returns to the railings. She's still there, unmoving, looking out to sea. Is she going to go away, or will she stay there for ever? Panic starts to bubble away inside him again. He doesn't know what to do.

He tries to watch the sea, but now there is something sinister about the way the waves never stop. Every time one reaches the rocks, there is another just behind, leaping along, waiting to take its place. Nothing alters, nothing breaks the pattern. Why is she here? What does she want from him? Has she walked all this way on crutches? Can't she see that he has no time for her? What happens if she doesn't go away?

What does she want?

He steps forward to the railings. He doesn't want her to see him, so he moves cautiously, but her position hasn't changed. He goes back in, out again, in again. He's sweating with fear, but the wind cools the sweat and he starts to shiver.

He returns downstairs to the room he uses as a study and sits at the battered table, which is covered with books and papers. He finds a pile of letters and makes himself read them through.

Dear Mr Straker,

Further to your enquiry of 26 May, I enclose details to the best of my knowledge. My parents have been greatly missed by three generations of our family . . .

I would be interested in reading your research on the 1979 crash . . .

Wayne's parents moved out of the area after the crash . . .

He reads each letter several times, but can't take them in. Just the first lines, forcing himself to concentrate, but they become random symbols, running in and out of his mind without meaning. He doesn't know how long he sits there, but it feels like hours. Eventually he stands up, stretches his legs, and runs up and down a flight of stairs several times, timing himself. Six seconds up. Five seconds down. Faster: five seconds up. Three seconds down. He runs up to the balcony again and leans over the railings.

She's still there. She's not going to go away.

He will ignore her. Presumably she'll disappear in the end. He doesn't need to go downstairs for days. He has enough food in here to survive. Stale doughnuts, bottled water, teabags, crisps, apples, bread and cheese.

He stares at her one last time. She appears very alone, separated from the rest of the world by her anger. She needs a hat. She doesn't know that the temperature is deceptive. It may not seem warm in the wind, but she'll burn. He examines the way she sits there, her shoulders drooping, somehow deflated, and sees that her anger has gone. She seems diminished without it, as if she doesn't exist. A carrier-bag with nothing to carry.

There's a photo on his desk of one of the children, Katie Flambard, sent by her mother two months ago. She's on the beach, kneeling in the sand, digging with a blue plastic spade. She's smiling at the camera, her blonde wispy hair frizzled by the salty air. Shiny patches of pink appear on the bony tops of her shoulders where she's starting to burn.

Maggie, a whisper from his dreams: 'Another failure, Straker?'

He returns to his living room, picks up a stale doughnut and a packet of tomato-ketchup-flavoured crisps on the way and walks heavily downstairs. When he unlocks the front door, he assumes she will hear him and come charging towards him, shouting. Nothing happens.

She doesn't move. When he reaches her, he sits down next to her. He doesn't think she sees him at first, but when she does, she's not surprised. He's irritated by her acceptance of the fact that he would eventually come out to meet her, so he doesn't do anything.

After a while, he hands her the doughnut and the packet of crisps, thinking she will probably throw them into the sea. But she doesn't. She takes the doughnut and bites into it without a word. The jam oozes out and streaks on to her cheeks. She wipes it off with her hand, then licks her fingers. They are short and stubby, and she doesn't wear any rings.

'It's stale,' she says, after two mouthfuls.

He nods.

'You're supposed to eat them on the day you buy them.'

She starts on the crisps and he can hear them crunching in her mouth. He keeps buying tomato-ketchup flavour by mistake because the packets are red like the ready-salted. He doesn't like them and there's an ever-growing pile in the store room he uses for rubbish. She seems to enjoy them, and he considers running back up and bringing her all of the packets.

'I haven't tried that flavour before,' she says, as if they were in the middle of a conversation. She eats politely, not putting in too much at a time, closing her mouth as she chews. 'They're disgusting.'

———————

They didn't eat like that in his family. His father had had a voracious appetite and would keep eating until there was nothing left. His mother struggled to feed him. She made enormous casseroles so that he could fill his plate over and over again, but he still complained that there wasn't enough. Pete and his brother used to watch him eat, see his mouth working non-stop like a cement-mixer. You could hear his jaw click as he chewed, and the food going round and round. When he spoke, they could see it in his open mouth, half recognisable, half blended. Then he would rush to swallow so that he could take another forkful. They had to eat at the table in the dining room, but their father was allowed to have a tray on his lap while he listened to the wireless. He would comment on the news as he ate, giving further glimpses of the breaking-down stage.

'That girl'll be dead when they find her,' he pronounced, into the stillness of the living room.

'Never trust a policeman,' he said, as he downed a roast potato. 'They're all crooked.'

They finished long before him and came to listen to the wireless. Their mother ran backwards and forwards with refills for him. The house was too big, the distance too great for this. They had a hall twenty yards long, with wood panelling and chandeliers hanging from the high ceiling.

'Self-made man,' he said, with satisfaction about some successful industrialist. 'Same as me.'

They watched, fascinated, as he speared a piece of steak with his fork, and bit a huge mouthful off the side.

'Is that it?' says Miss Doody. 'Don't you have anything more substantial?'

I didn't invite you to dinner, he thinks.

'It's my roof,' she says. 'I want to do it. I told Jonathan that I couldn't afford to pay someone, but he doesn't listen. Just because he earns pots of money, he thinks the whole world is stinking rich. He forgets too easily.'

She stops talking for a while. The wind blows her hair back towards the mainland. He can see darker roots below the blonde.

'I inherited the cottage from my godfather. Just like that. I didn't know anything about it until it landed in my lap. I was going to sell it. Jonathan offered to pay for the roof, but he won't do it really. He wants things to be a sound investment. He would take one look at the cottage and tell me it needs knocking down. Then he'd tell me to build a new house or sell the land. He wouldn't care. It'd just be an investment or a useful windfall. He only thinks in terms of money.'

Her voice is less harsh when she's talking properly. He sits further back than her so that she doesn't keep looking at him. But he has to strain sometimes to hear what she says.

'The thing is, I like the cottage. I don't see why I shouldn't do it up. It would be all mine. Not like where I live now – in a school.'

He knew she was a teacher. It was obvious.

'I can saw and hammer and paint. It's my job. Why can't I do the roof?'

He wishes she wouldn't keep going on about the roof. He'll take the sails down tomorrow.

'Children have no respect. I had one boy ready to punch me. Year six, eleven years old, his fist just under my nose. I could see the flicker of indecision in his eyes. Yes or no. Of course he would have been expelled, but that wouldn't have saved my nose, would it? It might have been worth it, I suppose, if I'd never had to see him again. Useless headmaster. Thinks I'm stupid. Wants to call me "dear", pat me on the head. He might do that to Doris the Lion Tamer, although I can't see her taking it. Was that your cat?'

Does she always talk like this? Too many words, not enough links, too loose a chain.

'I shouldn't have come. I suppose it was pretty stupid coming out here on my crutches. It's not broken, the ankle. I had it X-rayed. Just sprained. "Rest it," they said, but it's so boring. Haven't you got anything else to eat?'

He's not sure. He has to think. What does she like? Ricotta and spinach cannelloni? Alphabet spaghetti?

'I found you from the post office. Tall man with a beard, doesn't talk. The woman who works there was useless, but someone else knew you. Said you lived in a lighthouse. I wish it was me. Never having to talk to anyone.'

You'd have problems with that.

Tell her your name, Straker.

'People are so stupid, they drive me crazy.'

He realises that it's a long time since he last spoke out loud. Do you lose the ability if you don't keep it oiled?

'And you can always be higher than everyone else.'

He clears his throat. That makes a noise. Encouraged, he opens his mouth.

'I spend a lot of time on my school roof. You can watch without being seen.'

He hesitates, shuts his mouth, opens it again.

'Jonathan says they might be antique tiles. They could be worth a fortune.'

'My name is . . .' he starts to say, but no sound comes out. He coughs and tries again. 'My name is Peter Straker.' His voice sounds odd, as if someone else is doing the talking.

She doesn't even turn to look at him. 'I know that,' she says. 'They told me in the post office.'

A seagull swoops down in front of them, and lands two yards away. It must have smelt the stale doughnut.

Chapter 7

Mike folded his arms, stretched his long legs out in front of him and yawned loudly. He admired the way his jeans frayed at the bottom, the loose threads hanging over his trainers. The two children who had been sitting opposite him had gone to the buffet car, and there would be a few minutes of blissful space.

'Hand over your mouth when you yawn,' said Geraldine, next to him. 'You're setting a bad example for the children.'

'Sorry, miss.' He straightened and flashed a grin at her, knowing that he looked charmingly boyish when he smiled.

She frowned, her dark, heavy eyebrows coming together, almost meeting in the middle. He had never considered her to be attractive, but looking now at her pale brown hair, scraped back into a ponytail, he was unexpectedly stirred. The way the pearl of her ear-lobe glistened with downy gold hairs, the high cheekbones slightly flushed against the pale eggshell white of her forehead.

He turned away in a hurry. Careful, he said to himself. You can do without this now.

'Miss?'

They both looked at Sarah Wilson, who was standing by Geraldine.

'Yes, Sarah?'

'Wayne went to get a KitKat from the buffet, but when he got there he couldn't find the fifty pence piece in his pocket and he says me and Tracey pinched it, but we didn't, miss, and now the man is getting annoyed because Wayne opened the KitKat before he paid for it and he hasn't got the fifty pence and me and Tracey didn't have any money.'

Geraldine sighed and got up. 'Where is Wayne now?'

'In the buffet car. There's a big queue.'

'Show me the way.' Geraldine picked up her bag, grimaced at Mike and set off after Sarah.

Mike watched her lurching down the swaying carriage. There was something about the way her body moved that affected him. He knew it would be a bad idea to get involved with someone at school again, but even so . . . She had a gawkiness that he liked. It looked as if she knew she couldn't move naturally, but she was pretending she could, and in doing so, she became more awkward.

'Sir?'

Mike looked across at Leroy, who had slipped on to the seat opposite. 'Leroy?' He liked being called 'sir'. He felt he deserved the respect and sense of authority that had settled on him automatically as soon as he had started training. Eighteen months as a teacher. Pretty good, he told himself every now and again, when he stood facing the bathroom mirror.

'My dad says I can have a dog.'

'Great, Leroy.' It was getting dark outside, he noticed. He could see car lights on the road that ran parallel to the train. The cartoon figure of a sausage with a grinning face loomed against a red background on the side of a lorry. It was overtaking in the inside lane. Typical lorry driver, he thought. That's why he's not a teacher.

'What sort of dog should I have? A spaniel or a corgi or a beagle or a terrier or a red setter?'

Stop him, thought Mike. This is going to go on all the way home. 'You like dogs, then?'

Leroy nodded, his big eyes wide open and excited. 'My dad doesn't.'

'Right.' The conversation was dragging.

'My uncle likes dogs, though.'

'Great.'

They passed a station so fast that they couldn't read its name. Leroy's eyes darted backwards and forwards very quickly as he tried. 'Where was that, sir?'

'Your guess is as good as mine.'

'Was it Glasgow?'

'No, Leroy. Not Glasgow.'

Leroy sat quietly for a bit. 'Do you think a Dobermann pinscher would suit me? Or an Alsatian or a . . .'

Mike sighed. 'Stay with a spaniel.'

Leroy nodded. 'My dad says I can have a dog when I'm sixteen.'

'Ah. Right.' Only another seven years, then.

Simran returned from the buffet car. 'Sir, he's in my seat. That's my seat.'

'OK, Simran. Don't push him. He's going quietly.'

Geraldine came back and slid in beside him. He turned to look at her. 'OK?'

She nodded. 'He had the fifty pence all the time in his pocket. The man wasn't helpful, I must say. If he hadn't got so annoyed, Wayne wouldn't have panicked, and there wouldn't have been a problem.'

They could hear the general chatter of the children up and down the carriage, quieter than when they'd set off in the morning. The excitement had dissipated and most of them were content to sit and examine their souvenirs.

Mike watched Helen opposite him as she fingered a small model of the Statue of Liberty. 'Why did you buy that, Helen?' he asked.

'I like it, sir.'

'You know what it is?'

'Yes. The Statue of Liberty.'

'And where is the Statue of Liberty?'

'New York,' she said, without a pause for thought. 'I've seen it.'

Mike felt depressed. He leaned against Geraldine slightly

and was pleased that she didn't draw away from him. He could feel the warmth of her arm against his and he could see the shape of her nose in the corner of his eye. Sharp, angular, scrubbed clean, but somehow vulnerable.

'Fancy a Chinese takeaway when we've got rid of them?' he said.

She hesitated and he held his breath. 'Depends on the time,' she said. 'I've got to pick up some shopping for my mum.'

'We could do that first, if you like.'

She glanced at him with a slight smile. 'OK,' she said.

Yes! He examined his new trainers, observing with satisfaction that their pristine whiteness was already fading. Right now, at this moment in time, life was just right. He'd discovered this before. If you don't look forward and you don't look back, you can fix yourself in now and enjoy it. Never mind about Fiona, who would be spouting tears down the phone at him for the next three weeks, and never mind how he would introduce Geraldine to his flatmate, Barry, who had stipulated no more girlfriends for six months or he would chuck him out.

He was conscious of Geraldine's perfume. Devon Violets, he thought, infinitely preferable to Fiona's heavy Chanel No. 5. He admired her feet tied securely into Doc Martens. A practical woman. Someone who knew her own mind. Someone who would not want more from him than he could give.

'Fancy a coffee?' he said, good-naturedly getting to his feet, stumbling over her legs on purpose.

Chapter 8

Sitting next to Straker, eating his crisps, Doody realises that she's made a mess of things. She's not at all sure why she came. It seemed logical at the time, but now the anger has subsided, she can't quite recall her burning desire to confront him. When do the buses stop running? Even if she rings for a taxi, she can't avoid the difficult walk back to the road. She wishes she'd never set eyes on the man. 'It's all very well you producing food, but what am I supposed to do now?'

He doesn't answer. Of course. 'How does someone as stupid as you survive?'

She pushes the worry to the back of her mind. She walked here. She can walk back. Her shoulders ache from using the crutches, there are blisters on her feet, but she'll just have to get on with it. If she has to do something she'll do it, however hard it might be. She could walk to the North Pole, climb Everest, or sail round the world. She doesn't give up. She'll even take on the challenge of a roof.

She scrambles awkwardly to her feet and glares at Straker, trying to decide if he really murdered someone. 'I'll be off now,' she says.

He doesn't seem to know how to react.

'Could you pass me the crutches?'

He obeys. This pleases her enormously. 'Thank you.'

It's easier to use one crutch as a walking-stick and carry the other under her arm, as it eases the strain on her shoulders. She turns her back on the sea and looks up at his lighthouse. 'Have you thought about painting it?' she says.

If only it were her lighthouse. There's a certain satisfaction in being higher than everyone else, looking down. When she was a child, before her father died, she used to spend long hours in the old yew tree at the bottom of the garden, reading Biggles books. Jonathan used to search the garden for her, calling pathetically. She could just see the top of his head as he passed below, but she never gave in to the temptation to throw a berry down at him. Poisonous yew berries. She remembers the feel of them, squashing their waxy red between her fingers.

She starts walking. Not too bad. Everything aches a bit, but she'll loosen up. Nobody ever died of stiffness.

'Stop!'

She stops. She's tempted to ignore him, but it's always possible that he has a Land Rover stored away somewhere, and she doesn't want to reject a genuine offer of help. Ninety per cent of her doesn't believe in this, but she's prepared to give the other ten per cent a chance. She turns round. He's flapping his arms in his imbecilic way, and gesturing towards a cottage on the other side of the lighthouse. She waits to see what will happen.

'Get a move on,' she says. 'It's going to get dark soon.'

He nods and seems to want her to follow him to the cottage, but she stays where she is and watches him. Maybe he's just offering her a bed for the night, but the possibility of a vehicle still makes her wait.

He disappears inside and reappears pushing a bicycle with a large box on wheels attached to the back. 'Very helpful. How am I supposed to ride a bike with a sprained ankle?'

He shakes his head. He brings the bike over, takes the crutches from her, and puts them down on the grass. Then he pulls her towards the cart.

'It's not going to work,' she says. She's not very tall, but she's solid. He's tall, but not very solid. He's determined to try, so she gives up and climbs in awkwardly. There isn't enough room, so she sits on the bottom and hangs her legs over the side, balancing the crutches across the top. It's extremely uncomfortable.

'You'll never do it,' she says, as he gets on the bike.

She's right. He makes several attempts to start pedalling, but can't go fast enough to balance, so each time he falls over to the side.

'It was obvious it wouldn't work,' she says. 'Bikes aren't made for pulling human beings.'

She climbs out and sets off again on her own, feeling even more annoyed with him. Aren't men supposed to be useful? 'Thanks anyway,' she says, over her shoulder. 'Nice try.'

She doesn't look back. She's tired of him. This is all his fault. If he hadn't come into her garden, she wouldn't have chased him and she wouldn't have hurt her ankle. If he hadn't messed with the roof, she wouldn't have come out to this absurdly remote place. She wants to tell him all this, she would like to shout at him, but it would waste time, so she carries on walking.

Straker sweeps past on his bike and stops in front of her.

'Get out of the way,' she says. 'I've got a long way to go.'

He gets off and positions the bike so that it bars her way. She hesitates, not sure what he wants to do. 'It doesn't work,' she says. 'I'm too heavy.'

He pulls her by the arm until she's standing by the bike. He takes the crutches out of her hands and put them back into the cart. Then he bends down and pulls her leg over the bike.

'I told you. I've got a sprained ankle. I can't cycle.'

He ignores her and takes the bad ankle in his hand.

'Ouch!' There's a strap on the pedal, and he puts her foot into it. She sighs and looks at the sky. The man's an idiot. She knew that the first time she saw him.

'It's getting late,' she says. 'I don't want to be stuck out here in the dark. I don't suppose the council puts up street-lights just for dotty old men in lighthouses.'

He puts her hands on the handlebars. Then he takes her other foot.

'Hey!' she yells. 'Give me some warning, will you?'

They sway wildly, but he manages to hold the bike upright. He's much stronger than she'd realised, and she feels suddenly nervous. She'd forgotten that he might be dangerous. He's seemed so vague and woolly up until now that she hasn't worried seriously about him.

He fits her foot on the second pedal. Doody decides that he might know what he's doing so she stops resisting. He pulls himself upright, looks at her once directly with his blue eyes and starts walking, one hand on the handlebars and one on the back of the saddle. They move forward, precariously at first and then more smoothly as they both get the hang of it. The crutches bounce along in the cart behind them, clattering in protest.

Her feet move round with the pedals, but she's not controlling them, so she doesn't apply any pressure. Straker has to walk in an uncomfortable position, leaning to the side with his legs just missing the pedal.

'Yes,' she says, after a while. 'It works.'

He doesn't reply.

There's nothing left to say. He guides the bike and they travel bumpily but competently towards the main road. She worries about his blue eyes, and that he's more intelligent than he pretends.

Just before they reach the road, a bus appears at the top of the hill, heading towards them, moving fast.

'Quick!' she shouts. 'Where's the bus-stop?'

Straker looks up and sees the bus for himself. He swerves the bike suddenly and she nearly falls off.

'Hey! Be careful!'

He puts his head down and starts running, on a collision course with the bus. Doody manages to free one hand from the handlebars and wave wildly at the driver. She struggles to stay upright.

'You're going to kill us both!' she shouts at him, but he ignores her.

The bus slows down. 'It's seen us!' She's exhilarated by the race. 'It's going to stop!'

Unbelievably, it pulls up a few yards ahead of them. Straker runs the bike smoothly along the Tarmac on the side of the road until they're outside the opened door.

'Hang on!' she yells at the driver. 'Give me a second!'

'No rush, love,' he says, and leans on his steering-wheel as they struggle to get her off the bike.

Straker guides her on to the steps after he's released her from the pedals, and goes back for the crutches. As he hands them to her, the bus driver goes back into action.

'Hold on,' he says, and the automatic doors start to shut.

She leans against the bar as the bus edges away and struggles to find some money in her pocket. 'Do you go to Hillingham?' she asks.

The driver smiles wearily. 'There's nowhere else you can go, love, travelling in this direction on this road.'

'Don't call me "love",' she says. 'How can you love someone you don't know?'

He raises his eyebrows and concentrates on the road.

Straker has gone, already lost in the distance behind them. She feels unexpectedly guilty. Perhaps she should have thanked him.

She hops down from the bus in Hillingham and balances on her crutches while it drives off. The sun is low in the sky, but everything still looks bright and light. Curiously, she feels good. Sitting in the sun and the wind has warmed her and she feels relaxed and well, but hungry.

On the bus, she's been planning. It'll take too long to drive home tonight, and she's not sure if the ankle is strong enough after today's walk. She could buy something to eat, and spend the night in the cottage.

There's probably no electricity.

There's definitely no electricity.

The cottage will be creepy in the dark.

Candles.

She goes into a small supermarket (Open Eight Till Late) and fills a basket with bread, cheese, bottles of lemonade, cakes, apples and a bar of chocolate. She's the only customer, and there aren't any candles.

The woman at the till is elderly, grey-haired and red-cheeked. She has a label on her overall, identifying her as Sharon, but she must be too old to be called Sharon.

'I need some candles,' says Doody. 'Do you have any?'

'Oh dear, I don't know. I'll go and ask Fred.'

She gets up from the till and disappears to the back of the shop. This worries Doody. How does Sharon know if she's honest? Can she tell from looking at her?

A man comes into the shop and shuffles up and down the aisles, talking to himself. 'I told Poppy to leave the dog. "No," she said. "If I go, Rover goes." Golden Delicious, a quarter of ham, proper butter, none of this artificial stuff . . .'

He comes up behind Doody, clutching an empty basket, and stands there for a while, still muttering. She half turns towards him, but he has his back to her.

'Waste of time,' he says, after a minute of waiting, and puts his empty basket on the floor. Then he shuffles out of the door.

'I thought so,' says Sharon, appearing from the chocolate-biscuit aisle. 'Fred thinks he's got some in his office. If you want to go back and wait for him, he'll bring them down.'

'Shall I pay for these first?'

'No, no.' She flaps her hands at Doody. 'Go down Fruit and Vegetables. Potatoes on your left, baked beans on your right. There's a back door at the end, to the left of the fridge. Go and wait there. He says he'll bring them when he finds them.'

Doody walks to the back of the store, and realises that her ankle is not as painful as it was. If she walks slowly, she doesn't need to lean on the crutch. Thinking of Straker pushing her on his bike all that way, she fights down a sense of guilt. The fire of anger that keeps her alive is struggling to stay alight, on the verge of snuffing out, and it makes her feel insecure.

Fred appears in a white coat, looking like a doctor. 'Hello, madam,' he says. 'Fred Hopkins.'

He's probably expecting her to say, 'Imogen Doody,' so she says nothing.

He's small and old, with a high, domed forehead, and a rolling, bouncing double chin. His skin is tanned and leathery like the post-mistress's and he stands with a slight stoop. 'Were you the lady . . .?' he says, and stops.

'I wanted some candles,' says Doody.

He nods vigorously and produces a packet of twelve from his pocket.

'Brilliant,' she says.

He hesitates before handing them over. 'Were you expecting a power cut?'

'No.'

'Only I've found a whole carton of them. Perhaps we should bring them into the shop. In case everyone needs them in a hurry. If there's a power cut.'

'There isn't going to be a power cut,' she says. 'It's only my cottage that doesn't have any electricity.' Why did she tell him that? It's none of his business.

But he smiles suddenly, and his face disintegrates into hundreds of ready-made creases. 'I knew it,' he says. 'You're the lady at the cottage.'

Doody's annoyed with herself for destroying her anonymity. 'What cottage?'

'The cottage on the corner,' he says. 'Oliver d'Arby's old place.'

She's shocked to hear someone say his name like that, out of nowhere. 'Did you know him?' It's quite reasonable that people in the village should have known him, but it feels as if Fred knows all about her private life.

He nods vigorously. 'Odd chap. Flew aeroplanes, played the violin—'

'No,' says Doody. 'The cello.'

He looks confused. 'Maybe. He just disappeared, you know. Nobody knows what happened to him. One day he was in here, buying Mr Kipling Cherry Bakewells, and a pound of tomatoes. The next day he was gone.'

'You don't know what happened to him, then?'

He shakes his head. 'Nobody knew. He didn't tell anyone. A nice couple were living there in the last few years. Bob and Carol Macklethorpe. He's dead now, of course, and she's in a home in Exeter. I go and see her sometimes, but she doesn't recognise me. Alzheimer's. It'll get us all in the end.'

So the tidiness wasn't from Oliver d'Arby but an elderly couple. Doody's disappointed.

But if there were tenants, who had collected the rent? Someone must know where Oliver d'Arby is.

'Been empty for about five years now. Oliver's been gone twenty, twenty-five . . .'

He reminds her of Jonathan. More interested in his own conversation than hers. 'How much are the candles?' she asks.

'Oh, take them, take them.'

She's not sure if he's giving them to her or trying to get rid of her. 'So how much are they?'

'Nothing. Free. My pleasure.' He becomes more professional. 'Always good to see a satisfied customer. I'll have to charge you if you need any more, of course. Ninety-nine a box, or maybe one pound fifty.' He turns away as he talks and his voice drifts into a vague mutter.

Doody goes to pay at the till. 'There was a strange man in here a few minutes ago,' she says. 'He talked to himself about a dog.'

'Oh, that's Charlie. He usually comes in about now. He

never buys anything, but he's harmless. You think he's weird, you should see the man from the lighthouse.'

Why are they all so obsessed with Straker? It's as if they want him to have killed someone. 'What's the matter with him?'

'He never sleeps. Ever.'

'How do you know that?'

'His light's always on, up there in the dark, shining out non-stop.'

'That's what lighthouses do.'

Sharon smiles, but there is something nervous about the smile. 'Oh, no, it's not a working lighthouse. There's something very odd about him. Never speaks to anyone.'

Doody wants to tell her that he's spoken to her, but finds herself unwilling to admit that she's met him. 'What does he do all day?'

'That's another thing. He doesn't go out and do a day's work like anyone else. He just wanders around – up and down the beach, as if he's looking for something.'

'How strange,' says Doody, encouragingly.

But Sharon has said enough. 'Yes, strange, strange.' She smiles again, this time more openly. 'See you again, I hope,' she says.

Maybe. She probably wants Doody to smile back and give her name, so Doody says nothing.

As she comes out of the shop, holding a crutch and the carrier-bag in one hand, leaning on the other crutch, a car drives past unnecessarily fast. She watches as it goes round the corner, and steps out into the road, immediately colliding with a woman who is looking the other way.

'Sorry,' she says, and it's Mrs Whittaker who had given directions to the lighthouse.

'Hello,' she says, peering at Doody. 'Did you find Mr Straker?'

'Yes, thank you.' She doesn't want to tell her the details.

Mrs Whittaker looks over the top of her glasses. 'So, did he talk to you?'

'Of course,' says Doody.

Mrs Whittaker frowns. 'He's very odd, you know.'

'Yes, I think I'd worked that out for myself.'

'The police are keeping an eye on him.'

'Because he's killed someone?'

'There are other things . . .'

Doody feels increasingly frustrated by them all, their mysterious suggestions and suspicions. It makes her want to defend Straker. 'Like what?'

But Mrs Whittaker has registered Doody's irritation, and her expression changes. 'Oh, nothing. I'm sure you'll find out soon enough.' She turns and continues on her way.

Doody walks up the road to her cottage and thinks of Straker speaking to her. Mrs Whittaker and the post-mistress were wrong and she was right. That doesn't happen to her very often.

———

She unlocks the front door and steps in. The first thing she notices, which she doesn't remember from last time, is the smell. Damp, musty, unlived-in, old. She goes into the lounge with the intention of opening a window, but this turns out to be impossible. The windows are divided into small panes, and someone has painted them with too much enthusiasm, in the mistaken belief that rot will stop if it's painted. The paint has overlapped on to the glass and dripped down. It's coated the catches and welded them into a solid, impenetrable mass.

Doody is disappointed by Fred's information, and resents the intrusion of Bob and Carol Macklethorpe into Oliver d'Arby's dust, their presence in his silent spaces. Did the clothes in the wardrobe belong to Oliver or Bob?

She takes longer to examine everything this time, looking beyond the dust and cobwebs, discovering that things are not as they seem. Beneath a neglected but neat exterior, everything is dying, breaking down, corrupting.

The stair-carpet threads its way up the centre, leaving the edges bare and untouched. The pattern that remains beneath the layers of neglect is muddled and vague, a blurred geometric combination of grey and brown.

The stairs seem secure, but a cloud of dust puffs up with every step she takes. She grips the banister rail, convinced that her foot will go right through each step. Nothing is permanent. It all dissolves with time, crumbles into nothing, settles back into non-existence. It's difficult to find a place for herself in this dying, abandoned house.

Upstairs, it's darker than she remembered. The windows are too small to pull in much of the evening light. She should have brought a candle up with her, but she's unwilling to light one before it's necessary. Candles are all right as a last resort, but once you have a light, the outside turns into a frightening darkness.

There are two rooms and a bathroom up here. The larger room was presumably used as a bedroom by the Macklethorpes. The double bed that Doody had thought was Oliver d'Arby's must have been theirs. It looks completely normal – a high, dark wooden bed, covered with a grey-blue candlewick bedspread. Doody didn't touch it on her first visit because it seemed so normal and peaceful. In a state of readiness, expecting Oliver d'Arby to return at any moment to catch up on all those missing years of sleep. This time, she's looking for blankets, so she decides to pull back the bedspread. But when she touches it, a thick layer comes away in her hand. She steps back in alarm as it disintegrates and flies away into nothing. It takes her a while to realise that the bedspread is not made of candlewick, not grey-blue, but a smoother, paler blue. The surface consists of delicately interwoven dust that separates into vague strands when it's disturbed. Once she's worked this out, she holds the end of the bedspread and pulls it up and off as quickly as possible. Then she stands back to wait for the clouds of dust to settle. There are two blankets folded underneath, one pink with satin edges and the other green and blue tartan. She picks up the tartan one and sniffs it. There's a smell of oldness and dust, but nothing else. It might be all right if she bangs it up and down outside for a bit. She tucks it under her arm and examines the rest of the room.

There's a wardrobe against one wall, huge and dark, overwhelming in a small room. She opens the door, and is surprised to discover that it's almost empty, unlike many of the other cupboards in the house. In one corner is a pair of ladies' shoes, brown leather with small heels, and a strap that's fastened with a button. In another corner there are two wheels on top of each other – not quite large enough for bicycle wheels. The tyres are flat, the rubber loose and flabby. There's a small box against the back wall, which she pulls out. Knitting patterns. Cable jumpers, Aran cardigans, polo-necks. Men and women smiling out cleanly, frozen into the time of their origin by their hairstyles and their wholesomeness. The ceiling has collapsed above the wardrobe, and the wood on one side is swollen and discoloured where rain has poured in through the imperfect roof.

When she goes into the other room, smaller than the first, she finds what she found before. Here's the bureau, and the drawers with no underwear, and a small wardrobe with two empty suits, hanging dejectedly, redundant without a body to occupy them. These belonged to Oliver d'Arby. He must have put all his belongings into this room when he decided to leave. This was the room that he said goodbye to when he left with his cello to go to wherever he mysteriously went.

There's a larger hole in the ceiling here, and when Doody stands by the pile of debris and looks up, she can see pale gaps in the roof where tiles have gone, and where the plastic is now fixed. What was he thinking when he left? Did he expect to come back some time?

She walks over to the bureau and opens it, keen to examine the evidence of Oliver d'Arby's life. The front drops down easily to make a neat but strong desk. It smells very strongly of ink. Every compartment, every drawer, is stuffed with letters, bills, thrown in at random, with no apparent attempt at organisation. She picks out some to examine, but it's too dark to read. She feels a moment of excitement that she's standing by a desk that has not been touched for twenty-five years. A desk that belonged to Oliver d'Arby, the man who went out one day and never came back.

She takes a pile of papers to examine later. She wants to know about Oliver. If she can understand why he disappeared, perhaps she can get closer to the thoughts of Harry, who also never came home.

Downstairs, she takes the blanket outside, with two large cushions from the sofa, and bangs them against a wall of the cottage until the release of dust becomes less significant. Then she makes herself a bed on the floor of the sitting room. She lights two candles and sets them on either side. She lights another and takes it into the kitchen to look for a plate and a knife. There's a pile of blue and white china in a cupboard, still shiny, protected from the real world. There's cutlery in a drawer, yellow and tarnished, purchased before the invention of stainless steel.

She tries the taps, but nothing comes out, so she wipes the knife and plate with a tissue and sits at the kitchen table to eat her makeshift meal. She doesn't exactly enjoy it, sitting there in semi-darkness, the first human occupant for five years. She's not sure how safe she feels in this dying house.

When she lies down on the cushions, she hears whispers and rustling and scrabbling. Is it mice, or birds trapped in the attic? Do the sighs come from the trees outside, or the polythene inexpertly applied by Straker? She's nervous about insects, animals, mould, rot, but she's too tired to give any of it much attention. Her face glows hot and uncomfortable and she realises that she must have been in the sun too long. She falls asleep listening for noises, thinking about Mandles limping out of the cove where he crashed, looking for help.

She has a title now: Mandles and the Lighthouse.

Why would anyone live in a lighthouse? It must be so awkward doing the shopping. Does he have electricity, a phone? What about a loo?

Straker appears on the edge of her dreams and she tries to hear what he is saying. She finds she is unable to reproduce the sound of his voice in her mind.

Chapter 9

Patterns. Rhythms. Sequences. They are all around Straker and part of him. Even on bad days, there's a rhythm in the sea, the cloud formations, the shadows of the clouds on the water. Lying awake in the dark, he can hear the waves thudding against the cliff below, pushing further in, attacking the foundations of the lighthouse. They hammer and grind and pound away, and if he stays still and stops resisting, he becomes part of that movement, able to disappear into the patterns and cease to be. When the storms come, everything tries harder, gets angrier. The cliff retreats, and its substance is deposited elsewhere. The patterns shift with the fluctuations of the land, but they make new shapes and routines. As one shrinks, another grows.

Not everyone understands the patterns. The young people in their sailing dinghies know they're dependent on the tide, but they fight it, do things quickly, race against the inevitable. They can't win, but they don't seem to accept this at all.

Magnificent roams the area freely, believing himself to be unique, but he's as much a part of the natural processes as the sea. He leaves shifting traces of himself everywhere, baby Magnificents carrying his pattern inside themselves, the DNA.

It terrifies Straker that he carries his father's genes. Or that his father carried his. There's no escape. It's written inside him, indelibly. He will become more like his father as he grows older. And, since Straker is a murderer, his father must have possessed at least some of the genes of a murderer and passed them on, freely and inevitably. So why didn't he share the guilt?

When Miss Doody left on the bus, Straker cycled back to the lighthouse. He stood on the edge of the cliff, watching the sea and the seagulls, but there was something new about the way he saw it. Normally, if he turned his back for a while, then turned round again, it would still be the same, the buffeting wind, the taste of salt on his lips. Now he could feel changes that didn't fit into the existing patterns. A tremor of rebellion passed through the cliff-top and into his legs.

He was bothered by Miss Doody, by the fact that she had walked here, a mile over uneven surfaces on crutches, just to shout at him. What was it for, what did she want from him?

Darkness crept up on him while he was walking backwards and forwards in front of the lighthouse and a chill settled bleakly somewhere inside him. His mind had been drifting; there were no numbers clicking over inside him. With something like panic, he went inside and ran up and down the first flight of stairs. Ten times. Thirty-seven stairs, ten times up, ten times down. Seven hundred and forty stairs. He stopped at seventy-five, counted to ten, then resumed at eighty-six.

When he'd finished, he went upstairs. Crunching an apple, he sat at his desk, intending to read some letters and go over his latest notes on Sangita. But he was too easily distracted by the wind buffeting against the window, a sound that always reminded him of childhood holidays.

Every year, they went to the same hotel in north Devon, where the sea rolls in along great open beaches. Surfing waves, useless for swimming, big and frightening. It was unclear why they went to Woolacombe, because his father couldn't swim and refused to go into the sea. His parents would settle down on deckchairs in the dunes, sheltered from the wind, while Pete and Andy went off to the sea.

'Careful, don't splash!' their mother would shout when

they jumped in among them, shivering from the cold, in urgent need of towels, teeth chattering, lips blue. They would crouch down under their towels, eating the egg sandwiches the hotel had made up for them, tasting the salt, crunching the sand.

Their father wouldn't eat on the beach. When their mother put down her knitting and offered him a sandwich, he waved it away. 'We'll eat later in the restaurant,' he said. 'No need for that now.' Everything about his wife irritated him, whether they were at home or on holiday.

'Just a small one?' said their mother.

'Leave it alone, will you?' he said, and went back to his book. He read Agatha Christie. In all the black-and-white holiday photographs there was a Penguin paperback in his hand, the green and white edition – *The ABC Murders*, *Ten Little Indians*, *Miss Marple*. He never read anything else.

Their mother liked to bring a flask of tea with a small bottle of milk, and sugar in an empty honey jar with a screw top. Their father would accept his cup of tea, in a china cup and saucer, without pleasure or gratitude, drinking it all, despite his resentment.

'Collect shells,' said Andy to Pete, on their way down to the sea. 'Just the round white ones.'

Pete did as he was told, not minding too much, eager to please. He worried over every shell, never certain which ones were right, occasionally attempting to check with his brother. 'Will these ones do?'

Andy was not interested in hanging around with his brother. He would drift up to groups of children who were playing badminton, football, or jumping in and out of the waves, shrieking. They always accepted him, these other children, as if he naturally belonged with them, and in no time he would be taking over, issuing orders, improving the rules of the game.

The children gave him their names and addresses when they

left, but he couldn't possibly have written to them all. He wouldn't have had time. When he was older, they started to invite him to stay with them. His father would check out the address first, enquiring about the father's occupation before he agreed. Lawyers, doctors and accountants were encouraged; teachers, nurses and policemen were acceptable; everyone else was unsuitable.

'Don't want you mixing with the wrong sort,' he would say.

By the time he was twelve, Andy was never at home in the summer. His life was one long round of visits to his friends.

Pete stood on the side and watched, wondering how Andy did it, why the other children were pleased to have him in charge. Pete rarely spoke to anyone else, or joined in their games. They didn't seem to notice him.

Just once, as he stood on the edge of a game of football, holding his red bucket full of round white shells, a shorter boy with curly hair and freckles came and stood by him. Pete didn't know he was there at first. When he noticed him, he glanced quickly away and waited for him to move, but he didn't. Only after a long time did Pete look round at him again, his head barely moving, hoping he wouldn't be noticed.

But the boy caught his eye. 'Stupid football,' he said.

Pete was shocked. He waited for something to happen, for the boy to explode into flames or to sink into the sand. Football was sacred in Pete's family. They had to worship Aston Villa, bow down to the players, spend fifty per cent of their free time discussing it. Not even his mother would dare to call football stupid.

Nothing happened.

'I'm Brian,' said the boy. 'What's your name?'

'Peter,' he said.

'What shall we do, then, Peter?'

He liked the way he was accepted as Peter and not shortened to Pete. He felt less babyish, more an individual.

He's never forgotten that holiday. Sometimes he can go

through every conversation he had with Brian. Word by word, he's kept it all. Maybe what he remembers isn't right, stored in a faulty filing cabinet, but it still comforts him, even now. Pete was eight and Brian was nine. His family were camping. One day, when it was cold and drizzly, Brian's mum asked Pete's mum if he could spend the day with them.

'Oh, yes,' said his mum, and it seemed to Pete that a small light of pleasure glowed in her normally clouded grey eyes, her hollow cheeks flushing a little. Then she looked nervously at Dad.

Pete's dad hesitated, looking at Brian, eyeing his mum. Pete held his breath. They must be poor, he thought, because they're camping and not in a hotel, and he knew his dad wouldn't think much of that. But, for some reason, he was less aggressive on that day. He shrugged. 'He can go if he wants to,' he said, and went back to Hercule Poirot, sprawling across the sofa in the hotel lounge, his great hairy arms coarse and flabby against the pale pink brocade of the furniture.

They had two tents. A big one for Brian's mum and dad and a little one for Brian. The boys played in Brian's tent all day: spies; plotting Andy's downfall; the Incredible Hulk, changing shape as their shadows swelled on the sides of the tent. It was too small to stand up, so they crawled everywhere. Straker remembers the sound of the wind flapping the canvas, the light rain pattering across it, the musty smell. They had tomato sandwiches for lunch and fish and chips out of newspaper for tea. It was a great day.

Then Pete went back to his family and the hotel, which was quiet and disapproving. He knew his father didn't think much of tents, that he considered it important to be respectable, to look smart and imitate the other people in the hotel. Pete couldn't understand why his father wanted to behave like them, trying to eat the same meals or drink the same wine. He wouldn't even order until he'd heard someone's request at the next table. Sometimes they had to wait ages while he pretended to read the menu, waiting for a lead from another guest.

Andy didn't speak to Pete again until they went home. But it was the best holiday Pete had ever had. He met Brian every day on the beach and they did all the activities that he had observed Andy doing with other children. Swimming, running, exploring rock pools, catching crabs in their nets. He can still smell the tent today. It catches him unawares every now and again, and it shocks him. It's as if it all happened yesterday, while more recent events have gone straight out of the back door of his mind.

———————

Felicity is talking to Sangita. She is oddly articulate. 'We're the same really, aren't we? On our own, never getting married. We can be young for ever.'

Sangita: 'I wouldn't have married anyway.'

Felicity hesitates. 'No, nor me. There was a man once, Eddie, but he was much older than me. I didn't like him much. My aunt Lucy said I should of married him while I had the chance, because he was worth a fortune, but he wasn't nice. He couldn't stop touching me. My mum said he wasn't right for me.'

'I was only sixteen.'

'I was only eighteen.'

There is a pause. Sangita isn't good at conversation.

Felicity starts again: 'I might of got married later, I suppose. Once I'd given up my modelling. But I'd've been rich then. Wouldn't need to marry for money. Wouldn't need to marry at all, but if I met someone kind and nice, who loved me . . . you know, a boy-next-door sort of person.'

'I was already in love.'

'Who with?'

'Just someone.'

More silence.

'Do you remember apple crumble?' says Felicity. 'For school dinners. With custard.'

'I sometimes miss the peacocks,' says Sangita.

'Peacocks?'

'They were in the back garden. Six of them. My dad loved them. I think the neighbours would have come over the wall and strangled them if we went away for a holiday. They were so noisy.'

'Did they have those pretty feathers?'

'Oh, yes, the male ones. I always carried one with me to give to him – Rob Willow. When my parents came up after the crash, they'd been away for several days. I keep worrying that someone probably got the peacocks.'

A pause.

Felicity: 'We're lucky, really. We'll always be young and beautiful. Anyone who looks at my photos will see me at my best.'

Sangita doesn't reply.

'Frozen in time, that's us. No wrinkles, no fat, no arthritis. My mum would've been pleased.'

Maggie says nothing.

When the first flushed light comes up over the sea, pushing its way round the curve of the earth and arriving ahead of the sun, Straker wakes to find himself still sitting at the table, his legs and back aching. He stands up and stretches out his arms, yawning loudly, feeling cramped and exhausted. His mind echoes with the voices of Sangita and Felicity. They're still in his mind, inexperienced, unformed, talking about nothing.

Suleiman comes down the steps from the light room, padding lightly, his tail rigidly upright. Straker opens a tin of Rabbit and Game, and Magnificent appears from nowhere, apparently summoned home from his adventures on the headland by the smell on the wind. They like rabbit. It tells them that there is another life, away from the sea, where not all food tastes of salt.

Suleiman looks at Magnificent's food and thinks it's better than his, so he moves over. Magnificent doubles round behind him and they change bowls. Straker turns on the kettle, picks up two doughnuts and goes upstairs to the light room.

This is the best time of day. The sun is rising into a high blue dome of empty sky. The sea is less turbulent beneath this emptiness, and the world seems to pause. Straker nearly always wakes just before dawn and goes upstairs for this period of nothingness. Yesterday is forgotten, today has not yet started. He feels a newness, a freshness, as if he can start again and the past has never happened. This feeling usually lasts for five minutes before the seventy-eight come racing back into his mind, tumbling over each other in their desire to be noticed.

He can see two container ships on the horizon, silent and stationary, waiting. They frequently wait there, sometimes for several days, but he doesn't know why. They won't be able to see him – the lighthouse must be little more than a tiny grey speck in the distance. He imagines them out there, rolling in the waves, a handful of people in a great mausoleum of a boat, and wonders what they're doing. Eating, sleeping, playing cards? Do they take their wives along? Do they watch the sea like him and see the patterns of the waves, and take their thoughts from the sea, or do they ignore it all and pretend they're at home, living the same dull routine that they always do? Do they feel invisible or important, taking whatever it is they take from one side of the world to another? Does normal life go on without them? Would anyone notice if they never touched land again?

Straker does seventy-five press-ups, his knees creaking more than usual, then eats his doughnuts. He goes downstairs, washes, changes his socks, and runs down to the front door, shutting it behind him. He takes his bicycle out of the keeper's cottage, but then leans it against a wall and goes to look at the edge of the cliff. No change. No sharp, bright, clean break.

He returns to the bike, gets on it, stops, gets off, stands silently and tries to sort out his thoughts.

He's going to take the sails off Miss Doody's roof. He should never have interfered. She came all the way out here to say that, so she must have meant it.

He starts to cycle, but there's something wrong with the reasoning, however much he tries to analyse her intentions. Why would she want to leave holes in her roof so that the rain comes in? What does she really want? Should he go? Shouldn't he go?

He has no idea, and wonders if she does. There's something so irrational about all this that he can't work it out. Thoughts should be logical. They should run on straight lines so that you can see the beginning and the end.

He stops thinking and climbs down the cliff to his boat, which is just beginning to float on the rising tide. There's a powerful swell, and it takes some time, with the boat rocking alarmingly, to get the right balance before he starts rowing. But he can control it. He's stronger than the wind.

He moors alongside the pier as usual, and climbs up the ladder to the flagpole. The harbour is deserted. Too early in the morning, but he can see a woman pinning out washing further along the beach. She pushes her clothes line up with a prop and the washing comes instantly alive, ballooning out towards the sea, filling with invisible bodies, flapping triumphantly over the pebbles. He can't recognise her from this distance, and wonders if she's like him, unable to sleep.

The three gnomes are missing from the bench, and he imagines them at home in their beds. Do they lie alongside wives who don't know them? Wives who spend all their days away from the men, glad to see them out of the house for the day? Do they talk when they come together for meals?

Does anyone talk? He sometimes hears people's voices, but it always seems as if they have nothing to say.

'How much are those apples?'

'One twenty a kilo.'

'Kilos? Ridiculous. What's wrong with pounds?'

'The nectarines look nice.'

'Did you pay the milkman?'

'Can we buy some Mars bars?'

Nobody listens to anyone else. What's it all for? He must have done it once himself, along with the rest of the world, although he has great difficulty remembering details from his previous life. It now feels as if he'd only been acting, doing things without thinking because everyone else did them.

He walks up the hill to Miss Doody's house, his thoughts churning away too fast as he argues with himself. He is not at all sure he's doing the right thing. He tries counting, backwards from two hundred, in sevens, but he arrives at four too quickly and nothing has changed. When he reaches the gate, he stands outside for a while and studies the cottage. The sails don't look so bad. Their whiteness glows in the early sunshine, and they look somehow as if they are in the right place, a piece of the bright morning hiding the dilapidated structure of the cottage.

They haven't completely stayed in place. One end has come away and is flapping in the breeze, catching against the lilac tree. But the noise is not hostile. It feels right for the neglected nature of the place, and the sail billows out bravely, refusing to be contained.

He climbs the tree at the side, calculating the strength needed to counteract the wind. A wood-pigeon bursts out from the top of the tree, flapping wildly, threatening his balance. He steadies himself before carrying on.

Once on the roof, he hesitates and discovers that he doesn't want to do this. He looks round at his previous handiwork, and it's not bad. The bricks have stayed in place, even after the heavy wind in the night, and most of the nails have held.

He sits there for some time in the sun, starting to relax at last, tiredness creeping up on him. The sky is filling up with clouds, but the flashes of sun are warm and comfortable. He can see the lighthouse in the distance.

Maggie is still not talking, but she's there, somewhere close, listening, judging in silence.

'Here's to you, Pete,' says Justin, drinking heavily from a can of lager. 'You and me and Francis. Best mates.'

'You don't kill your best mate,' says Francis.

'He didn't kill us, did you, Pete? It was an accident.'

'Yes, an accident.'

Maggie can send her reproach through the air without speaking.

A long silence. 'OK. Not an accident,' I say.

Justin takes another swig of lager. 'Could have happened to anyone. Could have happened to me.'

'It didn't, though, did it? It was me.'

Francis joins Justin in his generosity. 'Wrong time, wrong circumstances, all came together at the wrong moment. Bad luck.' He and Justin laugh together. Cold and unreal. A dead laugh.

'No, not bad luck. Bad attitude. I can't escape judgement.'

Maggie is there. She always was. 'OK, Straker, step one. Confession. Well done.'

'Leave me alone, Maggie. I don't need you. I can work it out for myself.'

'I am your conscience.'

I know.

The wood-pigeon flaps back and wakes him up. He breathes heavily for a while, trying to calm himself, waiting for the sweat to dry. Maggie is closer to him than usual. She's eating into his mind, forcing him to confront things he doesn't want to confront. He licks his lips and tastes the fear that he's fighting to control.

Go away, Maggie. I need to do this in my own time. Leave me alone.

If I want to stay, Straker, I'll stay.

He needs to make a decision. What he would like to do is nail down the part of the sail that is flapping, then go away. He might as well finish the job properly. At least the sails stop the leaks and that will give her time to do some work inside. Then he can go back to his lighthouse and pick up his rhythms again.

Curiously, he's brought a hammer and nails with him as well as pliers. Did he know he was going to do this?

He climbs over to the loose part and folds it down neatly. He can see where it's come away from some rotted wood, so he feels along until he finds a stronger part and hammers it down, furtively looking over his shoulder, unable to shake off the feeling that he shouldn't be here.

The nails go in easily. He pulls at the sail, but it holds. He puts the hammer into his pocket and eases his way back over the roof.

'Straker!'

He stumbles and nearly falls. This cannot be happening.

'What in the world's going on?'

She's standing below, looking up at him, her face red and angry, in the same brilliantly blue blouse that she was wearing yesterday. Her hair glitters in the sun, shiny, almost metallic, hard and threatening.

'What are you doing?'

He freezes, trying to shrink back into himself, make himself as small as he can, willing himself to disappear.

'Have you got some hidden agenda?'

He doesn't know what to do.

'Get off my roof, Straker!'

Chapter 10

Anne was standing by the open train door watching a BR man in uniform approach. Where was Jerry? It didn't take that long to buy a newspaper. She was trying not to worry, but her legs were trembling.

'On or off?' said the man. He was wearing a turban and had a black bushy beard, streaked with grey. When he opened his mouth to speak, she could see that he had long, protruding teeth that made him look slightly menacing.

'No!' she said urgently. 'My husband!'

'Train's due out,' said the guard. He was very tall, standing too close and towering above her.

'I know,' said Anne. 'He's only gone to get— There he is!'

She watched Jerry shuffle across the platform, and relief flooded into her like the warmth of a cup of tea. Jerry running was an unusual sight, his hollow angular body struggling against its innate lack of rhythm. Even in her anxiety, she felt a stab of affection. He was academic, not athletic, she thought fondly.

The man turned and watched Jerry hurrying up to the carriage. 'Come on, sir,' he said. 'Can't hold the train up just for you. Next time you must arrive early if you want to buy a newspaper.' Unexpectedly he smiled, and the menace evaporated. He held the door while they both got on.

'Sorry,' said Jerry. 'I just got caught behind a—'

But the man wasn't interested. He slammed the door and moved on up the train.

They swayed through the carriage until they found two seats opposite each other. 'This'll do,' said Jerry, and sank down, still struggling to get his breath. He put the newspaper on the table.

'I don't know why you bothered,' said Anne. 'You'll have time to read it later.'

'You know I like a crossword on a train journey.'

He sat back, gave a sigh of relief and folded the *Guardian* on to the back page. 'Ah,' he said, after a few seconds. 'Of course,' and he wrote in his first answer.

Anne watched him for a while, knowing he didn't want her to say anything. When she decided that he was comfortable with his crossword, and possibly wouldn't speak again until they reached Birmingham, she settled back and got her knitting out of her bag. She hadn't forgotten to bring that. She held it up to admire. It was a navy jumper with a ship on the front, for Jeremy, her fourth grandchild, whom they had been to see today. She was very proud of the jumper. All her children had had one, and now she was knitting for the next generation. This was the ninth, each one a slightly different colour but the same design. She had photographs of every child wearing this jumper. There was a line of them up the side of the stairs. The children hated them. 'Take them down, Mum,' they had all said, at one time or another. 'They look like flying fish. They're in very bad taste.'

'Nonsense,' she said comfortably. 'I like them. They're my taste, so I don't care what you think.'

She smiled to herself and gazed out of the window as she knitted, so familiar with the pattern that she could do it by instinct.

'Excuse me.'

She turned her head and saw an elderly, bald man standing above her. She glanced at Jerry, but he was concentrating on his crossword.

'May I sit next to you?'

She looked around to see if there were empty seats anywhere else, but there weren't. She didn't really want to sit next to anyone. 'Of course,' she said, moving her bags and putting them on the floor.

'I wonder,' said the man, 'could I put my cello on this seat and sit opposite? I prefer to travel facing the engine.'

'Oh,' said Anne. She couldn't see a cello. 'Jerry,' she said. 'Move your stuff. He wants to sit next to you.'

'Sorry?' said Jerry, raising his eyes from the paper. 'Oh, yes, of course.'

The man went behind the seat and reappeared with his cello in an untidy leather case that was becoming unstitched on the sides. 'Thank you,' he said, beaming, and attempted to lift it. He did not look strong enough.

'Jerry!' said Anne.

Jerry looked up again. 'Oh,' he said. 'Let me help.'

He stood up clumsily, and together they lifted the cello on to the seat.

'Thank you,' said the man, and sat down. He had gone very red and seemed to have some difficulty breathing.

'Are you all right?' said Anne.

'Yes, yes, yes.' His little bald head bobbed up and down while he twisted himself to get a handkerchief out of his pocket to wipe his streaming face.

Jerry went back to his crossword. He had already completed a third clue, Anne noted with relief. He would be in a good humour if he could finish it on his own. She'd help him if he asked, but he resented it. He saw it as a matter of pride. She saw it as a matter of convenience. It wasn't her fault that she was better at crosswords than him. He might be very clever, but he didn't necessarily think in the devious way that was essential for crosswords. He was too literal, she liked to think. Too logical.

'It's tricky, taking the cello on a train,' said the elderly man.

'Yes,' said Jerry, without looking up.

'Do you have to buy a ticket for it?' asked Anne.

'Oh dear,' said the man. 'I haven't. I didn't realise it would take up so much room.'

Typical man, thought Anne. Lack of forethought. 'Never mind,' she said, smiling warmly. 'Let's hope the ticket collector doesn't notice.'

He leaned forward. 'I'm going on an orchestral course in Birmingham. Haven't played in an orchestra since I was at university. Quite an adventure, really. Always too busy working until now.'

'Wonderful,' said Anne.

'Do you live in Birmingham?'

'Yes.'

'Good,' he said, his head going up and down again. 'Good.' A toy dog in the back of the car, nodding every time they went over a bump.

Jerry put the newspaper on the table. 'It's not like you to forget the paper. It's very extravagant to buy two.'

Anne looked up from her knitting and read the paper upside down. 'Mother-of-pearl,' she said.

Jerry stared at her. 'What?'

'Two across. Mrs Oyster. Mother-of-pearl.'

He snatched away the paper. 'I know. I was just going to write it down.'

'Of course you were,' she said.

He looked at her suspiciously, uncertain if she was serious or not, then leaped to his feet. 'I'll get us some tea, shall I?'

Anne smiled at him. 'That would be nice, dear. Thank you.'

The little man had to stand up to let Jerry out. 'Sorry,' said Jerry, as he stepped on his foot. 'Sorry.'

'Get me something nice to eat,' said Anne. 'Some short-bread, or a KitKat or something.' She thought of her spreading waistline, then banished the guilt.

'Right,' he said, and waited to let some children pass. There seemed to be hundreds of them, in groups of four or five, swaying with the rhythm of the train, trying to work out their money as they went.

Jerry nodded towards his crossword. 'Don't do it, will you?'

'Of course not, dear. Why would I?'

He didn't trust her. He picked up the paper and tucked it under his arm as he followed the children down the carriage. Anne could hear him muttering to himself about children as he went. He had never liked children. Not even his own. Didn't know what to do with them.

She glanced at the man with the cello and he smiled at her. She felt tired, and decided to avoid his gaze in future. Smiling endlessly and pointlessly was very wearing. She thought of her children and grandchildren, planning their next family get-together like a military operation. She realised as she sat there that she was happy.

It wasn't her fault she was better at crosswords than Jerry.

Chapter 11

Doody pushes a chunk of crusty bread and a slice of cheese that she's hacked off with Oliver d'Arby's blunt breadknife in Straker's direction. 'You can have some if you want it,' she says, hoping he'll say no, but he takes it without saying thank you and starts eating.

'That's all right,' she says, taking a swig of lemonade. She wipes the top of the bottle with her shirt and hands it to Straker. He looks at it, looks at her, then gives it back. Fine, she thinks. Be thirsty, then.

She's brought out the two cushions she slept on last night and they're sitting on them with their backs to the wall. Bits of ancient white paint flake off and stick to their clothes. She's trying to stay annoyed with him, but it's proving difficult. She's fighting a growing sensation of relaxation, feeling the occasional shaft of sunshine on her face, and the proximity of Straker. She tries to imagine him robbing a bank, or mugging a vulnerable old man, but he doesn't have the right kind of menace in his face. You can't tell, she says to herself. That's the point. People are not what they seem.

A wood-pigeon hoots nearby and it reminds her of their old house – before they moved to the tiny three-bedroomed council house with no central heating. She used to go out early in the morning, when everyone else was asleep, and creep through the dewy grass to her yew-tree hideout. The wood-pigeon called from a distance, and she would doze off, secure in her aloneness. The garden was still and half lit, secret, only seen by her. She liked the distance that separated her from everyone else.

Judging by his breathing, Straker has gone to sleep. He's sitting with his eyes shut and his mouth open, peaceful except for occasional shudders that bring him almost awake, but not quite. She studies his face, now that he can't see her. The scar stands out clearly as it zigzags through his beard, old and shrivelled, pulling his skin inwards and distorting the left side of his face. He does look sinister – he'd make a good gangster, frightening people like Mrs Whittaker and Sharon in the supermarket.

Doody's mobile phone rings. Straker jerks upright and stares around in bewilderment. She pulls it out of her bag, irritated by its intrusion into the calm. 'Hello? Jonathan?'

'No, it's Mr Hollyhead here.'

'Hello, Philip,' she says. This name business still infuriates her. Doesn't she merit a small intimacy?

'Doody—'

'Mrs Doody,' she says.

'Yes . . .' He pauses. 'Have you managed to mow the playing-field? Only you did say . . .'

He knows she hasn't done it. He must be looking at it through his lounge window as he talks to her on the phone.

'If I say I'll do something, I'll do it.'

'Yes.'

Actually, she'd forgotten. 'I'll do it tonight. I'm out today.'

'Yes.'

' 'Bye, then.'

'How's the foot – the leg?'

'Terrible, but I don't suppose you want to know that if you're expecting me to mow the playing-field.'

'Are you up to it?' He sounds anxious.

She longs to say no, but he'll just get hysterical. 'Yes. 'Bye.'

She puts the mobile back into her bag. 'Headmaster,' she says to Straker. 'Pain in the neck.'

He doesn't respond. He looks as if he hasn't understood a word she's said.

'Well,' she says, 'since you've made yourself at home on my roof, I deserve an invitation to your lighthouse.'

He's a waste of time. He doesn't even pretend to look welcoming. She tries another approach. 'What is the extent of your knowledge about roofs?'

He still doesn't speak. Another man who doesn't know anything. A silent equivalent of Mr Hollyhead. So, general questions are a waste of time. He requires precisely worded questions, which can be answered with a yes or a no. It's such an effort. She'd prefer to throw words at him, and catch him out when he's not expecting it.

'I need some help,' she says. The words feel uncomfortable in her mouth.

He doesn't move, doesn't make a sound, but there's something different about him. An awareness. He's listening.

'I'm not talking about rubbish polythene. I want to do it properly. The tiles are too old – you can't buy them any more. Jonathan says I have to pay someone to retile the whole roof.'

He might be interested. Nothing obvious has changed, but his face doesn't seem to sag so much. Without moving, he looks as if he is sitting up straighter.

'I don't suppose . . .'

He nods.

'Can you help me?'

He nods vigorously.

'I can't afford to pay you.'

He shakes his head and jumps up, then walks up and down, stopping to look up at the roof, his lips moving silently. Doody can't make any sense of it, so she sits and watches him. He gives the impression that he knows what he's doing.

'Don't tell me what's going on, will you?' she says.

He moves his hand as if he wants her to be quiet, a

calming down, shushing movement that you might make to a child.

A spark of resentment shoots through her. 'Don't patronise me,' she says. 'If you want me to shut up, say so.' But he doesn't react to this.

It's starting to go chilly. The patches of blue sky are becoming less frequent, and without the occasional sun, the air is damp and unfriendly. Banks of clouds are building up in the distance, over the sea, and a cold wind is coming in ahead of them. Doody's not dressed for this. It's June. It's supposed to be warm.

He stops abruptly, as if he's walked into a brick wall. 'Thirty-seven,' he says.

She waits for more, but that's it. 'Yes?'

He looks extremely pleased with himself, as if he's been wrestling with a problem for days.

'You might think you're profound,' she says, 'but I think you're talking nonsense.'

He stands a few feet away, and acts as if he's chewing an unpleasant-tasting sweet. 'Just spit it out,' she says. 'You'll feel better then.'

'You need thirty-seven tiles,' he says, over-articulating like a foreigner who is just learning how to pronounce certain words.

'Don't be ridiculous. It's more than that.'

He pulls her arm until she gets up, then points at the roof, counting. 'One, two . . . fifteen, sixteen . . . twenty-nine . . . thirty-three, thirty-four . . .' He seems to think she can count every individual tile with him, but it's impossible. He could be counting the same hole thirty-seven times. When he's finished, he turns to her with an odd expression on his face.

'Thirty-seven tiles,' she says.

He nods eagerly, up and down, and it occurs to her that he might think he's smiling. 'OK,' she says. 'Thirty-seven tiles.'

He's almost trembling with excitement.

'But that's thirty-seven tiles too many. Where am I going to get them? They don't make them any more.'

He stops hopping and nodding and twitching and puts a hand on her arm. 'Come,' he says.

She studies him. Is he safe? Does he know something about thirty-seven antique tiles that she doesn't?

'All right,' she says, pushing his hand away. 'You don't have to maul me. Where do you want me to go?'

Of course he doesn't answer, but he heads towards the gate, turning towards her every few steps to make sure she's following. They go out of the gate in this strange, bobbing manner, Straker leading, stopping, turning, waving his hands vaguely while he waits for Doody to catch up.

'If you remember,' she says, 'I hurt my ankle not long ago. It is not completely better.' He slows down for a bit, but then speeds up again.

'Where are we going?' she says. 'You can tell me, you know, and there's a fairly good chance I'll understand.'

She rather hopes he might lead her down to the village so that all the local people can see she's got him tamed. It would be satisfying to prove that she's achieved something they couldn't do. But he turns away from the village and they climb a hill that leads towards open fields edged by lines of trees. She starts to feel hot and tired. The occasional car passes them without slowing down, and they have to jump into the ditch, which is almost dry, but not quite, so a cake of mud builds up on her sandals. Once a car has passed, Straker steps straight back into the road, the rigid set of his shoulders signalling his defiance. It's obvious that he doesn't think much of cars.

'You may not think much of them,' Doody says, 'but you should show a little more respect. As a safety precaution.'

She's reminded of the Pied Piper. Is it wise, following him like this? She still has to mow the playing-field. What if he never stops?

Doody stops. He continues, but when he turns round to check she's behind him, and finds that she isn't, he comes back, his face almost upset. He puts a firm hand under her elbow, and tries to ease her up the road.

'Don't touch me!' she shouts, pulling away from him. She hates people touching her – it's as if they are trying to get inside her skin, invade her thoughts.

Straker steps away, bewildered, but then has to jump back beside her as a Volvo roars past.

She glares at him, resisting the thought that she has over-reacted. He has, after all, touched her before, and she allowed it then. 'Look,' she says, 'I want to know where we're going. I'm tired. My leg hurts. Is there any purpose to this expedition?'

He stops pulling and stands with his long arms hanging loosely at his sides. He looks wrong, out of proportion. His blue eyes study her face, making her uncomfortable. He opens his mouth and it moves, but nothing comes out. He shuts it, then tries again. 'We only need thirty-seven tiles.' This time, his voice is deep and hollow.

'Well,' says Doody, 'I'm glad you told me that. I had no idea.' *We* is incorrect. 'Anyway, I need thirty-seven tiles, but you don't. It would be useful to have your help, but it's still my roof.'

He hesitates, pauses, then tries again. 'I know where there are some tiles like yours.'

She stares at him. 'Why didn't you say so?'

He doesn't answer, but starts walking again, not as fast as before. She wants to stand her ground, but she also wants the tiles, so she follows him. 'Are we nearly there?' she says, and he nods.

They stop by a wooden gate on the edge of the road. It stands across a path overgrown with enormous weeds. Doody regards the gate. 'Is this it?'

He almost smiles and looks pleased with himself. Then he climbs over the gate in one swift, easy movement.

'Hang on,' she says. 'Are you expecting me to do that? Why can't we open the gate first?' He doesn't react. She goes to the catch, but it seems to be rusted shut, and fiddling with it has no effect. Sighing, she places a foot on the bottom rung and puts her weight on it. It creaks. 'I'm heavier than you,' she says. 'I don't spend half my life in a gym, or jogging round the village at six o'clock in the morning. I'm not that sort of person.'

He waits and watches, but doesn't help.

She puts both feet on, holds her breath, and it supports her. Managing to sit on the top of the gate she swings her legs over inelegantly to the other side. Exhilarated by her success, she jumps down on to the grass on the other side.

'Ow!' She's forgotten her sprained ankle.

Straker bends down to help, but he irritates her. 'Get off,' she says, pushing him aside. He stands a few feet away and watches, making no further attempt to assist. The pain soon eases off, but she's not going to tell him that.

'All right,' she says, after rubbing the ankle for a while, and they walk more slowly.

The path fades out in front of an old brick building, ivy-covered, very large, with tiles on the roof that match the cottage tiles exactly. It's the kind of barn that would be big enough to store bales of hay. Straker stands still and waits. She knows he's feeling pleased with himself, so she tries to appear nonchalant.

'Well,' she says, walking up to it. 'What is it? A barn?'

He shrugs. They are on the edge of a neglected field, long and narrow, waist high with grasses and thistles. The barn, although weathered, looks more recently built than Doody's cottage, and in better condition, with no missing tiles. Straker might be working on a smile again, but it's difficult to be certain.

'Who does it belong to?'

He shrugs again. She can't decide if he knows and isn't going to tell her, or if he really hasn't a clue.

'But we can't just take the tiles, can we? They must belong to someone.'

He ignores her and starts to climb the horse-chestnut tree that is growing against a corner, its thickening trunk pushing against one side of the barn. She leaves him to it and walks round the building, easing her way through the bushes that are growing right up to the walls, trying to avoid the thistles and nettles. There are no windows. Three walls are brick, but the fourth, which faces the neglected field, consists of two huge wooden doors, padlocked together. She fingers the padlock curiously, wondering if it will just break with age and enable them to go inside, but it's completely secure. At the top of one of the doors, there's a number painted on, once white, now faded to a dirty grey: 21/7.

Doody puts her eye to a crack and tries to peer in, but the interior is completely black.

He's already coming down the tree with some tiles in his hands. He gives her one and she examines it. He's right. It's identical to the ones on the cottage roof. 'Are we allowed to take them?' she asks.

He doesn't seem at all worried, and climbs back up the tree to fetch some more. This time, she takes them from him before he comes all the way down, piling them at her feet. 'Thirty-seven,' she calls, after about ten minutes, but he doesn't stop. He collects a further ten. Then he climbs down and stands by the bottom of the tree. Is she supposed to pat him on the head and tell him he's a good boy?

'Is this your place?' she asks.

He shakes his head.

'But – aren't we stealing?'

He nods and looks pleased. She wonders if he has a secret grudge against the owner of the place. But it's obvious that nobody has been here for a very long time. She examines the roof. He hasn't taken all of the tiles from the same place so there's no obvious hole. Just small gaps that might have been caused by time and weather – like the cottage roof. Either he was trying to be discreet, or he was fussy and only took the best tiles.

'I want to go up,' says Doody.

He doesn't seem to understand her.

'Up the tree. I want to see inside.'

He shakes his head.

'Yes.' The tree appears easy to climb with lots of lower branches, plenty of footholds. She makes a start. Her ankle hurts, but not too much. He doesn't do anything, just watches.

It's a waste of time. She still can't see inside. She can pick out the shape of something very large, machinery perhaps, but it's impossible to identify. She climbs down. 'Do you know what's inside?'

He shakes his head, but she's not sure if she believes him. 'Number twenty-one,' she says. 'Stroke seven.'

He looks puzzled, so she leads him round to the doors and points: 21/7. The edges of the numbers are flaking, but they're still strong and readable, imprinted into the lichen dark of the wood.

He nods. 'Twenty-one,' he says.

She starts to feel angry again. 'Well, if you're going to talk, why can't you say something more useful? We go all this way in silence, no explanation from you, and then you tell me something I already know.'

He's watching her. His blue eyes are studying her face, searching for something, waiting for a reaction. She gives up. 'So, how are we going to carry the tiles back?'

———————

At the gate of her cottage, Doody watches Straker pushing his Sainsbury's trolley up the road, on his way back to the barn. 'We'll probably go to prison for this,' she says, as he rumbles it over the cobbles, but he ignores her.

She feels tired and deflated. They've been into the village, where he showed her the boathouse and his trolley, but they didn't meet anyone. The entire population seemed to have retired indoors.

'I don't know how you get away with it,' she said. 'Alarms are supposed to go off if you take a trolley off the premises.'

His face was blank, but she's beginning to read his expressions – when he doesn't want to respond and when he really doesn't know.

She sits down outside the cottage and nibbles a digestive biscuit. An aeroplane drones overhead. She pulls her notebook and a pencil out of her bag and sits on the grass.

The lighthouse had red and white stripes and dark green railings round the light at the top, and was surrounded by acres of deserted scrub.

She pauses, feeling the chill of the wind, conscious of a bird watching her from a nearby tree. What is she doing here? The country is not her natural environment. She's more familiar with concrete.

Doody's sister, Celia, was a gifted child. She did her O levels and A levels early. At seventeen, she went to Cambridge to do a maths degree.

She had white-blonde hair, perfectly straight, grey eyes rimmed with green, long fair curly eyelashes. She experimented with makeup for a while, but there was no need. Either way, she was beautiful. Even Imogen could see that.

She was brilliant. She was in all the school teams – hockey, netball, rounders, tennis. She could do mental arithmetic like a computer, memorise whole sections of text for exams. Grade eight piano and violin, a Mozart concerto with the youth orchestra. She nearly made the junior Olympic gymnastics team when she was younger. She won cross-country races, reached the finals of an under-sixteen national tennis tournament when she was twelve.

Their house was full of trophies and shields and cups and photographs of Celia smiling her innocent, victorious smile, holding another award, shaking hands with important people Imogen didn't recognise.

Celia was also not nice, but Imogen was the only one who knew that, because Celia was too clever to let anyone else see it.

Imogen wasn't nice either. They shared the loft, a dark room with open rafters and walls sloping into the roof. Celia's half was next to the dormer window, and her bed was always tidy, with its pretty flowered quilt cover and matching valance. Her nighties were folded precisely and put under the pillow, so that when she got ready for bed she always looked immaculate. White and clean and innocent.

Imogen's corner was dark and cluttered. She didn't put things away, and her clothes were creased and unwashed, her bed crumpled and unmade. She liked to drop her dirty underwear in the middle of the floor so Celia would have to walk over it.

'Imogen,' she would say. 'Knickers.'

Imogen would face the wall and make her breathing calm and even. Dead to the world. Can't pick up her own knickers.

Celia had different approaches. Sometimes she would step over them as if they weren't there. At others, she would pick them up with the edge of her finger and thumb and throw them on to Imogen's face. Imogen had to go on breathing calmly, wrapped in her own knickers or bra, pretending to be asleep.

Sometimes Celia stood in the middle of the floor. 'Imogen,' she would say gently, and her voice would be so sweet, so genuine that Imogen couldn't stop herself rolling over and opening her eyes half-way. She usually avoided looking at Celia, because her smile was irresistible. But however hard she tried not to, Imogen would go tumbling down into the trap Celia laid for her.

'What?'

'Could you clear up in the morning?' Celia's voice was so friendly – Imogen couldn't resist the offer of friendship. 'I thought we could make the room really nice and tidy over the weekend.'

Imogen grunted. Celia smiled and, although she didn't want to, Imogen started to like her again. She tried to fight it, but Celia had a way of making you feel special. She was letting you into her charmed world and offering you something unique.

People tried to be nice to Imogen, but it was a struggle when Celia and Jonathan were around. Jonathan was so much younger than them, and everybody thought he was sweet until he became a teenager and grew his unwashed hair down his back, never changed his socks and didn't have a bath for weeks on end. He talked to people in a patronising way, but they didn't mind because it meant he kept his distance, and keeping a distance from Jonathan in those days was a good idea. It wasn't much of a problem for Imogen, because she'd married and left home by that time. She didn't go to see Jonathan or her mother. Jonathan occasionally came to see her. They had nothing to say to Imogen. She had nothing to say to them.

Everyone loved Celia. They fell at her feet and worshipped her. But after their father died, she changed. They all had to move schools, because there was no way of paying the fees, and Celia found this difficult. She didn't make any new friends, and her old ones moved on without her. Two years later, she went to Cambridge and was only home in the holidays. She seemed to shine and dazzle in the same way as always, but Imogen could see it wasn't real. She stayed in bed longer in the mornings. Everyone thought she was working hard in her bedroom, but she wasn't.

She sat at her desk with books open, a half-written page in

front of her, but she didn't work. She didn't do anything. She just sat. She didn't even pretend to Imogen any more that she liked her.

'Celia, dear,' said their mother at lunch, 'could you help Jonathan with his maths? They haven't explained anything to him properly.'

Imogen could have helped him. She was good at maths, but her mother never asked her.

'Imogen, could you run down to the shop and buy some more bread?'

Celia got the interesting tasks; Imogen got the boring ones.

Later, in their room, Celia wouldn't go to bed. She sat at her desk all night, as far as Imogen could tell, until the early morning. Then she slid into her bed, fell deeply asleep and didn't wake until midday.

'Turn the light off,' said Imogen, several times.

Mostly, Celia ignored her, but once she came over to her bed and grabbed her hair very tightly.

'Ow!' shrieked Imogen, but Celia pushed her face into the pillow, so Imogen's cry was muffled.

'Shut up,' Celia hissed into her ear.

'Get off.' Imogen tried to move away from her, but she was too close.

'You don't know what it's like, everyone expecting you to be successful all the time, never being allowed to make mistakes.'

You don't know what it's like when nobody expects you to be successful, thought Imogen.

'Maybe I just don't want to be brilliant any more. Maybe I'm tired. What if they're wrong and I can't do it? What then?'

Imogen lay still, suspecting she wasn't required to answer.

'I don't see why I should be expected to perform just to please them.'

She can't do it any more, thought Imogen. The work's too difficult for her. 'Why don't you tell them?'

This was not the reaction that Celia wanted.

'I know what you're up to.' Imogen could sense the movement of Celia's lips almost touching her cheek. It made her feel sick.

'I know how you go around when I'm not here – sucking up to people, running me down, pretending you're better than me.'

'I don't,' Imogen whispered into the pillow.

'You're useless.' Celia yanked her hair even tighter. It sent shocks of pain down her arms. 'Don't ever forget that. You will never take my place. You're stupid, thick, ugly and fat.'

Imogen moaned. 'Let go.'

'Repeat after me. Imogen is stupid, thick, ugly and fat.'

She knew it was true, but she didn't want to say it. 'No,' she whispered.

'Yes.' She pulled even harder. Imogen's head jerked backwards and Celia put her face right in front of her eyes. Imogen tried to turn away but she was pulling too hard. She could feel Celia's breath on her face, the smell of the cauliflower cheese they'd had for supper. Imogen could see one eye, grey and hard, like a brittle, shiny marble. She could see Celia's nose, the open pores round the base, her loose, twisted mouth, only an inch from hers.

Imogen started to cry. Celia pulled harder. 'Go on.'

'I'm stupid, thick, ugly, fat.'

She let go suddenly and Imogen nearly bumped her head, but Celia turned away just in time. 'You disgust me,' she said.

Imogen cried silently into her pillow. She didn't want Celia to see she was upset. The light stayed on all night.

The next day, Imogen got out her supplies of yew berries, brought from the old house, kept safe in a tin under her bed. The tin had a picture of Sindy on top, so there was no chance that Celia would be interested in it. She squashed the berries and waited. They would have carrots for supper some day soon. She would offer to mash them.

Imogen wished so hard that Celia would die that she believed it would happen. She could see herself at the funeral. Imogen, her mother and Jonathan. No more money to inherit than last time.

Two days later, she came home from school to an empty house. Her mother was temping at that time, twenty storeys up in an office block. She liked it there and felt part of a team, she said. All typing away together. That was her last job. Jonathan must have been at a friend's house. Imogen took three custard creams (they were allowed only two) and made some orange squash. She put it on the tray that someone had given Celia when she went off to Cambridge, which she didn't like. Little pink pigs chasing each other round the edges. Big, fat, pink pig in the middle. Imogen carried it up to the bedroom.

She opened the door, balancing the tray in one hand, her schoolbag in the other.

She didn't see Celia at first. She put the tray down, kicked her shoes off and went to turn on the light. It was early November. The day was grey and dingy. Something brushed against her face and she turned irritably. It was one of Celia's feet, hanging with the rest of her from a rope tied to a rafter.

Imogen rubbed her cheek where Celia had kicked her. What's she doing up there? she thought. She might have told me she was in.

———————

Straker is taking too long to get back. He's probably got caught and is sitting at the police station, refusing to confess unless they give him paper and a pencil.

The wind has strengthened and there are dashes of rain in the gusts. Imogen thinks of the playing-field, which needs to be done now. She's cold and miserable. She writes a note for Straker and leaves it on the doorstep, held down by a stone. 'Sorry. Had to go. Things to do. Back on Saturday.'

Maybe, she thinks, she won't be back on Saturday. She hasn't decided.

Then she walks round the corner to her car and drives away. There's no sign of him in the mirror. She keeps looking back until she leaves the village.

Chapter 12

22 Westside Tower,
Edgbaston,
Birmingham 15.

14 June 2004

Dear Mr Straker,

I apologise for not having written earlier, but I still find it upsetting to have to think back more than twenty-four years. It should feel like a very long time ago, but I'm afraid the crash seems as vivid to me now as it was then. I wasn't on the train, of course. I was one of the ones waiting at home, watching the television, appalled at the disaster, expecting Maggie to appear at the door any minute, not realising she was on the train. Even now, after all this time, if I hear a ring at the door, I expect to see her coming straight in, full of energy, shoes off, ready to cook. We had a personal code. If either of us was late, we would ring three times and then come in, calling hello. It was so that we wouldn't startle each other, or perhaps it was just a habit that developed over the years without conscious thought. Just the pleasure of coming home, I suppose, and coming together again.

I was unsure about the validity of your project initially, and I have given it considerable thought. The idea of a book about famous crashes worried me. I was unhappy about the sensationalist nature of the project. However, on further reflection, I can see much to commend it. A celebration of the people who survived would be valuable, but also recognition of the dead. A chance for them to be heard. I like that. I would like Maggie to go on in the minds of those who read it.

I understand you want some details about Maggie. This has caused me great confusion. It is very difficult to know where to start. There were two sides to her, her working life and her family life. There were many other facets to her as well, of course, but you will not want to hear them. Some things should be kept private, I believe.

Maggie was a social worker, as I'm sure you will have discovered from the records. She was greatly loved by her work colleagues and by the families she helped. That was mentioned in the newspaper reports, but I imagine they say something similar about everyone who dies. In her case, I can confidently assure you that it was true. Hundreds of people came to the funeral, and I think I managed to talk to every one of them. I certainly hope that I did. They all had the same story to tell. Maggie had helped people through their difficult times, and I was stunned by their tears and their obvious affection. I realise that this sounds as if she were perfect, and of course she was not, but she did have an inner warmth and a genuine desire to reach all sorts of people. I still meet people today whose lives were transformed by her generosity. Of course, we are now a generation on, so children have grown up and people's lives have improved, but they still like to believe that Maggie played a part in their progress. Not everyone was saved by her, of course, but I think she gave something even to those who still struggle in today's fast, exhausting world.

On the subject of her family, we had two girls, Hilary and Philippa, and at the time of Maggie's death, we had four grandchildren. Three boys and a girl. There are great-grand-children now, and it is a constant source of regret to me that they will never know her. They can only visualise her from the pictures and my reminiscences. Maggie was very keen on the aural tradition. She had stories to tell about her grandparents, which took us right back to the nineteenth century. I think it would be true to say that she was the heart of our family.

Some people are able to give more than others, don't you

think? They are good parents, but then they find it easy to make room for grandchildren – they have an endless supply of affection, always making room for more people, building extensions, as it were, so that they can invite more people in. I'm afraid I'm not as good as Maggie. Less tolerant, more selfish. I try, but I need her push behind me. She made me a better person than I really am.

I hope I have given you enough useful information about her. Probably not, because I do ramble. I seem to become increasingly sentimental as I grow older. I can't decide if this is a good thing or not. Let me know if you need more. I enclose a few photographs if you are interested. I would like to purchase the book if it makes it into print. It's a good idea.

Please send me the details when appropriate.

Yours sincerely,

Simon A. Taverner

When the tide is out, Straker climbs down the rocks below the lighthouse and walks along the beach away from Hillingham. Strings of brown seaweed lie wet and glistening on the high-tide mark, guarded by clouds of hovering flies, which leap into the air in a frenzy as he crosses through them. The pebbles slope down steeply to a small shelf of sand that only appears at low tide.

The wind is fresh and he walks fast, counting his strides. There's no one else around so early in the morning, except the birds. Fulmars, gulls and kittiwakes sweep into the air, hurling themselves at the cliff behind him, screeching into the bleakness of the morning. Crunching over the shingle, he believes himself to be invisible. The birds don't react to him. He's an irrelevance in their precise balancing act between the sea and the sky. They skim the surface of the sea, dive for fish and rise again to hover in the wind, watching and waiting. One or two land on the beach. They stand there, uncharismatic with their wings folded, looking past Straker with disdain.

The seventy-eight are with him, as always. Sometimes he wants to forget them, throw them back into their rightful position of non-existence. Then he feels their personalities, asserting themselves again as he welcomes them back. He fears for the nine unidentified bodies, worries that their anonymity has caused them to disappear too easily into the wind.

When he's walked for fifteen minutes, he stops and stands motionless for a few seconds, unsure what to do next, then sits down.

The wind tugs at his hair. He can hear the pull of the tide as it drains to its lowest point, somehow drawing back the water from under the stones. Trying to suck the beach dry. The gulls fly past, round him, through him. If he stays here for long enough, the tide will come up, the days will pass, and seaweed will attach itself to him. The hard edges of his bones will be softened and smoothed. The kittiwakes will nest in his hair and raise their young.

He's tempted to do it. He closes his eyes, rests his head on his knees. Dreams come like the birds flying past, throwing themselves at him, careless with his presence. He smells the salt on his skin, the heat of the dreams.

———

'Straker . . .' Maggie's voice has changed. She's not angry, just upset – suddenly vulnerable. 'Why did you write to Simon? After all this time?'

'I don't know. I suppose I wanted to find out.'

'Find out what?'

'I wanted to know if you were still real.'

'Don't I remind you every night that I'm real? Don't I come to every dream?'

'Most nights, yes. Not every dream.'

'You don't know that, Straker. Think about it. I might be there all the time, listening, thinking.'

'Why do you come, Maggie? What do you want from me?'

'If I didn't talk to you, I wouldn't exist.'

'But you do exist.'

'Do I?'

'Yes. You still exist to Simon. He thinks of you now as much as he did at the time of the accident.'

'Simon is eighty-three years old, Straker. Old men live in the past. It's easier than facing the hard present. And when he goes, I do.'

'No, Maggie. You can't go.'

'Why not? Why should I keep talking to you once Simon has died? What's the point?'

It has never occurred to me before that Maggie might go. Empty dreams without her there to order things, to put everything into perspective.

'Scared, Straker? Can't you manage without me?'

'Of course I can.' I don't know. There is a tight, prickly fear creeping along my veins, my arteries, my nerve-ends.

'You were wrong to write to Simon. Why should he have to go over it again?'

'I just wanted to make some contact with him. I wanted to feel the way it was, and how he fitted with you.'

There is a long pause. Maggie's voice is quiet. 'We fitted well together. Very well.'

'And you have great-grandchildren.'

'They will never know me.'

'They already know you, because Simon has taught them.'

'Sentimental rubbish.' But her voice is not confident, and it frightens me.

'Maggie – I just wanted to make you more real.'

'You're fooling yourself. I'm not real.'

I shiver at her words. I want her to change back, to become

*the eternal mother again, telling me what to do, making me
think as she wants me to think. 'Don't leave me, Maggie.'*

'Maybe I will. Maybe not.'

*I think of Simon's words. Building new extensions, letting
more people in. Did she have a limitless capacity to expand?
Would the time have come when there was no room for even
one more person? Were her kindness and hospitality real or
was she pretending, building up an outer image to please
everyone? Creating an earth mother of boundless love and
energy to satisfy Simon?*

What is real?

There is no sound from Maggie.

Don't leave me, Maggie, please don't leave me.

I am cold and tired and lost. I want her to come back.

Straker is woken by voices.

'It's all right, Jen. There's no one else here.'

'Lee—'

'Jen—'

They are teenagers, but like children, walking hand in hand
along the shingle, stopping to gaze into each other's eyes, then
picking up shells. What are they doing here so early in the
morning?

'Watch this,' he says, picking up a flat stone and skimming it
across the surface of the sea. It bounces three times, then gets
swamped by an incoming wave.

She claps her hands. 'Cool. Do it again.' She's about sixteen,
wearing jeans and a bright red jumper. Her hair is dark and
curly, tied back into a pony-tail, and she's very pretty. The
cold of the air has sharpened her features, brought a pink flush
to her cheeks.

He's a bit older, perhaps eighteen, also in jeans, with a
leather bomber jacket over a T-shirt. He has two earrings in
one ear and a nose-ring.

Straker freezes and watches them, waiting for them to pass without noticing, hoping that he's as invisible as he would like to be.

But they don't go past. Jen runs towards the sea, trying to throw a stone like Lee, but after she has thrown it, she spins round and round, shrieking like a child, until she staggers and nearly falls over.

Lee catches her, holds her upright, and then they stop everything as his arms go round her, and they kiss – a deep, passionate kiss. His hands move down the line of her back and slide smoothly under her jumper. He knows what he's doing; it's obvious that he's done it before. She leans against him, pulling herself as close as she can, her back arching as they rock together.

Stop! Straker wants to shout. Don't do it, Jen. You're only sixteen (or less). You might get pregnant, catch dreadful diseases. He won't marry you. Wait. There are better things ahead.

He doesn't say any of it. He creaks slowly to his feet, intending to creep away, hoping they won't see him.

Jen sees Straker over Lee's shoulder. She goes rigid and screams. Lee turns and sees Straker. All three stand motionless for four seconds, the wind whistling round them. A gull swoops low over their heads and Straker turns and runs.

'Clear off!' shouts Lee.

'Dirty old man!' yells Jen. 'You're disgusting!' She's worse than him. More vicious, more shrill. She's still shouting as Straker runs away.

They don't run after him. He pauses briefly to look back and they're lying on the pebbles, their feet only a few inches from the returning sea, their hands and bodies intertwined, inseparable, just one more heaving mass among the crabs and flies and seaweed. A sculpture of lust in a landscape of sea.

Straker looks at his watch and starts to go faster, counting seconds. He needs to get back to the lighthouse in ten minutes and twenty-three seconds if he's to improve on the last run.

When he climbs the cliff back to the lighthouse, he sees that two more long dark cracks have appeared down one side, facing the sea.

It takes two days to mend the roof, working between the showers, and Straker is pleased at how easily the tiles fit into their new environment. It will be necessary to replace some of the wooden beams as soon as possible, though, and he starts making calculations – when he can get some wood, how much it will cost, how he'll need to remove the tiles again to do it. He takes the old sails back to the boathouse, returns to the lighthouse, carrying on in his normal routines, and waits for Saturday. He doesn't know if he should go and see her again.

He reads Simon's letter through five times every day, wanting to write back to him and reveal the truth. There's an unfamiliar feeling inside him, a fear that reality is catching up with him, forcing him in directions he's not sure he can go. He goes out in the pouring rain to count the cracks in the lighthouse, examines the doors, some of which won't close properly. Two upstairs doors jam, so he runs up and down with stones heavy enough to prop them open or shut. He measures the distance from the lighthouse to the edge of the cliff. Another foot has gone. He sets himself new targets for rowing, running, climbing to the top of the lighthouse and back. Numbers run through his mind, queuing up, calculating against each other – square roots, multiplication, division – clicking on endlessly, fighting each other for attention. They don't have the calming effect that he expects.

At night, he doesn't dream. The sleep is long and deep, and he wakes up with an empty mind.

'Your mother and I will stand by you,' his father announced, positioning himself in front of the marble fireplace. One of the logs newly placed on the fire cracked violently and sent out sparks, which bounced on to the back of his father's trousers. His mother jumped up from the sofa and patted his trousers with a cushion.

'Get off, woman,' he shouted. He believed he was immortal, that a few sparks couldn't touch him. Pete believed that too.

His mother sat down again. She was a small woman, but she nearly disappeared altogether on that day, her hands clasped tightly round her knees, her grey head leaning forward at an uncomfortable angle, ever-anxious, nodding in time with her husband's words. Her body was bowed, as if she'd spent her whole life scrubbing floors. In fact, she had. They had two cleaners, but every day after they'd gone, she could be found on her knees polishing the parquet, sweeping the stairs, scrubbing the stone floor in the kitchen. Today she wouldn't look Pete in the eye.

'I have appointed a solicitor for you, Pete. He's the best. Anthony Sullivan. Expensive, but we can afford it. No point in having money if you don't use it when you need to.'

'It was an accident,' Pete said, for the thousandth time, wanting to believe it. 'I just lost control.'

'Yes, yes.' As usual, he didn't seem interested. 'I've made an appointment for this afternoon. Three thirty. Got to go to his place. Wouldn't come here. Says he won't be needed for the inquest, but it's best to play it safe in case it goes further.'

Pete was twenty-eight and they were the same height, but his father still seemed enormous. Pete felt that he was shrinking next to him, unable to stop himself disappearing.

'And when this nonsense is out of the way, you get started on a proper career. A man of your age should be married with children in a respectable career. Sort out what you want to be – doctor, lawyer, accountant. Tell me what you want and I'll pay. You're never too old to train for something. Look at me.

Washing cars at fifteen, married to your mother at twenty, millionaire at forty.'

Watching him there in front of the fire, absorbed in his own greatness, Pete discovered with a jolt that he hated him. It rushed into him like a strong taste in his mouth, the bitterness of it infecting every part of his body. Pete saw his father's height, his huge weight, his florid complexion and Savile Row suit, and realised that he'd never even liked him. The man who'd always towered above him, manipulated his life, made decisions for him, was a fraud. He had so much money he didn't know what to do with it, and so much power that he had no idea how to use it.

'I don't want to see the solicitor,' said Pete. He wanted to say, 'I've changed my mind. It wasn't an accident,' but he couldn't.

'Don't be stupid,' said his father, walking to the door. 'The car'll be out the front at three o'clock.' He went out, slamming the door behind him out of habit.

Pete stood where he was, facing the fireplace. 'Mum,' he said.

She still wouldn't look at him.

'I don't want to—'

'All those people,' she said suddenly, in a low voice. Pete had never heard her speak like that before. Her voice was usually high-pitched and nervous, fluttering around the room, agreeing with her husband, never settling on anything, too restless and unconfident to find a sane pitch of her own. Something had changed. There was a new intensity about her, as if she'd just discovered something unexpected inside herself.

Pete tried to speak, but the words wouldn't come out.

Then she lifted her head and looked at him. Her eyes were unusually large. He'd never noticed before how blue they were. How could he not know the colour of his mother's eyes? 'Seventy-seven people have died,' she said. 'Maybe seventy-eight. Over a hundred injured.'

'I know,' he said.

'Because of you.'

He understood then, more clearly than he'd ever seen anything before, that she would never forgive him. He could see that it hurt her to force herself to look at him.

He couldn't speak. There was nothing to say.

She rose from the sofa, a small, slight woman who had spent a lifetime in the shadow of her husband. She'd found courage in herself to condemn carelessness in her son, to reject the child she'd delivered and nourished and nurtured for twenty-eight years. She looked at him once more, then turned and walked out of the room.

Everything that had anchored Pete's life slipped out of sight. The ropes that held him to the ground were loosened, the gravity that kept him upright in the world ceased to operate and he floated away. He was adrift without a rudder.

He had never before been so terrified.

———

'Hi, Pete. Remember me?'

'Of course I remember you, Francis. How could I forget?'

'Easily done, old man. Easy come, easy go—'

Justin interrupts: 'But we don't really go, do we? That's the point.'

Francis: 'Give us a break, man. Lighten up. Hang loose.'

I can't decide if he believes in all these clichés or if he's trying to be funny. Did he always talk like this and I didn't notice?

Francis: 'So there you go. Here and not here. Courtesy of Pete, stuck in 1979, destined never to grow old.'

'Immortality.' Justin sounds interested. 'Maybe you did us a favour, Pete.'

'With a bit of help from my friends. I didn't do it single-handedly.'

Francis jumps in quickly. 'It was your booze, your old man's cash, your aeroplane.'

Justin's voice alters, becomes more thoughtful. 'Should have been good, shouldn't it? The four of us in all that empty sky. How can you make a mistake when you're surrounded by space? You'd think we'd have missed everything, wouldn't you?'

Francis: 'Everybody's got to come down to earth. Gravity. Physics. Common sense.'

I want to ask them again. Can you remember what happened? But I don't, because I don't want them to tell me.

'We didn't have to come down precisely where we did, did we?' says Justin. 'It could have been a field, or the sea or—' He stops.

Francis chuckles. 'That's it, really, though. Field, water, roads, houses, people. Doesn't make any difference to us. Either way, we're dead.'

Justin: 'Except Pete.'

'Yes,' says Francis, after a pause. 'Did all right, mate, didn't you? Back to the old girlfriend, back to Daddy with all the money—'

Girlfriend? Did I have a girlfriend? I can't remember anyone.

'Mel,' says Justin. 'Alison, Liz, Helen, Pippa . . .'

'Daisy, Katie, Melinda, Ellen . . .'

'All those girls waiting for us to come back down. Wonder if they cried.'

'Bound to. They'd never have found anyone as handsome, clever, witty . . .'

'Experienced, able to give them a good time . . .'

'Good times . . .'

———

Straker goes shopping. Four bottles of Coca-Cola, an enormous bar of Cadbury's Dairy Milk, sardines for Suleiman and

Magnificent, toilet-cleaner, fabric conditioner and two loaves of thick-sliced Mighty White. He feels the need for the comfort of toast.

He works on the garden, washes his clothes and hangs them outside the lighthouse, letting them blow in the salt wind. He is trying to avoid thinking. He is waiting for Saturday and the return of Mrs Doody.

Chapter 13

Harry sat alone on the train and pretended to look out of the window. He had moved twice. The first time, he'd found a nearly empty carriage and sat down in a corner, looking out of the window, willing everyone to walk on past and find seats elsewhere. Within two minutes a crowd of children appeared from nowhere and flooded the entire carriage. He rose immediately, struggling to breathe, his knees trembling, walked to the end of the carriage and into the next. There he found a space that was not surrounded by people. But just before the train left, a middle-aged woman in a red coat climbed in, carrying a Debenham's carrier-bag, a large gnome and a medium-sized poodle.

She put the gnome on the table and talked to the dog. 'There we are, sweetie. You settle down there opposite the nice man.'

The poodle was a soft beige colour and appeared to have just had a perm. It sat on the seat facing Harry and stared at him. Its eyes were green and alert and interested. It put its head on one side, and Harry looked away. When he glanced back, the dog was still studying him with interest. The woman rummaged in her bag and produced a dried biscuit, which she put on the seat beside her. The dog snatched it with its teeth, and settled down, gnawing contentedly. It kept one eye on Harry as it ate.

'There,' said the woman to Harry, smiling cheerfully. 'Just in time.'

She's talking to me, thought Harry, and looked away.

'It was difficult to find a seat further up,' she said comfortably, getting a plastic container out of her bag.

The train started to move. Harry watched the station slide past, the backs of the people waiting on the other side of the platform, the piles of bags waiting for the Royal Mail train, the Coca-Cola adverts, the overflowing litter-bins.

He became aware that a plastic container was under his nose. 'Would you like one? Cheese and tomato.'

He looked down at the sandwiches and shook his head. He didn't trust himself to speak.

A cheese and tomato baguette, walking round Worcester when he was first married, having lunch with his new wife. They took a bite in turns, straight out of the paper wrapping, sharing their saliva, their germs. Polite at first with tiny nibbles, then more voraciously, taking huge bites, watching each other eat, laughing hilariously. Swans on the river, drizzle spotting the water, people huddled under huge multi-coloured umbrellas on their boat trips. Harry and his wife holding hands, dizzy with the sensation of pretending to be adults, experiencing a secret joy in the way they walked together through the rain, indifferent to the wet and cold.

Harry rose abruptly, did up the buttons on his coat and set off down the train.

'You're going the wrong way for the buffet,' she called after him, but he didn't turn round.

He walked as far as he could to the rear of the train and sank down on to an empty seat. The unoccupied seats around him were silent. The space soothed him, and he breathed more easily, watching his chest rise and fall. He was facing backwards, and it pleased him to see the passing world dropping away in front of him with no clue about what would appear and gradually disappear next. He wasn't sure why he was on the train but he had a vague idea that it was heading north. He remembered counting the last fifty pounds in his wallet and deciding to leave London. He might feel better away from the city, in the countryside or by the sea. There wouldn't be so many people ready to kick him off a park bench or throw him out of a shop entrance, waiting to rob him as soon as he shut his eyes. He thought he had probably been awake for about six weeks now, and he wasn't sure how long he could keep it up.

He held his head upright and closed his eyes. Nobody to watch here, a comfortable rhythm from the train, nothing to worry about. Just a blank in his head. A space.

He let go for the first time in weeks. He could feel his body grow heavy, sliding away from reality, into the lower levels of consciousness.

'Harry!'

He woke with a jolt, and looked up at the round face of Hassan.

'Your shift. I've had enough.'

Harry pulled his exhausted mind back to the present. His eyes were full of grit. He didn't know how to open them.

'You've got to do Mrs Grisham's blood test again. The lab has lost it.'

Harry forced himself out of bed in one quick movement and stood unsteadily, watching Hassan undress. 'What's the time?'

'Four thirty.'

'I'm not on till six. I've only just come to bed.'

Hassan stopped taking his socks off and looked at Harry. 'Sorry, forgot to say. Emergency. Multiple pile-up. At least ten seriously injured. They want everyone they can get.' He gazed into space for a minute. 'Except me. Johnson told me to get out of there before I killed someone.' He paused. 'I don't think he likes me much. He wants you, Harry, old man. You're more his style.'

He sat silently for a second and then keeled over, fully dressed and fast asleep.

Harry tried to dress, but nothing would go on right. His telephone rang. He tried to find it by the bed, but nothing seemed to be in the right place. He was grasping at the air, and the telephone stopped ringing.

Harry! Get up, Harry, emergency! Harry!

He woke with a start as the train lights flickered on. 'The train will be calling at Birmingham International, Birmingham New Street . . .'

Harry shook his head and put his hand straight into his inside pocket. OK. The wallet was still there. There was no one in sight, but he knew he had to keep watching. They might be behind him, waiting for the right moment, waiting for him to slide into sleep, the moment of surrender. They nearly got him then. He couldn't afford to let it happen again.

He thought of his wife. He didn't remember a great deal about her, but he had a picture in his mind. Small, puzzling, sometimes silent when he thought she should speak. She was too compliant, and it had worried him after a while. 'Don't just agree with me,' he'd said, over and over again. 'Argue with me.' But she had shaken her head, smiled and said nothing.

'I'll have to stay at the hospital when I'm on duty,' he had said. 'It's too far to travel.'

'You could work in Birmingham,' she said, smiling again.

'It wouldn't make any difference. I'd still have to sleep there.'

'Wherever you are,' she said, 'I am too.'

He hadn't really understood what she'd meant, but it had sounded good. 'I suppose I could look for a job here,' he said.

'Yes,' she said, and made him a cup of tea. It bothered him that she always made the tea.

'It'll be better now I'm qualified,' he'd said, putting an arm round her. She snuggled up to him, and he liked the way that they physically fitted together. It seemed right.

He shouldn't have done it. It was too much. The travelling. The tiny little bedsit where he left her, where he went home to. Damp seeping through under the front door, the dog barking in the flat below when he was just dropping off to sleep. The meals that she cooked to save money. Liver and bacon. Heart stew. Sago pudding, lemon-curd tarts. She wasn't very good at it. She read the cookery books and followed the instructions precisely. Upset tummies, getting out of bed in the middle of the night with diarrhoea.

'You must go to the doctor,' she said.

'I am a doctor.'

'You know what I mean. You shouldn't get upset tummies like this. I don't.'

Not enough sleep. Getting up to go to the toilet. Only two days at home and then back to the hospital.

'We'll buy our own place soon,' he'd said. 'When we've saved for the deposit.' London was so expensive. 'It'll be better then.'

'It's all right now,' she said. And she had smiled. The smile that had gone through him when he'd first met her at a party. It had been a smile that had told him all about her, right from the beginning.

'I'm Harry,' he had said, feeling big and clumsy.

'Hello, Harry,' she said. 'I'm Imogen.'

'Harry!' said his mother. 'She's only eighteen. She works in Asda, for goodness' sake. Stocking shelves.'

'No,' said Harry. 'She's on the tills.'

'Nevertheless,' said his mother. 'She's not suitable.'

Harry grinned. 'She doesn't have to be suitable. I love her.' And he did. He loved her big sad eyes, her dyed blonde hair. The way she spread and rippled her fingers when she didn't want to finish her sentences. 'Anyway, she's highly intelligent.'

'Then why is she working in Asda?'

'It gives her time to think. She's had a tragic life.'

'Wait two years,' said his mother. 'Then decide.'

He caught himself just as his head started to nod. Careful, Harry, he thought. Don't look backwards. Concentrate on where you're going. He felt in his pocket. The wallet was still there. There was nothing in it except the money. He'd got rid of all identification right at the beginning. He couldn't afford to be traced.

It was getting dark outside.

Chapter 14

It's dark by the time Doody finishes mowing the playing-field, and she's still shovelling wet grass on to the compost heap at the back of the school when it starts to rain. She is not obliged to cut the grass, it's not in her contract, but the council parks department is unreliable, so she does it in exchange for fruit and vegetables out of Doris Hollyhead's garden. The sharp, damp smell rises aggressively from the compost heap, making her sneeze, and her hands ache with the cold. So much for summer.

The phone is ringing as she enters the house. She picks it up, smearing the receiver with grass stains. 'All right, all right,' she says. 'It's done now, Philip. Wait until it's light tomorrow and you'll see the lines are straighter than usual. One of my better attempts, I think – despite the appalling weather conditions.'

'Imogen?'

'Oh, Jonathan.' She feels self-righteous, and wants some appreciation. 'I've just cut the grass.'

He doesn't reply immediately, and she understands the delay. It takes him time to adjust to the practical events in life that don't involve money. 'Well done,' he says.

'Don't be so patronising.'

'All I said was, very good.'

'No, you didn't. You said, "Well done."'

'So, what's the difference?'

There probably isn't a difference. They sound equally patronising when Jonathan says them. 'What's on tonight, Jonathan?'

'On? What do you mean?'

She's not fooled. She can hear television voices in the background, cutting off abruptly when he zaps them with the remote control. 'Are they demonstrating spinach and dandelion salad? Pasta with walnut sauce? Ciabatta bread? Who's coming to cook with you tonight?'

'Imogen, what do you want?'

'You phoned me, remember?'

'Oh, yes.' He'd forgotten, and a bubble of pleasure leaps up inside her. She loves to witness Jonathan's weaknesses. It almost makes her feel warm and protective towards him.

'Never mind,' she says. 'I expect you'd like to know about the roof.'

There's a silence. 'Oh,' he says, just as she's thinking about replacing the receiver. 'Yes, the roof. The offer's still open, you know. I could lend you some money for a bit if you're desperate.'

There. His original generosity has already devalued itself. Doody congratulates herself on having read the situation correctly. Too many ex-wives to cater for. 'Veronica and Gill will be relieved.'

'Sorry?'

'It's OK. The roof's taken care of. Thanks all the same.'

'Oh. Good.' She can see him lying there on the settee, his eyes on the walnut sauce, his mouth watering, wandering down the aisles of Sainsbury's in his mind, looking for dandelion leaves, sun-dried tomatoes, or tomatoes on the vine, whichever sounds more expensive to him.

'I've got dandelion leaves in my garden. Hundreds of them if you want to come and pick them.'

He doesn't reply.

'You know Oliver d'Arby? Do you reckon he had other things to leave? That he left them to someone else?'

'I think you were the only beneficiary . . .' He pauses for three seconds. She counts them. Got you, she thought. 'How would I know?'

'You opened my letter, didn't you? It came to you first.'

'It was addressed to you, not me.'

'That didn't stop you opening it, though, did it?'

'Imogen!' His voice goes up a perfect fifth. He's stopped thinking about sun-dried tomatoes. 'I hope you're not suggesting—'

'No, Jonathan, of course not. But did you know there were tenants in the cottage after he disappeared? What happened to their rent?'

'Really? That's interesting. Do you want me to find out?' She knows that he will think only men could do important things like write to solicitors.

'Yes, please, Jonathan. Could I leave that to you? I'd be really grateful.'

'Of course. I'll let you know what happens.'

He doesn't ask for the name of the solicitor. Exactly as she suspected. Further proof of his guilt. 'Sackville, Sackville and Waterman. Nice man.'

'Sorry?'

'The solicitors. You'll need to know who they are.'

'Good point.'

'Must go now. Haven't eaten all day.' Not true. But she doesn't want to give him the impression that she's anxious about money. If he isn't offering, she isn't asking.

'I'll speak to you later.' He's already turned the sound up again on the television. He'll enjoy writing to the solicitor.

' 'Bye, then.'

There's a pause. 'Maybe the solicitors have used the money on legal expenses.'

He would think of that. She puts the phone down. It's the right time for Mr Hollyhead to phone and thank her. He and Doris the Lion Tamer should have just finished watching *Peak Practice*.

The phone rings almost immediately. She picks it up. 'Philip! I thought you'd never ring.'

'Imogen, it's Jonathan. I know why I phoned.'

'Yes?'

'Can you phone Mother some time? She's complaining that you never speak to her.'

'Fine,' she says, and cuts him off. Why was it always her fault? Why shouldn't her mother contact her directly, instead of through Jonathan?

She dreams that Harry comes back. He flies over the cottage and lands on the road outside. She runs out of the front door, down the path and flings open the gate. 'Harry!' she cries.

He is climbing out of the aeroplane, unzipping his leather jacket, grinning like he did when she first knew him. 'Imogen!' he calls and opens his arms for her. 'Know any good jokes?'

She hesitates, struggling to think.

Why did the chicken—

There was an Irishman, an Englishman, a Welshman—

What do you get if you cross a kangaroo with—

A noise behind her makes her turn round and Straker is there, his eyes blue and intense. He is holding two tiles from the roof, offering them to her, almost smiling.

As she wakes, she turns back to Harry and he is fading, thinning out. She can look straight through him to the other side of the road.

'No,' she cries.

Once she is properly awake she gets out of bed and goes straight to the kitchen to make herself a cup of coffee, which she drinks before it cools down. It burns the roof of her mouth.

Occasionally, in a tiny corner of her mind, she unearths an unwelcome desire, a painful longing that Harry will turn up one day. She'll answer the door and there he'll be. 'Hi, Imogen,' he'll say. 'Shall we have another go?' And she knows

– although her logical mind resists the thought – that she'll say yes. That she'll leap straight into his arms and rediscover happiness.

Most of the time, she locks up that part of her mind with a large, expensive padlock. She hates to dream about him. Why would she want him back? He taught her all about disloyalty and abandonment. Because of him, she has had to learn about the comfort of anger, how to be self-sufficient, how to survive. What more could he possibly offer her?

When Doody returns to the cottage, she sees immediately that Straker has visited. The roof looks different. She walks round, examining it, unable to work out which are the new tiles and which the old. They're all equally weathered, but there are no visible holes. A shaft of victory pierces her. The cottage is safe: it can dry out and it's hers.

She goes indoors and upstairs, resolving to clear a bedroom and make it habitable so that she won't have to sleep on cushions every time she comes. She's brought a screwdriver and an old knife, with the intention of opening a window before she does anything else. She scrapes away at the painted catches, pushing and shoving until it suddenly, happily, swings open, and she is left hanging over the windowsill, breathless with pleasure.

With the fresh air, a change enters the room. As if the dust and stagnation of the last few years have given up, stopped resisting and allowed the present to reassert itself. The room no longer belongs to someone else. The air is chilly and damp after early-morning rain, but she doesn't mind and stands looking out. The lighthouse is visible from here.

Will he come back?

She has brought dusters and brooms. Cleaning is an art that she has only slowly come to appreciate.

When Imogen was first married, and Harry was away working, she would clean one room of their tiny flat every day. Sometimes he would be on call for eight days in succession, and when he came home, each room had been cleaned twice. She didn't know how often it should be done, how other people organised these things. Nobody had ever told her. Her mother stopped cleaning after Celia died, and she couldn't remember what it had been like before, when her father was still alive. Maybe her mother didn't clean then either. Imogen has a vague memory of a cleaning lady called Miss O'Malley, who kept going outside to smoke. The smell drifted round the garden and reached Imogen in the yew tree. She remembers the cigarettes more than she remembers Miss O'Malley.

She didn't think about cleaning as she grew up, until she became conscious of sticky surfaces on the kitchen work tops, and the fact that she had to do some washing-up if she wanted a clean plate. She was preparing her own meals then – baked beans on toast, egg on toast, pilchards on toast. She didn't know when her mother ate, or Jonathan, because they were seldom in the house at the same time as her. Or if they were, they were in the lounge in front of the television, silently absorbing *Starsky and Hutch* or *Monty Python*. They never laughed. That was the puzzling thing about them. They sat in silence, Mother on the sofa and Jonathan on the rocking-chair, staring at the screen as if it were their source of nourishment. As if it would solve all their problems.

Sometimes if Imogen came in late, she hoped her mother might say, 'What time do you call this?' But she never did. Imogen tried later and later. Midnight, one o'clock, two o'clock. Her mother would be bound to notice. But if she'd finished watching television, she went to bed. There was no hall light to welcome Imogen back. No voice from her mother's room. Nothing to indicate that she ever noticed if Imogen was there or not. In the end, Imogen gave up and came home earlier. She got too tired of hanging around after parties when everyone else had gone home, or too cold sitting on a wall round the corner waiting for midnight.

Harry's mother taught her about cleaning. Imogen and Harry came in one day while she was washing down the skirting-boards, and Imogen was amazed. She'd never noticed that there were such things as skirting-boards.

'Hello,' she said, as Imogen stood watching her.

'Hello.'

They didn't have much to say to each other – Harry's mother was always polite, but distant. She didn't like Imogen. She thought she was thick. She was wearing an apron, a scarf to tie back her hair and yellow rubber gloves. She scrubbed the skirting-boards with a wet cloth, which she kept rinsing in a plastic bowl of water. Imogen thought she looked like a real mother. For a brief moment she wanted to go and give her a hug. The moment passed.

'Don't slip on the kitchen floor,' she said, turning away from them. 'It's wet.'

'Why's it wet?' Imogen whispered to Harry.

He thought this was hilarious. 'Because she's cleaned it,' he whispered dramatically.

The kitchen was full of home baking. Containers of peanut cookies, lemon cake, ginger cake, mince pies, brownies, flapjacks. Harry had three brothers, so they must have needed an endless supply. Imogen had never before tasted such wonderful food, and would have spent hours in the kitchen, sampling new things, if Harry had not been so anxious to get out again before his mother came in and started to challenge her to an intellectual conversation. This was normal procedure. She wanted to show Harry that Imogen was too stupid for him.

'Do you think Margaret Thatcher will do anything about this European Community? Sort the money out properly? Terrible business, the Russian invasion of Afghanistan. What do you think?'

Imogen couldn't think anything. She would stand on one leg and look past her. 'I don't know,' she said.

Harry's parents did try. They invited her to Sunday lunch, and tried to find out what she was interested in, but she didn't know what she was interested in except their son. She concentrated on the food, and let the boys talk. They spent a lot of time arguing about nothing. Imogen always had second helpings. They knew when she was ready for more, and after a few weeks, they didn't bother to ask. They simply passed her plate over and loaded it up again.

'Why don't you talk to them?' Harry asked one day.

'I don't know.' She had nothing to say. There was plenty to say to Harry – about films, music, documentaries they'd seen on the telly – but nothing to his family. She knew they were only pretending to be friendly, and didn't see why she should contribute to the fiction.

But when they were married, and he came home for his breaks, she had to be sure that everything was the same, so that he wouldn't feel he was missing anything. The cake tins were full, the skirting-boards were clean, there was no dust under the bed.

'What do you do all day?' he said to her once.

'Oh, clean,' she said. 'And cook.'

He brought her books home then, because he thought she needed to be educated. Jane Austen, Charles Dickens, Charlotte Brontë. Imogen wanted to please him, show him that she was capable of fitting into his life, so she read them and thought about them, but didn't know what he wanted her to say about them. She felt too exhausted to think original thoughts.

'You've changed,' Harry said to her one day, when he came home pale and tired.

'What have I changed?' she asked, in a panic.

'We used to laugh all the time. You were so funny.'

Imogen didn't know she used to be funny. She didn't know

how to do it again, because she didn't know how she'd done it originally. She cleaned harder. She looked for more interesting things to cook. She searched her memory for jokes, but nothing seemed funny. She tried so hard.

She is drawn back to Oliver d'Arby's bureau. There's something so comforting about it, the way the front comes down so solidly to make a desk, the smell of ink. It reminds her of her father, although she can't remember the context. He must have had a fountain pen that he used when he sat in his study and they thought he was working, filling in all those forms, writing out the cheques that should have been paying their bills. He must have spent hours composing letters to people who were owed money, while he siphoned off more and more for his gambling. A small, gentle man, who used a fountain pen in a world of biros and quick bets, where television screens flashed up the results. Whatever had made him go into the betting shops in the first place? How had he discovered the thrill of it all?

Doody starts to sort Oliver d'Arby's bills into an order, the electricity bills, the telephone, the rates. Will she have to pay council tax? She pushes the thought away and goes on reading and sorting. She likes his writing. The little notes on the side of scraps of paper. 'Ring plumber'; 'Doctor, Wed 2.40'; 'Prune roses'; 'Bank'.

And then she comes across a collection of keys in a small cardboard box at the back. She sorts through them with interest, although there's no way of knowing what they are all for. She has her own collection at home, most of which lost their purpose years ago. Keys to missing padlocks, keys to doors that have had the locks changed, keys to clocks and cupboards that no longer exist. She never throws them away.

Locking and unlocking doors is the only thing Doody likes about her job. She enjoys being in charge, feeling the keys in her hand as she walks through the empty school, checking all the exits after the cleaners have left. It gives her a sense of authority and importance, and helps her stand up to Philip Hollyhead when he's in danger of becoming a dictator. He needs her to give him a sense of perspective.

Sorting through Oliver d'Arby's collection, she finds a large key with a luggage label attached, and a number on it that she recognises. Immediately, all her interest in the cleaning evaporates. She jumps up, looks out of the window and runs downstairs, hoping that Straker will appear miraculously. She's desperate to show someone, and he'll have to do.

Of course, there's no sign of him. Why doesn't he come when he's needed? He turns up often enough when she's not expecting him. His sense of timing is not impressive.

She makes herself sit down at the kitchen table and takes out her latest Mandles chapter. Cleaning isn't distracting enough. She can't waste all day waiting for the invisible man.

Mandles and his right-hand man, Ginger, have entered a deserted lighthouse, and are looking out at the surrounding countryside. They can see a barn, with tyre tracks leading to the entrance.

'I'll warrant there's a vehicle in that barn,' conjectured Mandles.

The image of Mandles is changing in her mind. He's no longer that young man with clear hazel eyes, waving a gloved leather hand as he takes off in his Camel. He's become older, and he has a scar on his cheek. She tries to erase the scar, rubbing at it irritably, but it refuses to go. All his youthful exuberance seems to drain away through it, and he's not flying a fragile biplane any more, but a modern, reliable monoplane.

She jumps up and goes to the living-room window, itching with impatience. Why isn't he here now? If he's got time to do roofs, he can hardly be pursuing a busy, stressful life in an office somewhere. Why doesn't he realise that he's needed now?

She climbs the stairs again and starts cleaning, watching out for him every few minutes. When his long, gangly body finally appears and hesitates at the gate, she makes herself walk downstairs without hurrying.

He shouts, 'Mrs Doody!' and she opens the door straight away, not wanting to appear too excited. She intends to thank him politely for the roof.

'Look,' she says, holding up the key. 'Look what I've found.'

This time they walk up the road together. Straker walks with less urgency than before, and when a car approaches, politely eases her in to the side of the road.

'Why did you call me Mrs Doody?' she asks.

'That's what you told the headmaster to call you.'

For a second, she thinks he's been talking to Philip without her knowledge, then remembers the call on her mobile. 'That's just him,' she says. 'He's irritating, so he's got to be more careful. You call me Doody.'

'OK,' he says.

She wants to walk faster, but he won't. He keeps the slow, steady speed that he set when they started walking, apparently not flexible enough to alter it according to circumstances. She would like to push him or drag him, but doesn't want the physical contact, so she makes herself stay calm.

'I've been stealing my own tiles,' she says.

She climbs over the gate in front of him. After all, she probably owns it. Outside the barn, she gives him the key. He inserts it, lets it fall out, tries again, drops it, jiggles it up and down, but can't turn it. 'Let me have a go,' she says, pushing him out of the way. She puts the key in again, but can feel that it hasn't gone far enough. She moves it backwards and forwards a few times until it's looser, then tries to turn it. Nothing happens.

'I should have brought some oil,' she says.

He takes the key from her and presses it firmly into the lock. 'Careful,' she says. 'You'll break it.'

He shakes his head and ignores her, pushing again. Nothing happens. Then there is a sound of creaking metal and the key turns.

They stand there and look at each other, and Doody finds she is holding her breath. Straker removes the padlock, lifts the catch and pulls at one of the doors. It's unwilling, partly because there are so many fierce weeds in front, but he forces it. They peer into the darkness, unable to see anything, so he opens the other door.

They walk in together and look at the object in front of them, which fills the barn, taller than them, long and wide enough to fill the entire space. She hears an intake of breath from Straker.

It's an aeroplane, an old-fashioned one, with double wings and a propeller. It stands on the floor of the barn in an attitude of ancient pride, its nose pointing up to the sky, the red underside of the wings looming over them. It's large but fragile, a giant butterfly dropped subversively into a world of helicopters and stealth bombers.

They stand in silence for some time, and Doody discovers that she's holding her breath. She makes herself breathe in and out, but it's an effort, and she's shaking with excitement.

'It's a Camel,' she says at last.

'No, an aeroplane,' he says, his voice deep and stilted.

'A Camel is an aeroplane. First World War.'

'Yes,' he says. 'But I think you're mistaken.'

She wants it to be a Camel. She wants it so much that she thinks she can change whatever it is by willpower.

She looks up at Straker. He is staring at the plane with shock in his eyes, as if he has been confronted with some terrible revelation. 'Pull yourself together,' she says, irritated by the drama of his expression. 'It's not going to attack us.'

She walks round the aeroplane slowly, pausing to examine

the propeller, the wires, the tailplane, although it's too dark to see much at the back of the barn. She smooths her hand across the surface of a wing and feels the fabric stretched taut under her fingers.

'Don't do that,' says Straker, sharply, and she withdraws her hand with embarrassment. The paint is flaking, revealing the threadbare fabric underneath. 'You could easily go through it,' he says.

He's right, but she still gently strokes the surface again, conscious that she's feeling a real aeroplane wing, one that was made nearly a century ago.

There's a canvas hood over the cockpit and she reaches up to unhook it. 'Come on. Don't just stand there. Give me a hand.' He comes round to the other side and helps her remove the cover, then carries it to the side of the barn.

At this point, she realises that it can't be a Camel after all, because there are two cockpits – one in front of the other. She stands still and contemplates this, waiting for the disappointment to hit her, but somehow it doesn't matter as much as she would have expected. This is a real biplane. It could still be First World War – a Bristol Fighter perhaps, or an Avro. They could fly this. Well, someone could fly it. Straker, maybe – he's touching and looking in a knowledgeable way. There is a reluctance in everything he does, but at the same time casualness and familiarity.

He climbs on to the left wing and into the back cockpit, standing briefly on the seat before sliding himself down into a sitting position. Doody watches him fiddling with switches, easing the joystick into different positions, examining the instruments.

'You know how to fly, don't you?' she says.

At first he doesn't reply. He's absorbed in feeling everything.

'You're a pilot.'

He looks up with a horrified expression, and starts to climb out. 'No,' he says furiously. 'No.'

He walks away, leaving her standing there, as if she doesn't exist. 'Stop!' she shouts. 'Stop!' She expects him to react to her authority.

But it's as if she hasn't spoken. He just keeps on walking.

She runs after him. 'Straker, stop! What's the matter?'

She tries to grab his arm, and he pushes her away. But she can be angry too. She feels it ignite inside her and now she's powerful, grabbing his arm again and hanging on. She refuses to let go, and concentrates all her strength into keeping her feet firmly on the ground. He keeps on walking, dragging her along behind him, her feet skidding through the grass and thistles.

'Ow!' she shrieks.

He stops.

She still doesn't let go. 'What do you think you're doing, going off like that? You can't just leave me here.'

He says nothing.

She takes a few deep breaths and forces herself to speak calmly. 'Come on. We've got this far. Why can't we stay and find out more about it?'

His expression becomes less frightening, his eyes less wild, and he relaxes. She can't see much else in his face because the beard gets in the way. He stops resisting her and she no longer has to pull to keep him in place.

'I know about biplanes,' she says. 'I've done a lot of research. You know Biggles? He flew Camels. I've got all the books.'

She hasn't intended to mention Biggles, aware that it's an invitation to ridicule, but he doesn't look contemptuous, just uninterested. Unlike Jonathan, who makes no effort to conceal his sneer whenever he comes across her collection. 'Please,' she says. 'Let's have a good look at it.'

They walk back to the aeroplane.

Doody stands patiently while he examines everything, not rushing him. They walk all round it again and back to the front, and still he says nothing.

'What do you think?' she says.

'About what?'

'The aeroplane, of course. Is it any good?'

He shrugs. 'I've no idea.'

Typical. He spends all this time pretending to be an expert, when he hasn't really got a clue. Doody forces herself not to break the following silence. If he can stop himself speaking, so can she.

'The fabric on the wings is rotting,' he says at last.

'Couldn't it just be repaired?'

'I shouldn't have thought so. There's not much sign of rust on the wires, though. It must be unusually dry in here.'

'Can I get in?'

'If you want to,' he says, without moving.

'So how do I do it?'

He walks round the side, and points to the edge of the wing. 'Put your foot there,' he says, 'and pull yourself up.' She's just about to do so when he grabs her arm and tries to help her up.

'Get off,' she says, and pushes him away.

He steps back hurriedly, and she regrets her sudden reaction.

She climbs on the seat, like he did, and then sits down. There isn't much space. She looks at the dashboard and tries to make sense of the instruments, which are more complicated than she expected.

She likes sitting there. It gives her a sense that she can be part of a history that is only just round the corner. It feels like when she writes about Mandles, as if she's present in that time, but not significant, not active in it, an observer only. She knows all the expressions, the words, the movements. Push the joystick back hard and the nose goes up, push it forward and you drop. She is a child again, looking out of her yew tree, watching Biggles come in to land. She can see him bumping along the grass, climbing out and wiping his greasy goggles.

'Altimeter.'

She jumps. Straker has been so quiet that she forgot he was there. But he's leaning over the side, pointing at the various instruments, his hands trembling slightly. 'Airspeed indicator, joystick, artificial horizon . . .'

She nearly tells him she knows, but realises at the last moment that he would like to tell her. 'Can we fly it?' she asks.

He steps away. 'No,' he says shortly.

'But it must be possible.'

'No.'

She doesn't like the dead, defeatist way in which he says this. 'Why not? Oliver d'Arby must have flown it once.'

Straker shakes his head several times. 'It must have been a very long time ago. You can see that from the condition.'

He knows about planes, however much he pretends he's not interested. Why is he so negative? 'Couldn't we just try to start it up? See if it works?'

'It won't.'

'Come on,' she says. 'Let's try it.' She is fizzing with excitement. A chance to enter her fantasy world, to become unreal like Biggles and to stop being herself. 'Please.'

He doesn't look as if he is going to co-operate. He is standing stiffly, a blank expression on his face, as if he is trying to hide something. A tic has appeared at the side of his left eye, above the scar, but he doesn't give any indication that he has noticed it.

'We could push it out. It can't be heavy.' She has pictures in her head of mechanics pushing the Camels out of hangars, ready for Biggles and Algy and Ginger.

'It can't go anywhere. The field is too overgrown.'

'Well, that's all right. We can't fly it anyway.' She climbs down. 'Come on, let's push it outside.'

She realises almost immediately that it won't work. The rubber has perished on the two wheels at the front, so that their rims are resting directly on the floor, and there isn't a wheel at all at the back.

'I recognise those wheels,' says Doody in surprise. 'There's another set in the cottage, in the wardrobe. They look in better condition than these.'

'They must be spares.'

'Shall we try and start it anyway?' she says.

'It won't work.'

'Why not? It might.'

'There won't be any fuel, oil, water. It's like a car engine. Everything would have dried up after all this time.'

He's right, of course. 'Couldn't we just swing the propeller, get a feel for the way it would work? You never know. It might just turn the engine over, if nothing else.'

He raises an eyebrow. 'You know all about it, then?'

'That's because of Biggles,' she says.

'Who?' he says, as if this is the first time she has mentioned Biggles. The man is unbelievable.

'They're children's books,' she says. 'There are hundreds of them – I've read them all.'

He looks puzzled.

'Didn't you ever read when you were younger?'

He shakes his head. 'No. My family weren't keen on reading.' He thinks for a few seconds in silence. 'Except Agatha Christie.'

'Similar period,' she says.

She bends down and looks under the wheels. There are yellow wooden triangles placed in front of each one, with rope attached.

'Chocks,' she says, pleased with her specialist knowledge.

'Yes,' he says. 'I don't think they'll be necessary.'

She climbs on to the wing and eases herself into the cockpit again. Placing her feet against the rudder-pedals, she leans over the side of the fuselage so that she can see Straker. 'Go on,' she says. 'Try the propeller.'

He reaches up to one of the arms of the propeller and pulls it down sharply. It moves a quarter of a turn, with an uncomfortable clonk, and then jams. 'It's not going to work.'

'No thanks to you,' she says, frustrated by her inability to bring the aeroplane to life in any way.

They cover up the cockpits again and lock the barn, walking back down the road without a word. There's a glow of excitement inside Doody, despite Straker's lack of enthusiasm. It's spinning around, churning up all kinds of emotions, soaring up into an unrealistically blue sky.

Chapter 15

10 Richardson Close,
Walkers Heath,
Birmingham.

Dear Mr Straker,

Who are you? Why have you suddenly decided to write to me out of the blue? I don't believe one word of your letter! The crash has got nothing to do with you! You weren't there, were you? Do you have any idea what it's like to lose a son in a crash? Robbie was nine years old, my life was destroyed by that crash, or tragic accident *as you call it. I haven't been able to live a normal life for over twenty-four years! Twenty-four years! My husband Jimmy left me after two years. Went off to Australia on his own, though I can't say I blame him. Nothing was ever normal ever again, I couldn't go upstairs to bed without going into Robbie's room to check on him. I couldn't cook meals without planning what he wouldn't eat. He only ate egg and chips, so I went on doing chips every day. Swelled up like a balloon. Jimmy refused to talk about it. We couldn't even have a row about it. I just sat in the living room and watched the videos we'd got of Robbie growing up. He was our whole life!*

It's taken me twenty-four years to get over it! Twenty-four years! I've been on medication most of that time. In and out of hospital with depression, breakdowns, alcoholism – you name it, I've had it. And now twenty-four years later when I finally begin to sort myself out, get a job, what happens? Your letter comes through my letter-box! And whoosh, bang, wallop, here we go again! My hands are shaking and I want a drink!

How dare you do this to me!! Go away, don't ever contact me again! It's nothing to do with you, it's private!

Unless you were on that train? Were you, or do you know more about it than you're telling me? You're not him, are you? Peter Butler? The mass murderer who got away with it because an ignorant coroner said there wasn't enough evidence. We all know what that means. He knew you were guilty but couldn't prove it.

If I'd found you at the beginning, you wouldn't be writing letters now. Disappeared into thin air, didn't you? Money I suppose, a rich father and a new identity. But you've given the game away, haven't you? Don't think I've given up!! Don't get the idea time heals. It's the anniversary soon. Quarter of a century. I'm not the only one, you know! There are lots of us. Lots and lots.

So, Mr Peter Straker, if you're Peter Butler, you'd better watch your back! Because believe me I will find you!!
Carmen Halliwell

It's impossible to accommodate seventy-eight people in your head at any one time. When they talk to each other in Straker's dreams, most of them get lost in the background. They don't make any noise, but he knows they're there. All those school-children shuffling, whispering words he can't hear, restless, fidgeting. You can't keep children still. Not even dead children. Robbie must be there among them. Does he know his mother is close by, on the trail? Would he even recognise her after all this time?

Sangita's parents have written to Straker. They've described how they drove up to Birmingham to identify her, puzzled by her journey to Birmingham, shocked by her collection of posters of Rob Willow, unable to believe what had happened to her. They returned home to their little part of India, partitioned off from the rest of England by the stone lions on either side of the gates, fountains in the garden, peacocks in the back (still alive) and lived the next twenty-four years in a condition of numbed bewilderment. Straker's letter of enquiry brought them back to life, made them want to talk about their daughter again.

He files their letter next to Carmen Halliwell's.

He now knows that everyone recognised Felicity – she was on the front page of the *Sun*. But there was no one really to claim her.

Straker pairs them up in his mind. It makes it all neater. Mike and Alan, Justin and Francis, Sangita and Felicity.

Except Maggie, who stands alone. Who has left him and no longer attacks him. Who has taken half of him away with her. He shouldn't have written the letter. He should have gone on in ignorance of her life.

They wander about in his mind, entering and leaving as they wish. His mind, but their choices. A record that keeps going round, caught in an endless groove, the speed uncertain. An old record, a seventy-eight.

When Pete was a child, he and Andy were given a gramophone – the type that you had to wind up, with needles as thick as nails. There were several records with it, but he only remembers 'Sailing On The Robert E. Lee' and 'There Was An Old Woman Who Swallowed A Fly'.

Pete and Andy thought it was wonderful for a time, and Andy used to bring all his friends home to play with it. They had a large toy room at the top of the house, filled with every toy that a boy could want, chosen by their father whenever he felt the need to walk into a shop and order the entire contents. There was a train set, mapped out on a huge table with stations, tunnels, sidings, turntables; a rocking horse, life-sized, stirrups, leather saddle, real horse's hair for tail and mane; shelves of books, stamp collections, ludo, cribbage, chess sets, jigsaw puzzles, magician sets. Funny about the books. There were so many but Pete can't remember ever reading them. Did they have Biggles?

When Pete was about five, Andy became obsessed by Enid Blyton, eventually bringing in friends to make his own Famous Five.

'What about me?' asked Pete.

'You've got to be the robber,' said Andy.

'I don't want to,' he said. 'I want to be the Famous Five.'

'Well, you can't. We can only have five, and that's the rest of us.'

Pete looked around at Andy's friends and counted. 'But there are only four of you.'

'The fifth is Timmy, the dog, I told you that.'

'Why can't I be Timmy?' He'd have liked that. He'd make a good dog.

Andy and his friends stood in front of Pete in silence while he went down on all fours and pretended to wag his tail. He tried barking, the harsh sound scraping his throat.

'You can't,' said Andy. 'We already have a dog.'

His friend Eric produced a fluffy toy dog from behind his back. 'Woof, woof,' he said, and pushed the dog into Pete's face. Pete fell over backwards.

They all laughed.

'I'm not going to be your stupid robber,' said Pete, and ran out of the room. He could hear them all laughing behind him.

He went downstairs to find his mother. It wasn't easy to find people in this house. There were so many floors, so many rooms. It must have been difficult for his mother to keep out of the way of the cleaners all day, so she often took a rest in her bedroom. Pete was never allowed to go in if she was in bed, so he sometimes sat outside the door, pretending that she was there and that he was having a conversation with her, even though it was only inside his head.

He tried this on the Famous Five day, sitting at the top of the stairs, hearing the gramophone upstairs, telling his mother about Andy and his friends. He thought he would quite like to be a dog. Regular meals, walks every day with someone who liked you, no homework, no cleaning teeth, sleeping all day if you wanted to.

'What are you doing here?'

It was his father, unexpectedly at home in the middle of the day.

Pete stared at him.

'Answer my question, Pete. Why are you here?'

'I don't know,' he said.

A strange eerie moan came from his mother's room. Pete stood up and watched his father. He didn't react.

'Outside, my lad, now.'

'What was that noise?'

'What noise? I didn't hear anything. Off you go.'

There was another moan and then a dreadful, piercing scream.

The door to his mother's room opened, and a woman Pete had never seen before in his life ran out. She stopped abruptly when she saw his father. 'Telephone for an ambulance, Mr Butler. Hurry.'

Pete's father stood completely motionless. Pete had never seen him so still before.

'Hurry, Mr Butler. She needs a Caesarian.'

Pete's father looked appalled. 'Are you sure?' he said.

'Of course I'm sure. Hurry – time is of the essence.'

He turned and ran down the stairs without another word. Pete could hear the gramophone start to play in the toy room upstairs.

> *There was an old lady who swallowed a fly.*
> *I don't know why*
> *She swallowed a fly.*
> *Perhaps she'll die.*

Several more loud screams came from his mother's room. Pete stood and looked at the lady who had come out. She wore a white apron, and there was blood on her hands. His mother had swallowed a fly – perhaps she'll die.

She looked down at Pete, paused, and unexpectedly smiled. 'Your little brother or sister's on its way,' she said.

Little brother or sister? What on earth was she talking about?

There were more screams, and the lady turned back to the room. Pete could hear her talking urgently, presumably to his mother. He wondered where the fly had come from.

He stayed there for a long time, hearing the siren as an ambulance drove up outside. Two men rushed up the stairs and took his mother away on a stretcher. The lady went with her, but his father didn't. He spent a long time in his study, talking on the telephone, asking for a tray at tea time. Pete went into his mother's room when she had gone and tried to work out what had happened. The bed was stripped back, and there was blood on the mattress. It seemed very easy to die.

Upstairs, the gramophone was still going:

There was an old lady who swallowed a spider,
It wriggled and wriggled and tickled inside her,
She swa-llo-wed the spi-der to catch the f-ly – —

The gramophone was winding down. The words stretched and distorted, until someone started winding it up again. The music started to go faster and faster –

I don't knowwhysheswallowedaflyperhapsshe'lldie—

They didn't get a little brother or sister. Pete waited for weeks, but no one ever turned up. Their mother came home and everything went back to normal.

———

Straker doesn't sleep much the night after the aeroplane. Whenever he dozes, he wakes with a violent jump after about ten minutes. He is dreaming of flying, the power of the engine under his feet and hands, showing someone the instruments – 'Altimeter, artificial horizon . . .' It's not Doody he's telling.

He wasn't ready for the aeroplane.

Sitting in the cockpit, he was shocked by the familiarity of it all. The controls were more primitive, but they felt the same. His hands on the stick in front of him, his feet on the rudders, checking the oil pressure, the compass, finding the throttle on his left. He felt as if he could just take off, hear the roar of the engine in his ears, smell the oil.

All those years ago, while his life on the ground had been wandering aimlessly in circles, flying was the one thing he could do that gave him a sense of authority and purpose. Now, briefly, for the first time in years, he had experienced the memory of that freedom, the belief that he could be in control.

'You're a pilot, aren't you?'

He looked down at her, round the cockpit he was sitting in, and knew that he shouldn't be in an aeroplane. The horror he had experienced when he first saw it hit him again. He climbed out as quickly as he could. With a few words, she had whipped away his control and sent him back loose into the world where he had no right to rest his feet.

What had happened over twenty-four years ago must all be somewhere in his brain, perfect and deadly in its accuracy, in brilliant, blood-red technicolour. It's just waiting for the best moment. Someone will press the right button, the film will start to play, and he will have to watch it all over again. Again and again—

A fear is growing inside him that he is nearly at that point. He has entered the cinema, the lights have gone down—

During the night Suleiman comes and sits on him. Straker feels his comforting weight, and hears him start to purr. He puts out a hand, and Suleiman obligingly rubs his head against it.

Straker scratches his ears. They lie there together for some time, waiting for dawn, wondering if it's worth pretending to sleep.

'Don't think you can sleep, Straker. We're all out here.'

'Who?'

'Guess.'

'I can't. Tell me who you are.'

'Think about it. There's me and five men and three women.'

'Have you talked to me before?'

'Yes.'

A woman's voice: 'No.'

First voice: 'You wouldn't know. We're here and we're not here. We just haven't joined in the conversations.'

The woman's voice: 'We're not important.'

First voice: 'Yes, we are. That's the point. We didn't know we were important then for all sorts of reasons, but we were really. Everyone's important.'

'Who are you? Were you on the train?'

'Of course we were. How many did I say?'

'One plus three plus five. Nine.'

'What do you know about nine?'

'The square of three. All the digits in the nine times table add up to nine. 2×9 equals 18. $1 + 8$ equals 9. 3×9 equals 27. $2 + 7$ equals 9.'

'You're missing the point, Straker. Think nine. Nine. Nine.'

'I don't know.'

'Yes, you do.'

Suddenly, unexpectedly, I understand. 'You're the nine unidentified ones.'

Congratulations all round. Nine voices talking together.

'Tell me who you are. I want to identify you. I would like to have names for you, characters, places in the world.'

'We can't tell you who we are.'

'You must.'

'We don't know. We're nobody. We only exist as nine. Dead bodies, non-people.'

'Someone somewhere must have lost you. Someone who doesn't know what happened to you.'

'Maybe there was nobody. We were the invisible. People with no past, no names, no ties.'

'Everyone must have had a mother.'

'You tell us who we are. Then we'll tell you who our mothers are.'

'But I can't. I don't know.'

'Then neither do we.'

I should know about these people. They deserve to have names. Everyone needs a name. How can they just come from nowhere and be nobody?

When Straker wakes, his head thumps, his arms ache, his hands hurt. Suleiman has gone.

He sits up. A dingy dawn is starting to seep into the lighthouse. The gulls are screeching outside, and he can pick out vague shapes in the room. He feels as if he has run a marathon. He slumps, exhausted, for a while and counts in thirteens. 13, 26, 39, 52, 65—

He stops. He should have known that thirteen was dangerous. He knows the factors of 78. He starts on fourteens. 14, 28, 42, 56, 70, 84—

OK. He can carry on.

He washes mechanically, following his normal routine without rushing, then takes two stale doughnuts on his way up to the balcony. Dawn hasn't yet arrived, but the dark is not impenetrable, and it's possible to see the shape of the rocks below the lighthouse. The seagulls seem very busy in the half-light, dipping and soaring, screeching past each other, but somehow, miraculously, never colliding. Flying by instinct. No crash landings.

The tide is out, and Straker watches the first hint of dawn

threading its way over the strands of seaweed, and the mud. Thin pink fingers pick away at the piles of pebbles, sorting through the dullness of the rocks and polishing them to reflect a generous light – yellow, orange, green and blue. The birds all seem to land at the same time, and there is a pause in the breathing of the early morning.

This is normally a good time. The five minutes of stillness. But today it's not working.

In the silence there is noise. Nothing today wants to be calm. Birds pecking at shells, water on the move, either creeping up or draining away, pebbles, creaking, creaking—

The creaking is coming from the lighthouse.

Straker stands up and balances with his legs apart, trying to listen and feel. Is it his imagination, or is the lighthouse moving? A tiny vibration creeping through the floor, a deep, secret engine starting to come to life. A shiver, a flexing of muscles. Is it slowly breaking away from its mooring, preparing to set sail?

He's not sure. Is the vibration in the lighthouse or in his legs? Everything seems insecure in this early morning. Nothing is constant. He's been here for twenty-four years, watching the cliff fall away, knowing that the end will come one day, and suddenly it is upon him. He's not prepared. What does he do? Try to go with it, of course. But what if he survives again? What happens to him without his home?

He shivers. There's a rising breeze. Magnificent comes and sits next to him, settling tidily with his tail wrapped round his legs. They look out to sea together. Perhaps he is worrying with Straker about their future.

Doody thinks that he can make the aeroplane work. Which is not going to happen. It's too old. But suppose it were possible. What then? Does he fly it? Could he still do that? Could he sit in the cockpit and pull the joystick and take off into that airy place of anonymity that he used to know? He wouldn't be allowed to. His pilot's licence ran out years ago. Or they took it away from him.

He can feel a tremor inside him that doesn't originate from the lighthouse. He identifies it as terror. An enormous churning fear of being in the air again, taking off, heading towards the defining moment of his life that he can't remember.

He doesn't want the aeroplane to fly. It should stay where it is, a monument to Doody's godfather, a useless relic.

If he refuses to help her with it, what then? The aeroplane stays in the barn, and she gets angry.

He rubs his tired eyes and knows he has no choice. Nausea rises in his stomach at the thought of flying. There is no debate. He can't do it.

He goes back down the stairs, leaving Magnificent at the top.

He opens a tin of salmon for the cats, and pours out some milk, feeling generous. He would like them to enjoy the day.

———————

He waits until he can hear the church bells. Ridiculous sound. Like someone striking one or two bells with a metal object. No pattern to it, no originality. He sets off after they have stopped for ten minutes. If anybody is going to church, they'll all be there by now, and everybody else will be indoors until the shops open. The fishermen will already have sailed on the early tide. Doody will be awake. Nobody could sleep through that racket. He's ready to do some work on the cottage.

Normally on a Sunday, he works on his garden, or his investigations if the weather's bad, rereading letters, making notes, putting photographs into files. Today, there is a certain exhilaration in turning his back on it, acting as if it doesn't matter. He runs from the harbour to the cottage, working out how long it takes, enjoying his long strides, feeling his heart pumping with clear, regular beats.

Once there, he leaps through the long grass to the door and knocks loudly.

Nothing happens.

He tries again, hurting his knuckles.

The house and garden are silent.

Perhaps he's got it wrong and she went home yesterday. Maybe he just assumed that she would stay overnight when she never really intended to.

He can visualise the files on his table at the lighthouse, open, expecting his attention. Sangita, Felicity, everyone else hovering, offended by his neglect. Except Maggie.

He walks up and down outside the cottage trying to decide what to do. He could make a start on some work before she returns next week. The window-frames need attention. B&Q sell sandpaper, wood filler, undercoat, white paint. He could fiddle that lock and get inside in seconds, have a look at the beams inside the roof.

The front door creaks, and Doody peers out with an annoyed expression on her face. She's wearing a striped nightdress – red and black, with the hem coming down on one side. Her hair is fuzzy round the edge of her face, tangled and confused. It looks impossible to brush out. It's not as blonde as he remembers, the roots darker and not so dazzling. Her eyes are green – the first time he's noticed the colour, but today they peer out between her frowning eyebrows, dark and impenetrable. The burnt pink patches on her nose and cheeks have faded into a softer tan, so that she appears slightly less out of place in her cottage.

'I thought you must have gone home,' he says.

She stares at him. 'Don't you ever sleep?' Her face is creased and puffy, oddly vulnerable. 'First those dreadful bells, and now you. It's Sunday, for goodness' sake.'

What's she talking about? 'We could clear the undergrowth, or I could paint the windows.'

She doesn't seem to understand. 'Go away, Straker. Come back in three hours' time.'

She shuts the door in his face.

He can't decide what he should do. He wanders around

the garden for a while, looking for the shed that was half demolished in the undergrowth. He pulls away some ivy, and discovers that two crumbling walls are still upright. In the corner between them, a spade, a rake and a scythe lie in an abandoned heap, all very rusty, but nevertheless intact.

He picks up the scythe. He's never used one before, but once he starts, he's surprised by its effectiveness, despite its age and rust. He goes back for the rake, which is little more than a few nails sticking out of a piece of wood, and sweeps the heaps of grass and weeds into manageable piles at the edge of the garden.

Tomorrow he could bring his own tools and start digging. It would all be cleared in a couple of days. Neat and ready to plant if she wants.

He works for some time, enjoying it. The sun comes out, and he stops for a rest. He sits with his back against the wall, and shuts his eyes, forgetting Doody.

———

'*Wake up, Straker.*'

'*Maggie! You're back.*'

'*Not for long. I want you to do something for me.*'

'*Anything, Maggie. You know that. I'll do whatever you want.*'

'*I want you to meet Simon.*'

'*Simon your husband? Simon A. Taverner?*'

'*Yes. I think you should make a connection and save us all.*'

'*Save you? How can I save people who are dead?*'

'*Easy. You let go of them. And if you speak to Simon, there can be some kind of resolution.*'

'*I don't understand.*'

'*No, of course not. That's the trouble with you. There isn't a lot you do understand. But there must be hope for you somewhere in all this.*'

'There is no hope for me. You know that.'

'Rubbish, Straker. You're just going down the cowardly road of self-destruction. Stop indulging yourself and do something useful for once in your life.'

'How could I meet him?'

'Get on a train. You know, a train like the one I was on. They usually manage to get there without crashing. Get off the train. Go to Simon's flat – you know the address – and ring the doorbell. Say, "Hello, I'm the man who killed your wife."'

'I can't do that.'

'Why not? My husband is a reasonable man.'

'He might not be by now.'

'You read the letter. You know he is.'

'I can't do it.'

'Why not?'

'I just can't.'

There is a long silence.

'That's it, then. Goodbye.'

'No, Maggie. No!'

Silence.

'Maggie! Maggie!'

———

He wakes with the sound of his own voice in his ears. He stares round in bewilderment, not knowing what he expects to see, certainly not the garden of Doody's cottage. Something terrible has happened, and for a minute, he can't remember what it was.

Goodbye.

He leans back with a terrible sick pain inside his stomach.

'So, who's Maggie?' says a voice above him.

He looks up and there's Doody, peering at him. She's holding a plate and a mug, pretending to be pleasant. But she is watching him, her eyes thoughtful and suspicious.

Chapter 16

So, who is Maggie?

He doesn't reply, and this annoys Doody. She's brought him some breakfast, but now she doesn't want to give it to him. She would prefer to throw it in his face. There's no reason why there shouldn't be a Maggie, of course. It's not as if he's talked endlessly about his single life. Why should she care?

He rubs his eyes with trembling hands, then blinks rapidly. He has the appearance of someone brought outside after a long confinement in the dark. Confused by the light, almost frightened. He's dressed neatly, but his face is crumpled and neglected. He really should trim his beard. Doody's not going to be fooled into sympathy. She can't bring herself to hand him the plate and mug, so she puts them on the grass beside him, and stands up quickly.

'Who's Maggie?' she asks again, refusing to give up. If he's got some woman up there in his lighthouse, she wants to know about it. Is this Maggie a prisoner? Growing her hair so that she can climb down it and escape?

He picks up the mug, takes a sip and swallows hurriedly. 'Coca-Cola,' he says, with surprise.

'What were you expecting? Coffee? There isn't any electricity, you know. You can't make coffee without heat.'

He picks up the slice of bread she's buttered for him and starts to eat, stretching out his legs in front of him. His right foot rocks backwards and forwards rhythmically.

Doody remembers her mother doing this at her father's funeral. Singing a silent song, she thought then. Her mother didn't care. She was bored with the funeral.

Doody shivers. 'I'm going indoors,' she says, a sharp, bitter taste coming into her mouth. 'It's cold.'

Straker pulls himself to his feet and follows her inside. It's dingy in the kitchen – the window is small, and needs cleaning – but it's warmer than outside. They sit at the table and Doody offers him some fruit cake. 'Made it myself during the week. Haven't made a cake in years.'

He nods and bites into a slice. She wonders if she's put too much fruit in it. It feels heavy, and a little sticky, as if it isn't cooked properly. 'I prefer it moist,' she says. 'It lasts longer.'

He doesn't reply. Doody's still waiting. 'Is she a prisoner?' she asks. 'In the lighthouse?'

He stops eating and stares at her, but she's not accepting this contrived ignorance.

'You know who I'm talking about. Maggie. Who is she? Is she your wife?'

He jerks his head up. 'No!' he says. 'Of course not.'

'Why of course not? People do marry. They do have wives, don't they?'

'Yes,' he says, 'but I haven't.'

'Did you once?'

'No,' he says again.

'You could have left her. She could have left you. You could be separated or divorced.'

'Yes,' he says. 'But I'm not.'

For a while he seems lost in thought. Doody waits for him to say something else, but nothing happens. 'Just as well,' she says, in the end. 'She'd have died of boredom every time she wanted to have a conversation.'

He drinks his Coca-Cola.

'I can't believe I own an aeroplane,' she says. 'A biplane. It's the sort of thing you dream about, isn't it?'

She gets up and goes to the sink. Last night, she found the stop-cock at the back of a cupboard in the kitchen, turned it on, and found that it worked. She rinses the plates and cups in cold water. 'Who is she, then?' she says, with her back to him.

'Who?'

'Maggie.'

He doesn't reply. If he was a child, refusing to answer her questions, she would march him to the headmaster. 'Here you are', she would say. 'You sort him out'. But you can't do that with an adult. Straker makes his own rules, and it infuriates her that she cannot shift them.

'We need to check the windows,' he says.

She turns round in surprise. 'What do you mean?'

'If the windows aren't sorted before winter comes, it'll be too draughty to live here.'

'Sorted in what way?'

'Some can be painted, but the others will have to be replaced.'

'I can't afford new windows,' she says coldly.

'No point in worrying until we know the situation.'

'No point in knowing the situation if I haven't got any money.'

They walk round and examine the windows. The frames at the back of the house don't seem too bad. Straker runs his finger along them, scratching the edges. 'These are OK,' he says. 'We can paint them.'

He spends longer on the front windows, poking them with a screwdriver that he produces from his pocket, running it along the join with the windowsill, where paint has been used to fill the gap. He pushes it into the side of the wood, which immediately caves in.

'Don't do that,' says Doody. 'You're damaging them.'

'They're rotten,' he says. 'It's the salt in the winds off the sea. They'll have to be replaced. I could probably do it.'

'Really?' she says. 'Are you a window man?' For some reason, she can't imagine him having a job. Now, it all seems rather odd. Does he work from home, doing something secret and mysterious in the lighthouse? But how does he find time for all this? Doing the roof when she's not here, wandering round the village, exploring neglected pathways, examining abandoned barns. He doesn't come over as a busy man.

He doesn't answer, his expression puzzled.

'Is that your work? Windows?'

He shakes his head.

'Then how do you know how to do it?'

'I don't,' he says. 'But I'm sure we could work it out.'

There he goes again. 'We'. She opens her mouth to say something, then shuts it again. At least he's offering. He's her best chance. 'It'll be expensive,' she says.

He shrugs. 'A bit at a time. We'll manage.'

His attitude is unexpectedly reassuring. Doody spends most of her life worrying about things that haven't happened yet. Maybe she should think like he does. We'll do this, and then we'll do that. Worry about it when they need to.

'So what is your job?'

He frowns.

'What do you do all day? What do you live on? Where does your money come from?'

Maybe he's a bank robber after all. He wouldn't need to do anything if he was – just sit in his lighthouse and spend the money. 'It's a pity you don't spend it on clothes, haircuts, shaving equipment . . .'

She looks at his face more directly, and his eyes slip past her, focusing on some distant point through the window. Extortionist? Murderer? Both? How can you tell? Is there some giveaway, a series of lines on the face, a hardness to the eye that indicates you've held a gun, plunged a knife into someone's heart, put arsenic in your wife's porridge?

Her pulse booms in her ears.

Do people do strange things if they are being poisoned? Does it make them commit suicide? Suppose they are only slightly poisoned: does that mean that they stop thinking rationally?

Imogen has asked herself these questions over and over again, but because she has never asked anyone else, she hasn't had an answer. What confuses her is that she can't quite remember what she did with the yew berries. She knows she mashed them up in the box under her bed, and she remembers going there every night, mixing them, stirring them, thinking of Celia. Did she sprinkle some on Celia's carrots one day at dinner? She should know the answer to that question, but she doesn't.

When Imogen found Celia, she stood for a long time just looking at her, unable to think clearly. After a while, she became conscious of a churning sickness in her stomach. She didn't know what to do. Should she run round to Mrs Gregory, their next-door neighbour, and knock on the door? What would she say? 'Can you come and see if my sister is dead?' But she might say no. She didn't like Imogen very much, and always ignored her if they passed in the street. She might be out.

Imogen heaved violently and vomited over the floor. She stood over it for what seemed like a very long time, struggling to breathe, cold and paralysed.

Once she could move, she tried to get Celia down, just in case she wasn't really dead, although she could see from her face that she must be. She climbed on to a chest of drawers, her legs shaking and jerking uncontrollably. But Celia was too heavy, and Imogen couldn't undo the knot that tied the rope to the rafter. She ran downstairs to find a knife, grabbed the breadknife, and tried to saw through the rope without any success. She cut her thumb, which started to bleed, and the breadknife wasn't sharp enough. Nothing in their house worked properly.

She needed to get help. She raced down again, tripping over

her feet, nearly falling head first, but saving herself at the last minute. She dialled her mother's work number, fumbling so badly that she had to make three attempts. It was engaged.

Should she ring the police? What would she say? 'I think my sister is dead?' But would they believe her? She wasn't sure if she could explain it properly. What if they thought it was her fault?

Imogen thought it was her fault. She decided to ring Janet, a girl who had been friendly with her at school for a time. Janet was a strangely slow person. She thought a long time about things before she did anything, and once told Imogen that she liked to keep her feet on the ground. This was literally true. She managed to avoid gym lessons when they were climbing ropes, refused to jump when she was aiming the netball at the net, and never ran if she could walk. But she was sensible.

Imogen dialled her number and waited, with the receiver jumping up and down against her ear. Echoes of the distant ring thudded and boomed inside her head, jangling harshly against the confused tangle of her thoughts—

'Hello?' It was Janet's mother.

'Hello, Mrs Franklin. Can I speak to Janet?'

'Imogen, is it?' She always changed her voice when she talked to her, trying to sound posh. Imogen didn't understand this.

'Yes. Is she there?'

'No, dear, sorry. She's off to the library.'

'Oh.' This was unbelievable. She wasn't there on the one day that she should be.

'Shall I give her a message?'

'No, it's OK.'

Imogen put the receiver down, picked it up again before she could change her mind and dialled 999.

Imogen didn't know if they believed her or not, but she started to cry and couldn't stop, so she had difficulty giving them the address.

'Is there anyone else with you?'

'No,' she said, wondering why it mattered.

'We'll get an ambulance there in a few minutes. And a police car.'

They knew exactly what they were doing. That was what was so frightening. They seemed to be prepared, as if they were expecting it. As if they knew all about Celia and Imogen, and there was a police car just round the corner waiting to come round, an ambulance five minutes away with all the right equipment for cutting down people hanging from rafters.

From the moment the police were at the door, nothing remained the same. There were people everywhere. They seemed to be rushing around, but in a kind of forced silence, as if nobody was allowed to speak above a murmur. They cut Celia down and were transferring her to an ambulance when her mother came home. Imogen was in the living room, staring at a cup of tea that someone had made her, pretending to sip it even though it had sugar in it and was disgusting. Her mother came through the front door, ran into the living room, grabbed Jonathan with a hysterical shriek and then saw Imogen. Jonathan was alive and Imogen was alive, so it had to be Celia on the stretcher.

'No!' she howled.

Her scream wasn't like an ordinary scream. Imogen kept searching for where it had come from. She couldn't believe that her mother could make that kind of noise. She hadn't made any noise when Daddy died. She had just been pale and brave.

Even now, she can see her mother's face when she realised that Imogen was alive and not Celia. The horror.

Imogen wasn't allowed back into their bedroom for ages. She had to sleep on the settee downstairs and couldn't concentrate on her homework with the television on all the time. A policewoman came to talk to her for a time, about Celia. She wanted to know what she had been like in the last few weeks. Nasty, thought Imogen. 'OK,' she said.

'Nothing unusual?'

'No,' she said. 'Except she didn't go to bed.'

The policewoman was interested in this. 'How do you know?'

'Because she was sitting at her desk.'

'Didn't you go to sleep either?'

'Yes, I went to sleep.'

'Then how do you know she didn't?'

Good point. 'She told me,' Imogen lied. Why did she feel as if the policewoman were trying to catch her out? Did she know about the berries?

Janet rang. 'Why weren't you at school today?'

'Something's happened,' said Imogen. 'Tell you later.'

'Tell me now.'

'No, I can't.'

Janet was annoyed and put the phone down. Imogen didn't care that much. They never had anything to talk about anyway. She suddenly longed for her old yew tree. She wanted to escape there, sit silently in the branches and construct Biggles stories in a world that didn't really exist.

About a week later, instead of going to school, she caught the train and went back to the old house. Other people lived there now – four pairs of faded jeans flapping on the line, a Wendy house beside the shed and a new cast-iron front gate. Someone had dug up all the cotton lavender near the house and replaced it with miniature conifers. The yew tree was still there, though. Once she could see that there was no one around, Imogen climbed the wall and jumped over. Then she sat in the tree and tried to forget everything. She closed her eyes and thought of Biggles.

But it didn't work. It didn't work properly again for years and years, until Harry had gone.

Nobody talked to her about Celia's death except the policewoman, but she heard her mother discussing it with the police. Apparently, Celia had been doing brilliantly at Cambridge, but hadn't made many friends. She was too young, really, they said, not mature enough to cope. She didn't relate to people. Well, well, well, thought Imogen. Why did no one spot that before? Now everybody knew what she knew.

'She may not have intended it to work,' said a policeman. 'She must have known her sister was due back. Pity she didn't find her earlier. Fifteen minutes might have made all the difference.'

Could poison unhinge the mind, drive someone to suicide? But Celia's mind had already been swaying, her behaviour erratic and strange, and nobody else seemed to have observed this. A new guilt wrapped itself round Imogen's thoughts. She should have told someone Celia was behaving oddly.

When Imogen was finally allowed back into her room, she went straight to the box under the bed where she kept the yew berries. It wasn't there. She lay on the floor for ages, stretching her arm in the dust, but couldn't find it. She pressed herself flat and peered under, certain that she had just underestimated its position, but the space was empty. Had the police taken it?

'What are you looking for?'

She sat up with a jump and saw Jonathan standing there looking at her. 'Nothing,' she said.

He stood there silently.

'What do you want?' said Imogen.

But he said nothing, and she knew then that he knew. Either the police had her berries, or he did, and either way, he knew about it.

———

Doody drives to B&Q with Straker. She's can't remember the last time she drove with a passenger and is nervous with him sitting beside her.

Straker looks out of the window to the side, away from her, and she tries to make herself concentrate on the driving.

'Is there a library near here?' she asks.

'It's the other side of Sainsbury's.'

'I'm going to look up aeroplanes, find out what it is.' She has been holding the image of the plane in the back of her mind all the time, but only visiting it occasionally for a treat, in case it wears out with use.

She knows it's not a Camel, but that's no reason why she shouldn't have one in her novel. That's the good thing about the writing – you can have whatever you want.

There's a Camel in the barn, about eight feet tall, wing span twentyeight feet, length eighteen feet.

The details are clear in her mind – it will be easy to insert them.

Straker seems to be fascinated by the row of terraced houses on the side of the hill and says nothing.

They are climbing in too low a gear and only just miss a woman who steps out without looking. When they reach the B&Q car park, Doody reverses into a space too fast and hits the bin on the wall behind.

'Stupid place to put a bin,' she says, still waiting for Straker to say something. 'I don't normally bump into things. I'm fairly safe as a general rule.'

He doesn't look interested.

'Do you drive?' she says.

'No,' he says. There's a long silence. 'I did once. A long time ago.'

He seems to be telling her something significant, so she waits for the rest. Nothing happens.

They go round B&Q with a trolley, putting in paint and paintbrushes. 'I can bring the tools from school,' says Doody. 'I don't need to buy any.'

He nods. 'You should get the electricity put on,' he says.

'Why?'

'Then we can use power tools.'

'It'll be too expensive.'

'No, it won't. You're hardly ever there.'

The trolley is alarmingly full. 'Do we need anything else?'

'Wood,' he says. 'I've got some odds and ends that we can use.'

'OK. Shall we drive out there? I'm sure we could get the car over the grass.' She wants to go inside his lighthouse. Find out if Maggie lives there.

He doesn't respond. 'I'll take that as yes, shall I?' she says.

They pass the village and leave the road, weaving across the uneven ground to the lighthouse. 'It's not that bad,' says Doody, as she wrestles with the steering-wheel. 'But I don't think you'd get a taxi driver to do it.'

She's enjoying the novelty of the drive. 'Geronimo!' she shouts, as they go up a particularly steep slope and drop over the other side.

'I hope the car isn't damaged,' he says, in a quiet moment.

'No, it loves it. Gives it a challenge. Can't you tell how much it's enjoying the exercise?' She glances at him for a second before quickly focusing on where they are going. He might be smiling.

Doody stops outside the lighthouse and turns off the engine. They sit in the car for a moment, uncertain in the sudden change of atmosphere, studying the lighthouse.

'Are those cracks on the side?' she asks. She doesn't remember seeing them before. The wind is buffeting the side of the car, rocking them from side to side. All around them, the grass is blown almost horizontal, away from the sea. 'It's windy here,' she says. A cat is sitting just two feet in front of the car, watching them, its ears pricked and its eyes round and interested. They must have only just missed it.

'I want to go and see the plane again after this,' she says.

'I'll be back in a minute,' says Straker, getting out and slamming the door shut behind him.

For a moment, she's disappointed, but then discovers that there's nothing to stop her going too. She gets out, closes the door, and follows him into the lighthouse.

There are even more steps than she expected, a long flight for each level, seemingly endless. She climbs quickly, wanting to get to the top before he knows she's come up, but soon starts to get out of breath and has to slow down. She passes through two levels that seem unused, and then arrives at a room with some furniture. He's not here, so she goes on up.

She examines the next room. There isn't much space. A mattress on the floor with a sleeping-bag, carefully folded and neat, and a basket at the end with another cat in it. Apart from that, there's a table and chair, and a cupboard along the wall, built into the roundness of the lighthouse, curved and narrow. She wanders over to the table. Several files are laid out on it, with photographs pinned to them. She picks one up, a picture of a middle-aged couple standing in front of a caravan. The wind is blowing, so that the woman's hair is blossoming out round her face and she's struggling to hold her skirt down. They are both smiling, and there's a feeling of health and happiness emanating from them, which makes them almost familiar. Then she notices the names under the photograph. Simon and Maggie.

She picks up the file and opens it. Inside, there's a list of dates, some newspaper cuttings, and a letter. She starts to read the letter.

'What are you doing?'

His voice is loud and very harsh. She freezes. 'Nothing,' she says. 'Nothing.' For the first time, she's genuinely frightened of him. He grabs the file out of her hand, and she is aware that he's a big man, and very strong. He's staring at her, his eyes fierce. She realises that she doesn't know him at all.

They stand like this for several seconds, and nothing happens. Doody starts to breathe again, slowly, self-consciously, still watching him. As she relaxes, she begins to think that he's waiting for her to say something. He doesn't seem to know how to proceed.

'Who are they?' she says at last, relieved to hear that her

voice doesn't sound too scared. 'All the people in these files. What are they to do with you?'

He's a spy, she thinks, and these are his targets. That's why he's so secretive. Or an assassin and these are the people he is being paid to kill. Her legs start to shake again, and she wants to back away down the stairs quickly and tell him she hasn't seen anything.

But then, at last, he moves. 'Sit down,' he says, and pulls out the chair from the table. She doesn't want to, but decides to do as he says. She watches him, trying to decide how alarming he still is. Whatever she saw there for a moment has gone, and he's just Straker, the idiot man who doesn't talk much, who mended her roof, who needs a shave.

Yes, she thinks, he mended my roof. He can't be all bad.

There isn't another chair, so he sits on the side of the table. 'There's something I need to tell you,' he says.

'About Maggie?' She doesn't want him to know that she was afraid for a moment.

'Yes. And some others.'

'The people in the files?'

He nods.

'So who are they? What have they got to do with you?'

He pauses. There is a long silence. Get on with it, she thinks, worrying that they're going back to square one.

'They are all people who died in a train crash.'

This is not particularly helpful. 'What have they got to do with you?'

He sighs, and his shoulders seem to droop. He looks somehow defeated. 'I killed them,' he says.

Doody thinks about this. 'You killed them?' she repeats. The villagers were right. He is an assassin.

'Yes.'

'How? I thought you said it was a train crash.'

'I caused the crash.'

His eyes are amazingly blue. 'You were the train driver?'

'No.'

'How, then?'

'I was flying an aeroplane and it crashed on to the train, which then came off the rails and fell into a housing estate.'

She cautiously starts to breathe again. He's not a murderer on the run. 'When?' She can't remember a train crash. He's making it up.

'A very long time ago.'

'Oh.' An enormous relief rushes into her. 'So it wasn't recently?'

'The people are still dead, whenever it happened.'

She nods. 'But it was an accident.'

He sighs again and sits silently for a long time. 'No. It was my fault.'

'Are you sure?' Why should he take all the blame?

He hesitates. 'Well, I can't remember anything, but I know it was my fault.'

'Did you go to prison?'

'No. There wasn't enough evidence to establish what exactly happened.'

'There you are, then. It was an accident.'

'No, it was my fault.'

He is determined to make himself guilty. If he doesn't remember, how can he be so sure?

'I'd been drinking,' he says.

She glances down at the files on the desk. There are an awful lot of them. 'Who's Maggie, then? Did she die on the train?'

'Yes. She was a victim.'

'So why do you talk to her in your sleep?'

'They all talk to me in my sleep. They are there every time I close my eyes.'

'Perhaps you shouldn't close your eyes.' This probably explains why he keeps dropping off during the day. 'How many?'

'Seventy-eight.'

She stares at him.
He looks steadily back.
'Seventy-eight?' she says.
He nods.
'That's a lot of people,' she says.

Chapter 17

As they drive away from the lighthouse, Doody doesn't speak. Straker watches her out of the corner of his eye. Her face is closed, slightly frowning, with a single straight line between her eyebrows. There's a hardness on the side of her jaw, as if she's clenching her teeth while she concentrates on the driving, and a network of creases runs up her cheek, intricate and well defined.

He counts the seconds of silence, missing out 78. On and up to 178, 278 – and nothing happens. What is she thinking? You can't ignore 78. You can't just pass it by as if it were irrelevant. The figure hangs above them from the roof of her ridiculous little car. Waiting. Watching. She must be counting too, running over the number in her mind. Has she realised the perfection of the figure? The addition of all the numbers up to twelve.

When they drove out here, she was so excited. Every time they jolted down a hole or hit a bump, she laughed with an abandoned joy that Straker had not seen in her before. He was moved by it. He nearly laughed himself. It was like being in a dodgem car for the first time, separated from Andy. He can remember the extraordinary discovery that he didn't have to sit and wait for people to hit him. He could hit them. He can still feel the thrill of chasing Andy, the judder that went through him when he made contact, the shriek of excitement that burst out of him. It was a time of innocence, a moment of true childhood. And when they drove out to the lighthouse today, it was almost the same. Uncomplicated.

Now it has all changed.

Everything is curling back inside him, back to where it came from, that twisted, foul interior, which will always swallow any passing innocence. The world inhabited by Sangita, Felicity, Sean and the others. They are there in his head, waiting – they want something from him, everything, more than he can give.

What can you expect? says Maggie. Except she doesn't. She remains silent, but he knows what she would say if she were to speak.

'Can we go to see the plane again?' says Doody.

He looks at her.

'Well?' she says. 'I do wish you'd answer my questions.'

'No,' he says. He doesn't want to think about the aeroplane. It makes him feel as if he can't breathe.

She drives straight past the cottage. 'Too late,' she says. 'We're going anyway.' She stops the car on the grass verge outside the gate. They sit and look at it for a minute.

'We ought to get the gate open,' she says. 'Then we could just drive up.'

'Yes.'

She smiles. 'But not today,' she says.

He's not sure why she smiles. Is she playing games? Pretending that nothing's changed? Or telling him that everything's changed?

They get out of the car. He's been over the gate many times, but never considered the latch. Today, he looks at it more closely, tries to move it, and it resists him. 'Oil,' he says. He wants to stay there, at the entrance to the field, thinking about the gate.

'Yes,' she says, and climbs over it.

He follows her unwillingly. With his feet, he feels the ruts under the weeds, and tries to decide if a car could come up here. It's so long since he's driven.

Everything is as they left it. Doody stands outside for a bit and examines the roof. 'You know the plastic sheets you put on the cottage roof for a while?'

Presumably she means the sails. He nods.

'I don't suppose you could put them on here? Where the gaps are. So the plane doesn't get wet.'

He doesn't want to see the aeroplane. The thought of it sends his insides into impenetrable knots. But he wants to please her, and patching up a roof doesn't involve going into the barn. 'All right.'

She is delighted, the lines on her face somehow weakening and lightening, and he feels better. 'I'll do it tomorrow,' he says.

She hesitates. 'You don't mind, do you?'

'No,' he says.

She turns her head away from him. 'I mean – don't you have to get to work? I don't want to take up too much of your time.'

'It's OK,' he says.

She waits for a few seconds. He looks at the barn roof, and the tree overshadowing it. It won't take long to put the plastic sails up there. He's familiar with the structure of the roof by now.

'Well?'

He's confused.

'So do you have a job? I'd just like to know.'

Oh. He hadn't realised that she was asking him about jobs. 'Well – no.'

'Unemployed, then. Right.'

Is he unemployed? He's not quite sure. He's never looked at it like that.

'But what do you do all day?'

What does she mean? He has a timetable, he's busy all day and every day, but it doesn't sound very much at all when he goes over it in his mind.

He has never been part of the world of working people. Even before the crash, he didn't have a proper job. Why work when there was an endless supply of money? A vast treasure chest that was going to waste. But it was more than that. He can't answer Doody. It's too complicated.

'Well, that sounds like an interesting activity,' says Doody. 'Don't know if it'll make you rich, though.'

She opens the doors of the barn and goes in to examine the aeroplane again. Straker stands outside with his back to the barn and looks across the overgrown field.

'What's the matter?' she asks, coming out again.

He keeps his eyes away from her, not wanting to speak, struggling with the dizziness that hit him as soon as she opened the doors and he caught a glimpse of a wing, the seized-up propeller.

She walks round in front of him and stands there, glaring into his face. 'What's going on?'

'Sell it,' he says, his voice low and harsh. 'It's probably worth a lot of money.'

'No. I want to fly it.'

'You can't.'

'Why not?'

'You don't know how to.'

'I can learn.'

'Do you have any idea how much it costs?'

She doesn't reply.

'Do you?' he says, louder.

She looks away. 'It's all right for you. You can do it – you know how to fly. I've never done anything exciting.'

A fragment of memory slips into his mind. Sitting at the controls, flicking a switch, someone beside him, Justin and Francis behind, the sudden roar of the engine—

He finds he is sweating and raises his hand to wipe his forehead. Doody steps back in alarm, as if she thinks he is going to hit her. Indignation flashes through him. 'What did you do that for?'

'What – what?' She is flustered, nervous, pretending it was nothing, that she hadn't misunderstood him.

He steps away from her and struggles to control his breathing. 'Sell the aeroplane,' he says unevenly. 'Get rid of it.'

'No,' she says. 'Why should I? I can do what I want.'

'You don't need it.'

'Don't tell me what to do.' Her voice is rising.

He turns away from her. He can feel an alien violence inside him, struggling to emerge, a desire to do something physical, a darkness taking over his mind. She's so stupid, so stubborn, so ignorant. He grabs one of the doors of the barn with both hands and hurls it shut. The crash blasts out into the air, the barn shudders and the door sounds as if it's ripping apart.

He watches it shaking for a second, then strides away, wishing he'd never met her, never seen the aeroplane.

Behind him he can hear her voice, shrill, strident. 'I might have known you'd be no use. I don't know why you pretend to know about flying. Crashing seems to be more your sort of thing.'

———

'Maggie? Are you there?'

Silence. Why does she always have to mean what she says? I'm not used to it.

'Maggie, I need to talk to you. I don't know what's happening to me. Please say something.'

Sangita is singing: 'Return home. Breakfast without you – coffee cannot wake me . . .'

Felicity: 'What are you singing?'

Mike: 'It's Rob Willow, isn't it?'

Sangita is thrilled. 'You know him?'

'Of course – he was a hero. Best singer/songwriter of our generation, according to New Musical Express.*'*

'Oh . . .' Sangita's voice is trembling with pleasure.

Felicity is annoyed. 'There's more to life than singers, you know.'

More to life? Does she know what she's saying?

'Where's Maggie?' It sounds like Anne, without Jerry for once.

207

So I'm not the only one who misses her.

'Maggie – I lost my temper today. I didn't know I could be like that.'

'She's gone.' Alan is around. He's older, he understands.

'Gone where?'

'I don't know. She's angry.'

'She's always angry.' Felicity's voice is petulant and childish today, bored, left out by Sangita and Mike.

'No, she's not,' says Sangita. 'I like her. We should look for her.'

'What a waste of time. She's dead.'

They're all dead. Maggie—

Sangita sings: 'The dust of muesli falls on your abandoned key. Return to me.'

———

Pete saw Andy only twice after the crash. The last time, Pete was just back from hospital with his right arm in a sling and a long, livid red scar down one side of his face. It was still held together by stitches. Mealtimes were difficult, and his mother had to cut everything into small pieces, but didn't offer to help him eat it. He juggled with his left hand to lift the food to his mouth. It required an enormous effort to control the trembling in his arm, and most of the time he wasn't willing to try. Eating didn't feel very important.

His father behaved as if nothing had happened, although he gave up television after the accident. 'They're all fools,' he said one day, when he crashed through the front door. Presumably he meant the news reporters at the gate.

So the three of them sat in the dining room, eating in silence. The dark, highly polished table could seat twenty, and there was a fifty-light chandelier suspended above it, which sent startled shivers of light darting in all directions if a small breeze or air current rustled it. The walls were covered with maroon and white Regency stripes, and antique mahogany sideboards were placed along the edges, dwarfed by the hugeness of the room. The heavy baroque curtains were draped in such a way that outside light hardly penetrated.

They didn't speak. At school, Pete had learned the habit of asking politely: 'Please could you pass the water?' 'Would you like the mustard?' And they had to wait until everyone on the table had finished before the pudding could be dished out. This had no effect at home. 'If you want something, take it,' said his father. 'That's how life is. If you don't grab it, someone else will get there first.'

He was probably right. Pete's good manners didn't get him anywhere, didn't prevent his fall from grace.

Andy's appearance on this occasion was unexpected. For some reason, they hadn't heard him drive up, so when he marched into the dining room and stood in front of them, it took a moment to register his presence. He waited to be welcomed.

'Andy!' said his father, leaping to his feet. 'Good to see you. Grab a plate.'

His mother rose to her feet at the same time. She didn't say anything, but she smiled and you could tell that she was thrilled to see him. Pete stayed sitting, feeling uncomfortable.

Andy was very successful, as everyone had expected. Unlike Pete, he'd gone to university and then into management at Marks & Spencer. He'd started at the bottom and gone up and up. They loved him there. He had so many contacts, friends from school who stayed in touch, and he knew how to take advantage of them. Last time he came home, he asked Pete why he wasn't working.

'I've got a job,' said Pete. 'I'm going to start working for Dad.'

'Well, well,' said Andy, with a grin. 'Giving up the playboy life?'

'Let's not get too enthusiastic,' said Pete.

'There are alternatives to working in the scrapyard, you

know,' said Andy. 'There's lots of other opportunities, even without a degree. You can work your way up. Lots of people do it.'

What he meant was, anything would be better than working in a scrapyard. It's not a proper job.

This was true, and they both knew it. Their father couldn't give his sons an expensive education and then ask them to work in a scrapyard. If he sent them to a place where they didn't fit, had them moulded into the shape of the school so that they became a certain type of person, he couldn't expect them to come home and fit into his world too. It didn't work. Pete ended up in limbo, not fitting into either world, despised on both sides.

The embarrassment of parents' nights, rugby matches, sports days, Founder's Day, school fêtes. His father dominated fathers' races, blindly ploughing through everyone else, scattering them in all directions. Pete couldn't bear to watch him thunder past, leaving injured men in his wake, always winning. He would run up and down the touchline when Andy was playing rugby, yelling abuse at all the other players, purple with inappropriate passion.

And their mother, dressed wrongly, small and ineffectual next to her husband. Pete never saw anyone talk to her. It was as if she didn't exist. All conversations were directed at her husband. She was just a breeze in the background, a shadow hidden behind him, a silent whisper that you would miss if you blinked. Sometimes, Pete just wanted to go and shake her. 'Speak to them, Mum. Say something. You're just as important as he is.' But he never said it, and never did anything to show that he appreciated her.

Her first act of rebellion was to reject him.

Andy didn't care. He had such charm, such a hold over other people, that he was able to place himself in his family and make them seem eccentric and lovable. He enjoyed his unconventional background. People admired him for his ability to rise above it. They talked to his father with respect because he was Andy's father. Boys in Pete's class thought his father was hilariously funny, and it was Pete's fault. If he had discovered alcohol earlier, if it had been available at school, he'd have started drinking then. To hide the embarrassment.

When he left school with five O levels and two failed A levels, he didn't keep in contact with any of the boys from his year. He hung around at home for some time, watching television late at night, falling out of bed at lunchtime. Nobody suggested work to him, although his dad occasionally asked him to come down to the scrapyard and help.

He hated it, working with the lads who had left school at fifteen, who lifted great weights effortlessly and manipulated machinery with nonchalant ease. They wore their strength with casual pride, unashamed by their lack of qualifications.

Pete felt stupid and uncoordinated when he was with them, unable to match their skills. Whenever he walked away, before he had even covered twenty yards, a great burst of laughter rose up behind him, a balloon of mirth that was only released once his restraining presence had been removed. It happened every time. It couldn't be a coincidence. So he stopped going.

When he was twenty-one, his dad gave him his house and a generous allowance. When he was twenty-five, he gave him a Piper Warrior, a four-seater single-engine aeroplane, and flying lessons. Pete learned to fly, and for the first time in his life, he felt that success was attainable. Meanwhile, he discovered alcohol, clubs and people who liked him because he was generous. He had a social life. He knew that if his money supply dried up, his friends would probably melt away, but his drinking warmed him and he was no longer alone.

He tried not to think about the pointlessness of his existence. Only at night, frustrated and unable to sleep, did he acknowledge the lack of direction and hope as depression came rolling in on silent waves.

When Andy came in to dinner with them several days after

the accident, he sat down opposite Pete and filled his plate. 'How are you?' he said. 'Arm any better?'

Pete shrugged. 'It's OK.' Andy had already been to see him in hospital, and joked about his injuries. 'You could have a career as a gangster with a scar like that,' he said. 'The one-armed bandit.'

'Jealousy will get you nowhere,' said Pete, struggling to keep up with the lighthearted manner of the conversation. 'I'm expecting the arm to get better.'

They had not discussed the crash.

Andy ate enthusiastically for a time, then looked up at him again. 'So?' he said. 'What really happened?'

'What do you mean?'

'The papers are saying it was your fault.'

'Ignore them,' mumbled his father, through his apple crumble and custard. 'They don't know nothing.'

'Anything,' said Andy, turning to his father, smiling.

His father took another spoonful. 'Whatever,' he said.

He wouldn't have answered like that if Pete had said it.

'So, tell me your story.'

Andy was studying Pete intensely, as if he could read his mind. Pete tried to look away, but found himself paralysed by his brother's silent interrogation, unable to think.

'There isn't a story,' he mumbled, wanting to glance down at his dish on the table.

'Of course there's a story. You need to be able to show the journalists that they're making it all up.'

Pete still couldn't answer him. 'I can't remember,' he said at last. 'I don't know what happened.'

But Andy persisted: 'You must have some idea. Do you think it was a mechanical failure, or were you careless in some way? What were you doing so close to the railway?'

'I don't know,' said Pete again.

There was a long silence. 'Well,' said Andy, 'I suppose the memory blanks out as a protection. It's not something you'd want to keep remembering, is it?' He turned to his mother. 'Shall we go for a drive in the car after lunch?' he said to her.

'Good idea,' said his father. He was always happy for his wife to be removed from under his feet.

'Terrible business,' said Andy. 'It's not just the ones who died, is it? It's the ones who were injured as well.'

Pete limped out of the dining room, trying not to fall over his feet. He was twenty-eight years old, but felt as if he were still twelve, stumbling over his untied shoelaces in his anxiety to escape the threatening presence of the boys in his form who instinctively knew he wasn't one of them.

Andy took his mother for a drive in his E-type Jaguar.

Pete sat in his room, desperate and aching for a drink, his mind unable to focus on anything else, not even having the energy to resent Andy and his rapport with his mother. But each time he reached out for the bottle, smelt the alcohol, his mind jumped back to that moment when he woke up, surrounded by mangled metal, bricks, bodies, blood. So he was sick instead.

When Andy and his mother returned, he dropped her off outside the house, but didn't come in. Pete watched him drive away, crunching down the gravel drive, and if he had known then that he would never see him again, he might have felt slightly less resentful.

———

Straker wakes in the hollow of the night, the bleakest hour, the darkest corner. For a long time he lies awake, listening, and wonders why there's nothing to hear. Where are they all? He can hear his heart beating, the cats dreaming of mice, but there is no other sound.

Why was he so angry with Doody? It was the aeroplane that set it off – not her. She will probably never speak to him again.

What is this hard, leaden pain inside him?

'Maggie?' he says softly, hoping she's there.

There is no Maggie. No Felicity, no Mike, no Francis.

Are they in collusion with each other? Are they all waiting with Maggie to see what he will do? Does everything depend on his response to her, his willingness to leave his place of safety and venture out for the first time in twenty-four years? Must he go? Could he do it?

He feels Magnificent sit up on the end of his bed, move around, scratch for a few frantic seconds. He curls down again, shuffles for a while, purrs briefly and goes back to sleep.

How would he get to the station? How would he know where to get off the train? What if Simon Taverner is not in?

What does Maggie want him to say?

The silence wraps itself round him – no other living person exists for hundreds of miles. He's protected from the real world by this cushion of nothingness, and has no desire to cut it away. The voices of the victims have never disturbed that comforting blanket. They have just crept in underneath and reinforced the remoteness of everything else.

He misses them.

———

He goes to the cottage early next Saturday, determined to face her, convinced she will tell him to leave.

She needs him to help her work on the cottage. She has no choice.

She's not rational. She won't even consider his usefulness.

He goes to Sainsbury's on his way, and buys some food, which he leaves on the front doorstep. He goes round to the back.

He works for about half an hour.

'Straker! Where are you?'

He puts down the tools and walks round to the front, where he finds her standing with her hands on her hips. Her loose silky top is bright pink and covered with blue elephants. Her hair is hanging down on her shoulders and looks freshly washed. The ends almost fall into curls, rather than the uneven chunks he remembers.

'What are you doing here?'

He can't reply.

'Well, I never thought I'd see you again.'

He watches her. She's not as furious as he expected. She's trying to be, but her words lack the searing heat that he remembers from their first meeting.

'Can I trust you?' she asks, pushing her chin forward, challenging him with her eyes.

'You are completely safe with me,' he says, trying to sound calm and steady.

'How can I be sure you're not going to murder me?'

'I don't murder people.'

She raises her eyebrows. 'Not counting the first seventy-eight, you mean?'

There is no answer to this.

She picks up the two Sainsbury's bags and holds them out from her body as if they are contaminated. 'What's in here?'

Isn't it obvious?

'Did you bring them?'

He nods, not sure what she's annoyed about.

'Charity now, is it?'

He stares at her.

'Or do you think you own me?'

He turns away and walks round to the back windows. She follows, but he ignores her and continues rubbing down the woodwork.

'Look, Straker,' she says, and her voice is more friendly, 'I'm sure you mean well, but I can afford to feed myself. I'm not entirely destitute. Unlike you, I have a job. Do I look as if I'm starving?'

No, she doesn't look as if she's starving.

'You probably think you're being kind, but I don't want to know about kindness. I don't believe in it. You don't have to

215

help me with the cottage if you don't want to. Only if you're interested, and if you are, I'll feed you. Get it?'

He nods, because she seems to be expecting him to. 'I'll take the bags away, then,' he says.

But, oddly, she doesn't seem happy with that either. 'Not much point now, is there? We might as well eat it as it's here.'

She contradicts herself at every turn, so everything he does is wrong, and can't be undone. It's good food. Not chocolate or biscuits, but fruit juice, muesli, wholemeal bread, butter, cold meat, oranges, apples, peaches, grapes. He'd thought she would be pleased.

'You must do something about the electricity,' he says, when they stop to eat. 'Everything would be much easier if we could use a drill.'

'You can buy cordless drills.'

'They're expensive.'

He decides not to offer to buy one. 'And you need a fridge.'

She's quiet for a while. 'I phoned Jonathan last night,' she says.

She's mentioned Jonathan before. Who is he? Is that what all the fuss about Maggie and wives was about? Is he going to turn up later today and want to know what Straker's doing here?

'My brother,' she says. 'He's an awful pain, but he'll know what to do to get the electricity on.' She pauses. 'He wants to look at the plane.'

'Why?'

'Jonathan knows about everything. He used to read fact-finders when he was little, and he hasn't changed. Facts, figures, money. Oh, and he watches television a lot. He likes the food programmes.'

Straker feels uncomfortable about all this. 'I'll go before he comes, then.'

She is surprised. 'Why? He won't mind you.'

How does she know her brother won't react like the boys at

school? They only had to see him to decide that there was something wrong with him. 'Watch it, Butler,' they would say, and kick him as they passed, just for being there. Is Jonathan going to be any different? He will probably object to Straker in the same way as they did. Just because he's here.

'You might like him,' she says. 'He's odd too.'

———

She has to meet Jonathan by the gate leading to the barn at two o'clock. 'We need to be on time,' she says. 'He will be.'

'Where's he coming from?'

'London.'

'He can't be that precise with the time, then.'

'Oh, yes, he can. You don't know Jonathan.'

Straker doesn't want to stay, but Doody insists that he waits with her. 'He won't be late,' she says.

At exactly two o'clock, a silver Audi TT drives up the road, and pulls in beside them. A tall, dark-haired man, dressed in a grey pin-striped suit and a white shirt, steps out and stands uncertainly on the grass verge. His tie has red and orange zigzags down it, bright and cheerful against his sober suit. He is out of place here, a man of the city, who never comes into contact with grass except when he pays the gardener.

'Imogen,' he says, as if he had not really been expecting to see her. 'You're on time.'

'Of course,' she says. They make no physical contact. No acknowledgement that they are connected except for the use of each other's name.

He eyes the pathway. 'Is that where we have to go?'

'Yes. Sorry about the weeds.'

'Never mind the weeds. Is it muddy?' He looks down at his shoes which are black and shiny, obviously very expensive. Everything about him indicates wealth.

'No. Not very, anyway. When did it last rain?' she says, turning to Straker.

He shrugs. He doesn't feel that he belongs in this conversation. Jonathan hasn't noticed him, and doesn't even make an acknowledgement when Doody talks to him. He is invisible. That's fine with him.

The sight of Jonathan negotiating the gate promises an interesting spectacle, but he manages to climb over with some elegance. They walk up the path, Doody and Jonathan in front and Straker behind.

'Will you be back in time for the dinner party?' says Doody. 'Who's folding the napkins?'

Jonathan doesn't reply. He doesn't say anything else until they open the barn and he steps in. 'Well,' he says, after a while, and there is excitement in his voice, 'what a wonderful thing.' He sounds genuinely impressed.

Straker waits outside and listens, keeping his eyes away from the aeroplane. His hands are shaking, and he puts them into his pockets. He hears himself talking to someone: 'It's a Piper Warrior.'

Jonathan and Doody come out of the barn, and walk over to where Straker is standing.

'I know a few people who would be most interested in this,' says Jonathan.

'I don't know if I want several people to be interested,' says Doody. 'It's my plane, not yours.'

'Don't be ridiculous,' he says. 'This is too important a find to hide away. It could be worth a fortune.'

'But is it definitely mine?'

'Oh, yes,' he says, taking a letter out of his pocket. 'The solicitors have confirmed it. Don't know why they didn't mention it in the first place. After I phoned them, they had to do some research of their own. But it's definitely yours. He left you everything.'

'Nice to know they write to tell you and not me.'

'Piers Sackville has written to you as well. The letter's probably at your home address.'

'Piers, eh? You're good friends, then.'

Jonathan doesn't reply.

Doody grins at Straker. 'Don't you wish you had a secret benefactor?' she says.

Straker thinks of his father, knowing how it feels to have someone give him money. He's not sure if it's such a good thing.

They stand together in an uncomfortable group, uncertain what to say to each other. Jonathan walks out and examines the overgrown field. 'Pretty good,' he says. 'You own this field and the one on the left as you come up the path. Prime land. You could sell it to the adjoining farms, or for building. They could make quite a nice little housing estate here.'

Straker nods in agreement. Sell it all. Forget it. He examines Jonathan thoughtfully. Has Doody described him too harshly? He's more sensible than he appears.

'Maybe I don't want to sell it. Why shouldn't I keep the plane and use it myself?'

Jonathan looks appalled. 'Don't be ridiculous. You don't know anything about it.'

'I could work it out.'

'Imogen, I have known you all my life. You are not a mechanical person.'

'Maybe not, but Straker is.'

Jonathan finally turns to him. His eyes are pale green and lacking in any real curiosity. 'Who exactly are you?'

Straker doesn't know where to begin.

'He's a friend of mine,' says Doody. 'He knows all about aeroplanes. He's a pilot.'

Straker wants to deny this. It's none of their business. But he can't open his mouth properly.

Jonathan shows some interest. 'Commercial, RAF or private?'

'Private,' says Straker after a pause.

Jonathan looks at him as if he's spoken in a foreign

language. Then he turns back to Doody. 'I must be off,' he says.

'Have you tried making fruit cake yet? I have a good recipe. Delia Smith.'

'I'll have a chat with some of my friends about the plane. I'll let you know.'

'It takes a long time to cook, but it has a lovely sticky centre.'

He walks away from them, back to his car, starts it up and drives away.

The field is very peaceful in the afternoon sunshine. Everything is still, even Doody, for a while.

'Housing estate,' says Doody, with contempt.

'It's not a bad idea,' says Straker.

'Don't be ridiculous,' she says, and turns back to the barn. Straker doesn't follow her. He sets off down the road.

'Straker!' she yells. 'Where are you going now?'

Chapter 18

Doody has tried to visualise seventy-eight people. In the three weeks since Straker told her about the crash, she's watched the children from the upstairs window of her caretaker's house, counting them, working out what a group of seventy-eight people looks like. She thinks about the relatives, how their husbands, children, parents never came home. At least they had an explanation. Surely it's better to know what has happened, even if the news is not what you want to hear. Would they have preferred to have uncertainty, so they could find comfort in hope? But hope is hollow. The missing person still doesn't come back.

———

Tony, Jonathan's associate – that's how Jonathan describes him, because he never admits to having friends, despite his dinner parties – comes to see the plane two weeks later. He's tall and gangly, like a teenager. He moves as if he's expecting to encounter awkward angles everywhere, sharp corners to catch on, holes to fall down.

'Hi,' he says, as they meet by the gate. He has long red-blond hair that flops across his forehead when he leans forward. Doody was expecting an expert to look older, somehow complementing the age of the aeroplane. She was expecting Biggles and she gets Ginger.

'Come on, Imogen,' says Jonathan. 'We haven't got all day.'

Rubbish, she thinks. You've got all the time in the world if it involves money. And you must have all day, since you've just driven down from London.

'After you,' she says. 'You've got to climb over the gate.'

Tony looks at her nervously. 'OK,' he says, and climbs on to the first bar. He hesitates, as if unwilling to go too high, then rises to the next bar. He has some difficulty in deciding which leg to put over first. He eventually settles on the left, turning himself sideways to do it, and nearly loses his balance. He saves himself just in time, swings one leg over, then the next, and misses his footing on the other side. He nearly falls, but just manages to keep himself upright. 'Oops,' he says.

Doody goes next, resenting the fact that she likes Tony. They don't wait for Jonathan as they walk up the path between the crushed weeds.

'This could be a very important find,' says Tony. He's walking slowly, but obviously itching to get there, only just managing to control his excitement. Jonathan treads delicately behind them, worrying about the mud.

'You could be wasting your time,' she says to Tony.

'I don't mind. Great to get out into the country. Makes it easier to go back to the office on Monday morning.'

What office? she wonders. An office full of people who know about First World War aircraft, an office in an antiques shop, or an office in a museum? 'How do you know Jonathan?'

'We're work colleagues,' he says, with surprise. 'Didn't he tell you? Money men.'

Doody is both disappointed and amazed. He bears no resemblance to Jonathan. He doesn't behave as if he inhabits the same world.

She unlocks the door of the barn, and they stand for a moment, admiring the front of the aeroplane. It seems smaller than before, only a few feet taller than Jonathan. The wings are black on top, red underneath, stretching out into the darkness of the barn, held in a twenty-five-year pose, ready for take-off.

'A Tiger Moth,' says Tony, in a delighted tone.

So it's not even a First World War plane. Doody feels cheated. 'When would it have been built?'

'First produced 1931. They used them for training pilots all through the Second World War. Instructor in the back, pupil in the front, so he felt as if he was on his own.'

Tony starts to walk round it, stopping every now and then to examine something, a wheel, a wire hanging loose. He runs his fingers along the fuselage and the wings, feeling for tears in the fabric. He pulls himself up to the cockpit and fiddles with switches, muttering to himself. After a while, he starts humming. 'Those Magnificent Men In Their Flying Machines.'

He climbs back to the floor, pulls down the engine cover and pokes around inside. 'Mmm,' he says. 'Amazingly good condition. I'd have expected far more deterioration than this. It's moisture that destroys them. The atmosphere must have been unusually dry.'

'There are good tiles on the roof.'

They look up and see the sails covering the holes, recently put up by Straker. 'That's only just happened,' says Doody. 'It was perfect up until a couple of weeks ago.'

'I suspect the aeroplane was renovated just before it was shut away. That would give some explanation for its good state of preservation.'

'We couldn't make it work,' says Doody.

'I wouldn't expect it to,' he says, his voice muffled as he bends over. 'The fuel would have evaporated years ago.' He reaches in and rattles something.

Jonathan says nothing. He probably resents experts. They make him feel inadequate.

Tony climbs down, catching his hair in one of the struts. 'Ouch,' he says, and disentangles himself. There's a pink flush on his cheeks. 'I think you may have something here,' he says. 'Of course, it'll be very expensive to restore, but well worth it.'

'So it's valuable?' says Jonathan.

'Oh, yes, worth quite a lot, I'd say. There are probably only about fifty left in the world. They chopped most of them up after the war and sold the rest off for twenty-five pounds each. Not a bad bargain.'

It's still special, even if it's not a Camel.

'I'd like to bring a couple of friends to see it,' says Tony.

'Why not?' says Doody. 'Invite the world. Might as well. What have we got to lose?'

Tony looks at her, and then at Jonathan, slightly perplexed. 'Is there a problem?' he asks.

'No,' says Jonathan. 'It's in good condition, then?'

'Remarkably intact, as far as I can see.'

'But the rubber on the tyres has perished,' says Doody. 'Everything falls apart when you touch it.'

'Small things,' says Tony. 'You'd expect that. It'll need a lot of work, of course.'

'Could you do it?' asks Jonathan.

Tony grins and shakes his head. 'No way. It would take years, even with other people helping. Regulations are very tight. If you want a certificate of airworthiness, you need the experts. Your best bet would be a restoration company.'

'But how much would that cost?' asks Doody.

'A huge amount, I'm afraid. Thousands.'

She feels stupid and defeated as her dreams of restoring and flying it drain away. 'So what should I do with it?'

'Sell it. It's still worth a small fortune as it is.'

'I don't want to sell it.'

'Let's consult your experts,' says Jonathan. 'See what they say.'

They stand for some time, looking at the aeroplane. It peers out of the shed comfortably, weak and vulnerable in its present condition, and somehow innocent. When it was built, nobody knew about nuclear bombs. Hiroshima was just a city in Japan, the journey to Australia took weeks in a boat, there was no such thing as a Boeing 747, the word 'hijack' was non-existent.

Eventually, they close the barn doors, replace the padlock and walk back down the pathway. Doody is next to Jonathan this time.

'You know Oliver d'Arby?' she says.

'No,' he says. 'I never met him.'

'You know what I mean.'

He frowns. 'Yes.'

'He disappeared, didn't he?'

'Yes.'

'Who made the decision that he was dead, so that I could inherit the cottage?'

He shrugs. 'I don't know how these things work.'

'I don't believe you. Mother said you sorted it out.'

'Did she?'

She waits for more, but he's silent. She wants to shout at him, but she's aware of Tony just behind. They climb over the gate, and this time Tony rips his trousers on a splinter.

'Ouch,' he says.

Doody prises the fabric away from the wood with her fingers. 'It doesn't look too bad. I'm sure it could be mended.'

He smiles at her. A good, easy smile. 'My wife is used to it. All my clothes are covered in little patches, masterfully disguised by her needle and thread.' Doody smiles back. He's a likeable man.

'Come back any time,' she says to him, as they hover by his car. 'Bring your friends.' Did she really say that? She's not interested in other people's friends.

'I'll be in touch,' he says out of his window, as he drives off.

Jonathan hovers by his car. 'Do you want a lift?'

'No, thanks, I prefer to walk. It keeps me fit.'

'Let's find out how much it costs to restore it.'

'I won't be able to afford it.'

'No, but I might.'

'You?'

'Why not? I've got nothing else to spend my money on. Maybe I could learn to fly.'

'What about the ex-wives?'

He looks almost cheerful. 'No problem. We've made arrangements.'

'Well, that's news to me.'

'We all move on, Imogen. We're grown-up people.'

'Don't patronise me.'

He pauses. 'Anyway, I think I could afford it.'

Doody feels irrationally resentful. 'Then it wouldn't be my aeroplane.'

'We'd be equal partners.'

Why is he interested? This is Jonathan standing here, her brother, the man with no feelings. Is it possible that some previously unknown part of him has woken up, seen the romance of the Tiger Moth, stirred him into making a genuine commitment?

'Maybe even you couldn't afford it.'

'You'd be surprised,' he says.

He doesn't seem to want to go. 'When do you have to be back at school?'

'Tonight,' she says. 'I have to be there for Monday morning.'

'Do you have a spare key to the barn?'

She nods, unwillingly.

'Could you lend it to me? In case I have to be here to show the experts?'

Reluctantly, she hands him the key. 'What if I want to be here?'

'Would you be able to come during the week?'

'Some of us have to work.'

'By the way,' he says, 'I asked the solicitors about the rent.'

'And?'

'There isn't any. They think those people must have been squatters.'

Doody sighs. Can she trust the combination of Jonathan and someone who works for Sackville, Sackville and Waterman? 'Funny kind of squatters,' she says. 'Aren't they meant to be young and revolutionary? I don't think we could quite put the Macklethorpes into that category.'

'Who?' he says, and looks past her. She can see he's not listening. 'I only wanted you to have what was rightfully yours,' he says. 'That's all I did, try to help you.'

So he had interfered. 'It's none of your business.'

He shifts uncomfortably on the muddy grass. Despite his best efforts, his shoes are not maintaining their normal immaculate state. 'I was sorting out papers for Mother,' he says, 'and I came across a letter from Oliver d'Arby about the will. I just thought it would be worth enquiring. I only wanted to help.'

'Why? I'm all right, aren't I? I can help myself.'

'I know that. I just thought any money or property would be useful to you. So you don't have to be tied to a dead-end job if you don't want to be.'

'A dead-end job? Is that what you think?'

He sighs. 'Look, Imogen. You're my sister, and I'd like you to be happy. All right? I thought that if some property was rightfully yours, you should have it. What you do with it is entirely your decision. All I did was make it possible for you.'

She stares at him, not knowing what to say. 'So what if I am your sister? I can manage my own affairs.'

'Fine,' he says, and gets into the car. 'See you,' he says, as he turns on the engine. He waves out of the open window as he drives off.

Doody doesn't understand. Why would he try to help her? He must have a motive, but she can't work out what it is.

As soon as the term ends, Doody drives down to the cottage and races up to the barn without even stopping to see if Straker has done more work on the cottage windows. The hedges lining the pathway to the field have been cut back, presumably to allow access for a lorry. The gate opens properly now, so there's no longer any need to climb over it.

The barn doors are closed, but not padlocked. She doesn't have to pull the door open very far. The Tiger Moth has gone.

Doody stands in the field, her arms crossed, angry and disappointed. Jonathan making all the decisions again. It's her field, her gate, her aeroplane, and someone takes it away without telling her. She wants to phone Jonathan immediately and tell him to put everything back as it was. But she knows he won't listen. He's probably already having flying lessons. He won't be any good. He's not a practical man. He only pretends to build his own kitchen.

As she walks back down the narrow road to her cottage, she passes two women who look vaguely familiar.

'Good morning,' says one, and Doody recognises Mrs Whittaker. She half smiles at her and tries to pass without stopping, but Mrs Whittaker wants to talk. 'You're doing a wonderful job on the cottage,' she says, laying a hand on Doody's arm.

Doody wants to push it away, but makes herself smile, stretching her lips outwards, just refraining from baring her teeth. A car drives past too fast, and they all step back together.

Mrs Whittaker brings her face closer and looks into Doody's eyes. 'Nice to see you're getting on with Mr Straker,' she says.

Doody removes Mrs Whittaker's hand and glares at her. 'I'm not,' she says. 'He's just useful. I pay him.' She turns away. 'By the way,' she says, over her shoulder, 'he talks to me all the time.'

———

Straker appears later in the day, and they start to paint adjacent window-frames. She's quicker than him, but he's neater.

'They've taken the plane.'

'Good,' he says.

'Am I right in assuming you don't want it to be restored?'

He doesn't answer, but she notices that he is speeding up, making mistakes and breathing more heavily.

'You missed a bit,' she says, pointing. 'It'll take a few weeks before they bring it back.'

He stops. 'They're bringing it back?'

She grins, knowing he's annoyed. 'Jonathan's paying.'

He goes back to the painting, slow again, controlled.

'How can you be so sure the crash was your fault?' she says, after a while.

'I just know.'

'Very convincing. You just know.'

'Yes,' he says. His manner is odd – even odder than usual. He's hiding something. He's not telling her the whole story.

'You've got paint on your beard.' Although he hasn't. She just wants to irritate him.

She throws him a rag and he wipes the beard, but can't find any paint. He looks puzzled, standing back from the window and touching his beard nervously with his fingertips. He's wearing a white shirt and grey trousers, old and threadbare, but immaculately ironed. His forehead creases into a frown as he gives his beard one last examination; then he picks up his paintbrush again.

'Maybe at the last moment someone else took over the controls, or there was some kind of mechanical failure. Or it was just bad luck, the wrong place at the wrong time.'

'No. I caused the crash. It was my responsibility.'

'But you can't remember. That's what you said. Were there any witnesses?'

'Yes, but nobody could work out exactly what happened. Lots of different stories, no evidence.'

They say nothing for a while and continue to paint. It's becoming clear that although the little panels in the window look picturesque, they're a lot of trouble. It might be worth changing them when they do the windows at the front. Never mind period detail. She wants to be able to see through them, let in lots of light. That's all that matters.

'I can't see how you can really know.'

'The voices in my dreams. They're there all the time, telling me.'

'About these voices. Are they supposed to be ghosts?'

He thinks for a bit. 'No. I don't believe in ghosts.'

'Neither do I.' So there's one good thing. 'But they have conversations with you?'

'Yes.'

He probably doesn't want to pursue this, but Doody thinks they should. 'Are they real voices? That you can hear? Like mine now?'

'It's only in my dreams,' he says. 'Not during the day.'

'Not schizophrenic, then?'

'No. Just nightmares.'

'But you believe them?'

'They're very persuasive.'

'Like Maggie? She's like a real person to you?'

He hesitates. 'Maggie won't let me forget. She makes me face up to it.'

'But she's dead.'

'Yes.'

They go on painting. Doody tries to make sense of it, but can't. 'Why do you write to all their relatives, keep files? What's it for?'

'I have to keep them alive. I can't let them disappear or be forgotten. It's important that I see them all as if they're still here, that there's someone to hold on to them in case everyone else walks on past.' His voice is low but urgent, rushing through the information compulsively. 'People do that – after five years, ten years, they move on. They might marry someone else, have another child, grow old without

230

them, so I want to hold all those people in my head to stop that happening.'

He's taking on too much. 'You can't do it,' she says. 'You can't carry seventy-eight people round with you. It'll make you mad.'

'Perhaps I am mad,' he says.

It's a distinct possibility. 'It doesn't make them alive again, though, does it?'

'No.'

'But it's not as if you meant to kill them all.'

'No.'

'Well, there you are. It wasn't premeditated murder.'

'It might have been.'

'More like carelessness, I'd have thought. There's a world of difference between Hitler, who meant to kill all those Jews, and . . .' She tries to think of another accident, but can't. Aberfan, *Titanic, Herald of Free Enterprise* . . . They seem a little extreme, since hundreds of people died, and they've become historical landmarks.

'How come so many died?' she says instead. 'It's not usually that many in a train crash.'

'Fire,' he says harshly. 'It engulfed two carriages of the train. They couldn't identify some of the bodies because they were so badly burned.'

Doody tries not to see the blackened, wrecked train and the unrecognisable victims. They paint in silence for a long time and the tension of the conversation begins to dissipate. There's a faint rustle in the lilac tree, a car passing in the distance, voices of children calling to each other in a faraway garden. Doody likes this awareness of things going on, the feeling of someone beside her working. She can hear the swish of his paintbrush, the slurp as he puts more paint on it, the creak of his knees as he bends to do the lower level. She can hear him breathing, moving to one side, the ease of his presence. She remembers the first day when he invaded her garden, the sharing of silence with someone else. It's the same again, but more comfortable. The rhythm of sounds around them, the soothing nature of being together without speaking.

————————

On the first day when Harry didn't come home, Imogen wasn't worried. Sometimes he would turn up and she'd forget he was coming. She'd be cleaning, wiping all the skirting-boards, which didn't need doing, and he'd be standing there, watching her, when she turned round, scaring her to death. Then they would hug, and she would take his coat off, get him to sit down while she made him a cup of coffee. She'd go into the kitchen and worry about what to cook for him, bring down all the recipe books, check what tins she had and what was in the fridge. By the time she'd worked it all out, and produced the coffee, he would be sprawled out on the sofa, his mouth open, snoring away.

That was all he ever did in the end. Sleep.

Sometimes she stood over his inert body and allowed herself to be angry. She'd waited all that time for him to come home. What had happened to their life together? The conversations, the fun? It wasn't all her fault, surely?

At first, she thought she'd made a mistake. On the second day, she started to worry, and went through his papers to see if he had a timetable, a list of days on and off. He'd never shown her anything written down. He used to just tell her, 'Back on Thursday late'; 'I've got three days at home'; 'Don't bother with dinner. I have to leave by five o'clock.'

After three days, Imogen summoned the courage to phone the hospital and spoke to a receptionist. 'You want Dr Doody?'

'Yes, Harry Doody.'

'Hold the line.'

She waited until she was cut off.

After two hours, she tried again, her hands shaking so badly that she had to keep redialling. 'Please, I need to speak to Dr Harry Doody.'

'Hold the line.'

'Please can you be quick? I got cut off last time.'

'I'll do my best.' She could hear the receptionist's irritation.

'Hello?' A man this time. 'To whom am I speaking?'

'It's Imogen Doody. Harry's wife.'

'Well, Mrs Doody, you can tell Harry that if he wants to keep his job, he'd better get right back here.'

'What do you mean?'

'He let us down in a crisis. You don't do that in medicine.' Imogen could hear his annoyance pulsating through the phone line. 'He has a duty of care. Tell him that.' And he put the phone down.

She didn't know what to do. She still thought Harry would just walk through the door. Every time the post was delivered, she was there, expecting him to come racing through. 'Imogen!' he would call, in the urgent way she liked. 'I'm home.'

She would find herself holding her breath, listening, thinking perhaps she'd missed the sound of his key in the door. She lay awake all night, imagining she could feel the weight of him sliding into bed beside her, careful not to let him know that she was awake, so that he would drop straight into his exhausted, desperate sleep without knowing that she wanted to talk to him.

For another day, she forgot to eat, wash, or go outside. She went to bed, got up, waited, listened, and he didn't come back. She didn't know how to think about it. All she could do was wait.

Then the phone rang. At last. He was letting her know that there had been a delay. He didn't want her to worry.

She ran to pick it up. 'Harry!'

But the voice wasn't Harry's. 'No, Imogen, it's Stella.' Harry's mother. He was with her. He'd asked her to phone and say that he'd left her. Imogen didn't want to talk to her and have it confirmed. It was better not knowing, thinking that she'd made a mistake and that he'd be arriving any minute now.

'Can I speak to Harry?' Imogen said.

'But I was going to ask you that.'

'Oh.' Imogen had to pause and think. 'He's not here.'

'When do you expect him back?'

She didn't know what to say.

'Imogen, are you there?'

'Yes.'

'When will I be able to catch him? I need to check arrangements for our wedding anniversary.'

'Sorry?'

'He has told you, hasn't he? November the second. It's our twenty-fifth.'

'Oh, yes.' Imogen didn't know anything about it.

There was a pause. 'Imogen, could you just tell me when I can speak to him? I haven't got all day.'

'I don't know.'

'What do you mean, you don't know?'

'I don't know where he is.'

And that was it. That was when Imogen realised he wasn't coming back. His mother phoned all the hospitals in the area in case he'd had an accident. She phoned the police. The police came to talk to Imogen, and it was Celia all over again.

Nobody had any idea where he was. The last person to speak to him had been Hassan, who was his best friend, they told Imogen. Harry had never even mentioned Hassan. They'd got married suddenly, out of the blue, in a few hours without telling anyone, so there had been no wedding reception, no best man, no speeches in the marquee in the garden. Just her and Harry with two strangers they'd picked off the streets to be witnesses.

Stella was distraught, furious with her. 'Why didn't you call me? He might have had an accident, be lying somewhere injured. We could have saved him. Now it might be too late.'

She couldn't accept that Harry would go away willingly without telling her. But Imogen knew that he'd just walked off one early morning and kept on walking because he couldn't cope with it all. The job, the travelling, the lack of sleep, Imogen. She'd known, right from the beginning, that he wasn't coming back, which was why she hadn't rung the police or anyone else.

After the police had been through the house, Imogen searched again, looking for clues, examining his clothes, his pockets, his books, his drawers. She piled everything in the centre of the living room, a great pile of non-existent Harry, the man who had ceased to be. She became increasingly frantic, tearing the clothes with her hands, throwing them on to the pile, screaming at them if they wouldn't come apart.

She tore up his papers, his lecture notes, screwing them into tight balls and hurling them on to the pile. She ripped pages out of his books, pulled the tapes out of his cassettes, long shining ribbons of his favourite music, tangled and twisted.

When she couldn't find anything else that belonged to him, she started to kick it all viciously.

'Traitor!' she yelled. 'It's no use having good manners, or a posh voice, or a private school if you can't look after your wife! Call yourself a doctor? What about kindness, compassion? What about me?'

Overwhelmed by the desire to destroy everything connected with him, she picked up a box of matches. They wouldn't light – they must have been damp. Then one stayed alight. She held it over a sheaf of papers, her hand trembling.

She started to cry. Tears poured down her cheeks, dripping on to the match, just before the flame reached her fingers.

She cried and cried and cried.

Then, the next day, she did the same thing as Harry. She left the flat and everything in it, and walked away. She took a small suitcase with essential clothes, and, as an afterthought, one of Harry's textbooks. To prove to herself that he had really existed. *Advanced Studies in Neurology*.

She caught a train and went to Bristol where she had never been before and knew no one. She walked into a labour exchange and saw a job for a school caretaker. She went to the interview, said she was a widow, ready to start immediately, and they gave her the job. She gave them two references: an old friend of her father, who was a lawyer and would sound convincing, and her former headmistress, who could at least back up Imogen's claim to exist. While she waited two weeks for the house to be vacated, Imogen slept in shop doorways, under bridges, walked everywhere, looked at everything, and decided that she didn't mind living as long as she didn't have to be close to anyone.

She liked the idea of being someone new. Starting again, being a different person. Strong, hard, in control. Nobody messes with Doody.

She kept her new-found knowledge of anger. She carried it around with her, nursing it, polishing it, holding it ready. And every now and again, she opened the lid and let it out. It had an amazing effect. People backed away from her and apologised. Children cowered and confessed. Men put their hands into the air and surrendered. No one came near the space she manufactured around herself. For the first time in years, she felt safe.

Once she'd moved in she rang home. Jonathan answered the phone.

'Hello, it's Imogen.'

He sounded surprised. 'Imogen? Where are you?'

'Bristol.'

'Why?'

'I fancied a change.'

He was having difficulty thinking of something to say. 'Shall I fetch Mummy?'

'No, I'll give you my phone number.'

'OK. Have you got a flat?'

'No, a house.'

'Oh, good.'

' 'Bye, then.'

'Imogen – what happens if Harry comes back? How will he find you?'

'He won't come back.' She put the phone down. What did they care? They'd only met Harry a couple of times anyway. She was right. On the rare occasions Imogen rang her, her mother never once mentioned Harry, or his disappearance. She had always thought he was too good for Imogen.

'Why in the world did he marry you?' she'd said, after Imogen first brought him home as her husband, and her surprise was so genuine that Imogen had had to leave the room in frustration.

Jonathan started to phone instead, and he's always been the one to contact her ever since. He must have had some feeling that they should pretend to be a family, since they were the only ones left.

Imogen never spoke to Stella again.

———

Doody and Straker are working on the garden when she decides to tell him about Harry, without knowing how she arrives at this decision. He's digging and she's working behind him, picking out the weeds with a trowel. They should be inside the cottage, making it warm and habitable before the winter, but the weather is fine, and it's pleasant out here, smelling of freshly turned soil, as they pile up weeds and fallen leaves.

'So if you're not married,' she says, 'what about your family? Do you have brothers, sisters, parents, nephews, nieces?'

He doesn't say anything, or make any acknowledgement that she has spoken.

'I was married once,' she says.

He continues to dig, but the shape of him changes. His movements become less fluid.

'He was a doctor, but I think he must have had a breakdown.'

He gives no sign that he's interested. Does he even want to know?

'He was tired all the time – he spent most of the time sleeping. He had to travel a long way to the hospital. I think it was just too much for him. The flat was cold and damp, and we never seemed to have enough money – although things would have got better, since he'd just qualified.'

He stops digging, but doesn't look at her. 'So where is he now?'

'I don't know,' she says. 'He disappeared.'

'What do you mean?'

'Well, you know, there one minute, gone the next. Just a space where he used to be.'

'What did you do? Go to the police?'

'Not straight away.' It sounds foolish now. No wonder Stella was so annoyed with her. 'At first I thought he'd been delayed.'

'But he didn't come back?'

'No.'

'Never?'

'No.' It sounds final. More final than it's ever felt. It's the first time she's told anyone about it, admitted that she'll never see him again. He must be a different person by now, and if he turned up at her door, she wouldn't recognise him. He'd be twice as old as she remembers. In her mind, he's still twenty-five. A young man.

She has stopped weeding, her hands poised over the freshly turned earth. Harry at fifty. She has never thought about this before. He would be the same age as his father was when she last saw him, bald, probably. The Harry she knew is gone.

'Did you tell the police?'

'Yes – yes. They didn't take it very seriously. They said lots of people just disappear. He was under stress from work – there was a major accident that night, apparently. A big pile-up on the M25. Or he had another woman somewhere. I told them that wasn't possible, because I'd know, but they didn't believe me. They pretended to, but they didn't.'

Straker goes back to his digging. 'So how long ago was this?'

'A long time.'

'How long?'

'I don't know. About twenty-five years.'

He stops digging.

'What's the matter?' she says. 'Did you know him, then?' Silly question. He doesn't even know Harry's name.

He looks at her and his face is pale and shrivelled.

'What's the matter?'

'Twenty-four years?' His voice has changed, become strangled, thick and uncomfortable.

'No, twenty-five.'

He drops the spade and backs away from her. She doesn't understand what's happening.

He starts to walk away.

'Straker! Come back! What's going on?'

His walk turns into a run.

'Straker!'

He turns round when he gets to the gate. 'Don't you see?' he shouts.

She stares at him blankly.

'He was on the train, wasn't he? I killed him. He was one of the seventy-eight.'

'No,' she shouts. 'It wasn't the same time.'

'Yes, it was. About twenty-five years, you said.'

'It can't have been. Nobody said anything about crashes. They know who died on the train, don't they?'

'There were nine unidentified bodies.'

She doesn't know what to do. He opens the gate.

'Straker!' she shouts. 'Straker, come back!'

But he's gone. The gate is open, the spade lying abandoned on the earth, and she's alone.

Chapter 19

Straker runs all the way to the lighthouse. It is only when he arrives there that he realises he's left the dinghy by the pier in the harbour. He stops by the door and tries to think. Does it matter? Should he go back and fetch it? Nothing is clear in his mind. His thoughts roll round in circles, pretending to be articulate, but ending up at the beginning again, making no sense whatsoever.

Suleiman comes out through the cat-flap, perplexed, not expecting him to be there. They stare at each other as if they've both been caught in some accusing spotlight. Suleiman gives in first and goes back through the cat-flap. Straker remains standing, looking at the empty spot where Suleiman has been, trying to remember what he should be thinking about.

After a while, he walks to the edge of the cliff, counting his steps. Nineteen yards, much closer than last time he counted. When did the last five or six yards go? How had he missed their disappearance? Has he forgotten to check for the last few weeks, or is it going more rapidly? He balances on the edge, watching the sea. The wind pushes him constantly backwards, and he has to put all his energy into standing upright. The sea is hurling itself against the cliff with desperation, and spray shoots up at regular intervals. The waves seem to know that they can bring the cliff down and are competing for the privilege of delivering the final blow. Beneath his feet, there is a feeling of the cliff moving. Shifting, crumbling, preparing for destruction, and there's nothing he can do to stop it. He looks back at the lighthouse and sees more cracks, more evidence of its vulnerability. From a distance, it looks invincible, but in reality it is dying, struggling to hold on to its last breath.

He stands for a long time, counting the waves as they come in for the attack, swaying in the wind, maintaining an unwilling balance in the unpredictable gusts.

What does he do now?

He has no idea. It feels as if everything has stopped.

When he turns back to the lighthouse, he's still counting. First waves, then lighthouse steps. He goes up and down, up and down, leaving out seventy-eight. He treats it as if it doesn't exist.

Later, much later, he stops on the top floor and watches the sun set. He's exhausted, but unable to eat anything. He sits down and leans his back against the wall. Magnificent comes to rub himself against him. He gives a little chirrup when Straker puts out his hand to stroke him.

Now, finally, he realises the one thing that he hadn't understood before. There may have been seventy-eight victims, but if you know one of them, the other seventy-seven become irrelevant. All his research, his letters, the replies, should have told him that, but he hadn't somehow put the strands together.

This should not be true. Some of the victims are more real to him than others. Maggie, of course, Felicity, Alan . . . They have all become part of his thoughts, but they started from the position of being dead. Today he's had a conversation with a real person, and everything has changed. There was only one passenger on that train who has any direct relevance to his life, and he doesn't even know the man's first name.

He remains outside after the sun has gone, and darkness rolls in. He discovers that his face is wet. Looking round in surprise, he wonders why he hadn't noticed that it was raining. Magnificent is beside him, lying on his back. He's sleeping blissfully, the soft fur on his stomach exposed, and he isn't wet. The floor around them is dry.

Straker is crying. He can remember only one other time

when he cried as an adult, and that time has led to this. Tears pour out of his eyes, down his cheeks, and he feels their wetness, tastes their saltiness, not even attempting to wipe them away.

Speak to me, Maggie.

There's no one there. Not even Sangita, Felicity. Where have they all gone?

I'm listening, willing myself to sleep so that I can hear them, straining inside my head, longing for a voice, a faint whisper, the rustle of a movement.

Nothing.

I imagine I can hear a small voice in the background, interfering with my normal dreams, and I stop the action, call a halt in the filming, listening, listening, expecting Felicity to come into the dream. Felicity can't stop talking. She's always there.

Nothing.

What has Maggie said to them? Why are they all so obedient? What hold does she have over them, that if she doesn't speak, neither do they?

Maggie, please come back. I'll go to see Simon. I've listened to you, I've understood. I'm trying. I'm changing – I can feel it inside me. I'm doing what you want me to do. Please come back.

During the following week, he walks up the road from the village, past Doody's cottage, towards her field, where there are signs of serious activity. A mechanical digger has been brought up the pathway and left on the side of the field, presumably to redo the runway. Straker resents the people who've come here and taken over. If he meets them, he's afraid he'll be angry, threaten them, frighten them so that they'll go away.

Every day, it becomes more urgent that he talks to Maggie's husband. So, two weeks after he ran away from Doody, trying not to think too hard about it, he takes a bus to Exeter. He's never travelled on one before, but he's seen them with EXETER on the front, stopping in the village.

He steps up behind the other passengers and watches them pay. When Straker reaches the front, he waits to see what the driver will say. He sits slumped down, only half looking at Straker, and doesn't say anything.

'Exeter,' says Straker at last, struggling to breathe evenly.

'Where in Exeter?'

'The station.'

'Which station? Bus or train?'

'Train.'

'Central or St David's?'

Why are there two stations? 'I don't know.'

The driver shifts irritably in his seat. 'I'll tell you when we're at St David's. You can sort yourself out from there.'

Straker gives him the money and goes to sit down, wishing he'd never started. He looks out of the window and shuts his eyes, waiting for the sweat to dry on his face.

'Excuse me.' A small, thin woman in a pink and white tracksuit is leaning over his seat and holding something out. 'You forgot to take your ticket.' She has very big, earnest eyes.

He takes it from her and tries to smile. She doesn't react.

Once at the station, he goes to the ticket office and stands behind a queue of people who seem to be in a desperate hurry. He moves aside as each new person arrives, waiting until they've all gone, but they're never all gone. People keep coming, an endless trickle, and he steps forward to join the queue. When he reaches the window, he leans forward.

'A return ticket to Birmingham,' he says loudly, to the man behind the thick glass screen.

He's convinced that the man can't hear him, but he feels unable to shout.

'New Street or International?'

He can't go through this again. 'New Street,' he guesses.

'What day are you travelling?'

Straker looks at him blankly. He has no idea. Maybe he never will. Maybe he's only pretending.

'Well?' says the man, impatiently.

'Today,' says Straker.

'When are you returning?'

This is none of his business. Straker can hear people muttering behind him, with urgency in their voices. 'Today,' he says.

Once he has the ticket, he stands looking at it for some time. People are still arriving, rushing up the steps to other platforms. He discovers screens that show arrivals and departures, so he studies them for some time, until he sees a train to Birmingham and a platform number. The train leaves in ten minutes, and he follows a group of people up the stairs to the bridge over the platforms. On the way up he passes a young girl with two heavy suitcases, struggling to lift them up the steps.

Somebody should help her, he thinks, as he passes her. He pauses at the top to see if anyone does, but they all ignore her. He walks away. He can't force people to take notice. Half-way across the bridge, the thought comes to him. He could help. He stops. Can he do it without talking? No. He continues on the bridge, then stops again. He should offer. If she doesn't want help, she'll say so.

He goes back. She's paused half-way up to have a rest, so he walks down to her. 'Can I help?' he says.

'Oh, yes, please.' She smiles.

He has done the right thing. He bends down, picks up both her bags and climbs quickly up the stairs. The cases are heavy, but not impossible. He can hear her sandals clicking on the floor as she runs to keep up with him. 'It's very good of you,' she says breathlessly. 'I always mean to take less, but somehow it just mounts up, doesn't it.'

He can't think of a suitable response.

'The others'll laugh at me when I meet them, because I always take too much.'

She doesn't look old enough to be travelling on her own.

Once they reach the platform, he stops, realising that he didn't know which platform she wanted. He turns to her, ready to ask, but she seems satisfied, so he must have guessed correctly. 'Thanks ever so much,' she says. She's pretty as well as young. He feels her examining his face, and a hot flush spreads through his cheeks. Her expression seems to change. She pretends to keep smiling, but it's not the same.

'Oh, look,' she says, 'there's Jamie. Thanks awfully.'

And she's gone.

What did she see in his face? Is it possible to tell that he's a mass murderer? Does he have '78' written between his eyes?

———

When the inquest ended with an open verdict because of insufficient evidence to bring a prosecution, Pete's father was jubilant. He hustled Pete past the waiting hordes of press. 'Gangway!' he yelled, as if they were standing in a market and he was pushing a trolley into people's backs. For some reason, they parted to let them through.

A man pulled Pete's arm and stopped him. He was a small man with very greasy shoulder-length hair and thick-rimmed, dark glasses. 'Pete,' he said into his ear, and Pete stopped at the familiarity of his tone. Did he know him? 'What are you going to do now?'

Pete stared at him. Who was he? Was he asking him to go out for a drink with him? He tried to think if he had met him before. His father pulled his arm. 'Come on, Pete,' he said. 'What are you messing about for?'

'Fifteen grand,' the man said, speaking fast. 'Think about it.'

Pete didn't know what he was talking about. The man

reached up and put a card into his top pocket. 'Ring me,' he said.

There were voices all round, people shouting Pete's name, the flashes of endless cameras. He lost his bearings. He didn't know which way to go. His lawyer had disappeared completely. He was supposed to be making a statement on Pete's behalf, but Pete didn't know how he would manage it with this terrible noise around them. He stood and tried to make some sense out of all the heads, the voices, the garbled words that came flying through the air at him, but nothing connected. It had the surreal atmosphere of a nightmare where everyone was talking in a foreign language. They could all understand each other, but not Pete, even though he had something important to say.

'Pete!' He heard his father's voice, and there he was again. 'Over here.' His arm grabbed Pete and pulled him forwards. They arrived at a car and he shoved him in. He tried to force the door shut, but they drove away with it still slightly open, a man's face leering in at them through the window, the almost human face of his camera pointing at Pete.

'Get down,' said his father, pushing his head on to his knees just as a click set off a blinding explosion of light. They drove away, slowly at first and then faster, leaving the roar of the crowd behind them, a forced calm settling over all of them in the car, as if they'd just escaped from a war zone.

There were more reporters at the entrance to Pete's parents' house, but his father had guards at the bottom of the drive by the electronic gates. Ian, whom he had known for years, stood there in his uniform and pressed the button to open the gates, while Neil stood in front of the other vehicles, preventing them following. They glided through and Ian shut the gates again immediately. Pete looked into the mirror and could see them standing in front of the closing gate with their arms crossed, twice as big as any other man he had ever met, except his father, obviously getting enormous pleasure out of the confrontation.

Pete hadn't wanted to go back to his parents' house again. He thought it would have been better to go home, to his bachelor house, the place where he did as he pleased – played records, watched TV, drank and drank and drank. But he had no choice. His father was directing operations. Pete's preferences were irrelevant.

When they entered the front door, Pete thought his mother might be there, waiting for them, worried about the outcome of the inquest. But she wasn't. In all the time Pete was in the house after the inquest, he never saw her. He didn't even know if she was there at all. She might have been in one of the twelve bedrooms on the first floor, or the attic rooms. Maybe she stayed in her room the whole time, watching the garden through the window, measuring the height of the roses in her mind, seeing the grass grow, the buds forming on the late marigolds. Maybe someone took her meals up on a tray. There were plenty of people working around the house. Pete didn't recognise most of them. He didn't ask about her, and his father didn't volunteer any information.

Pete stayed indoors for about three weeks. There were always reporters at the gate. Most of them left after a few days, but one or two remained, apparently convinced that patience would reward them. He didn't know what to do with himself. He prowled round the house, looking at the people by the gate, wondering what would happen next. He seemed to be surrounded by a fog of unreality that he couldn't shake off. He slept very deeply every night and woke late in the morning, his head thick and heavy. He spent long periods sitting and doing nothing, finding it almost impossible to rouse himself to go to meals. He tried watching television, but couldn't take it in. How could he be interested in people wandering around on a screen pretending that they were going through crises? What did they know about disaster? Time moved slowly, slowly, plodding with heavy feet, refusing to rush.

Then one day his father came to find him when he was sitting in the library pretending to read a magazine about boats.

'Pete,' he said, without any preliminaries, 'I've found you somewhere to go.'

'What do you mean, go?'

'Well, you can't stay here for the rest of your life.'

Why not? 'I'll go home, then.'

His father shook his head and looked at him with a glance that he presumably thought was wise. Pete had seen it many times before when his father was right and Pete was wrong. 'No good, son. They'll never leave you alone. I've put the house on the market.'

Pete thought that he should be annoyed, but couldn't manage any emotion. Did his father have the right to do this? He'd paid for it, but given it to Pete as a present. 'How much for?'

His father put back his head and laughed, a great booming, tycoon laugh. 'That's my son,' he said. Pete didn't believe in the laughter. He could see that it was unreal. Always had been. He watched his father from his new perspective and thought what an unpleasant character he was.

'I've bought you a lighthouse,' he said.

Pete stared at him. 'A lighthouse?' He couldn't understand what he was talking about.

'Yes, Pete, a lighthouse. You can go there in disguise, give yourself an alias, and nobody will know who you are.'

'Why?'

'Why do you think?'

He had no idea. 'You want to get rid of me.'

His father laughed again, loudly, and Pete could see that that was exactly why he wanted him to go. 'Of course not, Pete. But we can't all go on living like this, under siege, afraid to go out in case they molest us, or follow us. You have to think of me and your mother.'

'Why?'

He didn't manage such a confident laugh this time. 'I'm a businessman. I have work to go to. If you stay here, we can't get on with anything.'

Shame about me, thought Pete. Shame about all those dead people.

'It's a decommissioned lighthouse. North coast of Devon. Grow a beard, take a different name, they'll never recognise you.'

'How do you get food in lighthouses?'

'Oh, it's not one of those sort. It's on land. Just a bit remote, really. Long way from people. Just the kind of thing you need. You'll like it there.'

How did he know what Pete would like? What did he know about his son? Pete looked at him, and saw that he was just a man. Taller and wider than most people, but still just a man. Not even worth hating. Why had Pete always been afraid of him? 'All right,' he said.

They smuggled Pete out in the back of a small delivery van, covered with a blanket, pretending he didn't exist. They changed cars twice, stopping in strange out-of-the-way places where the next car was waiting for them with the engine running, until they eventually reached the M5 in a BMW. It all seemed a bit melodramatic – there weren't men out there waiting to abduct him, or murder him – but his father obviously enjoyed the cinema-like way of doing things. It made him believe in himself and his importance. They didn't talk at all, until they were on the final stretch and needed to consult the map. His father was a bit put out by the last mile when they had to leave the road. He must have expected them to put down Tarmac once they knew he was coming.

When they arrived, he turned off the engine. They sat in the car and looked at the lighthouse. It towered above them, red and white stripes gleaming, the green canopy at the top ornate and somehow mystical. Inside the car, they could feel the force of the wind, buffeting the windscreen, exposing the sharp edges of the grass. Pete got out of the car and looked up. He felt dwarfed by its height, and excited by its bleakness.

His father got out too. He gestured to a keeper's cottage. 'You can live in there,' he said. 'There's some basic furniture.' Pete didn't want him to come in with him and his father didn't suggest it.

He held out his hand and gave Pete a set of keys. Pete removed from the boot his small, nearly empty case – he hadn't been able to think what he needed for his exile. He just wanted to forget he had ever existed in any other life. His father unloaded four bags of groceries from Fortnum and Mason.

'Just something to keep you going for a bit,' he muttered. He waved his hand vaguely in the direction of the nearest village. 'You can do your shopping over there. There's a new Sainsbury's. It's a long way, but it'll give you something to do. I've made out a standing order – should be enough to live on. If you need anything let me know. Money no object, of course.'

Of course. Money solves everything.

He stood in front of Pete. 'Well, son . . .' Pete looked at him. He wasn't going to help him. 'You'll be OK. Just give it time. They'll all forget in the end. These things have a habit of dying down eventually.' His manner was hesitant. He didn't seem to know what to say.

He was useless once you took away the outer layer. There was nothing underneath. A blank. A non-person. As Pete stood there, watching him, he saw him shrink. This man, who had been such a huge influence in Pete's life, had been caught out, wrongfooted by his son's behaviour. Money hadn't solved the problem, and he didn't know what else to use. His resources had dried up.

'Well, son . . .' he said again. He leaned towards his son and, for one terrible moment, Pete thought he was going to hug him. But he stopped just in time. 'Goodbye,' he said, and held out his hand.

They shook hands as if they were strangers who had only just met, and then he got into the car. Pete stood outside the lighthouse with his small suitcase and the Fortnum and Mason food and watched his father's car bouncing back to the road. He hasn't seen or heard from him since.

Straker sits on the train and watches the scenery passing. His father hadn't approved of public transport. 'Dirty,' he would say. 'If you don't have to share with the rest of the world, then don't. That's what money buys you.'

Straker has not thought of his parents properly for twenty-four years, but finds that a new space has opened up inside his mind. Tentatively, he explores this unexpected pathway, unwilling to experiment very far, conscious that any wrong move will result in a jolt of pain. Did his father intend never to speak to him again? Had he expected twenty-four years to pass without any contact? Has he forgotten his son altogether, or have the years just passed by mistake? Does his mother ever think of him? Are they even still alive?

Opposite Straker, there's a young mother with two children. She is reading to them from a book called *Mrs Pepperpot*. The little boy sits nestled on her lap, dozing off while she reads. The girl, who is older, is leaning against her, studying the pictures. On the other side of the gangway, there is a man reading a newspaper, his legs crossed so that one sways out into the aisle, and two middle-aged women, who are playing Scrabble on a tiny board where the pieces slot into little holes. They are talking about a wedding.

'Lovely flowers,' says one.

'Didn't like the bridesmaids' dresses, though. Salmon pink doesn't suit everyone. How about that? EXPORT – triple word score. Excellent.'

'Seventeen times three. Fifty-one points. Well done. I thought Sally was lovely in the pink . . .'

Three young men in pin-striped suits lurch up the aisle towards the buffet car.

All trains must look like this. If there was a crash, these people would die. They would become Maggie, Sangita, Mike . . . He examines all the people around him and tries to imagine them dead. Would they then become more real? Would they take on a life in his head like all the others? Should dead people become more real than live ones?

When Straker reaches Birmingham, he looks for a news-agent and buys an A–Z. He gets caught in a hustling, driving mass of people and follows them along until he comes out into daylight. Finding a corner away from shop entrances, he examines the map.

Simon A. Taverner apparently lives not far from the city centre. If Straker can get the direction right, and cross the big traffic systems, it must be only about two miles to the flat. He'd intended to take a taxi, but he walks that far every day.

He stands and stares up at the block of flats. They look expensive and difficult to penetrate. Perhaps they have security men, or a caretaker. There's a row of bells with names beside them. Should he ring and say, 'Let me in, I'm the man who murdered your wife'? That's what Maggie suggested. It doesn't seem an ideal introduction. But, then, what is?

While he stands there, a woman approaches, carrying bags from Safeway. She puts the shopping down and punches out a series of numbers on the dial to the side of the door. Straker watches her and memorises the pattern. Looking ahead, im-patient for the door to open, she doesn't see him. She picks up her shopping and pushes through the unlocked door, disap-pearing inside.

He goes up to the panel and reproduces the pattern of her

numbers. C3562X. Easy to memorise. Three and two on the outside. Add them for five, then multiply for six. The door doesn't make any sound, but when he pushes, it opens immediately. He goes in and lets it lock behind him.

Inside, there are two lifts, one for even-numbered floors, the other for odd. The hall is carpeted, and dark. Not quite as luxurious as promised from outside.

He takes the lift to the sixth floor, but twenty-two is on the one below. He finds the stairs, walks down, and stands in front of number twenty-two, then waits for a very long time, not sure how to proceed. Several times, he turns to go away, but doesn't quite lift up his feet to do it. Why is he here?

Then, abruptly, not allowing himself to think about it, he puts up his hand and rings the doorbell. He can hear it chiming inside.

Nothing happens and he starts to breathe again. He can't talk to a man who's not in. He's about to walk away, when he realises that if he doesn't talk to Maggie's husband now, he will have to repeat the same journey another day. The thought of returning is exhausting, so he puts up his hand and rings the bell again.

This time he can hear something, a shuffling, a muttering, a clinking of keys and the door opens slightly. It is restricted by a chain. Straker can just see the face of an elderly man with grey eyes and a florid complexion. 'Yes?' he says.

'Mr Taverner?'

'Yes.'

'Mr Simon Taverner?'

'Yes?' He opens the door a little wider. He has a friendly face, the face of a man who has lived a long time, and is not afraid of what might confront him on his doorstep.

Straker likes the look of him – he's a comfortable man. 'My name is Peter Straker.'

Taverner freezes visibly with shock. He doesn't speak for some time, conflicting emotions drifting across his face. He studies Straker intently, his frank gaze penetrating and painful.

Finally, he relaxes and produces a half-smile. 'I see,' he says, taking the chain off the door and opening it properly. 'You'd better come in.'

Chapter 20

Steve sat in the aeroplane, unable to believe that this was really happening. Pete occupied the seat next to him, handling the controls as calmly as if he were driving a car. Justin and Francis shared the back seat and stared out of the windows nonchalantly, unaware of the excitement that was bubbling away inside Steve's chest. He had known them for less than a day, and here he was, in a private aircraft, joy-riding in a far more sophisticated way than any of his mates at school had experienced. Their talk of stolen Minis suddenly seemed rather childish.

So much had happened in the last two days that he felt breathless. One minute, there he was with his mum, who used to be OK, and his stepfather, Roger, who was never OK. Things had not been right since Roger had burst into their house, propping up his golf clubs against the fish tank in the kitchen, leaving his racing bike in the hall for everyone to fall over. Rugby or football on television whenever possible.

'Why don't you come cycling with me one of these days?' said Roger, almost every night. 'You'd be surprised how good it can make you feel.'

'The only thing that would make me feel g-g-good would be getting my house b-b-back to myself,' said Steve, deliberately knocking over Roger's fresh orange juice.

'Oops,' said Roger, fetching a cloth. 'I can understand how you feel,' he said gently, mopping up the juice.

You're only pretending, Steve wanted to shout. Your niceness isn't real. But he said nothing and walked out of the kitchen without finishing his breakfast.

Everything had changed since the wedding six months ago. Steve had watched his mum become distracted, lose her softness and, at the same time, throw herself at Roger, ready to do anything to please him. Steve couldn't understand it. She no longer seemed like his mum.

'Please be back by six for supper, Stevie. Roger likes us to eat together as a family.'

Family? Not in a million years.

'Just going for a drink, Stevie,' his mum had called up the stairs two days ago. 'Back in an hour.' More like a hundred drinks, thought Steve, more like four hours. He hated them drinking. Roger didn't change much – if anything, his voice softened, and he became even more caring. But his mum changed. She alternated between laughing wildly and singing. Steve couldn't bear the sound of her voice when she was like that. He had to fight an overwhelming urge to slap her face, to force out the wild looseness that took her over.

They returned late, talking at high speed. He could hear them coming through the front door, his mum giggling and Roger shushing her. The crash as she walked into Roger's bike. He saw the light come on in the hall.

'Come on, Barbara,' he heard Roger say. 'Let's go into the kitchen. We don't want to wake up Steve.'

Why should you care? thought Steve.

He lay for a while, looking at the light from the hall reflected on his ceiling. I have to go to school tomorrow, he thought. Why didn't his mum think of his needs any more? It hadn't been like this when Dad was home. Their house was like everyone else's then, his mum quiet and in during the evenings, chatting to him before he went to bed.

A shout of laughter came from the kitchen, quickly suppressed. Why did she laugh so much now? Roger seemed to have some strange power over her. He could make her perform to satisfy his own desires, change her personality and transform her into this drunken, hysterical woman.

Another crash came from the kitchen and more laughter. The golf clubs this time.

Steve swung his legs out of bed. He wasn't going to stand for this any longer. He went downstairs and threw open the kitchen door. 'D-d-do you know what t-t-time it is?' he said, making his voice as deep as possible. Then he stopped.

Roger was backed up against the fridge-freezer and his mum was leaning against him, her blouse undone and her skirt discarded on the floor behind them. She was wearing stockings and suspenders, her plump legs bulging out over the top of the stockings. She looked ridiculous.

They both turned to him, their faces rigid with disbelief. Then, slowly, Roger eased himself out and straightened his clothes, picking up the skirt from the floor in one smooth movement and handing it to Steve's mum.

'Steve,' he said, in the friendly voice Steve hated, 'is everything all right?'

Steve tried to speak, but when he moved his mouth, nothing came out. He seemed to have lost all his saliva.

His mum stepped into her skirt, but made no attempt to be pleasant. 'How dare you?' she said slowly, as she struggled to pull up the zip, her voice low and icy.

'Barbara . . .' said Roger, laying a restraining hand on her arm.

But she took no notice. 'Don't I have any privacy in my own house? As if it isn't bad enough to come home and have you scowling at me all the time, disapproving of everything I say or do, being rude to the man I chose to marry. This is my house, too, you know. Go straight back to bed, Steven, and don't let me see you again until the morning.'

Steve stared at her, unable to think. It was as if his mother had turned into another person, talking in a foreign language. She used to be nice to him. He looked at Roger, who grinned half-heartedly.

'We'll talk in the morning,' he said. 'It's all a bit late now.'

Steve turned and left the kitchen.

But at the bottom of the stairs, he changed his mind and stopped. He groped for his shoes under the hall table and pulled them on. Then he grabbed a coat, and walked out into the night, shutting the door behind him.

Half an hour later, he wished he hadn't been quite so hasty. It was very cold in his pyjamas, even with a coat over the top. There must be places you can go, he thought, if you can't live at home. But he had no idea where. He went round to the back gardens and found a neighbour's shed that wasn't locked. He huddled down under a shelf of seedlings and curled himself up tightly for warmth, then dozed, waking with a sudden jump every now and again.

Six hours later, when his mum and Roger had left for work, he broke the window of the downstairs loo and crept indoors. It occurred to him that he needn't have spent the night outside, because they would have assumed he was still in bed and left him there. They wouldn't want an argument before work. Moving swiftly round the house, he packed some clothes, took as much food as he could carry and stole twenty pounds, sixty-seven pence – Roger's beer money, which he kept in a butter dish at the back of the fridge. Then he walked away, believing he would never return.

He met Justin and Francis and Pete outside a nightclub, at the end of a long, frightening day. He'd been walking past, nervous, panicky, wondering where he would sleep, but was diverted by the music blasting out on to the pavement. It was the Village People – 'YMCA' – a single that he'd played over and over on the record-player in his bedroom. He was suddenly overwhelmed by a desire to go home. The three men got out of a taxi. Two of them looked drunk, unsteady on their feet, loose-limbed and disjointed. The third stood slightly apart, remote, somehow unconnected with the others. One of the drunken men swayed towards Steve and almost knocked him over.

'Get out of the way,' he said.

Steve stepped back, scared by the attention that was being paid to him, but someone was right behind him and he trod on his foot. He turned round, terrified, and found himself facing the second man, who leered at him, breathing alcoholic fumes directly into his face. He leaned forward and was sick all over Steve.

'Now look what you've made me do,' he said, shaking his head with confusion.

The third man came up to them and sighed heavily. 'Justin, you're disgusting,' he said, pulling him out of the way. Steve avoided his eyes. He tried to work out his chances of dodging round all three men and running.

'I'm Pete. Who are you?' Steve brought his eyes back round and stared up into the man's very blue eyes, which were fixed on him steadily.

'S-S-S-Steve.'

'OK, Steve. We'd better get you cleaned up. Come with me.' He led the way to the door of the nightclub and then stopped. 'How old are you?'

Steve knew he had to be careful. 'F-f-f – eighteen.'

Pete roared with laughter, longer than seemed necessary, as if he didn't know how to stop. 'OK, eighteen-year-old Steve. Follow me.' He guided Steve in front of him, but at arm's length. The bouncers nodded at Pete with respect, but stepped back with disgust as Steve went past them.

'Phew!' said one, waving the air in front of his nose.

'Hope you know what you're doing, Pete,' said the other.

'Thanks, lads,' said Pete, and Steve saw him hand over a twenty-pound note.

Pete's friends followed them in and he led them to the toilets. 'Come on, Steve, we'll have to do the best we can to clean you up.'

He directed Steve to the basins and gave him a handful of paper towels. 'You too, Justin,' he said to the third man. 'Otherwise we'll never get a cab home.'

Steve tried to clean himself by wetting the towels and wiping them over his coat.

'Look,' said Pete to Steve, 'let's get a taxi. I'll pay the fare. Then you can get your mum to wash these disgusting clothes.'

Steve tried to imagine his mum's face when he arrived. All he could see was her bare flesh bulging over those stockings. He could still hear her talking to him very slowly and nastily. He wanted to cry. 'No,' he said. 'It's all right.'

Pete seemed annoyed. 'She'll be wondering where you are.'

'I don't think so,' said Steve.

Pete hesitated. 'OK,' he said. 'Let's go back to my place. We're having a party. You can have a bath there. Call us a cab, Francis.'

'Right,' said Francis, and disappeared.

The taxi driver didn't want to take them, but Pete seemed to have so much money stuffed into his wallet that he eventually agreed. He drove fast and carelessly. Nobody in the taxi spoke.

Pete's house was amazing. It was carpeted throughout in white, with black walls, and there were life-sized Disney characters everywhere he looked. Mickey Mouse by the front door, Bambi hanging from a chandelier, Pinocchio on the landing half-way up the stairs. The ceilings were tiled with mirrors. In the bathroom, the mirrors were on every surface, including the floor. Steve stood in the middle and saw hundreds of images of himself reflecting each other back, all soiled with sick, all stinking. Shere Khan looked at him disapprovingly from the end of the bath.

Pete turned the taps on. 'Help yourself,' he said, and wandered off, shutting the door behind him.

Steve stepped into the enormous bath, and lay back. The hot water was wonderful after his day on the streets, and he let it soak into his skin, feeling his whole body relax. He nearly dozed, but jerked awake when he remembered where he was. He wondered if his mum was feeling guilty. Let her, he thought. After a while, he climbed out and wrapped himself in a fluffy black towel. He didn't think he should put his clothes back on, so he went to find Pete. He found the three men lounging on sofas in front of a huge television screen, surrounded by empty beer cans, laughing at *Fawlty Towers*. Two women were squashed together on one sofa with Grumpy the dwarf and Cinderella.

Pete was gazing up at the ceiling, his eyes unfocused, not laughing with the others. Steve froze for a moment when he saw him, shocked by the bleakness of his expression. It was as if he was not really there, unaware of what was going on around him. Then he turned and saw Steve, his face slipping back into amiability. 'Hi,' he said. 'Have a drink.'

'Um . . .' said Steve. 'I haven't got any clothes.'

Pete nodded. 'Down the corridor, third door on the right. Help yourself.'

Steve found a room whose sole purpose was to store clothes – rows of shirts, suits, shoes, socks, underwear, jumpers, T-shirts. It was like walking into a shop where you didn't have to pay. Winnie-the-Pooh smiled at him from the side of the door. After much indecision, Steve chose a yellow T-shirt and some beige trousers. They were a bit big for him, but he found a belt, which held them up. He went back to the living room and sat down behind the others, trying to make sense of what was happening.

'What's your name?' asked one of the women, who was wearing a long, green dress that shimmered as she moved.

Steve opened his mouth.

'He's called Steve,' said Pete, without turning his head.

She smiled at Steve. 'My name's Ellen, sweetheart,' she said. 'Would you like something to eat? Some popcorn?'

She thinks I'm a kid, he thought. He couldn't take his eyes off her.

She looked over his head at Pete. 'How old is he?'

Pete shrugged. 'Says he's eighteen.'

She studied Steve's face and he had to turn away. He could feel her closeness, smell her perfume, a female smell that both alarmed and excited him. 'He's having you on. You're not eighteen, are you, Steve?'

Steve couldn't respond. He sat and studied the floor.

Pete answered for him again: 'Leave him alone. He's all right. Reminds me of myself at his age. He's older than he looks, I expect.'

Ellen withdrew from Steve and went to whisper to Pete. Steve could just hear their conversation.

'Pete – he's under age.'

'So?'

'We might be accused of kidnapping him.'

Pete's voice rose indignantly then fell again. 'He wanted to come. I gave him a choice.'

'What about his family? They must be wondering where he is.'

'No – there's something wrong there. He doesn't want to go home.'

'I think you should take him anyway.'

'No way. I like him. He can stay with us tonight. We'll take him home tomorrow – have a look at the family.'

'You're crazy.'

He drained his bottle of beer. 'Probably.'

Steve breathed a sigh of relief and settled back into a chair. He needn't worry until tomorrow now. Feeling very daring, he opened a can of lager. The smell was unpleasantly familiar, reminding him of his mother's recent behaviour, but he couldn't feel anything strange happening to him as he sipped it. Everything seemed normal.

The party seemed to go on all night, but they all succumbed to sleep in the end, sprawled around the room. Steve kept his eyes on Pete and Ellen, in case she decided to send him away.

Pete finally stretched out on his back on a sofa, breathing heavily through his mouth. His eyes stayed open, but he didn't move, so Steve curled up on the floor by his feet and slept.

The confusing thing about the whole situation was that nobody seemed to care whether Steve was there or not. Ellen cooked breakfast for them all at about twelve o'clock in the morning. She stood over the stove, still in her long green dress, breaking eggs into a frying-pan, with the air of someone who did this every day of her life. 'Scrambled eggs?' she said to Steve, who was extremely hungry.

'Yes, please,' he said.

She gave him an approving smile. 'Polite boy,' she said, and went off to mix up the eggs.

They sat round a vast marble table in the kitchen to eat. Cereals, orange juice, coffee, scrambled eggs, toast, fruit – there was an abundant supply of food. Pete didn't eat anything. He lounged over the table with bleary eyes, his face grey and exhausted. He looked as if he hadn't slept. Steve kept an eye on him, ready to follow if he left.

'Let's go flying this afternoon,' said Pete, as he finished a mug of coffee.

'Can we come?' said Mel, the other woman.

'Why not? Let's all go while we've still got the chance.' He thought for a moment. 'Oh, sorry. You can't all come. I've only got four seats.'

'You can't go anyway,' said Ellen to Mel. 'We're going shopping. Remember?'

Mel screwed up her face. 'I want to go flying.'

'There's always tomorrow,' said Ellen. 'And we'll have to go home to get changed.'

Justin chuckled. 'Just us, then. The three of us.'

Francis grinned at the girls. 'You can wait here. Have the dinner on, the wine opened, the beds warmed.'

'Forget it,' said Mel, tapping his nose with a spoon.

Steve watched, waiting for them to decide to take him home.

Pete turned to him. 'You can come, Steve. Ever been flying before?'

'No,' said Steve. He couldn't even pretend about this.

'I thought we were taking him home,' said Ellen.

Pete looked irritable. 'After,' he said, picking up the phone and dialling. 'Hi, Dean,' he said. 'Pete here. I want to take the Warrior up this afternoon. Could you wheel it out for me? Great, thanks.' He put the phone down and picked it up again. He dialled, listened and replaced the receiver. 'Weather's good all day,' he said. 'Let's go. Can you drive, Justin?'

'Where's your car?' asked Francis.

Pete frowned at him. 'It's out of action.'

'What do you mean? It was fine yesterday.'

'Well, it isn't now.'

'Do you want me to look at it?' said Justin. 'I'm good with cars. Ask my dad.'

'Just leave it, will you?' said Pete, his voice hard and dismissive as he walked out of the room.

It was half-way through the afternoon by the time they set off in Justin's Aston Martin. Francis waved to the women through the open window. 'Back later,' he said, blowing them a kiss.

'We may not be here,' said Mel.

They had cans of beer with them and everyone was drinking freely. Steve drank too, and wondered what had made him think that drink was a bad thing. There was a light, unreal sensation about everything, as if he were living a dream, but he felt exhilarated and careless of consequences. He was so far from the memory of Roger and his mother that they might never have existed. He watched Pete's every move, but it wasn't necessary. Pete seemed to have adopted him and made sure he was close by him all the time.

'I'm like you,' Pete said quietly, in the back of the car. 'Shy. You have to pretend – nobody else notices.'

Steve couldn't make sense of this. Pete behaved with such certainty, such confidence. He didn't seem shy at all.

It was five o'clock when they arrived at the airfield. The aircraft was out and waiting for them.

'It's a Piper Warrior,' said Pete to Steve, as they walked round it. 'We need to check it over before we go up.'

'What for?'

'Anything. Could have been knocked by another aircraft in the hangar – bashed something on the way out.' He fingered the lights, and the edges of the wings, running his fingers over surfaces. 'OK,' he said eventually.

He led the way into the aircraft, stepping on to the back of the wing, then opening a door in the side. He eased himself into the seat on the left, in front of the controls, and gestured to the place next to him. 'Sit there, Steve.'

Steve hesitated, seeing a steering column in front of him and foot pedals. He looked at Justin and Francis worriedly as they settled themselves on the back seat.

'Oh, don't bother about them. They've been up thousands of times. They're out of it. Come on, I'll show you how it all works.'

Steve slipped into the seat, noting with relief that most of the dials were only in front of Pete. It didn't look as if he would need to do anything.

'Seatbelts,' said Pete. He put on a set of headphones and flicked a switch. 'Request taxi clearance for a VFR flight to the south,' he said clearly.

'Roger, Golf Bravo Romeo.' The voice made Steve jump. 'You're cleared to taxi to holding point of runway one eight.'

Everyone was quiet while Pete continued his conversation with the control tower and they taxied to the edge of a runway. Steve watched Pete's movements, listened to all the words, impressed by his knowledge and authority. He seemed more alert, no longer so tired.

They stopped at the end of the runway while Pete pressed

several switches. The engine revved up dramatically, and the cabin started to judder as if they were taking off, but they remained stationary. Then it all died down.

Pete turned to Steve. 'Power check,' he explained. He spoke into the radio. 'Golf Bravo Romeo ready for departure.' His voice was serious.

'Roger, Golf Bravo Romeo. You're cleared to line up and take off. Surface wind one seven zero degrees, ten knots.'

Pete pressed more switches, moved his feet, and the engine noise increased. They started to move along the runway, slowly at first, then faster, louder. Steve held his breath as Pete pulled back on the control column and they lifted smoothly into the air. The column in front of him moved with Pete's. They kept on climbing in a straight line until they levelled off. Pete sat back and undid his seatbelt. 'Pass me a beer, Justin,' he said.

Justin chucked one over and he caught it neatly. He flipped the catch and drank the whole can in one go. He laughed, but the sound was brittle and forced. 'Just what I needed,' he said. 'Chuck me another one. Look, Steve.' He pointed at one of the dials. 'That's the artificial horizon.'

Steve could see the straight line across the dial, looking exactly like the division between earth and sky.

'Watch this.' Pete turned the control column to the left and the aeroplane banked slightly. The artificial horizon began to slip to the left. Then he brought it back to the level. He pointed to each dial in turn and explained its function. Steve heard the words, let them flow around him, and appreciated the fact that Pete was talking to him. It didn't matter that he couldn't follow it all.

'Where shall we go?' said Pete, after a while.

'France,' said Justin.

'Italy,' said Francis.

'Not likely,' said Pete. 'My dad hasn't got over Austria yet. Where do you want to go, Steve?'

Steve was thrilled to be asked, but had no idea what to say. 'I d-d-don't know,' he said. He couldn't believe they were in the air, flying without knowing where they were going. The world below him looked like a model village – tiny dolls' houses, fields divided up geometrically with plastic hedges.

Pete kept laughing, his voice growing louder after each drink, and Steve found that he could watch Pete getting drunk and not mind.

'There's a train,' said Francis, pointing.

They all looked down and could see the lights of a train snaking across the evening landscape. It was approaching a raised embankment that would lead it over a bridge in the distance.

'I bet you . . .' said Justin slowly.

'Yes?' said Pete, swilling beer out of his can.

'See those pylons?' There was a row of pylons running parallel to the train line in the field below the embankment, a Lego housing estate on the other side.

'Yes?'

'Bet you can't get under the cables and over the railway line before the train gets there.'

'How much do you bet?' said Pete.

'Hundred quid,' said Justin.

'Two hundred,' said Pete. 'Get your money ready.'

'Another two hundred from me,' said Francis.

'Done,' said Pete. 'Let's give the driver a thrill.'

'It'll scare him to death if we shoot up over the side of the track just before he gets there.'

'Hope he can handle it.'

'Course he can,' said Francis. 'He's a train driver, a skilled professional, years of specialised training. He'll have logged hours and hours—'

They all roared with laughter.

'OK,' said Pete. 'Let's go down there.'

Steve could feel a tightness in his stomach. Surely they didn't really mean it? It didn't look possible. They'd have to go incredibly low to get under the overhead lines, then come up very fast on the other side to clear the embankment and the railway line before the train reached that point. He had never been in a situation like this before. He was a boy who believed in rules – a law-abiding citizen. What would his mum think of all this?

The tightness inside him was tying itself into a tangled knot, but as he watched the intense concentration on Pete's face, he relaxed a little. Pete knew what he was doing – he could be trusted to make the right decision.

Pete pushed the stick forward and they started diving rapidly, the sound of the wind louder than the sound of the engine. Steve was exhilarated by the speed, his caution evaporating with the thrill of it all. 'Hoorah!' he shouted, hearing his voice disappearing behind him.

They went between the pylons, under the wire, almost scraping the ground, then Pete pulled the stick back hard and they were climbing very steeply, losing speed as the engine roared on full power. They were pushed back into their seats with the force of the climb. Steve held his breath, willing the Warrior upwards, his mind straining with the effort.

The embankment was in front of them, getting closer and closer. Where was the top? Surely they must be there.

They burst over the peak of the embankment with a great throaty roar from the engine.

'Bravo!' shouted Francis from the back.

Then, unexpectedly, they swung to one side, and there was a sharp crack.

'Look out!' yelled Justin.

The world turned upside down. There was a sound of splintering, fracturing, metal screaming, everyone shouting at once. Steve was thrown violently to his left, then to his right.

We'll be all right, he thought. Pete's looking after us.

He was hit by a searing pain as they stopped moving, a

suffocating pressure above him. He could hear Pete's voice in the distance. 'Get out! Get out!'

The thunder of the approaching train drowned all other sounds.

Chapter 21

'Mother? It's Imogen. Jonathan said you wanted me to phone.'

'Did he? How strange. Perhaps I just wanted to know if you're all right. I can't afford to phone you very often with my limited income.'

'My job isn't well paid either, you know.'

'No? Well, I'm sure it's more than my pension.' There is satisfaction in her voice because she likes to be worse off than everyone else. It makes her feel better.

'So, how are you?'

'Bearing up. You remember that pain I had in my hip?'

No. 'Yes.'

'The doctor thinks it could be arthritis. He might send me for tests.'

Doody doesn't believe her. The doctor must be wise to her by now. She's had tests for heart disease, lupus, MS, ME and osteoporosis in the last year. 'Well, never mind. I expect it'll clear up soon.'

'What do you mean by that?'

Doody experiences an unexpected pang of sympathy for her mother. She's lonely, and needs her illnesses. They're just a familiar fantasy world that she can control. The trips to the doctor give her something to do, and her pills are comforting. 'Nothing, Mother. Let's hope it's not too serious.'

'Yes, because—'

'Have you heard about my cottage yet?'

She brightens up at the prospect of good news. 'Yes, Jonathan told me. How wonderful. A cottage by the sea.'

'It's not that wonderful. It needs a lot of work.'

'Oh, I'm sure you'll manage. You're very capable.'

'Mother, it's more than just painting a few doors. It's major work. Roof and windows and things.'

But she doesn't want to hear this. 'And it's all thanks to Jonathan.'

But it's Doody's cottage, her aeroplane, her life. She doesn't want to be grateful to Jonathan. 'I'll have to go, Mother. Mr Hollyhead is waiting for me to discuss a hole in the fence.'

'Yes, of course. You mustn't keep your headmaster waiting.'

It's hard to know what irritates Doody most. Her mother remembering who Mr Hollyhead is, calling him her head-master, or thinking Doody shouldn't keep him waiting.

'Goodbye, Mother,' says Doody, and puts the phone down.

She shouldn't have phoned before settling down to work on the Mandles novel. Now, instead of thinking calmly, she is humming with frustration, itching with resentment of Jonathan, her mother and Philip Hollyhead.

She's worried about Mandles. The story is slowing down, losing its momentum. Something needs to happen, a dramatic development that will bring back some of the sparkle she felt when she started writing.

Determined to solve the problem, she picks up a pencil.

Mandles froze as he felt a cold barrel placed carefully at the back of his neck. A gun! 'Good afternoon,' remarked a cool, level voice that he had never heard before. 'Welcome to our little party.' Rough hands came from behind Mandles and tied his hands tightly behind his back. A wad of material was shoved into his mouth and a scarf was fixed uncomfortably round his face in a vice-like grip.

This is better. Some real action.

'*You got it wrong, Imogen.*'

All week she has been pushing away thoughts of Harry. He seems to be hovering at her shoulder, whispering into her ear.

'You did walk out on me,' she says out loud.

He laughs. '*But you can't be sure.*'

There's the problem. She can't be sure. She has always believed that he left voluntarily because he didn't want to live with her any more, and the leitmotif of rejection has been drumming away in the background ever since.

If he was on the train, killed off by Straker, everything changes. The world has been picked up, twisted slightly and put down again. The same, but not the same. She has mis-judged him, found him guilty in his absence.

'You left me. There's no question about that. The crash was later.'

'*But I might have come back.*' His voice is cool and level, mocking her.

He shouldn't be here. He doesn't know anything about her life and has no right to challenge her like this. He's somewhere else, in a large house in the suburbs, making money, being a doctor, living the middle-class life he was destined for. He's married to someone who doesn't know he's a bigamist, and has four children at private schools.

Or he's dead.

Doody jumps up and puts on her coat. She can see Doris the Lion Tamer out in her garden, taking in the washing, so she doubles round the front of the house to avoid her and walks down the road to the shops.

Her mind slips sideways to Straker, who may have killed her husband. Why does he refuse to believe the crash was an accident? Does he enjoy being responsible, or does he just feel better saying it was his fault? He wants to be a martyr, like her mother. How can one person cause the death of seventy-eight people? It seems almost self-indulgent of him to insist on it. If he can't remember what happened, why does he insist on blaming himself?

We're all guilty, thinks Doody, half running along the road. She had mashed the berries. She had wanted Celia to die. Perhaps she could have saved her if she'd done something quicker.

Her mother had implied that once. 'Did you phone the ambulance as soon as you found Celia?' Imogen was washing up at the time, the marigold gloves letting in warm, damp soapsuds because there was a hole in each thumb. Whenever she thinks back to this conversation, she remembers the feel of her hands, wet and somehow contaminated inside the gloves.

'Of course I did,' said Imogen, too quickly. Had she delayed on purpose? Was that why she couldn't decide what to do?

Her mother must have detected something in her voice. She pulled Imogen round and put her hands on either side of her face, looking very hard into Imogen's eyes. Imogen could smell her breath. It reminded her of Celia. 'Are you quite sure? You were seen coming home at least fifteen minutes before you phoned the police.'

Imogen hadn't given herself away. Her mother had known all the time. 'I told you, I didn't find her straight away.' Imogen could hear the panic in her voice. She knew that her mother could hear it too. She could feel the redness in her cheeks, the sweat gathering on her forehead.

Then her mother's hands fell away, and she stepped back. 'It wasn't your fault, Imogen.' Her voice had changed. It had become less raw, more controlled.

Imogen stared at her, not sure how she should respond. Did her mother mean it, or was this a new tactic? A trap?

'You mustn't blame yourself. I'm sure those fifteen minutes wouldn't have made any difference.'

But they might have done. Imogen had heard the conversation with the policeman and her mother would not have forgotten it.

'We should remember that it was Celia who made the decision, not you,' said her mother, turning her face away, but not managing to disguise the catch in her voice. 'We must remember that,' she said again, as if she were trying to persuade herself.

She's only pretending, thought Imogen. She doesn't mean it.

In her memory, her mother is there, holding her face again, close like Celia. And she does blame Imogen.

———————

'Hello? This is Stella Doody speaking.'

Doody opens her mouth and tries to speak, but nothing comes out.

'Hello? Who is it?'

'Imogen.'

'Imogen? Imogen? I don't know any – oh—'

Doody tries again: 'It's Imogen.' Her voice doesn't sound right. She's talking to someone from her past who doesn't know her as she is now. She doesn't know how to give the impression that she's no longer the tongue-tied, naïve girl who destroyed the life of Stella's son.

'Imogen,' says Stella, and her voice has lost some of the authoritarian sharpness. It's a little softer, even kinder, perhaps, but this may just be Doody's imagination. 'What a surprise. How are you? We didn't know what happened to you.'

'I went to Bristol,' says Doody. She wonders how hard they tried to find her.

'I see,' says Stella. 'And are you there still?'

'Yes. Although – I also have a cottage in Devon now.'

'Oh. You have done well for yourself, then.'

'No, not really. It's not as good as it sounds.' Why does she tell her that? Her outer layer is dissolving, and she's allowing Stella to penetrate the inner, private part that should remain hidden. She can't seem to stop herself.

'Have you married again?' There's tension in Stella's voice. As if she doesn't want to know that Doody might have replaced Harry with someone else. Another rubbing out, another denial of his existence.

'No,' says Doody. 'I live on my own.'

'Ah.' Stella probably wants to say 'good' but realises that it would be inappropriate.

Neither of them speaks for a while. 'Well, it's nice to hear from you, Imogen,' she says. 'Did you phone for any particular reason?'

'Harry didn't come back, did he?' says Doody, thinking suddenly that maybe he had returned to his family years ago, and nobody had bothered to find her and tell her.

'No, of course not. We would have contacted you if he had.' Her voice is brisk and sensible. She's a decent woman. She would never have lied, or pretended that things were not as they were.

Doody nods. 'I just wondered . . .'

'Yes?'

'Do you remember a crash, about twenty-five years ago?'

'A crash?' She sounds confused. 'What sort of a crash?'

'It was a train. A private plane hit a train, which collapsed on to a housing estate. There were lots of casualties. Seventy-eight dead.'

'Why are you asking me this?' Her voice has lost its softness. 'Is this something to do with Harry?'

'Yes,' says Doody. 'Well – I don't really know.'

Stella is silent for some time, and Doody begins to worry that she has gone. 'Are you still there?'

'Imogen, I would appreciate it if you would get to the point.'

Doody swallows. 'It's just that the crash was round about the time that Harry disappeared, and I wondered if you had considered it, that's all.'

Stella lets out a sigh. 'I do remember the crash, as a matter of fact. It was a train from London to Birmingham, but it was some time after his disappearance. We'd hardly have ignored something as obvious as that.'

Doody is relieved. Of course they would have thought about it. They were all sensible people. 'So he couldn't have been on it?'

'It was at least three months later. Why would he have been?'

Doody is uneasy. It's not as obvious as she suggests. Harry vanished first, then the train crashed. 'But we don't know where he was. He might have been on the train. Maybe he went somewhere for a short time, and always intended to come back, but then went on the train.'

'They will have identified all the people on the train.'

'No. There were nine unidentified bodies. Nine people who didn't belong to anyone.'

'I see.'

'Do you think they could still check? With dental records and things?'

There's another long pause. 'Look, Imogen,' says Stella, 'perhaps we should meet. Shall I come down to your cottage in Devon?'

'No,' says Doody, imagining her coming through the front door of her cottage, eyeing the rotten window-frames, the dust-filled furniture. 'I'll come and see you.'

'Fine.' She sounds relieved. 'We're still in the same place. When would be convenient? A weekend would suit me best.'

Doody hesitates, not sure if she wants to meet Stella again and go back to a version of herself that she would prefer to forget. 'I can come next Saturday,' she says.

'Good. Come for lunch. One o'clock.'

Doody puts the phone down and wonders what has happened to her. Did she really telephone Harry's mother, the woman whose dislike for her always permeated her scrupulous politeness? Has she really accepted an invitation to lunch? Stella won't recognise her. Will she recognise Stella?

———

Harry and Imogen had set off to Stratford as two separate people and returned as man and wife. Till death us do part. Or at least until Imogen drove him away with her inability to remain funny. Harry wanted her to come in with him when they arrived to break the news to his parents, but she refused.

'I'll wait in the car,' she said. 'It'd be better if you go and tell them first.'

'There's nothing to be ashamed of,' he said. 'I'm proud of my new wife.' He leaned over to kiss her, and she breathed in that vague, antiseptic, hospital smell that he carried around with him. She could feel the sharpness of the bristle on his chin against hers, the intensity of his presence.

'You don't have to be ashamed,' she said. 'I'd just prefer you to tell them first before they have to speak to me.'

He gave in eventually, and left the car with a breezy wave. 'I'll be back in no time, you'll see,' he said. 'They'll be delighted.'

Imogen knew they would be appalled, and it thrilled her to think that he'd brave their wrath for her. She sat in the car, an old Cortina, and waited. All around her was evidence of Harry. Chewing-gum wrappers in the ashtray, lecture notes stuffed into the glove compartment. There were bits of grit caught in the mat where he placed his feet, slivers of nails that she'd seen him bite off and drop on the floor. She touched the gear stick and felt its shiny surface, worn smooth by all the previous owners. Now Harry's left hand had taken over, polishing away the past. The steering wheel had old cracks that had become his cracks, where he had held it and turned it, letting it slide easily through his hands.

She couldn't drive then – she learned much later. Harry had once opened the bonnet and explained the internal combustion engine, pointing out the various parts and their functions. She pretended to understand, but the information came too fast, with too many alien words.

'How do you know these things?' she asked.

He looked bewildered. 'Well, I don't know. You just pick it up . . .'

It shocked Imogen to discover that people all over the country were picking things up, examining them, remembering them, while she'd wandered along carelessly, missing the details, not even aware of their existence. She was glimpsing a new landscape through an open door, perceiving that her world was tiny compared to the great other world outside.

Harry came back, looking pale and angry. 'Come on,' he said. 'They're delighted.' He smiled at her, but his mouth moved without the rest of his face. Imogen could feel the tension beneath the smile, his determination to be positive.

They walked in, holding hands, and found his parents drinking in the living room.

'Sherry, Imogen?' said her new father-in-law, Arthur.

She was going to refuse, but could see Harry nodding beside her, so she took a glass, and they sat down on the sofa opposite his parents. She tried to think of them as Arthur and Stella, but it wasn't possible. They were too far away from her.

'It should be champagne,' said Harry.

'Yes,' said Stella uncomfortably. 'Of course. Do we have any?'

Arthur frowned. 'I don't think we have, dear. Shall I pop up to the off-licence?'

'No,' said Harry. 'It's all right.'

Imogen was disappointed. She'd never tried champagne, and this might be her only chance.

There was an awkward silence. 'So,' said Stella, 'you're married. To each other.'

'Yes,' said Imogen, and smiled.

'Mummy and Daddy are delighted, aren't you?' said Harry.

'Yes, of course,' they said together, and Imogen could feel how hard everyone was trying.

'So, where are you planning to live?' said his father. 'Harry hasn't qualified yet, you know.'

'Qualified?' said Imogen. She didn't know you had to be qualified before you got married.

'My job,' said Harry, squeezing her hand. 'As a doctor.'
She felt foolish.

'He has another six months at medical school.'

'Oh, that's all right,' said Imogen, eagerly. 'I earn good money at Asda. They like me there.'

'Good,' said Stella.

'We thought we could rent a flat here until I'm qualified, and then I can look for work in Birmingham,' said Harry.

Did they think this? Imogen couldn't remember discussing it.

Arthur was nodding. 'Good, good. You'll be settled in no time.'

'You need to be in London, Harry,' said Stella. 'You'll have to finish your course.'

'I'll come back at weekends,' he said.

Imogen stared at him. Why wasn't he planning for them to be together all the time? Surely that was what happened when you got married. 'But I can come to London,' she said.

'No, no,' said Stella. 'You don't want to give up your job. The cost of living in London is so high. There's far too much unemployment at the moment. Anyway, Harry will need the time to study. He'll be back in no time.'

How had this happened? How had they persuaded her not to go to London? Imogen has wondered about this a lot since. She had just done as she was told when she should have protested. But now she suspects a conspiracy between them, a deal they did with Harry. Sending him away from her all week was a kind of test, to demonstrate that he didn't need her, and could be perfectly happy away from her. Perhaps they thought he would meet someone else when he was in London during the week. What did they offer him that Imogen didn't know about? Financial help, some gentleman's agreement that he had to honour if he wanted to keep on seeing them?

Had Stella and Arthur plotted to remove her? Do they feel guilty about it now?

Doody drives up to Birmingham from Bristol on Saturday morning, wondering if Straker has turned up in the last two weeks and found the cottage empty. What would he have thought? Would he have taken her absence as acknowledgement that he had been right and Harry was on the train?

She feels uncomfortable about this. She doesn't want him to believe he killed Harry if it's not true. But there is so much uncertainty. Harry seems to have strolled in twenty-five years too late and messed up everything again. Why should she care? What does she owe him?

She has no difficulty finding the house. The road is as wide and leafy as ever. Large houses standing back from the road, tall and elegant, sheltered from hardship and economic struggles. There are more cars parked on the drives than there were then, but nobody has plastic windows. Theirs are wooden, well looked-after, painted regularly, free from rot. The road is quiet and remote when she turns off the engine – any sounds from traffic are muffled, far away, irrelevant.

She doesn't have the nerve to pull on to their drive in her little Fiat – ten years old, rust spreading on the wings. They have two cars – a BMW and a smaller Fiesta, both brand new – on the drive, so she parks on the opposite side of the road. She's very nervous, and doesn't really want to do this. She should have tried to find more information about the crash before she arrived, but it's too late now.

She sits in the car, watching Harry's old home for some time. It's a wonderful house. There are three storeys, with the top floor built into the eaves. Harry had a room up in the attic, and his brother, William, had the other. They were the largest rooms in the house. Harry had once given Imogen a guided tour when no one else was there. They looked at his other brothers' rooms, Nick and Gavin's, and then he took her into his parents' room. He leaped on to their bed and persuaded her to come and join him. He clearly found it erotic to think of them making love on his parents' bed, but Imogen couldn't do it. She was too terrified by the reflection of them in his mother's elegant three-way mirror, under the shadow of his father's red check dressing-gown hanging on the back of the door.

What she learned, when he showed her round, was that other people had untidy houses too. She'd thought that because the house was so big, because they obviously had so much money, and his mother cooked and cleaned, everywhere in the house would be immaculate. It was a shock to discover that they left things lying around, that the basin in the bathroom had soap smeared on the taps, that Harry's father would leave a shirt in the middle of the floor when it needed washing.

Doody steps out of the car, shuts the door and locks it. She walks across the road and on to the drive beside the Fiesta and the BMW, skirting the delicate yellow roses in their beds beside the hedge. She climbs the steps to the porch and reaches up to ring the doorbell. The sound echoes through the house in the way that it always did, an old-fashioned bell that goes on jangling for some time so that it can be heard by everyone wherever they are in the house. She can picture the hall inside, with its uncluttered, magnolia walls and the thick pile carpet that cushions all unexpected noises.

When the door opens, it takes Doody a few seconds to realise that the old woman in front of her is Stella. She's shrunk. Her hair has gone white and her skin has shrivelled. She looks like someone dying, so frail you could blow her away.

She leans forward and makes an attempt to kiss Doody's cheek. Doody freezes. She wasn't prepared for this. 'Imogen,' says Stella, and her voice is instantly recognisable.

'Hello,' says Doody.

Chapter 22

Straker follows Simon Taverner down his narrow hall and into a large room at the end. Once inside, he looks round, examining each item in turn, making himself see everything slowly. His hands are shaking and he needs time to calm himself.

The room has tall windows looking out on to a leafy area of large houses and gardens. There are a few similar blocks of flats nearby, all about six storeys high. Most of the windows in the flats opposite have net curtains, but where they haven't, it is possible to see inside the rooms. This glimpse into other people's lives is unnerving, and Straker moves back from the windows in case he can be seen.

In Simon Taverner's room, the carpet is wine-coloured, dotted with tiny yellow daisies, flattened with age, but very clean. Two brown leather sofas are creased with wear, moulded and hollowed into the shape of invisible bodies, comforting and welcoming. A long, low coffee-table is over-flowing with open, well-thumbed reference books, all on the subject of battleships. Around them, several sheets of paper are scattered, covered with indecipherable handwriting, a pair of glasses lying on top of everything. There's a cabinet of china and glass, including several intricate models of ships, a piano, several bookshelves, all overcrowded, and there are photographs everywhere. They fill all the remaining wall space, the shiny black wood of the piano, the top of the cabinet, some even on the floor.

Once Straker stops to look at the photographs, he can't see anything else. Maggie is here, in the room with him, beaming out of every surface. Maggie at a daughter's wedding, holding on to her hat as she's caught by a gust of wind, squinting into the sun; sitting before a table of food in a restaurant, sipping wine; pretending to stand to attention next to a guard outside Buckingham Palace, tiny next to him, but still significant; sitting in the car of a Big Wheel, her arm round a child, her face fixed into an expression of forced delight. Maggie in gardens, sitting in deck-chairs, smiling at a newborn baby in her arms. Different children in every picture, boys, girls, babies, toddlers, older children sitting by her legs, teenagers towering over her, standing awkwardly, but somehow belonging to her, the family resemblance drifting through all their faces. Did this woman ever stop smiling?

'I see you recognise Maggie,' says Simon Taverner, making Straker jump. He's been unconsciously counting the photographs. Forty-two so far. 'Wait there,' says Simon, and goes out of the room. He returns a few seconds later with armfuls of books.

'Look,' he says, and opens them on the floor. They are photograph albums. Straker kneels down and starts to turn the pages slowly, chronologically, watching Maggie's life grow before his eyes. He sees her in black and white as a girl, a young wife with her first baby, her second, her third, her fourth. The children grow up, and she gets older, less glamorous, but more motherly, warmer and more comfortable with the passing years. Her waistline expands, her hair begins to go grey, but she remains the same, the real Maggie, the voice he knows from his dreams. She's exactly as he imagined. He feels that he has known her all his life. As if she were his mother. The children grow tall and rebellious in their appearance – jeans, long hair, casual neglect – but they are still drawn to her, and she still accepts them. You can see this in the way they gather round her for the photographs.

Then the weddings. Two of them, everybody present, a family that knows how to grow together and is happy to welcome new members. And the grandchildren. Babies, toddlers, cats, dogs . . .

Then it changes. There is no more Maggie. The family goes on without her. They still seem to be close, to support each other, but Simon is now at the centre without her, growing older, loved, but somehow lost.

Straker reaches the end and looks up at Simon. He's sitting on one of the sofas, pouring tea out of a silver teapot into two china cups. 'Tea?' he says.

Straker gets up off the floor and rubs his knees. 'You know who I am?' he says.

Simon nods. 'Do sit down, Mr Straker.'

He takes the mug of tea that is offered. 'I mean, you know who I really am?'

'Yes. I know who you really are.'

Straker doesn't know what to say. Why is he here? Simon seems almost to have expected him.

They sit together, sipping tea.

Simon's movements are slow and careful, as if he's afraid of a sudden weakness in his hands, which will send the cup tumbling to the floor. He's almost bald, with just a few wisps of white hair above his ears. He has a kind face, wrinkled and worn, like his room, but not hostile. He exudes a benign, fatherly air that is very reassuring.

'Let me explain,' he says. 'When I received your letter, enquiring about Maggie, I had a strong feeling that it was important to you to find out about her. Why, I thought, would you need to have more details about my wife? Because he's a journalist, I said to myself, and that's what journalists do. But at the back of my mind was the idea that this was not quite the full truth. I picked up an intense desire to look more deeply into Maggie's life, more than you would expect from a journalist. It was almost as if you knew her and had some feeling for her, as if you were tied in a more intimate way. An old friend, I thought. But I know her old friends. They all came to the funeral, most are still in touch – or dead. So – someone who thinks he has something in common with her, with the way she died. And then it hit me that what I could feel coming out of your letter was guilt. Once I realised that, I knew who you were.'

He stops talking. Straker can't look him in the eye. He studies the carpet between his knees, the way it has faded from vacuuming and scrubbing and the sun.

'Mr Straker,' he says, 'please don't think that I want vengeance. If there was one thing I learned from Maggie it was that you accept people as they are, and you don't demand more than they want to give.'

'She talks to me,' says Straker.

'Really?' he says, with surprise. 'A ghost?'

'No. In my dreams.'

He sighs. 'I see.' He pauses, then nods. 'Yes, I see.'

'But you're right. I do feel as if I have known her.'

'Help yourself,' says Simon, putting a plate of chocolate biscuits beside him. Straker takes one and bites into it.

'I expect you think I'm a potty old man,' says Simon. 'Well, I probably am. But I'm not amazed by what you tell me. Maggie's personality was so powerful that she could easily still influence somebody after all this time.'

Straker clears his throat and tries to talk sensibly. 'I don't know what you want me to say. I'm just following instructions from Maggie in my dreams. Go and see you, she says. But why? What for?'

'It's not Maggie,' he says. 'It's your conscience.'

'No, it's not.' But of course he's right. 'Why should I come here?'

'You are the only one who can answer that.'

'Well, I can't. I don't remember what happened. I just woke up in hospital and they told me we crashed. You know what they said at the inquest. Insufficient evidence to bring a prosecution.'

286

'So why do you feel guilty?'

'I don't.'

'I think you do. That's why you write letters.'

'I just want to know about them, that's all. So they don't get forgotten.'

Something strange is happening. Straker knows he was responsible for the accident. He wakes up every morning with the weight of it pressing him down on his mattress, pushing him towards the floor. He counts the numbers, he debates with the victims all night.

So why is he disowning his guilt now?

Simon looks out of the window. 'Do you really think any of them would be forgotten? What about their husbands, wives, girlfriends, children, mothers, fathers? How do you imagine people react when they lose someone they love in violent and unexpected circumstances? Do you think we're sad for a bit, and then carry on as if they never existed?'

'No, I don't think that.'

'Then why do you think you have to take on the burden of remembering all of them?'

'I don't know.'

'Guilt,' he says.

'I think I'd better go,' says Straker. 'I don't know why I came.'

'Stay a bit longer. I know why you came.'

'You don't know me. You have no idea.'

'I think you want forgiveness. Absolution.'

Straker stands up, frustrated by Simon's presumption of his guilt. 'How can you be so sure there's something for you to forgive?'

Simon pauses and picks up a chocolate biscuit. 'I imagine your assessment of the situation is very similar to my own.'

Straker sits down again, somehow defeated. It's the photographs – they have unsettled him. 'Look,' he says, 'I'm sorry about Maggie, I really am. If I could change things, I would. But I can't. It's too late.'

'It was always too late, from the time she got on that train and said goodbye to our daughter and her baby, and from the moment you took off in that plane.'

'You mean it was fate?'

'No, I don't believe in fate. I just mean that once the events were set in motion they carried on happening, and once they had happened, nobody could undo them. Whatever you feel now, it's irrelevant. You can't alter the fact that you've changed the lives of all those people. Seventy-eight died, but there were many more relatives and friends who were affected by the deaths.'

'You've already said that.'

'My point is that it is arrogant of you to believe that knowing the victims better makes any difference to anyone.'

'So what would you have done?'

He smiles. 'I have no idea. I'm grateful for the fact that it was you and not me.'

Is he feeling sorry for Straker? Does he appreciate how impossible it is to live a single minute of a single day without thinking of the seventy-eight?

'Which doesn't mean that I absolve you. I haven't made a decision on that yet. I confess that I spent many, many years after the accident bitterly resenting you, and the effort of it has worn me out. The ache of losing Maggie has never truly left me, but I have gradually learned to accept it. You have to let things go in the end, or you don't survive. I think I've changed again in the last two years, although I'm not sure why. I have been thinking about it more, going over the details in my mind, trying to understand what really happened.'

This is curious. It was just over two years ago that Straker saw Felicity in the poster outside Sainsbury's, and started his investigation into the victims' lives. Did the air between them start to vibrate, sending silent and invisible messages, eventually leading them to the same place? Has Straker been waiting for nearly twenty-five years to end up here, facing this old man who would have good enough reason to murder him if he could summon the strength?

Simon gets up. 'Come with me,' he says, walking to a door at the side of the room.

Straker watches him, unsure if he trusts him. 'Why?'

Simon opens the door. 'There's something you might find interesting.'

Reluctantly, Straker follows. The room is a little study, as cluttered with books and photographs as the living room. He's surprised to see a computer set up on a desk just under the window.

Simon looks pleased with himself. 'My hobby,' he says. 'There's a whole world of information out there and I can sit in my own flat and access it. You can find out anything you want to, you know.'

He sits at the computer and presses a few buttons. With a rush of sound, a picture appears on the screen. He starts typing, very fast, clearly familiar with the keyboard.

'Sit down,' he says, indicating a second chair. 'I often have a grandchild with me when I use the computer. Although it's usually one of them sitting in the driving seat, while I'm the spectator. They seem to know so much, these days. They work everything out for themselves.'

Straker watches as Simon types on to the screen: *www. disaster25.9.79.co.uk*. The date of the crash. He begins to feel very uncomfortable. There's a pause, and then the screen changes to a cartoon picture of an aeroplane, a train, some houses, separate from each other but linked by a series of dramatic lines. Then he clicks something and the screen changes again. Now it's a kind of written conversation, like a play, with the writers' names at the beginning.

Simon grunts. 'Sorry,' he says. 'Wrong page.'

The screen changes several times and then stops. 'Right,' he says. 'This is what I think you should read.'

Straker leans forward.

```
TWENTY-FIFTH ANNIVERSARY - 25 SEPTEMBER 2004
Schedule: 8.30 coach leaves birmingham, should
arrive in hillingham by 12.00
  please make every effort to be there, this may be
our one chance of finding out the truth, the chance
to let some of it go
  Carmen Halliwell
```

Straker reads it several times. Carmen Halliwell. He remembers her. She responded very badly to his letter. What does she intend to do? Come and find him? She won't be able to. The letters go to a post-office box number, so she won't know his address. Nobody can find him. How does she know he lives near Hillingham?

'What do they want from me?'

Simon shrugs. 'I don't know. I won't be accompanying them, I assure you. I'm too old for that kind of thing.'

'Will anyone go?'

'Possibly. The website has been set up for some time now, and they've been corresponding regularly.'

'They write to each other?'

He smiles. 'Yes. But it's a kind of open letter. The site has been growing rapidly in the last couple of years. There must be hundreds of people registered now.'

Straker stares at the screen. 'Hundreds? Who are they all?'

'Relatives.'

'But there were only seventy-eight victims.' He's never said that before. Only seventy-eight. The number has always seemed too big.

'I've told you. Every person is surrounded by people. When they die, the people all come together, people whose lives have changed for ever. I was introduced to the site by a great-grandson.'

'He can't possibly have known Maggie.'

'No, but he's been affected. Grief spreads down through generations, ripples outwards. If you lose a parent, it affects the way you bring up your children, which then affects the way they bring up their children. It would take generations to obliterate the damage. It never goes away, never gets any easier. You just get used to living with it. You have to.'

Straker imagines a growing pyramid of people, Simon at the top, old and shrivelled, babies at the base, squirming, crawling, all of them looking for someone, aware of an emptiness in the centre. 'Do you think they want revenge?' Is that what he's wanted all this time? Not forgiveness, but justice? Has he been waiting for the hand to come out of the darkness to kill him, so that he can join the seventy-eight?

Simon shrugs. 'Who knows? I don't suppose they know themselves. It gives them a purpose, a common focus. They've hated you for a very long time. It's not unreasonable that they would want to see you. You stirred them all up with your letters. I wasn't the only one to realise who you were. It took them some time, but they arrived at the same conclusion as me.'

'You didn't tell them?'

'No. I don't write to them. I just read the messages.'

Straker feels trapped. 'So, what do I do?'

'I can't advise you. You must do whatever you feel is right. Go away, hide, call the police, stay there and confront them. I can't make that decision for you.'

Straker puts his head into his hands and runs his fingers through his hair, while studying the floor. 'I don't know,' he says. 'I don't know.'

Simon turns to face him. 'I forgive you,' he says.

Straker experiences an unaccountable stab of resentment. 'Why should your forgiveness make any difference to me?'

'Nevertheless, I forgive you.'

———

Before he catches a train back to his lighthouse, Straker investigates the shops in Birmingham. He's unexpectedly invigorated: all his tiredness has evaporated, and he feels as if he will never need to sleep again. Everything round him is sharp-edged, highly coloured, more real than he's used to. He goes into a café and orders a pizza and ice-cream. He buys a book, a novel about a man who lives in a lighthouse, which is illustrated on the front cover. It's not the same as his. Wrong colour. He buys two shirts, one blue, one green and patterned, and two ties to match. Then some leather gloves, wool-lined, and a hat that makes him look like a gamekeeper. He looks at the computers in Dixons and wonders if he should consider buying one. If Simon Taverner can do it, why shouldn't he? Maybe there are things in the world that would divert his mind from numbers if he could find out about them. He buys a clock for Doody's kitchen, and a set of six glasses. If she doesn't want to talk to him, he can leave them on her front doorstep. Then she can throw them away if she wants to.

He goes down the escalators to the station and works out the time of the next train home.

―――――――

Back in his lighthouse, he tries to sleep, lying in his sleeping-bag with Suleiman and Magnificent curled up beside him. It's a very still night, and through the window he can see the sliver of a new moon standing out piercingly against the black sky. It produces a surprising amount of light. He moves restlessly, and Suleiman starts to purr. He reaches down and strokes him. Suleiman responds with a little chirrup.

Straker dozes.

―――――――

'OK, Straker, you did it.'
Yes. I did it.
'Thank you.'

I can't speak. I have dried up.

Maggie has run out of words too. I can hear voices in the background, chattering away, but they seem less distinct than usual. They are fading, like the sound of a train once it has passed, just a mumble, just a whisper in the distance.

Nevertheless, I forgive you. It's Simon's voice that comes calmly into his mind.

Straker tests himself, thinks of seventy-eight. Nothing happens. The number is sitting there in his mind between seventy-seven and seventy-nine. He waits for the familiar panic and nothing happens. His thoughts are calm.

But Maggie was more than his conscience. She was his mother.

He sits up suddenly, and Suleiman and Magnificent spill on to the floor. He doesn't even know if his mother is alive. Or his father. He knows nothing about them. What are they doing? Is his mother still there, disowning him, hating him, quietly going about her cleaning and her pruning? Does she ever think about him? Does his father continue to work, heaving rusty old cars around in his old age, training another young man to be his heir instead of Pete, aware that Andy will never do it? And where is Andy? Does he have children?

Twenty-four years is a very long time. If Straker had been put in prison for life he'd be out by now. Why should his family have assumed he was guilty when nobody really knew what happened? The fact that he believed in his guilt shouldn't have meant that they automatically assumed it. If Simon can forgive him, why shouldn't they? Perhaps he's been forgotten – missing, presumed dead. Just taking the monthly allowance.

He gets up and dresses rapidly, without his usual care, putting on yesterday's shirt because it's easier. His mind is swirling, patterns shaping and reshaping, thoughts tumbling over each other in urgent competition with each other. His family are probably just the same, alive and functioning, carrying on as before but without him. He's starting to feel resentment. Why should they keep him shut away for so long?

And he needs to speak to Doody. To explain. To apologise, take responsibility for the death of her husband, and allow her to make the decision about whether she wants to speak to him again.

He leaves the lighthouse while it's still dark, and feels his way across the headland to the road. He's familiar with the ground and doesn't need any extra light.

He walks into the village where the street-lights draw attention to his isolation. Most of the village is sleeping, but some upstairs lights are glowing brightly. Fishermen preparing to go out on an early tide, perhaps. High tide is due just before dawn. A good way to start the new day.

Nevertheless, I forgive you.

Chapter 23

In Doody's mind, Stella has always been tall and authoritative, perpetually condemning her for ruining Harry's life. Doody used to have imaginary arguments with her after he went. 'I didn't make him like he is.' 'You're the one to blame if he doesn't live up to your expectations.' 'Try examining yourself first before attacking me.' None of it was ever said out loud. She hardly spoke to Stella before Harry left, not at all afterwards.

Stella leads her into the kitchen. Slowly, rolling from side to side on unstable hips. She must be about seventy-five, but looks much older.

The kitchen has deteriorated. On every available surface there are piles of dirty dishes. Tins and cartons of food have been left out, all at one end of the table, as if swept aside this morning. Several of them are on their sides, their contents leaking out gently into sordid puddles. Doody goes over and stands them all upright. The floor in her memory had pale blue and white ceramic tiles, but it seems to have been resurfaced in a dull, uncertain colour. Then she realises that the tiles are the same, but they haven't been cleaned for so long that they're dark with grime and neglect. Clothes are hanging out of the washing-machine. Half in, half out, abandoned on their journey to cleanliness.

Stella's personal appearance has changed too. It was inevitable that her hair would be grey, but it's also unkempt. She doesn't appear to have used a brush for some time, and strands hang down in ragged, uneven lengths, as if she's been hacking away at it herself with scissors.

'Do sit down, Imogen,' she says, enunciating clearly. That feature of her voice hasn't changed, although it is slower. She puts two paper plates on the cleared corner of the table with knives and forks and spoons in a confused heap, then brings over several little plastic containers from Marks & Spencer.

'Help yourself,' she says, waving her hand vaguely over the food.

Doody takes a spoonful of salad out of each container and pushes them back to Stella, who doesn't take anything. Doody is disappointed to discover that she's still nervous in Stella's presence. Her hands tremble as she lifts her fork and she's the eighteen-year-old Imogen all over again, overawed by the size of the house and the air of privilege and taste that leaks from the furniture, the heavy curtains, the subdued colours. Strangely, the years of neglect haven't cancelled out those earlier impressions.

'How's Arthur?' she says.

Stella looks surprised. 'Didn't you know? He died. Eleven years ago. He never recovered.'

How could Doody possibly know, when she hadn't seen them for twenty-five years? No need to ask what he didn't recover from. 'I'm sorry.' She is genuinely sorry. The picture of Arthur that remains with her is of a kind man who had somehow been left behind by the energy of four boys and a highly organised wife.

'And the boys? William, Nick and Gavin?' Of course, they're not boys any more.

Stella takes a sip of water. 'William's a barrister. Nick is in property, and Gavin—' She stops.

Is Nick an estate agent? The idea appeals to Doody. Not quite what they would have had in mind for him. It's obvious that Stella is unwilling to tell her about Gavin, but she wants to know, so she waits.

'Well . . . Gavin has not had a happy life. He was influenced by others . . . ' Like Harry, she means. Led astray by some unsuitable girl. 'He's got himself into trouble.'

What sort of trouble? Drugs, alcohol, crime? Doody's shocked, but at the same time a thin, vicious needle of elation shoots through her. Harry wasn't the only disaster. Gavin couldn't have been influenced by her: he must have managed it all on his own. Then she feels ashamed. Gavin was a sweet boy, eight years younger than Harry, the youngest of the four, and the most friendly. Harry treated him with a gentle, casual affection, so he would come and join them if they sat in the lounge and watched television. Doody always thinks of *Cagney and Lacey* when she thinks of Gavin. And the *Nine O'Clock News*.

'Do any of them still live at home?' she asks.

Stella looks surprised. 'Oh, no, of course not. William's married, two children. Nick lives with a nice girl. Gavin comes home occasionally, in between prison spells.'

So it was crime. How could this have happened?

'Do have some more salad,' says Stella, pushing the containers back towards Doody. 'There's plenty here. They've opened a new Marks and Spencer's food hall quite close. So convenient.'

'Are you not eating with me?'

She looks vague. 'Oh, yes, of course.' She pulls the top off a carton of raspberries in jelly and eats it rapidly, swallowing the mouthfuls without chewing.

Stella used to know exactly what she was doing. She cleaned thoroughly and efficiently, she cooked and baked for an army of men, and there was an abundance of food available, far more than necessary. Doody always thought that this was how the family had felt cared-for. Stella was her role model. Doody cooked because Stella cooked, and her failure was that she couldn't reach the same standards. Everything she did for Harry was in imitation of Stella, knowing that she would never be good enough. Looking at this now, Doody realises how foolish she was. She could never have won in a direct comparison. She would have been wiser to go and buy takeaways every day, and Harry might have liked that more.

'So you live on your own now,' says Doody. 'Like me.'

'Oh, yes,' she says. 'Bit of a problem when Gavin's around, though. He wants me to look after him, but I don't do cooking any more. Can't be bothered. Far too busy. He sometimes pretends to prepare a meal for himself, but he's not much good. Just makes a mess. Much better to go to Marks and Spencer's.'

A great sadness seeps through Doody. She used to come here for the house, the efficiency, the food. And now it reminds her of her own home with her mother and Jonathan, from which she was so desperate to escape. The lack of interest, the chaos, the neglect. She would never have believed that such a strong household could descend so far.

'I've been to the police,' says Stella.

Doody swallows her mouthful of couscous. Why is she talking about the police?

'About the crash.'

'Oh – yes, of course.'

'They said they could do DNA tests and check dental records against the unidentified bodies from the crash.'

'I thought the bodies would have been destroyed years ago.'

She nods. 'But they keep records of things like teeth. Any personal details. So they can check.'

'How long will it take?'

'No idea. They just said they would let me know.'

So that's it. All they can do now is sit and wait.

'You look surprisingly well, Imogen.'

Doody can hear resentment in her voice. 'Thank you.'

Stella seems to shrink even more. 'It was the waiting that destroyed us, you know. The not knowing.'

She must be offended that Doody looks well, wanting her to say that she, too, has suffered. But why should Doody explain about her life? It's none of Stella's business. She had made no attempt to keep in contact.

'He was my firstborn. You always feel closer to your first child, you know.'

Doody freezes in horror. She doesn't expect sentimentality from Stella.

'We did try to find you, but your mother didn't seem to have any idea where you'd gone.'

'Jonathan knew,' says Doody.

'Jonathan? Oh, yes, your brother. We didn't think of him. He was only a child, wasn't he?'

'A teenager.'

Stella has become like Doody's mother. Only able to see the world through her own eyes, indifferent to everybody else. With Doody's mother it was Celia, and with Stella it was Harry.

'Arthur changed. He went out and found a ladyfriend.'

Arthur? Harry's father, Arthur? Solid, dependable, reliable Arthur, who tried so hard to keep things amiable between them all?

'He didn't keep it secret. He took her openly to restaurants, booked into hotels, even took her to friends' parties. You'd think they would ostracise him, wouldn't you? Disapprove. But no. They invited him and her without me. One or two did invite me after a while. Thought we'd all arrive as a happy threesome, I suppose. Didn't go, of course.'

Doody doesn't want to hear this. She doesn't want to know the details of their loss of dignity and the final fall.

'She wasn't our sort, of course. She worked in Tesco's, on the checkout. People seemed to like her for some reason. Ghastly woman. Laughed very loudly. I could hear her all over Tesco's when I was doing my shopping, chatting to everyone, telling them her business. My business as well, of course. People queued for hours in her line because she took so long talking. Called them "love" and "darling" and "sweetheart". I had to change shops in the end. Drove another five miles to Asda. Nuisance. Didn't stock the right kind of marmalade.'

Doody drinks some water, unable to speak. She pictures this woman in Tesco's, bright and happy, chatting away to everyone. It's obvious why Arthur would have been attracted to her. The opposite of Stella.

'Called Tracey. What more can you say?'

Doody had come here to discuss the possibility of Harry being on the train. But Stella's already embarked upon the inquiry, so there's nothing to do. Doody had thought they might remember him together, talk about him, imagining that they might be able to communicate at last, or understand each other – or something.

'He died of a heart-attack, you know. Sitting in a dodgem car with her at Blackpool. Dodgems at his age! Pretending to be twenty instead of seventy, lost all sense of respectability. They had to prise him out of the dodgem car because he was so fat. His legs had got wedged in, and she sat with him for ten minutes while they waited for the ambulance. She kept talking to him as if he were alive for those ten minutes. Never shed a tear. That's what she tells everyone in Tesco's, anyway. Probably still talks to him as if he's alive. That would be about her level.'

Doody feels sorry for the unknown Tracey, and wonders what happened to her. Presumably he didn't leave her anything when he died. Stella still has the house and a brand new car parked in the drive.

A door slams in the hall. Stella ignores it.

'Has someone come in?' asks Doody.

'Oh, that'll be Gavin. He's in and out. When he's not in prison.'

The kitchen door opens and Harry walks in, carrying a yellow bucket. Seventeen years older, but with that same droopy look that comes from being very tall. The floppy brown hair that won't stay in place, that nervous tension round the eyes. Doody stops breathing and stares at him.

'Hi, Imogen,' he says carelessly, as if he sees her every week, and his voice is Harry's too.

'There's some food, Gavin,' says Stella, with a brief enthusiasm. 'Marks and Spencer's.'

'Great,' he says. 'Put it in the fridge and I'll have it later.' He flashes a grin at Doody, a charming, debonair smile that pierces her with a physical pain. He fills up his bucket with water from the tap. 'See you around, Imogen.'

Then he's gone. The front door bangs again and the house descends back into its lost, sterile silence.

'I told him you were coming,' says Stella.

'Would you mind . . .' says Doody, after a while '. . . would you mind if I looked at Harry's old room? I'd just like to see it again.'

'I don't see why not,' says Stella. 'You'll find it the same as it always was. There was never any point in changing anything. We didn't use it again.'

Doody waits at the door, expecting Stella to follow her, but she remains sitting. 'You don't mind, then?' says Doody again.

'No, no, go ahead.' Stella flaps at her with her hands.

Doody climbs the stairs, and discovers that nothing in the house has changed. Nobody has ever repapered, or painted, or even dusted. Looking back down to the hall and landing below, she can see dust collected on the lightshades, thick and black and almost solid. It must date back to the same period as the dust in Oliver d'Arby's cottage. Contemporary dust.

Once Doody reaches the top floor, she enters Harry's room with some trepidation. The main feature is a large, dark desk, piled with papers and books, apparently abandoned in midstudy. She walks round and examines everything, the books on the bookshelves. Enid Blyton, Just William, Jennings, Billy Bunter, all collected in series, well thumbed, well read. And Biggles. Doody remembers these, not daring to tell Harry that she'd read them all, that she knew them word for word.

There are posters on the wall, of Abba, Eric Clapton, Olivia Newton-John; an old guitar in a corner. She hadn't known he possessed a guitar, let alone played it. But now she realises that she didn't see most of the contents of the room. She just saw Harry's face. When she came here, she had no curiosity for his life. Only for him.

Photographs are lined up on the mantelpiece. She picks one up and rubs off the dust, searching through the faces until she recognises Harry. A team photograph. He looks so young, just a boy. This group of pretend men in their rugby kit, arms folded, hairy legs lined up neatly, looking earnestly into the camera, bursting with health and energy. She'd forgotten Harry played rugby.

She examines with surprise a photograph of their family in front of a lighthouse. The boys are all young – Harry must be only about ten – and they look clean, healthy, full of sun and fresh air, an idyllic family holiday. It looks exactly like Straker's lighthouse, the heavy wooden door behind them, the keepers' cottages on the side.

She opens the top drawer of a large chest of drawers. Inside there are piles of underwear, balls of socks, rolls of ties. Why didn't he bring all his worldly possessions when he moved in with her? Did he only ever enter into a world with her half-heartedly? Did he come back here sometimes, when she thought he was working in London?

Doody sits on the bed, which she remembers well. It's old-fashioned, with a high dark oak headboard and base. Sitting here, she accepts finally that she never knew him. The Harry who inhabited this room, a young medical student who lived a privileged life, was not the man she had married. She only ever saw a pretend Harry. A young man of jokes and fun, who did not really exist. Their marriage was untrue. Did he think he needed to assert himself as an adult? What was it all for?

She sits on the bed and tears spring into her eyes, not of anger, not of betrayal, but of sorrow for the eighteen-year-old

Imogen, who had had no idea. She had been so innocent that she couldn't see any of it.

The real Harry had been so far away from her that she never had a chance to find out about him. If he hadn't disappeared, or died in the crash, he would never have stayed with her. He would have reverted to his old life, which was centred here in this room, waiting for him to pick up where he left off.

She goes out and shuts the door. On her way down, she glances into the other rooms. None of them has been left like Harry's. William's and Nick's rooms are nearly empty. They must have taken their possessions with them when they left, with no sense that they would return. Gavin's room, she sees by peering through the half-open door, is in a state of chaos. Books, papers, magazines, CDs lying around on the floor. Piles of unexpected things, like kettles, fans, stationery sets, quilt covers, all wrapped and in boxes, apparently brand new. Stolen goods? Or does he run a market stall?

Downstairs, every other room seems abandoned, full of unwashed plates, mugs, soiled clothes. It looks as if Stella has worked her way through them, abandoning each one as it overflowed with rubbish, moving on to the next.

She is still sitting in the kitchen when Doody gets back. In the same place, in the same position. There is a portable television on the dresser opposite her, so she must be used to sitting there and watching. Has she regressed intellectually so that she now enjoys games shows, soaps, chat shows, anything that's on? Doody sits down opposite, and starts to worry about her. 'Do you have any friends?' she asks her.

'Friends? What are those?'

'Does anyone come and see you at all?'

She laughs, uproariously, with her mouth wide open. 'Don't be ridiculous.'

'Are you well, Stella?'

Stella looks at her suspiciously. 'You've changed, Imogen.'

'I'm older.'

'When did you ever notice anyone else?'

Doody is shocked. What does Stella know about her interest in other people? 'Will you let me know when you hear from the police?' she says.

Stella nods. 'Leave me your telephone number.'

She can't be as incapable as she looks. At least she went to the police after Doody's phone call, and she did manage to buy some lunch.

'Thanks for the lunch,' says Doody, moving to the kitchen door.

Stella stays on her chair. 'Thanks for coming.'

Doody goes out through the front door, and finds Gavin outside, washing the big BMW. It belongs to him, not Arthur, as she'd thought.

'Hi,' he says, looking up. 'Great to see you.' He smiles, a friendly, boyish smile. 'Great weather,' he says. 'I like to do my car myself. No one else does it properly.'

He doesn't look like a criminal: he's too open and generous to be involved in violence. What can you go to prison for that isn't violent?

'Is your mother all right?' says Doody.

He stops polishing and straightens up. 'I don't know. She's just the same as she always was.'

'I don't think so.'

He frowns – like Harry – so that his eyebrows meet in the middle. 'It's a long time since you last saw her, Imogen.'

'I can remember what she looked like then. Probably better than you.'

'Maybe you're right. Maybe I don't notice properly any more.'

'Well, you're not around, are you.'

He laughs, a huge, infectious laugh that sounds as if it comes from someone who is comfortable with his place in the world. 'She told you, then?'

Doody nods. She feels that she should offer some practical

advice, an older sister's protective words, show him that she cares. But she can't think of anything. She stands looking at him.

'Well,' he says, 'we can't help who we are. It's all in the genes.'

'The same genes as Harry?'

'Yes, why not? Maybe he was nursing a secret vice, drugs or something. Easy to get supplies when you're a doctor. Maybe that's why he disappeared.'

'No! He wasn't like that.'

He laughs again. 'Only joking.'

He seems so innocent and naïve. How can Doody be sure that Harry wasn't like that? 'So what do you do?' she says. 'I mean, in between . . .'

'Oh, this and that. A bit of this, a bit of that.'

'Well, this and that seem highly profitable.'

'Are you referring to something in particular?'

'The car. Not everyone can afford a brand new BMW.'

He winks at her. 'I haven't paid a penny for it. They'll come and take it away once they realise.'

He is Harry with a bend in the middle. A slight twist that makes him into an imperfect image of his brother.

'Don't worry about Mum,' he says. 'She's OK. She's been like this since Harry left. Serves her right. She shouldn't have had favourites.'

'Does she manage the practical things, like eating and washing?'

'You mean does she ever clean anything? No, of course not. She never washes up. She piles all the stuff in the rooms she doesn't use, and when she wants more mugs or plates, she goes out and buys some.'

Is he joking?

'Honest. Good idea, I reckon. She says she always hated washing-up. Why should she have to do it if she doesn't want to? Every now and again I fill a few bin-bags and take them to the tip.'

So the one good thing she remembers about Stella, the cleaning, that wonderful sense of order and cleanliness, was not real either. Doody wants to say something to Gavin. Something that will tell him it matters that he is involved in crime, that he keeps going to prison, but she has no words.

''Bye, Gavin,' she says.

''Bye, Imogen.'

Chapter 24

Straker sits at the end of the pier with Doody's clock and glasses beside him, watching the sun rise. The tide is out and the first hints of half-light separate the beach from the water, picking out clumps of black seaweed and the dark, abandoned shapes of the grounded boats. The shoreline is steely grey, then purple, and then copper-brown as the sun pushes up from the horizon. Water murmurs in the pools between the mud flats. The mud sucks and gargles, rolls the sea round in its mouth, then spits it out again. He can hear the day coming, the rush of activity as birds and shellfish emerge into the new warmth of the morning.

The wires on the flagpole rattle and hiss in the slight breeze as gulls appear from nowhere and whirl in flurries across the mud, watching the distant channel of low water, waiting for it to expand and creep towards the harbour. Straker can feel their excitement as they soar into the fresh blue sky. Flying is the one good memory he has of his younger self. The anticipation of real pleasure as he climbed into the cockpit, that surge of joy as the wheels left the ground and he rose effortlessly upwards.

The tide turns while he's sitting, and the water starts to approach at a surprisingly fast rate. Behind him, the village is waking up, the fishermen coming down and preparing to cast off as soon as the water is deep enough. A good day for them, setting off early on the tide, plenty of time to get out to sea.

Will they come and find him, the relatives? What do they want? What will they do?

'Are you Mr Straker?'

He turns in surprise and finds a boy standing behind him, dressed in jeans and a warm jacket, hood up and pulled tight round the face, his hair hidden. He's holding a fishing-rod and looking amiable, but slightly nervous.

'Who's asking?' says Straker.

'Nicholas Turner.' He holds out his spare hand and they shake hands.

'Where are you from, Nicholas Turner?'

'Over there.' He waves in the direction of a large house up on the cliffs further along the shore. A metal staircase winds down the cliffs to the beach, with a padlocked gate at the top and another at the bottom.

'Do your parents know you're here?' He doesn't look old enough to be out on his own.

Nicholas shrugs. 'How should I know? They're still in bed.'

They can hear the fishermen, sorting sails, stowing nets, waiting for the tide to pull them off the mud.

'The thing is . . .' Nicholas pauses. 'I've forgotten the maggots. They're the best – cost me a fortune. I bought them yesterday, but my mum wouldn't let me bring them indoors, so when I got up and it was still dark, I forgot them.'

'Can't you go back for them?'

'I'm going to, but Duggie Hollingworth will pinch my place.'

'Does it matter?'

'Of course it does. The best place is at the end in the middle, where you're sitting.'

'I see.'

'Only – could you save it for me? So if Duggie Hollingworth gets here before me, he can't have the space.'

'OK. How long will you be?'

'I'll be really quick.' His forehead wrinkles. 'Have you got time, or do you have to go? It doesn't matter that much if you do, only it'd be good if you could keep the space for me. That is, unless you want to stay here anyway.'

He's like boys Straker used to know at school. Earnest, educated, polite. Nice boys, who played with him if asked by adults, even when they didn't want to.

'I'll save it for you.'

An enormous grin fills his face. 'Thanks,' he says, putting down his fishing-rod beside Straker. He runs back down the pier and along the beach to the locked gate. He leapfrogs over without opening it, and races up the steps. Straker feels unexpectedly pleased with himself. He can't remember the last time he spoke to a child.

It's inconceivable that his brother Andy is not married with children. He was so good with people. But if Straker's an uncle, he'd like to have been told. Why have they made no attempt to contact him? Are they waiting for him to take the first step?

Nicholas returns with his maggots, and shows them to Straker proudly. There's something fascinating about their frantic pink and blue wriggling. Straker tries to estimate how many there are in the tin – fifty, a hundred?

'No sign of Duggie,' he says.

Nicholas grins. 'Great. He always gets here early, and I hardly ever beat him.'

'What are you hoping to catch?'

'Fish,' he says.

'Right.'

Straker gets up to leave, letting Nicholas take his place. 'I thought you didn't talk,' says Nicholas.

'You were mistaken, then, weren't you?'

'Yes,' he says. 'I suppose I was. I'll tell my mum she got it wrong.' He picks up his fishing-rod. 'Duggie says . . .'

'Yes?'

'He says you're dangerous, that you kill people and eat them in your lighthouse.'

'Does he?'

Nicholas studies him from under his hood. 'Is he right?'

'What do you think?'

'I don't know how you can tell.'

'Nor me.'

Nicholas starts to fiddle with his fishing-rod. 'You don't look like a cannibal,' he says.

'Good,' says Straker. 'You show remarkable discernment.' He turns to go. ''Bye.'

''Bye,' says Nicholas, without turning round. 'Thanks.'

The church bell starts to chime. Another bell joins in with a hollow, half-hearted attempt to sound welcoming. It must be Sunday and Doody should be at the cottage. She always comes for the weekend. Maybe she's upstairs in bed. Straker walks round the edge of the village, anxious to avoid anyone going to church, but the roads are deserted. Most houses have their downstairs curtains still drawn, and there is little sign of life away from the harbour.

The cottage garden feels empty. He leaves the glasses and the clock on the doorstep, and goes round to peer through the back windows. Now that it's light, he can see in properly. The kitchen appears to be different. The walls have been painted pale yellow and there's a frieze at eye level, with large hens walking round in single file. He's impressed by these hens. They are bold and stylish – they tell him that she knows what she's doing, and she doesn't need any help from him. A yellow and orange cloth covers the table, and dishes sit in the drainer on the side of sink. It looks like a kitchen where someone lives. A vase of flowers stands in the middle of the table.

He steps back and takes a breath, shocked by the flowers. He knows flowers are sold in Sainsbury's, but he's never given them much thought, accepting they are for confident, knowledgeable people. People who think about appearances, who know what they want.

He stands behind the cottage for some time and thinks about this. The world he doesn't know. The world he never

310

knew. How does Doody understand what to do? She's not exactly conventional.

It's her unpredictability that he likes.

He goes back to the front and sits on the grass in the sun with his back leaning against the wall. He shuts his eyes and thinks of Simon Taverner, feeling oddly attached to him – protective, even. Simon is so old, so frail, so in need of support. Straker starts planning to return, offering to do his shopping, do some repairs for him, decorate his flat, put down carpet . . .

It's Maggie. Whenever he sees Simon in his mind, she is there too, smiling up from the photographs, her presence still tangible after all this time.

Can he put the accident into some kind of perspective, go on as if it never happened? Or does forgetting mean not thinking about it, letting other things crowd in, take its place? Does he need compartments in his mind? Rooms that are occupied, that he needs to visit only occasionally? Not forget, just walk past, seeing through the open door.

'Maggie, I need to speak to you. I know you said you were going, but I think I'm getting somewhere.'

Silence.

Francis: 'We're here, old man. Holding the fort.'

'Do you two have relatives?'

Francis laughs. 'Doesn't everyone?'

Justin: 'Aunt Amy, Uncle Fred. Dreadful – my dad used to go out when he knew they were coming.'

'But what about your mum, your dad – you had a sister, didn't you? Penny, wasn't it?'

Justin's voice becomes softer, more vulnerable. 'So? Everyone's got a mum and dad.'

'How old would they be now?'

'Work it out. You're the one with the brain.'

'What about you, Francis? What about your parents?'

'*What about them?*'

'*Do you think they'll come and see me? With all the other relatives? Apparently they're coming here.*'

Justin and Francis yell with laughter. '*Hey, terrific. The showdown. The Gunfight at the OK Corral. Can we watch?*'

I discover a curious emptiness inside me. My parents won't be there. '*I don't know what they want.*'

'*Calm down, Straker.*'

'*Maggie! You're listening.*'

'*Only occasionally. Only if I want to.*'

She's watching over me! '*I wanted to tell you. About the door, the open door, the room. I don't always have to go into it, you know.*'

'*Careful, Straker. You might be growing up.*'

In the next two weeks, he visits the cottage several times, always expecting to find Doody there but missing her on each occasion. There is evidence that she has been, but they don't meet. Is she deliberately avoiding him? He needs to talk to her, but doesn't know how to find her. He has no phone number, no home address. Their paths only converge at the cottage. Will she ever speak to him again? It's nearly the end of August, and the school term will start soon.

One Sunday, he decides to cut the lilac away from the windows, and he has just started when a man opens the gate and walks up the path. If Straker had seen him coming, he could have gone round the back and avoided speaking to him. As it is, there's nothing he can do except stand up and wait for him to get within speaking distance.

'Hi,' says the man. He's tall and thin, and has straight ginger hair that flops over his forehead. 'Is Imogen in?'

'I don't think so,' says Straker. 'No.'

'She should be here. They're bringing in the Tiger Moth today. She won't want to miss it.'

So it's a Tiger Moth. Straker wonders if Doody's happy with that.

'Look, are you a friend? Of Imogen's?'

Straker hesitates.

'You know about the aeroplane?'

'Yes.'

'Do you want to come and watch? She's been renovated and they're delivering her today. Flying her in. Should be any time now.'

'No,' says Straker.

But the man doesn't seem to hear him. 'My name's Tony, by the way,' he says.

Straker feels pulled in two directions. He doesn't want to see the aeroplane again. He's afraid of what it symbolises, afraid of the dreams and sensations that may return to him. At the same time, the thought of seeing it fly thrills him, sending a tingling sensation down his spine. He dithers between the two.

Tony gives him no choice. 'We'd better get a move on.'

Straker finds himself walking up the road with Tony, who talks without waiting for a response. 'My wife's getting fed up with the whole thing. I've been down here every weekend working on the field. We've had diggers in, levelling it out, and now it's all turfed. She says if I don't stop soon, she'll divorce me. Of course she doesn't mean it. It's just her way of telling me she's had enough. We don't believe in divorce. I mean, all our friends are splitting up, and you should see their children. Swamped by material possessions, two homes, sets of clothes and toys for each home, but they don't know whether they're coming or going. It makes you grateful for what you've got, doesn't it?'

'Well,' says Straker, 'I don't really—'

But Tony is too diverted by his own conversation. Straker wonders if he could just run away.

'Funny Imogen's not here. I phoned to tell her the date.

Maybe she got the day wrong. She's been busy at home – packing to move down here, I gather. I couldn't make it yesterday. My daughter was taking part in a show. They all go to holiday clubs. Odd concept. Didn't do it like that when I was a child. They do everything now, you know, gym, bands, drama, things like that. Keeps them occupied all through the summer holidays. I've only got three children, but they go to everything. Sally does ballet and gym in term time as well. They say she has to choose one and drop the other, but she won't. She's too good at both of them.'

So Doody is going to move down to the cottage.

They arrive at the pathway, and Tony opens the gate properly, with the catch. He stands back to let Straker pass and then shuts it. 'Ouch!' he says, and sucks his finger. 'Must be a splinter.'

They walk up the pathway, which has been cut back and widened considerably. 'Dreadful job getting the lorry up here to take her away,' says Tony. 'Luckily the wings are hinged – don't know what they'd have done otherwise.'

The field has been transformed – flattened, turfed, a windsock up at the end. Four men are standing by the barn with a small tractor containing a fire extinguisher. It all looks painfully familiar to Straker – a more amateur version of the airfield he remembers.

'Any luck?' says one of them to Tony, as the two men approach.

'No sign of her, I'm afraid,' he says.

He introduces them. 'This is Ben, Frank, Terry, Kasra . . .'

Straker shakes hands with them all, but can't look into their eyes. They seem too young, too eager, too friendly. 'So it's a Tiger Moth?' he says.

Tony smiles. 'Yes. Imogen thought it was a First World War aeroplane. Bit disappointed, I think, but it's still quite a find. I don't think she's decided what to do with it yet, so we're bringing it back here for the time being.'

'It's been restored, then?'

'Specialist firm,' says Tony. 'You need that nowadays. The safety laws are so stringent.'

Straker's legs have started to tremble. He tries to be calm. 'What was that about the wings being hinged?'

Tony laughs. 'Unbelievably clever design. They made them on hinges so they'd fold back, like a moth's. It meant more flexibility about where you could keep them.'

'Right,' says Straker, incapable of producing the necessary interest. He turns away, panic threatening to swamp him. 'Sorry, I've got to go. Something I forgot—'

'Here she comes,' shouts Tony, pointing to the south-west. They follow his finger and see a tiny speck coming out of the sun, hear the little engine puttering away. It grows quickly, the shape becoming clearer until they can see every detail – the flimsy wings, vibrating wires, even the pilot's face looking down at them through his goggles. He raises a gloved hand and waves.

He circles the airfield once, disappears behind some trees at the end, then emerges suddenly over the hedge, ready for the approach to the landing strip, directly into the wind.

Within seconds, the wheels touch, bounce slightly, touch again, then stay. It runs a short distance, slows, turns round 180 degrees, and taxis towards them at the end of the field before stopping.

The pilot stands up, steps on to the wing, then jumps down. There's oil on his face, with white rims round his eyes where the goggles have protected his skin. He looks like a giant panda.

Everyone is talking at once, crowding round him and slapping his back. He pulls off his goggles and grins at everyone. 'Great flight. Handles beautifully.'

Straker stands back and watches them. He sees himself a long time ago with Justin and Francis, climbing into the Warrior—

'Tony!' Doody's voice floats over from some distance away. She's striding across the field towards them.

Shock forces Straker to move. It's so long since he last spoke to her that he finds he can't do it. It's not the right moment. She's angry. She's come to shout at Tony, not him. He turns away quickly and dodges round the side of the barn. While she storms up to Tony, he runs round the back and down the path to the road, certain he hasn't been seen. He can hear her shouting.

'I can't believe I missed it. It's my plane. I wanted to be here when he flew in.'

Straker can just hear Tony's voice, calm and apologetic: 'I'm so sorry, Imogen. I went to look for you. You can't always time these things exactly . . .'

There's a new voice in my dreams.

'Pete, Pete.' It's very distant, not as confident as Maggie and the others.

'How do you know my name?'

'I don't know. I just do.'

He is someone who was there. Someone who can tell me what happened. I don't want to hear him, but I do want to hear him.

'Who are you?'

'I don't know.'

'You must know who you are. What's your name?'

'I'm not sure.'

'Everybody knows their own name. What's yours?'

'I'm confused, I'm not sure.'

His voice seems to be fading, growing weaker.

'Your name, I must know your name.'

I can hear him going away, but know it's important. 'Your name, your name . . .'

'Steve.'

Straker wakes up with a jerk, the name in his ears. Steve. He knows a Steve. He knew a Steve. Who was he? There was no one on the list of victims called Steve. Was he one of the unidentified nine? But he knew Straker. How? Was he on the plane with him? Steve . . . Steve . . .

He rolls off the mattress, surprised to find that the sun is high in the sky and washing the room with a clear, benign light. Why is he in bed during the day? Magnificent comes through the door from the stairs, rubbing his face against the crooked doorpost and arching his back. Straker puts out a hand and ruffles the thick softness of his fur, and tries to concentrate.

He has no recollection of coming home. He remembers the flight, the breathlessness, the terror and running away from Doody, but he can't remember rowing back across the bay, climbing the stairs of the lighthouse or getting into his bed.

He gets up and goes to the window, his whole body aching. The tide is up, and a fresh wind is whipping the tops of the waves into white, urgent foam. It must be early afternoon. He picks up Magnificent, letting him snuggle into his shoulder, and they climb the steps to the light room. He goes out on to the balcony and stops.

Doody is sitting on the grass at the foot of the lighthouse, gazing out to sea. Her car is parked nearby.

She's come to confront him over her husband. Now he has the chance to speak to her and apologise – but he's afraid. The idea seems rational and civilised, but it doesn't take account of Doody's unpredictability, the level of her fury. He steps back, out of sight, and breathes hard, trying not to make a sound, knowing she can't possibly hear him up here anyway.

He leans forward to check, wondering if he imagined it. No, she's still there, gazing out to sea, looking surprisingly relaxed.

She turns round and sees him. He steps back, but he's too late.

'Straker!' she shouts.

He can't hear her, but presumes she's shouting his name.

She calls again, putting her hands round her mouth in the way that children do, believing it will make their voices carry further.

He runs down the stairs, faster and faster, not sure why, but rushing to open the door for her. Then, when he reaches the bottom, he hesitates, suddenly nervous.

He turns the lock, and the door swings open on its own, because it no longer fits properly. Doody is standing outside. They face each other, and Straker can't think of anything to say.

'Have you got anything to eat?' she says.

He nods, and she follows him upstairs. He finds some Penguins and a packet of Scotch eggs. He still can't think of anything to say, so he starts to make coffee on his portable stove.

She takes one bite of a Scotch egg, chews for a second and then fixes Straker with her green eyes. 'I'll never forgive you,' she says.

So her husband was on the train.

'I wanted to be there when he flew her in. I wanted to see it. And you saw it without me.'

He breathes again, and pours out the hot water. He's only got one mug so he'll have to wait until she's finished.

'There was a hold-up on the M5. I should have had plenty of time – couldn't even use my mobile because we were moving slowly all the way.' She starts to eat more rapidly. 'I'm so hungry,' she says, between bites. 'Why didn't you stay?'

He looks at her in amazement. Did she really want him to be there? The murderer of her husband?

'And where have you been? I haven't seen you for weeks.'

'I thought—'

'What? What did you think?'

Straker takes a breath. 'Your husband,' he says.

She says nothing for a while, and just eats. 'How do you get up there?' she says. 'Where I saw you. By the light.'

He waves at the corner. 'Up the stairs.'

'Can I go up?'

'If you want to.'

'Come on, then.'

He leads the way. They emerge, panting, into the light room and then go out on to the balcony. Magnificent is still there, lying on his back, fast asleep with his paws dangling in the air, exposing his most vulnerable parts, wind ruffling the white hair on his stomach. The great warrior.

Imogen walks round the light several times, stopping to look out at the sea, leaning over the barrier. 'Wow!' she shouts into the wind. 'You can see the cottage.'

There's an oil tanker on the horizon, apparently stationary but maybe moving fast. It won't be possible to tell for a few hours. The roar of the sea is louder up here, and the wind rattles the loose window-frames, whistles through the railings.

Imogen says something, but he can't hear in the wind. He looks at her blankly, and she moves closer. 'It's all right about Harry. My husband.'

He's not sure what she means.

'I don't know if he was on the train or not yet. But, anyway, it's OK.'

'So he might not have been on it?'

'I'm waiting to find out.'

It must take time to identify an unidentified body. He still could have been on it.

'Let's go back in,' she shouts.

'Go down the stairs backwards,' he says in her ear. 'It's safer.'

Once inside, they have to wait a while to let their hearing return to normal.

'I've been to speak to his mother,' she says. 'I haven't seen her for years and she's completely changed – not the same woman at all.' She takes a breath. 'I never knew him.'

'Who?'

'Harry. He was a figment of my imagination.'

'But I thought you were married to him.'

She shrugs. 'Doesn't mean a thing. I realised when I went back that we'd been children. We had no idea what we were doing. I don't think I ever knew the real Harry.'

Straker doesn't fully understand what she's telling him, but she seems pleased about something, so he lets her go on talking.

'It was the photographs.'

For a shocked moment, he thinks she had been somewhere behind him in Simon Taverner's flat, watching him go through all the old photographs of Maggie.

'The rugby teams. He played rugby, and he's sitting there in the photographs, arms folded, his great hairy knees in front of him, looking directly at the camera, completely serious with all those other boys, and I thought, I never knew him. We lived in different worlds. I can't imagine why he ever got caught up with me. I was so unsuitable.'

'So what happened to him?'

'I've no idea, and I don't think I care any more. It was all too long ago.'

Nevertheless, I forgive you.

She's standing in front of Straker, all flushed and excited, and she seems to glow, her eyes sparkling more than they used to. There's gentle pink in her cheeks, and she appears quite different from when he first met her. Has she lost weight, become fitter and browner from working at the cottage, less sharp-edged? He's not sure about this – he needs to think—

There's a sharp crack above them, followed by a long, drawn-out groan, louder than the howl of the wind, from everywhere and nowhere. 'What's going on?' says Doody in alarm.

'It's breaking up – the lighthouse.'

'You mean it's going to fall down?'

'Yes.'

'What? Now?'

'No, not now.'

'When, then?'

'When it wants to. There's nothing I can do about it.'

'But what if you're in it when it goes?'

He opens his mouth to say that he doesn't mind, that he's been waiting for it, happy to go with it, but something stops him.

'Well?' she says.

'It won't happen in one go. Things never happen that dramatically.'

She relaxes. 'So are you going to come back to help me at the cottage?'

'I left something for you.'

She nods. 'Yes, yes. I thought it must be you. Thanks.' She sighs. 'I wish I'd been there. I really wanted to see the Tiger Moth land.'

'Go to an air show. They have lots of old aircraft. You can see them all landing and taking off.'

'You've never wanted me to keep it, have you?'

Straker looks away. He can't explain.

'Jonathan wants me to sell it. It would pay for my windows.'

'Then do it.'

She says nothing for a while, as if she hasn't heard him. 'I thought Jonathan was going to take flying lessons, and now he's suddenly changed his mind. He was probably no good at it.'

'That seems possible.'

'So?' she says. 'What do you think?'

'Sell it.'

'You're useless. I want the windows. I want to keep the Tiger Moth.'

'It's not practical.'

She sighs and sits down on his mattress. 'I know, but it's

exciting. Anyway, I need to sort out the cottage now, and I can't afford it.'

'I could pay for the window frames.' He looks away from her, out to sea. Two gulls are chasing each other in circles, and he can hear their desperate cries. They're playing, but they sound desolate, as if nothing in the world will save them. Straker wants to pay for the windows. He knows that they're not really connected with the Tiger Moth.

She's quiet for such a long time that he thinks she's gone. 'I don't know,' she says. 'Shall we wait a bit and see?'

It's dark outside and the wind has died down, but Straker can still hear the whoosh of the waves, pounding away at the cliffs below. He sits at the table, everything focused on the pool of light thrown out by the Calor gas light. He's surrounded by screwed-up pieces of paper.

He knows what he wants to say, but he doesn't know how to say it. He doesn't know what he wants to say, but he wants to say something. He tries again.

Dear Mother,
I know you will surprised to hear from me . . .

Chapter 25

Rows of cardboard boxes from the supermarket stand around Doody's front room, but she is finding very little that she wants to pack. A few clothes, the Biggles books, her unfinished novels. Otherwise, she hasn't kept things. She likes going to the tip, emptying away anything that could be considered unnecessary to her requirements. She doesn't believe in sentimental value. She has acquired very little in her life that she wants to keep. She picks up the textbook that she rescued from the pile of Harry's belongings. *Techniques in Advanced Neurology*. She hesitates, nearly puts it into the box of Biggles first editions, then changes her mind and tucks it into the waiting bin-bag of rubbish.

While she is sorting, her mind is wrestling with the problem of Mandles. She's written herself into a dead end, and can't think how to resolve it. He's tied up, blindfolded, in the back of a plane, about to be thrown into the sea. What are his options? Excitement seemed a good idea, but how does he realistically escape?

She worries away at the problem, a tight, inhospitable knot that doesn't want to be untied. She contemplates giving up. Another unfinished novel, another failure. No, there must be a way out of this.

She throws a lamp into a box, unsure if she wants to keep it. If it breaks, she'll throw it away. If not, she'll keep it. The bulb shatters, and the pieces slip, tinkling attractively, down the side of the kitchen plates.

Doody dials her mother's number and listens to the phone ringing in the dark, joyless flat. She pictures her sighing, turning *Coronation Street* down, hesitating before she picks up the phone, which is right by her chair next to the fire, close to the remote control. She'll be hoping that it will stop ringing. Doody calls on purpose during *Coronation Street*, wanting her to know that her daughter is more important, more immediate than the soaps. That there is a real life out there, where people have original thoughts and carry out non-fictional actions and do things that affect other people.

'Hello?' Her mother's voice is little and faint, clearly mindful of her potential heart condition.

'It's Imogen.'

'Oh, hello, Imogen.' Now she tries to inject some warmth and feeling. 'How are you? It's *Coronation Street*, you know.'

'I'm fine, thanks.' Suddenly Doody doesn't know what to say. She's unwilling to ask about her mother's health, because it would lead to a one-sided conversation and she's forgotten why she phoned. There may not be a reason. It may be her conscience telling her she should try to communicate with her mother more effectively.

'I'm giving up my job and moving down to Devon.'

'Oh dear, do you think that's wise?'

'Yes. I've inherited a cottage, remember. I don't need to pay rent.'

'You don't pay rent now.'

Doody sighs. They've had this conversation before. 'I do pay rent. It's rent in kind. I have to do things, be available, be around. It's the price of my free accommodation. That's why my salary is so low.'

'As I'm sure I've said before, you should have aimed higher.'

Doody knows how hard it has been for her mother, telling friends that her daughter is a school caretaker, when their children are doctors, dentists, vets. Jonathan is the ideal offspring. He's much more in her conversation than Imogen.

'I'm sure you were always quite right, then.'

'Imogen?' Her voice sharpens. 'Are you being facetious?'

'No, Mother.'

There's a pause while Doody fights down the resentment that is churning up inside her, knowing that her mother is watching the screen to find out what's going on, who's hitting whom, or who's having an affair with whom. You don't really need dialogue for that. Pictures are sufficient.

'So what are you going to do instead?'

'I haven't decided yet.' Doody wants to give the impression that she's choosing, that there are twenty job offers out there, and she would like to consider them all before making a decision.

'You know, you really should try to get some qualifications. I've always said you're wasting that brain of yours. You could have done so well if you'd tried.'

Has she always said that? The only discussions that Doody can ever remember about brains concerned Celia and Jonathan. She wasn't aware that she was supposed to have been given a generous portion of the genes.

'Maybe I'll do a college course and get a degree.'

'Oh, yes, Imogen. What a lovely idea. You're not very old. You've got plenty of time for a new career.' There's an impression of alertness, of her mother sitting up straighter, taking more interest. 'You could be a teacher.'

A teacher. Doody has a brief picture of herself in front of a class full of Bens and Helens, fighting them off, shouting over their screams, watching in despair as they wreck the classroom for the fifth time. No, thank you. 'I think I'd prefer to be a doctor,' she says.

There's a pause while her mother tries to believe this. 'Your father always thought you would be a teacher.'

Doody is shocked into silence. Her father? Is her mother talking about her husband, Doody's father? She has hardly ever mentioned him since he died – she usually behaves as if he'd never existed. 'Are you feeling all right, Mother?'

'Well, since you ask, the doctor tells me that I will have to take things a little easy in future . . .'

Doris the Lion Tamer is working in the garden when Doody goes round to the headmaster's house. She's bending over the potato patch, digging up handfuls of weeds. Her feet are firmly planted on the ground in wide-toed leather sandals, sturdy brown legs visible beneath khaki shorts. She's wearing a baggy red T-shirt and a floppy cloth hat. She likes her garden. You can see that pleasure in the easy movement of her body, bending and pulling, comfortable in its proximity to the earth.

'Doris!' calls Doody. 'Is Philip in?'

Doris straightens up. 'Hello,' she says, and Doody watches her pretending to look pleased, slipping automatically into her role as a headmaster's wife. She has to be nice to everybody – to be on the safe side. 'How lovely to see you.'

'I need to speak to Philip. Is he in?'

'Go and knock on the back window. He's only reading the paper.'

He might not like Doody knocking on his window, so she goes round to the front and rings the doorbell. She can hear him moving inside and feels his reluctance. He resents being disturbed on a Saturday evening. The door opens. 'Hello, Doody. What a surprise. It's not often we see you here at the weekend.'

She smiles happily. 'No, I'm down in Devon a lot.'

She follows him through the hall and into the lounge. There's a good view of the garden from here. Doris is visible through the window, still working on the vegetables.

Philip sits down and waves Doody to a seat, but she remains standing. 'I've been meaning to ask you, Doody,' he says, 'do you feel that perhaps you're absent from the school a little too often?'

'That's what I came to see you about.'

'Ah.'

'I'm giving up the job. I have to give a month's notice, so I've already written to the LEA.'

She enjoys telling him even more than she relished writing her letter of resignation. No more cheeky boys, no more blocked loos, no more balls on roofs. Freedom. She never wanted to be a caretaker, and she'll never need to do it again.

'The cottage, I suppose.'

'Yes. I'm moving down to Devon.'

'And you have a new job?'

'No, but I'll find one.' She can do anything. Clean, work in Sainsbury's, drive a taxi. She won't have to pay rent or a mortgage. She might sell the field, not work at all. She's a woman of property now.

'Well, I admire your courage. Starting a new life at your age.'

'Which is considerably less than yours.'

He shifts uncomfortably in his seat. 'When are you going?'

'Two weeks' time.'

'That's a relief. I thought we'd have to start the new term without a caretaker.'

'I've agreed to wait until my replacement can start.'

Doris walks in. 'Haven't you given Doody a drink yet, Philip?'

He goes apologetically to his cabinet. It's wonderful watching him obey Doris. 'What would you like, Doody?'

'Nothing for me. I need to get back.'

'I'll have a whisky, thank you, darling,' says Doris. 'Neat.'

Philip pours her drink and hands it to her. 'Doody's leaving us.'

'I knew something was going on. We've hardly seen you this summer. What exciting plans have you made?'

'I've decided to move to Devon.'

'We'll miss you, Doody.'

'Yes.' She won't miss them. Well, perhaps Doris – a little.

Doody looks out of the window. 'What's that bush called, with the little pink flowers?'

Doris joins her. 'I think it's Weigela you're looking at.' Her tanned face suddenly fills with colour, glows with a new light. 'Of course, you've got a garden. How exciting. Before you go, come round the garden with me. We can take some cuttings, and dig up a few plants that have spread, divide some perennials.' She starts to wave her hands, making shapes, wild gestures of digging, cutting, moving things from one place to another.

This is all new to Doody. She's learning about the life of a home-owner.

'You could have cuttings from the buddleia, the hydrangea, the potentilla, the mahonia – I'm sure the geraniums would take if we dig up a root or two, and the periwinkle, the one with the variegated leaf, although it can get a bit rampant. You'd have to keep an eye on it and cut it back.' She's speeding up, the names slipping out effortlessly.

Doody has never seen her so animated. The garden always looks so regimented that it appears to be obeying orders. The lawn is neat and weedless, attended to by Philip, painted with exact stripes from the mower, razor-sharp at the edges. The bushes are never permitted to stray over the lawn, the flowers colour-co-ordinated and organised in precise patterns and shapes. Doody had not understood how much passion it inspired in Doris.

'Thank you,' says Doody. 'I'd like some plants. Any time now, really, because we've started to dig the garden.'

She stops, aware that she's said something wrong. They're both looking at her with a new alertness. 'We?' says Doris, a fraction of a second earlier than Philip. 'We? My dear, I didn't realise . . .'

What is she talking about? 'What? What didn't you realise?'

Philip folds his paper, lining up the corners carefully. 'We didn't realise someone else was involved.'

'There isn't anyone else involved.' How do they know about Straker? Have they been talking to Jonathan?

'Oh.' Doris lets out a short but audible breath. 'We thought perhaps there might be someone – an attachment.'

An attachment? What's an attachment?

'A boyfriend, perhaps?'

Doody's mind fizzles and sparks with outrage. How dare they make such assumptions? Do they think she's some young girl who goes around getting crushes on people, making secret assignations in her cottage in the country? She's never thought of them as the kind of people who would concern themselves with things like that. Why have they formed judgements about something they don't understand?

'I can assure you that you've completely misunderstood,' she says, with dignity. 'My brother Jonathan comes down to help me occasionally.'

Their interest subsides as quickly as it came. 'So sorry, dear,' says Doris, but with no sign of guilt. 'We shouldn't jump to conclusions, should we?'

'No,' says Doody. 'That's absolutely right.'

'Jonathan, eh?' says Philip and opens his newspaper back up again. They know Jonathan and approve of him. Bettered himself, they think. More socially acceptable than Doody.

'Hello?'

'Imogen? It's Jonathan.'

'What's the matter? Have your friends got bored with cooking?'

'Mother says you're going to move.'

'Yes, I thought I'd live in the cottage you so kindly made available to me.'

'That's great news.'

'Maybe.' Doody feels tired. She still doesn't trust him.

'And Mother says you're going to college.'

So how long had it taken her to tell him? 'I didn't say that. She did.'

'Oh.' His voice flattens, almost as if he's disappointed, which doesn't seem likely.

'Why does it make any difference to you?'

'I wasn't thinking of me, I was thinking of you.'

'What do you mean?'

'Imogen, we've had this discussion before. I want you to be happy.'

'What's the connection?'

'You're clever. You've wasted all these years since that disastrous marriage.'

'It wasn't disastrous, it made me happy.' That should please him. She's lying, of course, but she's not going to let him know anything about her recent doubts.

He sighs. 'Whatever. But you need to do something more fulfilling, use your abilities, make some money.'

'Ah, money. Now I see where you're heading.'

'Stop it, Imogen. You're undermining everything I say. I think college is a good idea.'

'So does Mother.'

'Of course. She wants the best for you.'

'So that she can tell her friends she finally has two educated children. That's the only reason she's interested, you know.'

He hesitates. 'Actually, that's not true.'

'How do you know?'

'We talk about it, of course, and I know she wants you to have a better life.'

'She's never said that to me.'

'You wouldn't let her, would you?'

Doody stops to think about this. Do they sit there talking about her, cosy together in her mother's dark little flat? What do they say to each other? *Imogen is such a clever girl. Yes, she should be doing something much more fulfilling.* How long can the conversation go on when they have so little information, and she's not there to tell them anything new?

'She mentioned Father on the phone.'

'Really?' He sounds pleasingly amazed. 'She never mentions him to me.' His voice drops, sounding small and jealous.

Doody feels an unfamiliar sense of sadness for him. She waits for the usual accompanying irritation, but it doesn't come. 'The college was only a joke. I wanted to get her going.'

'Imogen.' His voice is solemn and she knows she's going to get a lecture. 'You must stop all this. You know we worry about you. Why do you always choose to pretend we don't care? We're your family. We feel a connection with you. Don't you think you could make an effort to make a connection with us? Mother may not be here for much longer—'

'What does that mean? Is she ill?'

'You know she is.'

'She's always ill. Why should we take this one more seriously?'

He sounds young, vulnerable, worried. 'I don't know. I'm not sure. But she does seem different . . .'

Doody is astonished. It has never occurred to her that her mother might be genuinely ill. Logically, it's not impossible. Some of the symptoms might be real ones. Maybe her doctor is intelligent after all, able to tell the difference. 'But she didn't say anything to me.' At least, she did. But, then, she always does. She was the same as usual.

'Well, she wouldn't, would she, because you wouldn't believe her?'

Doody needs to think about this. 'I have to go, Jonathan. I have an appointment. I'll speak to you later.'

She should have told him about the Tiger Moth. He paid for the repairs, and has a right to know it's finished. But he must know already. He doesn't need her to tell him. They'll have sent him the bill.

———

Straker and Doody are examining the windows again. They're standing with their backs to the sea and the lighthouse, looking up at the upstairs front windows, which are reflecting the setting sun. They look magnificent, pools of limitless colour, red, fiery, enormous. But even as Doody looks at them, she's conscious of Straker beside her, aware that she feels safer with him there. With some shock she realises that she missed him. She has never missed anyone before in her entire life.

Except Harry.

How could she miss Harry, when she didn't even know who he was? Did she miss him coming home, the meals eaten together, the presence of someone else in the flat? She can't remember. She can't recall a similar feeling to the one she's experiencing now, a warmth, a comfortable feeling of being in someone else's company. Why she should experience this with Straker is a complete mystery. It's not as if he says very much.

'Stimulating conversation isn't exactly your strong point, is it?'

He says nothing for a while. 'You think I should talk more?'

'No, of course not. Well – yes, maybe.'

'I see,' he says, and falls back into silence.

Doody wonders if she would miss Mandles if she stopped writing about him. He's still stuck there in that aeroplane, in imminent danger of being thrown out, and every time she tries to solve the problem, her mind drifts away from it. She's no longer sure that she wants to save him.

The windows will have to be replaced. They have decided this together, and Straker suggests they do it now, before winter sets in. 'I know about winter storms,' he says. 'You'll really suffer with frames like that. The wind'll come whistling through, then the rain, then the ice, and before you know where you are, you'll be freezing to death.'

'How do you keep warm in the lighthouse?'

'The windows are in better condition.'

'I thought it was falling apart.'

He shrugs. 'Yes. Well – I'm used to it.'

'So am I.' Not strictly true. There was central heating in the caretaker's cottage. Not very efficient central heating, but it was heating of a sort. She's not experienced real cold since the days with her mother and Jonathan in the council house after her father had died. That was cold.

'I could pay,' says Straker.

'What with?' she says.

'I have an allowance. From my father. I don't use it all. Most of it sits in the bank, waiting to do something useful.'

'Father? It's all revelations today. I didn't know you had a father. What's he got to do with all this? Do you ever see him?'

Infuriatingly, he stands next to her, looking up at the windows, and says absolutely nothing.

Doody's mobile rings. She rummages around in her bag, pulls it out and turns it on.

'Mrs Imogen Doody?'

'Yes.'

'This is Birmingham Police, Sergeant Bill Waitley.'

'Yes?' Doody has contacted the police herself. She knows that if she waits for Stella to pass on any news, she could wait for ever. She's not convinced that Stella even went to the police station.

'None of the unidentified bodies from the train crash was Harry Doody.'

'What?'

He speaks more slowly. 'None of the unidentified bodies from the train crash was Harry Doody.'

Doody tries to absorb this. She had become almost certain that he was on the train, that this was the rational explanation she'd been expecting for twenty-five years. 'But he must be.'

'I'm sorry. We've done tests on various items from Harry Doody's home, and they don't match up.'

So Stella had contacted them after all. She would be the best person to provide DNA samples, with none of Harry's belongings touched since he disappeared, nothing cleaned. They must have done a DNA test of Stella herself as well. 'Are you sure?'

'Absolutely positive. Mrs Doody supplied us with plenty of items from his bedroom and there can be no doubt whatsoever.'

'I see.'

She turns off the phone and stands looking at it. Straker doesn't say anything. She keeps thinking about Harry leaving her. He knew what he was doing. It wasn't a mistake.

'He wasn't on the train,' she says to Straker.

'Who?'

'Harry.'

'Great,' he says. He sounds unusually cheerful. 'Then I didn't kill him.'

'No.'

'So he must be still alive.'

'Maybe.'

'You don't sound pleased.'

She's not. It shouldn't matter to her now if he's alive or dead. Their marriage had never been what she thought it was. He means nothing to her. He never did. And yet—

Straker seems very close. She can hear his breathing right by her ear. She should move away, because she dislikes being so close to people, but she doesn't.

'So if he didn't die in the train crash, then he knew exactly what he was doing. He didn't come back because he didn't want to.'

'He might have had another accident.'

'No. He was running away from me. He hated me.'

There are tears running down her cheeks, pouring out, cascading over her face. She hasn't cried for Harry for years and years. She thought she had finally reached the stage where

334

she didn't mind, that it was all a childish dream and she had never really cared for him at all. She tries to wipe the tears away with her hands, but they keep coming.

Straker stands next to her, not moving, but solid and permanent. Like a lamp-post.

Chapter 26

It's a fine, sunny day, the sky pale blue and hollow, with tiny wisps of cloud drifting lazily up from the horizon. A jumbo jet climbs effortlessly upwards, leaving a trail of white behind it, which breaks up easily into streaks of pretend clouds.

Carmen Halliwell stands at the door of the coach. She's tall and thin, the bones of her face standing out sharply, accentuating the look of neglect that she likes. Her hair is dyed a solid black and cut very short, with tufts sticking up on top. She spends hours in front of a mirror every day, cultivating this look of deliberate dishevelment. She's dressed completely in black, despite the hot day, in a long-sleeved T-shirt and a skirt down to the ground. A striped rucksack sits at her feet, containing all her papers.

She ticks her list as people appear, and provides each with a name badge. She knows the history of everyone, but can't recognise them until they give their names.

A very tall young man, slightly droopy, with his hands hanging loosely at his side, approaches her. He gives the impression of great strength, harnessed and controlled. He has hazel eyes and a pony-tail.

He grins at Carmen. 'Hi,' he says. 'James Taverner. Grandson of Maggie.'

This could be my Robbie, thinks Carmen. A bit younger than her son would have been, but her insides still flutter at his attractiveness.

'I just thought I'd come along for the ride,' he says. 'Out of curiosity.'

Mrs Mehta, mother of Sangita. She is elderly and very small, with round shoulders, her hair grey and thick. She's wearing a bright red sari and dangling gold earrings, which end in large, pear-shaped diamonds. They look very expensive. She's dressed up, special, ready for an important event.

'I don't really expect anything,' she says, 'but I want to see him, know how he feels, isn't it?'

Jack Tilly, father of Fliss. He's short, with wisps of white hair on the edges of his largely bald head. He insists on shaking hands with Carmen, and his grip is strong and authoritative. He looks unreliable, slightly threatening, although she can't work out why.

'He's guilty,' he says, in a low voice, leaning close to her face. 'That's what an open verdict means. They know he did it, but couldn't prove it.'

'I know,' says Carmen, backing away from him, uncomfortable with his familiarity.

She watches them all boarding the coach and feels the familiar anger inside her. It's still there, burning hot, but cleverly concealed, brought lovingly to maturity, ready for this day. The most important day for a quarter of a century. All that wasted effort trying to find him in the early years. The frustration of trying to trace someone who has completely disappeared. Then the letter through the post and the realisation of who the writer was. She can still taste the triumph she felt when she was writing to him and suddenly made the connection.

She tries to see Robbie in the moment of clarity that she can usually reproduce in her mind – on the bouncy castle, suspended in mid-air, his hair spiking upwards as he descends, a look of pure joy on his face as he smiles at her. But today the image is stubbornly absent and she can only find a blank space where she expects him to be. She knows there's something missing inside her, a hole that has grown bigger and bigger over the years, and the only thing that can fill it is this anger, this raw, incandescent rage that has been building up its temperature for so long – a furnace, white-hot, powerful enough to melt iron.

———

10 a.m.

Straker and Doody stand in the office of the window-manufacturer and look through their brochures.

'UPVC windows are best,' says the sales rep. He's a very young man, the son of the owner, he tells them, but Doody thinks he doesn't look old enough to be working. It's probably just a Saturday job – earning his pocket money.

'They're plastic,' she says.

He smiles at her and looks even younger. He's called Edward, and has acne on his chin. 'Everyone says that at first,' he says, 'but have you looked round the village? At least fifty per cent of the cottages have UPVC now. They look good and they're very low maintenance – no painting. They don't rot, you can have them in any shape and design you like, and they're no more expensive than any other material. You can have aluminium, of course, if you prefer, or seasoned wood, but it'll cost you more.'

'I suppose you get more commission if we have plastic?'

He smiles again, not in the least offended, and Doody's slightly annoyed about this. She would feel better if he stopped being so nice. People are less slippery if you know you can annoy them. 'What do you think?' she asks Straker.

There's a long silence. He's not going to say anything, she thinks in a sudden panic. Finally, he opens his mouth. 'The lighthouse windows are metal,' he says.

Edward looks interested. 'Are you from the lighthouse?'

Straker nods.

338

'You live there?'

He nods again.

Edward's enthusiasm is real. 'You must be Mr Straker. I should have realised. I'd love to live in a lighthouse. My boyhood dream, I suppose.'

But he's still only a boy.

'I've heard it's going to fall down one of these days. The cliffs are crumbling, aren't they?'

'Maybe,' says Straker.

Doody is proud to be acquainted with a lighthouse-dweller. She wants Edward to know that she's been there and he hasn't. 'The doors don't fit any more, and it creaks.'

'Cool,' says Edward.

'I don't think metal windows are a good idea,' says Straker.

'Why not?' says Doody.

'They're cold. You get ice inside.'

She has a sudden bleak memory of their council house. She sees the ice in great thick layers over the metal frames, hard, shiny, impossible to remove, then the pools of water that dripped off the windowsills when the sun shone. 'Not metal, then,' she says, with relief.

'The question is—' says Straker, and stops. They wait for the question, and it seems to take for ever. 'Is wood likely to last?'

Edward is immediately enthusiastic. 'Yes, if you have seasoned wood, although I don't think it's as good as it was years ago. There are houses in the village with windows that date back one or even two centuries. Solid oak, seasoned for years before it was used. Or mahogany – real hardwood – but you can't get it now. Sustainable forests are the new way forward. They don't make window-frames like that any more. I shouldn't tell you this, really, but I think it's best to be honest.'

His father comes down the stairs with two mugs of tea, and hands one to Edward. 'How are we doing?' he says. 'Edward looking after you all right?'

Doody doesn't want him to know that she likes Edward, so she nods briefly and turns to Straker. 'You decide,' she says. 'You're paying.'

The father turns immediately to Straker. 'Go for the UPVC,' he says. 'You won't regret it.'

'What windows do you have in your own home?' asks Doody.

'UPVC,' they say promptly, almost in unison.

'You've been asked that question before,' she says, and they smile together – the same smile, the same creases round the mouth.

'OK,' says Straker. 'We'll think about the plastic. But we'll have to have prices.'

So he doesn't want to pay after all. It might be too much. He's just been pretending. 'Yes,' says Doody. 'The price is important.'

'We'll have to come out to the cottage,' says Edward. 'Measure up and then give you a quote.'

'OK,' says Straker.

Doody is annoyed that he hasn't checked with her. Maybe she doesn't want them in her house, looking at her things, being nosy. 'Can't we give you the measurements?'

The father shakes his head. 'We need to do it ourselves. If there are any mistakes, we accept full responsibility.'

'What about the fitting?' says Straker.

'We'll quote you for that.'

'I mean, can we buy the windows, then fit them ourselves?'

Edward and his father look at each other. They're thinking, Pair of idiots here. Wasting our time.

Edward starts to explain in a slow, patient voice: 'It's not really in your interest to fit them yourselves because we couldn't guarantee them. You get a much better deal if we do it.'

Why are they being so unhelpful? Does this mean that they're dishonest? Doody looks at Straker, who seems to be thinking the same thing.

340

Straker nods. 'OK,' he says. 'Come and give us a quote.'

If Doody was paying, she could walk out of the shop now and go elsewhere. She's not used to someone else making decisions. 'We'll think about it when we've got a quote,' she says.

They nod and smile. They know there aren't any other window suppliers for miles around. 'Come on,' she says to Straker. 'Let's go.'

Edward gets out his diary. 'You'll have to give me the address,' he says, still smiling, apparently unaware of her change in mood. 'Then we need to fix up a date.'

10.30 a.m.

The coach stops at a service station, and everyone gets off to stretch their legs.

A young man approaches Carmen, taller than her, with blond hair cut very short, almost a crew-cut, and moulded to his head.

'Jeremy Ainsworth,' he says, as she looks down at his name badge. 'Grandson of Jerry and Anne Ainsworth. I was named after my grandfather.'

He's very good-looking, like James Taverner, but not as old. Maybe all young men are good-looking, she thinks. Especially if you once had a son yourself. 'You can't be old enough to remember,' she says.

'I'm twenty-five. It's my birthday today.'

'You were born on the same day as the crash?'

'My grandparents had come down for the day to see me. If they'd waited a day, they'd still be alive.'

'But how did they manage that? To come on the same day?'

'I was born at one minute past midnight.'

She studies his face, trying to read in it some evidence of his mistake, his badly timed birth. She can't find anything. 'I'm glad you decided to come.'

341

'Well, I'm glad you started the website and organised the trip. My father was never the same after the crash, according to my mother – distant and uninterested in us, and she says he wasn't like that before. I think he blamed me. If I hadn't been born, his parents wouldn't have been on the train and they'd still be alive.'

'That's ridiculous. It wasn't your fault.'

'No, but people don't always think logically, do they?'

Carmen is saddened by him. He seems too young to have such profound thoughts. As he walks away, his long legs striding out with authority, she looks inside herself again, to reassure herself that the flame of anger is still alive. Small, but definitely there, flickering with impatience, poised, waiting for its moment.

Kieran Fisher, son of Alan Fisher, takes Jeremy's place. He's a short, hunched man in glasses, who has so far managed to lose his glasses on the coach, spill a flask of coffee and fall down the steps when they arrived here. His brother, Stuart, is also on the coach, but they sat at opposite ends, and don't seem to have spoken to each other.

He leans forward, his face too close to hers, and she backs away in alarm. 'What if he's not there?'

'Who?'

'Straker. Or whatever he calls himself.'

Carmen peers into his grey, flecked eyes, which are staring at her unblinkingly. She has to turn away. He's too intense. 'He will be,' she says, and knows this to be true. She has waited a long time for this day. Nothing will go wrong.

'How did you know his address?'

'Easy. He wrote to me.'

'But it was a box number.'

She grins. 'There was a postmark on the envelope. He posted it from Hillingham.'

He thinks for a while. 'But you still don't know his exact address.'

'Yes, I do. He lives in a lighthouse.'

He's clearly impressed. 'How did you find that out?'

'I rang the post office and pretended I was an old friend.'

'What if it's not him?'

'It is him.'

'But what if it isn't?'

She can feel herself getting annoyed, but she doesn't want to. It's not the right moment yet. 'Of course it's him. Nobody behaves like that. Writing to people, asking questions. It's him.'

'How can you be sure he'll be there?'

'It's the anniversary. He'll be thinking about it, the same as us.'

'Maybe he doesn't care.'

'He cares. He wouldn't have contacted us if he didn't.'

'Maybe he's just a researcher, as he says.'

Her hands are trembling with the desire to hit this man. 'If you don't think it's him, why did you come along?' she says, her voice rising in pitch.

He stands back and spreads out his hands as if he's being unjustly accused. 'I didn't say I didn't think it was him. I just wondered what we'd do if it wasn't.'

'We'll go home,' she says over her shoulder, as she walks away.

---

11 a.m.

Straker is not sure why Doody won't talk to him. Something about the window place, but he doesn't know what he did. 'We haven't committed ourselves,' he says. 'We're only getting a quote.'

She doesn't answer. It's moodiness. He knows all about that. His father was frequently moody – unexplained and frightening. He would announce arbitary decisions with no prior warning. Like the day before the crash.

Pete's mother had telephoned in the morning and woken him up.

He sat up in a dazed panic. In his dream, he had been sitting in an exam, unable to answer a single question. The bell rang – it was the end and he had failed to write anything. He fumbled with the receiver, dropped it and managed to put it to his ear, his head throbbing. 'It's only –' he squinted at the clock on his bedside table '– ten past ten.'

'It's very late to be in bed, Pete.'

'I wouldn't call this late.'

'Your father gets up at six o'clock. He says that's why he's successful.'

'Yes,' said Pete. A wave of lethargy washed through him at the thought of six o'clock in the morning. He couldn't remember ever being awake that early.

'He wants to see you at twelve o'clock.'

'What for?'

But she had put the phone down.

It must be the speeding, he thought.

He sat on the edge of the mattress, fighting the urge to get back into bed. That was all he wanted to do these days – sleep. Everything else felt like an intolerable effort. Another few pounds added to the crippling weight on his back that was already crushing his ability to move.

He forced himself to dress and shave, creeping about the house, trying not to make any sudden noises. He couldn't get the dream out of his head. It was a familiar, recurring dream, but it never became any easier to bear. It was as convincing after fifty instalments as it had been the first time. Still terrifying. The desperate, sinking realisation that he couldn't do the exam. That he was incapable and would be found out.

The phone rang again and he picked it up.

'Pete, it's Justin. What time are we meeting up?'

'I don't know. Seven, I think.'

'OK. See you then.'

If I survive, thought Pete.

He dressed in a suit, aware of the need for respectability. He tried to prepare a defence for his fast driving, but he knew what his father would say. 'You shouldn't have got caught.'

He drove over to his parents' house and arrived ten minutes late. His mother was hovering by the door as he went in. 'Hi, Mum,' he said.

She smiled at him, but he could sense her nervousness, so he walked past her without another word. She blended in with the wood panelling of the hall, only there for the décor, fading into an insignificant background.

His father was waiting for him in the office – an imposing room with bookcases lining every wall, and a large executive desk in shiny dark wood. Books were displayed in sets, according to colour, with leather binding and gold lettering. Pete had never seen his father take one out to read.

'You're late,' said his father. 'Sit down.'

Pete sat opposite the desk, the soft warmth of the leather welcoming and enclosing him. He was now lower than his father. He waited for the onslaught.

His father swivelled from side to side without saying a word. He looked smug and superior, exactly as he should look, the managing director of a firm he had singlehandedly set up, developed and expanded. A very rich man who could buy whatever he wanted. His eyes were fixed on Pete, but he didn't speak.

Pete moved uncomfortably and felt his mouth go dry. What was it all about? He cleared his throat. 'Did you want something, Dad?'

His father reacted to this. 'Did I want something? Am I

345

happy to see you sitting there doing nothing? Perhaps you'd care to tell me what you're going to do today.'

This wasn't what Pete had expected. He didn't plan his days in advance. 'I'm not sure. I haven't really—'

'What do you mean, you're not sure? I pay you a generous allowance. You have everything you could possibly want, a car, a house, a plane, and I pay for it. Don't you think it's time you started to think about earning your own money?'

Pete's insides shrivelled with misery as he recognised the old familiar conversation. They went over this every few months. It always resulted in his father's anger building up to boiling point and spilling over. The room became white-hot with fury, the surrounding air throbbing with accusation. 'OK,' he said, his voice small and insignificant next to his father's. He stood up, anxious to resolve it quickly. 'I'll go down to the labour exchange today.'

'Sit down!' his father roared, and Pete sat down. 'I want to know what you're going to do with your life.'

'It's all right,' said Pete. 'I'll get a job. You'll see – I'll soon be offering to lend you money.' He smiled, willing his father to see the joke, to abandon his headlong rush down the motorway and turn into a smaller, gentler country road. 'What a relief. I thought you were going to tell me you'd been made bankrupt, or diagnosed with cancer, or something important like that.'

'You don't think this is important?' His father got up, came round to the front of the desk and perched himself on the edge. He had put on weight in recent years, and was even bulkier than he used to be, yet he was still nimble on his feet, bursting with energy and strength. His physical presence was over-powering, and Pete found himself pressing into the back of the chair, intimidated by his closeness.

'Your mother and I—'

Mother? What did this have to do with his mother? He followed his father's eyes and turned round. She had crept into

346

the back of the room and was standing watching them. She gave him a smile again but it had no power. Why didn't she say something? How could she stand there and let her husband bully him? But then he saw again the way she stood, closing in on herself, small, fragile and inward, and he knew he was asking too much.

'Your mother and I are very angry that you've been caught speeding by the police,' said his father. 'Again. Way over the limit. How irresponsible can you get? You're a grown man and you behave like a teenager.'

'Everyone speeds,' said Pete. 'You do.'

'I don't get caught.'

His mother stepped round the side of Pete's chair. She must have been edging forwards during the conversation. 'You were going over a hundred miles per hour. You could have killed someone.'

'You'll probably be banned,' said his father.

His mother's eyes slid away to the side, refusing to look at him. She was fiddling with a handkerchief in her pocket, as if she had never spoken.

'Look, son,' said his dad, and his voice softened, 'this can't go on. My deal is, you can come and work for me, properly – in at eight, a full day, or I cut off your allowance.' He smiled, as if everything had been miraculously sorted out. Everybody manoeuvred into the correct position. End of discussion. Close the file.

Pete was shocked. 'What do you mean?'

'No more money.'

'What? None? What am I supposed to live on?'

'There won't be a problem. You're going to start earning your wages, grow up, act your age.'

Pete could feel panic rushing through his body, scorching and abrasive. They were being perfectly reasonable, of course. Most men of his age earned a living. But he had long ago discovered a fundamental weakness in himself – an inability to achieve anything of value. He lacked Andy's natural talent. 'I do try,' he said.

'No, you don't,' said his father. 'Look how well Andy's doing. You don't get that kind of success by sitting back and expecting someone else to supply all your needs.'

Pete rose from his seat. 'I see,' he said, anger and resentment giving his voice more strength. 'Andy's the golden boy, as always, and I'm the rubbish.'

His father nodded. 'You've said it.'

Pete pushed away the chair and walked to the door. 'Fine. I'll get a job – I've already said that. You think I can't do anything, but just wait and see.' He pulled open the door. 'I'll show you.'

He heard his mother cry as he left the room, 'Pete—'

He pulled the front door shut, intending to slam it, but it was too heavy and surrounded by insulation. The sound was weak and ineffectual.

He jumped into his car, turned on the ignition and put his foot down hard. The tyres shrieked as he pulled away violently over the gravel. He swung out of the gate.

––––––

'You didn't have to tell them you were paying for the windows,' says Doody.

'I didn't tell them. You did.'

'You didn't have to agree.'

Maybe she hadn't meant to tell them and it had just slipped out. So she's embarrassed – a matter of pride. 'Look,' he says, 'it doesn't matter. For all they know, we could both own the cottage. I could be your brother. I could be Jonathan.'

'No, you couldn't. You told him you lived in the lighthouse. He even knew your name.'

She strides ahead and he follows her back to the cottage. They're going to the barn this afternoon. Tony will be flying the Tiger Moth to an airfield where there's a prospective buyer.

Of course. That's the problem. She doesn't want it to go.

'Biggles wouldn't have sold it,' she says.

It would be better if she stopped thinking so much about a non-existent person.

'I always thought Mandles— Biggles would come and save things. After he escaped.'

'Biggles isn't real.'

'I know that,' she says, glaring at him.

They reach the cottage and go in through the gate.

'Supposing he's never rescued?'

He doesn't know what she's talking about. Who's Mandles?

'There he is, kidnapped by smugglers, bound hand and foot and bundled into a converted Camel.'

'Sounds like the Trojan horse.'

'Does it matter if they chuck him out into the sea, or if he gets out of the ropes, struggles with the pilot, crashes into the sea?'

'A bit cold. Not good, crashing into the sea.'

'But at least you survive if you crash on to water. It's a softer landing, surely?'

'Depends if there are any rocks, how cold the sea is, whether he can swim, how long it takes for the rescue services to arrive.'

'Oh, not long. They all know he's been kidnapped.'

'He should be OK, then. At this time of year, when the sea's warm.'

'Yes. On the other hand, should he just stay there for ever, waiting for the climax? What if there is no climax, no ending? Who cares? I thought I did, but now I'm not so sure. He's not real, is he?'

'No,' says Straker. He doesn't understand what's going on here. But at least she's talking, and she doesn't sound quite so miserable as before. 'He's not real.'

'It's just a story.'

She gives a sigh, and he examines her face for longer than

normal. He knows her now. She's not a stranger, but someone he wants to buy windows for. This is the extraordinary thing that has happened to him. He wants to buy windows for someone.

'There's something I need to tell you.'

She looks at him sharply, somehow knowing it's serious. 'You're not going to confess to another seventy-eight, are you?'

───────

Pete took the corner too fast, but he didn't care. He wanted to shut his eyes, put the accelerator down as far as it would go and roar into oblivion. His anger had subsided almost as soon as he pulled out of his parents' drive. Sleep was beckoning him again. Deep, dreamless sleep where he wouldn't have to keep tasting the bitter failure that had accompanied him all through his life.

The tyres skidded, he swung the steering wheel, and lost control. The car careered off the road, and rolled down the bank, turning over three times. It came to a halt on its back, wedged against a tree.

Pete lay dazed for a while, tangled in a heap on the upside-down roof of the car, then slowly and uncomfortably tried to extricate himself. He moved with great care, uncertain if he was still in one piece, but everything seemed to function so he eased himself out of the open window. He was in a small wood, some way from the road, and completely alone. The car groaned as he left it – creaked and settled. He sat down among the brambles and stared into silence. Everything around him seemed artificial. The blood from a scratch on his hand was too red, the sky unnaturally blue, all in primary colours, lacking subtlety, like a child's painting.

After a few minutes, he put his face into his shaking hands, and started to cry. It was not shock that was affecting him, or fear. It was an overwhelming sense of failure.

He had been on the edge of a black, welcoming void, desperate to fall down it. Now that void had moved away, out of his reach, and he remained on the outside as always, abandoned, lost, with no possible pathway back home.

Chapter 27

12 p.m.

All faces are turned to the windows on the right of the coach, watching the sea. It's a calm day, with a faint breeze rustling the edges of a gentle swell, which rises and falls rhythmically. It's an idyllic scene, seagulls circling and diving, the sun transforming the metallic surface of the water into a brilliant blue reflection of the sky.

'There it is!'

Everyone leans over and stares. The lighthouse is silhouetted against the sea, calm and in control, almost elegant, despite the fairground implications of its red and white circles. It's pointing up at the sky, surrounded by space, superior in its isolation.

'How close can you get us?' Carmen asks the coach driver.

He's already slowed down, examining the cropped grass bordering the Tarmac. 'I might be able to get us on to the edge,' he says. 'But I couldn't risk anything more than that.'

'OK. That'll do.'

He swings the wheel sharply and they lurch on to the grass, levelling out, until they're parallel with the road. 'Sorry,' he says. 'That's as far as I go. As it is, I've broken a few rules.'

'That's fine,' says Carmen. 'Thank you.'

They climb out of the coach and on to the grass, standing around at first, stiff from the long drive, squinting into the brightness of the sun. After a few minutes, they organise themselves into small groups and set off towards the lighthouse. Carmen finds herself taking the lead with a group of young men, while the older ones walk more slowly behind, stumbling over the unevenness of the ground.

'What if he's not here?' says Kieran Fisher.

Carmen takes a deep breath. 'We've already had this conversation,' she says.

'Ignore him,' says a calm voice on her other side. 'He's always like this. Can't leave anything alone.'

'I'm sorry?'

'You've forgotten me already, haven't you? Stuart Fisher. Kieran's my brother.'

'I don't know why he came,' she says. 'He doesn't believe we'll find him.'

'He never believes anything. Never did. He's a compulsive doubter. You should try living with him. It's no fun, I can assure you.'

'Don't believe him,' says a voice in her other ear. 'He can't tell the truth. He's the compulsive one. He lies to make himself look good.'

'See?' says Stuart.

'He even fools our mum,' says Kieran.

Carmen finds herself unable to judge between them. She stops and looks round. 'We should wait for the others,' she says. She can see Mrs Mehta struggling in the rear, her high heels sinking into the turf. Geraldine Pendlestone, one of the few survivors of the crash, goes back to help. She used to be a teacher until she lost the entire class in her care. Carmen waits for them to reach her, and the brothers walk on without her, several yards apart, acting as if they don't know each other.

'Are you all right?' she says to Mrs Mehta. 'I'm sorry, I didn't realise it would be such a long walk. My directions weren't very precise.'

'I am good,' says Mrs Mehta. 'What is a little discomfort? A little pain for my daughter, isn't it?'

'What do you expect to get out of this?' asks Carmen.

Geraldine shrugs. 'Who knows? I just think we owe it to

ourselves to find out what we can while we've got the chance. I suppose there will always be unanswered questions – nobody can know everything. But I'd like to see him again.'

'Do you think we'll recognise him?' Carmen has a folder full of blurred newspaper pictures in her bag, but she knows he won't look the same.

'Was he evil or stupid? That's what I want to know.'

'I don't see how he can go on living a normal life. How would you live with yourself?'

Geraldine looks át her. 'So what are you saying? He should be dead? Kill himself for our sakes?'

Carmen flushes. 'I don't know.' She fights down the flames of her internal fire. 'Well, why not? It doesn't seem right that he should be all right when our children aren't.'

'I lost a whole class of children. You never recover from that either. But I'm not sure that knowing he was dead would make it any easier.'

They weren't your children, thinks Carmen. It's not the same.

'What I have discovered,' says Geraldine, 'is that I want him to be evil.'

Carmen nods slowly. 'He is evil.'

'The trouble is, he may not be.'

'He must be. All that blood on his hands.'

'He might regret it.'

No way, thinks Carmen.

There's shouting from ahead, and they see that the younger ones have already reached the lighthouse. They're standing at the bottom, looking up.

'They might have waited until we all got there,' says Carmen.

'They probably feel they've waited long enough.'

They walk a little faster, half carrying Mrs Mehta between them, until they are all congregated at the base of the lighthouse.

'He's not here,' says James Taverner.

Kieran tries the handle on the door, and it swings open. 'We could go in,' he says.

'I don't know . . .' says Geraldine, but nobody takes any notice. They race inside and up the stairs. Carmen and Geraldine follow. They can hear the footsteps of the others pounding up the stairs above them, stamping in their anxiety to be there first.

'Oh, well,' says Carmen. 'What have we got to lose?'

'Suppose we have the wrong person?' Geraldine seems genuinely worried. 'Thirty-two people hounding an innocent man.'

'Too late to worry about that,' says Carmen, and they start climbing the stairs.

12.15 p.m.

Doody and Straker prepare some lunch in the cottage kitchen. The hens prowl broodily round the wall on their frieze, clucking in silence. Doody fills a jug of water at the sink and puts two glasses out with the plates and knives. Straker gets the breadboard, unwraps some pâté and puts it on a plate.

Doody thinks about what Straker has just told her. 'So you think you crashed the car on purpose?'

'That's how I remember it.'

'You wanted to die.'

'Yes.'

'But it didn't work.'

'No. I just got up and crawled out. Apart from a few bruises, I was completely unhurt. The car didn't catch fire.'

She half smiles. 'Bad luck, then. Couldn't even kill yourself properly.'

'No. I had another go the next day.'

She is about to sit down, but stops and looks at him. His

beard is shorter than it was when she first met him, and neater. He's started to trim it and she hadn't noticed. He looks younger than when she first met him.

'You mean you did it deliberately? The real crash? The aeroplane?'

'Well – the evidence is fairly incriminating, isn't it?'

'But that was different. I mean, there were other people involved.'

'If I'd tried it once, I could have tried it again.' He looks past her. 'I was a fool. No common sense, no concept of responsibility.'

She sits down and looks at the plate in front of her. Oliver d'Arby's china. White with two blue circles round the rim. 'My sister committed suicide.'

His eyes turn to her in surprise. 'I didn't know you had a sister.'

'I haven't. She's dead.'

He watches her. 'Why did she do it?'

'I couldn't understand it at the time. She was very clever, a gifted child, everybody said. Maybe she couldn't keep it up. I suppose it must be a huge strain, having to be the best all the time. You're not allowed to be lazy, or careless. Everyone's expectations must be so high, and if things don't go right, they're all so disappointed. I think she tried to explain it to me once, but I wasn't listening. We didn't get on.'

'So she was too clever and I was too stupid.' His voice is low and exhausted. 'I can't remember what was going on in my mind – only the despair, the feeling that there was no way out.'

'But you had an easy way out. You could have gone to work.'

'I know. It doesn't make sense, does it? I told them I would work. But that wasn't really what it was about. I couldn't seem to do anything right – nothing would please them . . .' He pauses and smiles bleakly. 'I was like a self-indulgent, spoilt child, I suppose.'

'But you still don't know what happened on the next day when you crashed the plane. It could have been completely different.'

He is silent, and they start to eat their lunch. Doody needs to consider what he's just told her before she can make any comment. She likes the fact that they can think together but they don't need to share the words.

Did she share any silence with Harry? Even in the last few weeks when he seemed depressed, Doody had talked to him all the time, filling the spaces, trying to make the flat homely and comfortable with her life, her thoughts, her existence. Somewhere he would want to come home to.

Except he didn't.

Harry and Imogen had talked non-stop to start with. About everything in the world. It was as if neither of them had talked before and they just poured it out, endlessly. Did they listen to each other? At the time, she had thought they did, but perhaps she was wrong, and they were just concentrating on their own thoughts. Maybe they had both found it so exciting to have a person to talk to that they forgot they should have been listening as well.

The liberating thing about Straker is that she doesn't have to try. There is nothing that she must do or say. She can talk to him or not and he accepts both.

'How old are you?' she asks.

He looks up in surprise. 'I'm not quite sure. I'll have to work it out.'

'Well, you're good at numbers. Think of a number, double it, multiply by three, divide by two, take away the number you first thought of.'

He shakes his head and smiles. 'Fifty-three,' he says.

'Ten years older than me.'

'Really?' He bites into his roll. She watches him chew. She normally can't bear people eating, hearing food rolling round in their mouths, breaking up, liquefying, watching them swallow, seeing it go down their throats. All horribly intimate and physical. But every time she sits with Straker, she doesn't mind. It seems perfectly natural, as if she's eating and all the noises and movements are her own.

Biggles doesn't seem important any more.

'It's an impressive record,' she says. 'Surviving two crashes in as many days.'

---

1 p.m.

They swarm over the lighthouse, crowding into the tiny rooms, overflowing from one level to the next, squeezing past each other on the stairs. The young ones race up to the light room and lean over the railing.

'What a way to see the world every time you wake up.'

'Cold in the winter.'

'You can see for miles.'

They have to shout to make themselves heard. The wind is booming overhead and tugging at their T-shirts and jackets.

'Does it seem completely upright to you?'

They try to stand up straight and gauge the vertical position of the lighthouse against the church tower in the background.

'It's an optical illusion.'

'No, it's not right.'

'You're imagining it. It's fine.'

'It makes me feel sick. I'm sure it's leaning over, like the Tower of Pisa.'

'Look how close we are to the edge of the cliff. That can't be right.'

'Do you reckon it's going to fall over?'

'I'm sure of it. I'm an architect. I know about these things. Believe me, the edge of the cliff is too close. It'll be much more eroded lower down – undermining the foundations.'

They look at each other, alarmed. 'Is it safe?'

In the room below, Carmen and the older ones are peering round curiously. They move awkwardly, with the embarrassment of intruders, but at the same time they want to see how he lives, to find proof that they have the right man.

'Look,' says Geraldine, picking up several files from the floor. She puts them on the desk and opens them. Photographs spill out, news cuttings, letters from them to Peter Straker, lists of names, communications from experts, times, dates . . .

'There you are,' says Jack Tilly. 'What more evidence do you want? It's him all right.'

'We knew he had all this information. We gave him most of it. He could still be what he says he is, a writer,' says Geraldine.

Carmen doesn't believe this. She never has. She knows that Peter Straker is Pete Butler. In her mind they are the same person. She felt it from the first moment she received his letter and she trusts her instincts on this, absolutely.

'But where is he?'

'Yes,' says Carmen. 'That's what I want to know.' The thought that they might miss him altogether haunts her. They have found the lighthouse, his home, his notes. All they want is the man.

'We could just wait here for him to return.'

Carmen hesitates and looks at her watch. One fifteen. She makes a decision. 'Let's go and have lunch. We'll all feel better when we've eaten, and we can ask in the village if anyone knows where he is. We can always come back.'

She calls the young ones down from the light room and they emerge from the stairs dishevelled by the wind and excited.

'Phew!' says Jeremy Ainsworth, breathing deeply. 'Great place to live.'

Something like a groan begins somewhere deep within the building. It starts softly, a delicate whine of protest, polite still and controlled, then it rises in volume and becomes a shriek, more violent, like the protest of a man screaming in agony.

Gradually, the sound subsides, settles back into the low groan, then stops. Everyone is motionless, looking round with shocked horror.

'What was that?' says Kieran into the silence.

'The lighthouse is dying,' says Stuart. 'It's about to collapse.'

Jack Tilly bolts for the stairs. 'I'm out of here,' he says.

'Well, probably not quite that soon,' says Stuart, watching Tilly's departing back. There's a shout of laughter, mixed with relief, then they all dash after him, tumbling over each other in their anxiety to escape.

They drive back into the village, subdued, grappling with the discovery of Straker's notes, the crumbling lighthouse, the realisation that they are in the right place and that they have been breathing the same air as the man they have all been hating for twenty-five years.

Chapter 28

Doody marches through the cottage gate and turns towards the field and the aeroplane that Tony is about to fly away. Straker follows her reluctantly, wishing it was all over and the Tiger Moth gone.

'I've changed my mind,' she says, turning round to wait for him. 'I'm going to keep it.'

Naturally.

'It's a dream, isn't it? Why should I sell my dream?'

'Because it's cheaper.'

She stops walking. Straker is learning to recognise that dangerous glint in her eyes, the rigid set of her mouth and the way she stands, hands hanging loose at her sides, deliberately not clenched. 'So why shouldn't I do something extravagant? I've spent most of my life getting things wrong without meaning to. This cottage is the best thing that ever happened to me. Aren't I allowed to make my own mistakes for once and not just wait for circumstances to get me anyway?' She stops, takes a breath and relaxes now that she's said it all. 'If I can't have Biggles, I want the real thing.'

Surely Biggles has already been disposed of in the sea.

'It's not just the cost of learning to fly. You have to keep paying out for maintenance.'

She glares at him. 'Stop being so practical. You live in a lighthouse. You should be more visionary.'

A large crowd of people is walking up the road behind them,

some on the cobbled pavement, but most on the road. Straker and Doody stop to let them pass.

Straker is still thinking about the crash. He wishes he could remember more, bring back what was going on in his mind just before it happened.

Unexpectedly, he feels Doody's hand on his arm. He waits for her to remove it, assuming it is a mistake, but it stays there. He can feel the warmth from her seeping through and penetrating his skin.

'You can't change things, you know.' Her voice is unusually gentle.

He raises his eyes.

'It happened. Nothing stops that, whatever you were thinking at the time.'

'I don't know what I was thinking.'

'You probably weren't that stupid. Crashing a car with just you in it isn't the same thing as destroying a train full of people. Most potential suicides don't decide to take everyone else with them.'

'I wish I could remember. What sort of person was I? I can only see myself now.'

'And you wouldn't do it now. That's the important thing. I used to worry about Harry. Maybe if I'd done it better, he wouldn't have gone. But that's just how it is. You pick yourself up and carry on walking.'

'An open door,' says Straker. 'You don't have to look through it every time you go past.'

Doody stares at him. 'That's right,' she says. 'That's it exactly.'

Straker moves over to let the group of people pass, but Doody remains standing in the road, refusing to allow them more space. He examines their feet. There are trainers, normal for the sailing lot, and smart shoes – suede, leather. Older styles too, with flat heels, one-inch heels, three-inch heels, even higher in one case, although these are stumbling to keep upright on the road, which is not much smoother than the cobblestone pavement. It's the diversity of ages and styles that is disconcerting. They don't look as if they ought to be together.

Straker becomes aware that the feet have stopped walking, and they're all around him and Doody. There's an odd silence.

'Straker?'

Who are they? How can they possibly know his name? He raises his eyes to their faces.

In front of the group, there's a woman who reminds him of Doody. She has that same aggressive way of standing and staring at him that makes everything his fault. She moves closer and he tries to back away, but there's only a stone wall behind him.

'Who's asking?' says Doody.

'Who are you?' says the woman, half turning her face to her.

'I asked first.'

'Is your name Straker?'

'It might be.'

The woman turns back to Straker. 'I don't think so,' she says slowly.

He looks at the woman's face. She has pale, almost transparent skin, and her short, spiky hair is so black that it's difficult to see any individual strands of hair. Her unnaturally bright eyes, heavily rimmed with black makeup, are staring at him with an intense, hungry expression. She's prettier than Doody, and thinner, but there's a hardness about her that's almost familiar – although not quite. He realises that Doody's anger must be cultivated and controlled, because it's nothing in comparison to the reality of this woman's anger.

'I'm Straker.'

She smiles unpleasantly. The people round them are breathing, listening, waiting.

'Does the name Carmen Halliwell mean anything to you?' she says.

He knows the name, but he can't think clearly enough to work it out.

'Or Pete Butler?'

He swallows hard.

'I'll tell you who we are. Listen to the names, Straker. Think about them. Kieran and Stuart Fisher, sons of Alan Fisher. Jack Tilly, father of Felicity. Felicity Tilly. Jeremy Ainsworth, grandson of Jerry and Anne. James Taverner, grandson of—'

'Maggie,' he says. 'Maggie!'

There's a sudden silence, as if they are taken by surprise. There appear to be hundreds of them now, crowding round together, although no one actually touches him. Straker is finding it difficult to breathe.

'Yes,' says a calm voice. 'Maggie. She was my grand-mother.'

Straker looks at his face. A tall young man with a pony-tail, somehow very strong and confident. He's undoubtedly a Taverner, a younger version, one of those faces in the photographs that Straker pored over in Simon's flat. It is possible to see Maggie in him. And Simon. Looking at his face, Straker believes he can see the loss, the absence of something.

'What about the others?' shouts another voice. 'My Helen.'

Then all the voices join in. 'Yes, what about Leroy?'

'Paul!'

'Johnny!'

They are all names he knows. He's conscious of the fury of the names, throwing themselves at him, slamming him against the wall. He tries to push them away, and feels Doody's reaction as she moves closer.

'What's going on?' she says. 'Clear off! How dare you come here and harass us?'

He wants to tell her that he understands what's happening. He doesn't recognise any of them, but he knows who they all are. He's been diverted by other memories and briefly forgotten Simon Taverner's computer – the conversations on it, the plans they were making . . .

'What do you want from me?' he says at last, struggling to make his voice work properly. Half of him is afraid and the other half is strangely liberated, as if this is what he's been waiting for all these years, a chance to confront them, to explain, or give them something back. If he dies here, now, it won't matter. It would be fair. After all, there's no real justice for someone who's killed people. How can there be? You can't bring them back. There's nothing you can do. Once it's done, it's done.

'We've come for you,' says Carmen.

'I know,' he says.

'We want to know what really happened, not what you told the court.'

'I don't know what happened,' he says.

'Rubbish,' says a voice from the back. 'Stop being a coward and face up to it. Tell us the truth.'

Doody, at his side, is tensing, but not speaking. She must realise by now who they are.

'It's the same as then,' he says. 'I can't remember.'

'Don't give us that. It's just a cop-out.'

'I know it seems like that—'

'Stop messing about and tell us the truth.'

But there isn't a truth. Or if there is he doesn't know what it is. He only has the information that they all have, the result of the inquest, which is that nobody really knows what happened. The truth must be locked somewhere inside his brain, and he doesn't have access to it. He doesn't know a way to get to it.

'Go away!' shouts Doody, right by his ear. 'This isn't a court. You've no right to come here.'

'Don't talk to me about rights!' yells a voice from the back. 'Did he think about my rights when he killed my daughter?'

'How does it feel to kill all those people?' says a soft voice by

Straker's other ear. He turns and sees a man in his thirties, who's screwing up his eyes and twisting his mouth into an expression of revulsion. He appears to be about to hit him, but he doesn't. 'How does it feel to be a murderer?'

'It wasn't murder,' says Doody. 'Murder is premeditated. It was an accident.'

'What do you know about it?' shouts a woman.

'As much as you,' yells Doody.

'Seventy-eight people,' says the voice by Straker's ear, and his stomach starts to roll. He has managed to not think of the seventy-eight for some time, but now they come back to him eagerly, burrowing their way into his head, tumbling around his mind: seventy-eight, seventy-eight.

Jonathan looks at his watch. 'What time are you taking off?' he says again to Tony, although he's already asked the question several times already.

Ben and Kasra have just brought the aeroplane to the take-off position, one on each wing, guiding it into the right place, with Terry controlling the trolley at the back, supporting the tail skid.

Now it sits comfortably on the grass, facing the runway, neat, polished, immaculate. Tony is wearing a leather jacket and has goggles hanging round his neck. 'Got to look the part,' he had said, with a grin, when he first greeted Jonathan.

'It's supposed to be two fifteen,' he says. 'She's done it again. We'd better hang on a bit.'

'Reliability isn't Imogen's strong point. I spend my life waiting for her.'

'I can't understand why she's late again. Give her a few more minutes.'

Jonathan walks round the Tiger Moth, running his hands over the wings. 'They've done a good job,' he says.

'Careful,' says Tony. 'It's only fabric. You could go through that, easy as anything.'

Jonathan hastily withdraws his hand. 'Are you sure you couldn't take me up as a passenger? In the other cockpit?'

Tony shakes his head. 'Sorry, it's not on. Regulations are very strict these days. If you want to keep the certificate of airworthiness, you can't take passengers. I've got ballast in there to get the weight right.'

'We'll give her another five minutes,' says Jonathan. 'Then you'd better go.'

'I can wait a bit longer than that. She'll be very disappointed.'

'I'll be very disappointed if you don't take off before I go. I've driven all this way to see it, and I've got to get back. I've got an appointment later on today.'

Tony looks interested. 'On a Saturday? Are you still on that deal with Harold Harrington?'

Jonathan nods. 'Promised I'd meet him for drinks tonight. I can't miss it.'

They stand by the aircraft with Ben and Kasra and Terry. Jonathan checks his watch, shifting his weight from one leg to the other. 'Imogen's seen it in the air,' he says. 'She told me.'

'She missed the landing.'

'Yes, but she saw it flying. I won't see it at all if she takes much longer.'

A gentle breeze ruffles the short grass at their feet. The windsock comes briefly to life.

'Perfect weather conditions,' says Kasra.

––––––––––

2.20 p.m.

A sharp object hits Straker, and he falls backwards against the wall, his hand to his head. There's something wet dripping down his face. Blood. They've got guns! With silencers. He's hit again and again, knocked back each time, convinced he must be dying. But it doesn't hurt enough. He brings his hand

367

down to look – it's coated with something yellow and slimy. For a second he thinks his blood has turned yellow. Then he realises he's being attacked with eggs.

They're coming rapidly, but from only one person. A tiny Indian woman in a bright red sari, with dangling jewellery and ridiculously high-heeled shoes. She's getting the eggs out of a carrier-bag one at a time and throwing them, putting all her energy into the action. Everyone else has stopped to watch her, amazed by her ferocity.

'You took away my Sangita,' she's shouting, tears running down her cheeks. 'She was a beautiful girl, my only one, just a little trip to India, her father and me, come home, no lovely girl, you kill her!'

She leaps at Straker, spitting, her long painted nails attacking his face, scratching him, grabbing at his clothes. He tries to fend her off, but he's afraid of hurting her – she's so small. Doody doesn't seem to have any reservations, however, and she throws herself at the woman, trying to pull away her hands, which is almost impossible, since her nails are locked into his jumper.

The situation descends into chaos. There are people everywhere, disembodied hands clawing at him, fighting each other for a position, voices screaming, feet pushing against each other, and in front of all these, the Indian woman refusing to let go with her nails, her voice hoarse and shrill. 'Murderer! Killer! Assassin! Manslayer!'

She screams the four words over and over again, and her high-pitched voice carries above all the other shouting. Straker keeps trying to untangle her nails, but as soon as he removes one, another hooks on. Doody is pulling at her viciously, while, at the same time, they're being lunged at by people in the crowd. It's a maelstrom of voices, arms, legs, heads, open screaming mouths, kicking legs, scrabbling hands—

2.30 p.m.

'We're going to have to get going,' says Jonathan. 'I wasn't expecting to wait.'

'Well . . .' says Tony. 'If you're sure.'

'I'll just go and see if she's coming.' Jonathan jogs to the top of the field, looks down the pathway to the gate, and runs back. 'Sorry,' he says, panting. 'There's no sign of her. I think you'd better go ahead.'

Tony zips up his jacket, climbs on to the left wing and into the cockpit, then lowers himself into the seat. He organises the harness and clicks the five points into place. He looks out over one side and then the other. 'OK,' he shouts, and pushes down the brass switch on the side to start the electrics.

Ben and Kasra move to the front and stand by the propeller, which is set at a ten-to-four position. Then, together, they reach up and pull the propeller down very hard. Nothing happens. They try again, and this time it rotates twice, hesitates and stops. They do it once more, and it roars into a violent and powerful life, while they jump out of the way.

Tony moves the joystick, looking round to check that the elevators are moving correctly, and tests the pressure on the rudder pedals. He can see the ground beneath his feet, the grass he spent so much time preparing. He moves the ailerons. Then he pushes up the throttle to full power for the engine test. The sound is deafening, and the cockpit vibrates uncomfortably around him.

2.35 p.m.

There's a new sound, confused with everything else at first, gradually becoming more dominant. A strident, ear-shattering blast, on and on – a belligerent car horn. Some people are drawing back – there's a sense of space appearing around Straker.

'Look out!' shouts a hysterical voice.

'A lorry!' screams someone else. 'Quick, get out of the way!'

The lorry is big and orange – a Sainsbury's lorry – and it's not making any concessions as it heads towards the people in the road. They are scattering in all directions. Straker can't see Doody anywhere. The Indian woman still seems to be attached to his jumper.

'Run!' says a voice in his ear. Doody. He tries to turn and speak to her, but there's no room to move in that direction. He can just see her arms pulling the Indian woman off him with a final yank, and then he's free.

'Run!' she yells.

He runs. He pushes through the people who are hovering in bewilderment and pounds up the road, squeezing through the narrow gap at the side of the lorry. He puts his head down and counts his strides – twenty-five, twenty-six, twenty-seven – his mind calming with the rhythm. He doesn't know where he's going – he just knows he's running away. He can hear Doody's voice behind. 'Run! Run!' She may not really be shouting at him, it may just be in his head, but he keeps going.

He has no idea if anyone is following. The hysteria seems to fade slightly as he approaches the gate to Doody's field. He swerves off the road and leaps over the gate without pausing. He can feel their feet behind him, their panting, their breath on his neck, their desperation, and he runs faster. Up the path, into the field where the Tiger Moth is waiting to take off.

'Stop!'

He can't stop. They're behind him, they're nearly upon him, and he has to escape.

2.40 p.m.

Tony pulls back the throttle, reducing the power. He looks round the side of the cockpit at the field, unable to see directly ahead. The aircraft is still vibrating, the wires twanging, and he can see movement on the wing surface – a fluid rolling of the fabric, almost like water.

He pulls his goggles over his eyes and waves his arms to indicate that he wants the chocks removed.

Ben pulls the rope from one side, then Kasra pulls from the other side. The yellow chocks come away easily. Tony looks into his mirror to see Terry holding down the tail empennage. The Moth is straining to go. He can feel its readiness, and when he waves, Terry lets go.

Figures appear in his mirror, someone out in front, racing towards the aeroplane, waving his arms, followed by a crowd of other people, surging after him.

He turns round to see what's happening.

———

2.41 p.m.

Straker runs past Jonathan and the other helpers to the aeroplane, and can't believe what he's seeing. The engine is already running, the propeller moving, ready to take off. Tony is climbing out, looking anxious.

'What's going on?' he shouts. 'I thought you were—'

Ignoring him, Straker runs round him and starts to climb into the Tiger Moth.

'Hey!' shouts Tony. 'You can't do that.'

He grabs Straker's arms, then his legs, and pulls him down off the wing.

'Get out of the way,' screams Straker, and his voice seems to belong to someone else – a terrifying madman.

He tries to climb up again, but Tony pulls at him violently. He's stronger than he looks.

Straker turns back and pushes him hard. At first Tony resists and struggles to keep his balance, then falls over, his mouth in a round O and his eyes wide behind his goggles.

371

Straker climbs back in, settles down in the seat and takes hold of the joystick. Yes, he can do this. The controls are not so different from his old Warrior. He finds the lever for the throttle on the side.

As the Tiger Moth begins to move, he turns in his seat and sees the whole vast crowd of people rushing towards him. Tony is still on the ground, staring up in shock.

'I'm sorry!' he yells. 'I'm sorry.'

Probably no one can hear him, but it's true. He's always been sorry.

He opens the throttle and the Moth moves forward over the stubbly grass, down a gentle gradient and into the wind. It rocks precariously. The engine roars as he picks up speed and the tail lifts. Will it take off? The pilot who delivered it flew it successfully – there's no reason why Straker shouldn't manage it. By luck the wind is in the right direction – although, of course, it isn't luck. Tony will have worked it out. Straker pulls the stick back gently, holds his breath, and slowly, slowly, he feels the wheels leave the ground.

There is a great rumbling in his ears – it may be the sound of the engine, or it may be the crowd of people below him. He gasps with relief, then sees the end of the field, and the row of cypress trees, looming up in front of him. He pulls the stick back hard, as far as it will go, forcing the nose up, shuts his eyes and feels the plane press upwards, the engine straining with effort.

Then he's clear. He opens his eyes, and the trees are below him, while he soars up into the blue sky. A huge space opens up inside him, and a freedom that he'd almost forgotten greets him like an old friend. There is emptiness all around, almost weightlessness, a sense that nothing else matters. It's exactly the same as it used to be, when he was younger, when he could forget all the squalid, boring details of his life and feel that he was worth something.

He experiments with the ailerons, and banks sharply so that

he goes back over the field. When he looks down, he can see them all in a group together, staring up at him, a crazy pavement of upturned faces, pale and featureless. They're unknown to him as individuals, but their accusations are floating up to him through the clear air. Only one person is familiar, Doody, and he can't distinguish her from the others.

'Sorry!' he shouts again. 'Sorry!'

At that point, he realises that he doesn't know where to go. He has no plan.

He circles, flying lazily over the village. Out to sea? He spots the lighthouse, which looks small and vulnerable, and perilously close to the edge of the cliff. He goes round several times, until Suleiman and Magnificent emerge through the cat-flap. They sit outside, tiny ornaments, surprisingly close to each other. Their faces are turned up at the sky, their tails sticking out long and thin behind them. Do they know it's him?

Why is the lighthouse still standing when everything else is coming to an end? He banks and heads out to sea, not knowing what he wants.

Doody. She comes charging into his mind, angry, yelling. 'Don't give in to them,' she's shouting. 'Make your own decisions. Do what you want to do.'

She's right. He didn't decide to do this. He was driven here by them.

He deserves it. He killed all those people.

How do you know? Nobody knows what happened.

But he knows it was his fault.

So? Can he change anything?

No.

Can he make it up to them?

He's spent all this time writing to them, talking to them in his head, justifying himself, trying to make himself understood, but really there's nothing he can say. It happened. He made it happen, and he doesn't remember how. It was his fault, but he can't replay it and make it better. It's done.

He thinks of Simon Taverner, of Carmen and the fury of the tiny little Indian woman who must have nurtured all that hate inside her for so long. Will she feel better now that she's attacked him? Maybe that was what she needed. Maybe they'll all go home thinking they have achieved something. Would anything he does make any difference?

The space that opened up when he took off into the sky grows wider and fresher and more welcoming than before. He can breathe. The air is rushing into his lungs freely. He has to keep wiping his eyes, brushing away the spots of oil that blow on to him from the engine.

Maggie has forgiven him.

Doody is here now, taking over from Maggie, her voice concerned, no longer angry. 'Well, you'd better come down, then, hadn't you?'

Yes, he can face them now. He will speak to them.

He attempts to bring the Moth round, ready to return to the airfield, but she doesn't respond as he expects. Instead of turning to the right, the wings waver slightly, and they continue to head out to sea. A knot of anxiety tugs at his mind.

The engine misses a beat, almost imperceptibly. He listens, straining his ears, and it happens a second time. Why didn't he notice it before?

He tries again. The Tiger Moth responds a little more willingly, and Straker leans over to help it turn. The sea is swaying below him, closer than before, the waves tipped with foam, alarmingly close.

Sluggishly, the aircraft turns, and Straker relaxes a little, although he doesn't stop listening. As he heads back for the land, there's a strong breeze in his face, and he has to screw up his eyes uncomfortably, aware that the engine is fighting to maintain its power against the wind. It's almost impossible to fly without goggles. Hot, leaking castor oil is pouring into his face in a steady flow, and he can taste it in his mouth – vile and bitter. He tries to wipe it away, but his hand becomes too greasy and it is increasingly difficult to see anything.

He pushes the nose down, trying to build up speed, so that he can get back to land before anything else goes wrong, but the throttle is not responding normally, and the engine starts to whine with the strain. Then, suddenly, it cuts out altogether and he's plunged into complete silence, the aeroplane gliding down towards the sea. He presses buttons, pulling the controls in an attempt to jolt the engine back to life, but it's not a modern aircraft – there's no electronic ignition. He's dropping rapidly, the only sound the whistling of the wind through the struts, a wailing from the wings as the speed picks up, the groaning of the Tiger Moth as it unwillingly surrenders.

Oil is all over his face by now, and he can't see anything. There's nothing he can do. So this is how it feels to die. He's glad it's him and not Tony, who's got all those children. It's not so bad. Was it like this the last time he crashed, before he hit the train? If he survives, will he forget this too?

His mind fixes on an image of Doody, standing in front of him, ferociously angry as ever, and it's as if he can feed off her anger. There's something wonderfully alive and urgent about her that nourishes him and makes him see himself in a way he's never experienced before. The numbness of twenty-five years has melted, he realises, and Doody has brought him back to life. Just in time to die.

'Do something, Straker!' he hears, as he hits the sea. And it's Doody's voice, not Maggie's.

Chapter 29

Doody wanted Straker to run, to escape from those vindictive people, and following him up the road in the direction of the field, she realises she must have known that he was going to end up flying her aeroplane. She whoops with pleasure as he picks up speed along the field, and the moment the wheels leave the ground feels like the moment she's been waiting for all her life. She stands and watches him take off over the trees, the most beautiful thing she's ever seen. It wipes away all her years of frustration and nothingness.

She shades her eyes with her hand and watches Straker head out to sea. She's surrounded by this crowd of people, the relatives who've come to get him, but she doesn't mind, because she's not really here. She's with him in the Tiger Moth, soaring into the sky. Everyone has gone quiet, and they stand together, gazing up, watching him gain speed and height.

'Imogen,' says an urgent voice at her side. She turns round and Tony is beside her, confused and dishevelled. 'I'm sorry. I couldn't stop him. He knocked me over.'

She blinks, trying to see him more clearly after the glare of the sun. 'Are you all right?' she says.

He nods. 'Yes, it was nothing, really. He didn't hit me very hard. But the Tiger Moth—'

'It's all right,' she says. 'It doesn't matter.'

'But all that work, all our time.'

'I'll pay you,' she says. 'I don't mind.'

'I don't want money,' he says. 'It's not about money.'

She watches the speck of the Tiger Moth in the distance. 'Of course not,' she says.

'Imogen.' Jonathan is also standing beside her. 'What's going on?' He's wearing a maroon sweater, brand new, and sparkling white trainers. Imogen has never seen him out without a suit.

'Jonathan! What's happened to your clothes?'

'I knew you shouldn't have trusted Straker. Now look what's happened.' He's still calm and controlled, but there's a wildness in his eyes.

'It's insured,' says Doody. 'You insisted, remember?'

'What's going on?' he asks again, indicating all the people round them.

'It's complicated,' she says.

'That's obvious.'

They can still hear the drone of the engine in the clear emptiness of the afternoon sky.

'He'll crash it,' says Jonathan.

She's surprised by this. 'No, he won't.' But then she realises that she hasn't thought beyond this moment. What will he do? Will he come back here? If not, where will he go? 'No,' she says again, not sure if she believes herself. 'He'll just bring it back.'

As the plane disappears from sight, the people round her lower their heads and start to talk to each other again.

'That's it, then,' says a man in glasses. 'I knew nothing would come of it.'

'Rubbish,' says someone else. 'We confronted him. That's what we came to do.'

'Didn't get us anywhere.'

'Yes, it did,' says Carmen, the woman in black. 'He knows how we feel.'

'Actually,' says another, older woman, 'I feel better.'

'He said sorry.'

'No, he didn't.'

'Yes, he did. He shouted it lots of time before he took off.'

'You wouldn't have been able to hear that.'

377

'I heard it.'

'And me.'

'You must have been lip-reading.'

'Anyway, what else did we want from him?'

They are all slightly bewildered, shaking their heads, as if they've woken up from a collective dream.

'What do we do now?' says someone.

'Go home, I suppose.'

The little Indian woman who was so ferocious with the eggs is sorting out her bag, muttering to herself in another language. She gets out a pocket mirror, and applies lipstick meticulously, calm and contented. She straightens her sari, brushes her hands down the silk, rearranges her shoes and smiles to herself.

'That's it, isn't it?' she says, to no one in particular.

'He's coming back!' shouts a voice from the back of the crowd. Everyone goes quiet again, and Doody can just hear the sound, the hesitant putter of the little engine in the distance.

'There!' shouts a voice, and they follow his pointing finger. A minute speck appears in the blue of the sky far out to sea.

'See,' she says to Jonathan, grinning uncontrollably. 'I told you it would be all right.'

'That's hardly the point, is it?' he says.

What is the point? It seems as if they lost the idea of there being any point hours ago.

'Well,' says someone, 'we can check with him again, can't we? See if he's really sorry.'

'Of course he is. Why else would he come back?'

'Scared he'll crash.'

'Yes,' several voices are muttering, but it's not clear what they're agreeing with.

The Tiger Moth gets closer. It looks painfully precarious, tiny and fragile, far too primitive to fly.

'He's in trouble,' says Tony.

A sharp pain stabs Doody's chest. 'What do you mean?' she says.

'Listen.'

She concentrates very hard, and at first doesn't notice anything unusual. Then there's a faint cut in the sound of the engine, as if it's stopping and starting again. Like a cough, a clearing of the throat. 'What's happening?' Doody asks Tony, without taking her eyes off the aeroplane, fear making her voice sharp.

He hesitates. 'Don't know. Could be something, could be nothing.'

The Tiger Moth has nearly reached land, but just as Doody manages to breathe normally, it falters, pauses in the sky, coughs again, hesitates, and then there's silence. It hangs there, motionless, like a seagull on a thermal, waiting for a breeze, hovering, uncertain. It starts to sink, gliding first, then faster and faster, dropping towards the sea.

Biggles! thinks Doody. 'No!' she screams.

Nobody else is saying anything. It feels as if she's in a vacuum, just a shaft of light linking her to him, while everyone else round her fades into nothing.

She can just hear Jonathan's voice in the distance. 'He's coming down.'

'Come on!' She starts to run. They need a boat. He doesn't have to drown. 'Phone the police!' she yells to Tony as she runs. 'The coastguard, the helicopter-rescue service!'

People are following, but she doesn't care about them. Jonathan is beside her, struggling with his mobile phone. 'Which way?' she shouts. 'Where's he going to come down?'

'Near the harbour, I think. He can't be that far out.'

It's better if he comes down in the sea. There's a better chance of survival than if he lands on something solid.

Not good, crashing into the sea.

But at least you survive.

Depends if there are any rocks, how cold the sea is, whether he can swim, how long it takes for the rescue services to arrive . . .

The sea can't be that cold. It's a sunny day, the sky is blue, this is not the North Sea.

There must be rocks. That's why there's a lighthouse.

He'll miss them. He has to.

Doody races down the road to the harbour, faster than she's ever run before, her heartbeat deafening in her ears. She can't see the Tiger Moth any more. It must have crashed already. As they reach the harbour, other people from the village join them, wanting to know what's going on. Groups of them stand between the upturned, beached boats, all looking out to sea, shading their eyes against the glare. The tide is up, and water is lapping against the side of the pier.

They run along the pier, pushing through the crowds of spectators. 'Get out of the way!' Doody shrieks at them. They're enjoying it. They want to witness a disaster.

'There he is!' says Tony, pointing.

The Tiger Moth is a tangled, crumpled mass of wire, wood and fabric, awkwardly collapsed in on itself, hovering on the surface of the water. Even as they watch, parts are sinking below the surface. Doody can just distinguish a figure hanging on to a random strut of wood, and an enormous relief rushes through her. 'He's alive!'

'Can he swim?' says Jonathan.

What a stupid question. 'How would I know? I've never asked.'

A large rowing-boat is moored at the side of the pier, with a bewildered boy sitting in it. He's staring at the crowds of people in consternation.

A young man has already climbed down the metal ladder and now he jumps into the boat. 'What's your name?' he asks, with calm authority.

'Connal.'

'OK, Connal. I'm James Taverner. Can you row us out there?'

Connal looks frightened and uncertain.

Jonathan follows James into the boat.

'Hey!' says Connal, turning round in a panic.

'Get moving,' says Jonathan. 'You can't leave him there.'

'Wait for me!' Doody scrambles down to join them and the boat lurches alarmingly as she jumps in. Water laps over the side, soaking them all. Jonathan pulls her up beside him and she struggles into a sitting position. Gradually, the boat stabilises. Doody breathes in and out, afraid to move.

'I can't go,' says Connal. 'I'm waiting for my girlfriend.'

'So you'd rather see someone drown?' Doody shouts at him.

'But she'll think I've gone off without her.'

'She's got eyes. She can see what's going on.'

He still just sits there, like a child, stubborn and unmoving.

'Get on with it!' screams Doody. 'He may not be able to swim.'

'Wait!' There's a voice behind them and another person drops into the boat. They rock wildly again, and everyone grabs the sides in alarm.

'Stop it!' says Connal. 'This is my boat.'

'Will we be able to get one more in?' asks Jonathan.

'No!' shouts Doody. 'There won't be room for Straker.'

'That's who I'm talking about.'

At last Connal starts rowing.

'Hurry,' says Doody. 'It's sinking.'

They move slowly and the boat feels heavy and cumbersome. From a distance, the water looked blue and calm, but in reality it's very choppy, throwing them uncomfortably from side to side as they head into the waves. Doody clings to the side, trying to see where they're going.

The last person to jump in was Carmen. She sits rigidly on the back seat, white as a sheet, her eyes black and intense, refusing to look directly at anyone else, and there's something

381

frightening about her, a desperation, the single-mindedness that must have brought her here in the first place. James Taverner is more composed, his blue eyes steady as he sits easily in the front of the boat, turning every now and again to see where they are. He obviously knows about boats. He's like Harry when Doody first knew him. Calm, confident, in control. Well, appearances can be deceptive. He'll probably try to kill Straker as soon as they get near him.

It's difficult to tell if Straker is all right, although as they get nearer, they can distinguish the details of the wrecked aircraft. He's still there, leaning over a wing, hanging on to a strut, while the rest of the Tiger Moth continues to sink. Can he swim? Wouldn't he swim towards them if he could?

'Can we go any faster?' asks Jonathan.

'It's all right for you,' says Connal. 'I'm doing all the work.' There is something slow and laborious about him – an inexplicable lack of urgency, an inability to react with speed.

'Do you want me to take over?' says James Taverner.

Connal scowls at him. 'No.'

'Let me know, then. I'm ready whenever you want me.'

They're nearly there.

'Better be quick,' says Jonathan. 'If it all goes down, he might be sucked down with it.' As if he knows about these things.

Straker is staring around blindly, his face completely black.

'He's burnt,' Doody cries, in a panic.

'No,' says James. 'It's oil.'

'Oh.' But she doesn't feel relieved. Where has the oil come from?

'Straker!' shouts Jonathan. 'Over here.'

Straker turns towards them, but doesn't seem able to respond.

'What's the matter with him?' asks Doody.

'Don't know. He might be concussed, confused, hurt.'

'I'll get him,' says James Taverner, calmly. He bends down

and removes his trainers. Then he takes off his jacket, folds it neatly and puts it on top of his shoes. He stands up, balances himself against the rocking movement, and dives into the water. The boat almost submerges as he goes, then leaps up again.

He slices through the water with an easy, competent crawl. Once he has reached the aeroplane, he holds the wing and persuades Straker to drop down into the water with him. Then he lies back, holds Straker under the chin and pulls him to the boat. It's all very professional.

As they approach, Jonathan leans over to help pull Straker in. He puts out a hand to grab the side, and suddenly Carmen comes to life.

'No you don't!' she shrieks. She seizes an oar from Connal and waves it wildly through the air in an attempt to hit Straker on the head. It's too big and she can't manoeuvre it properly.

Doody throws herself at her. 'Stop it!' she shouts, and tries to pull the oar from her. Carmen pushes her away. Jonathan is struggling to get Straker on board. James is warding off the oar. Carmen swings it round again, screaming all the time. 'That's for Robbie, and that, and that!'

But she misses every time. Doody lunges at her and grabs her hair. The boat rolls to one side and she loses her grip as Carmen kicks her and scrabbles for the oar again. Doody grasps her legs and pulls her back, trying to contain her arms so she can't reach the oar. The boat rolls even further on to its side and they're tipped out into the sea.

They go down together in a flurry of fighting, frantic, swirling arms and legs. Then Doody loses all contact with Carmen as she goes on sinking, distracted by a great roaring in her head. She can't swim. She flaps her hands in panic and rises to the surface. As she comes out of the water she takes a huge breath to scream, but she goes back down again and the roaring in her ears is overwhelming. Gradually the sound subsides. She can feel herself falling and doesn't know how to stop it. A curious calm starts to settle over her, and nothing matters very much any more . . .

There is a pressure round her, resistance to her downward passage, strong arms pulling her. Someone has come to help.

She breaks the surface again, gasping for air, retching, spitting out the water, and she is supported this time. She gradually becomes aware that it's Jonathan. He pulls her to the boat, and more hands haul her in. She collapses on the bottom, coughing and choking.

Someone else is beside her, coughing in the same way, and she realises it's Carmen, no longer aggressive, limp and crying. 'Robbie,' she's whimpering. 'Robbie, Robbie . . .'

In the end, Doody puts her arms round her and pats her gently, as if she's a child, both of them shivering with cold, squeezed into the tiny space between everyone else's feet. Straker is at the back of the boat. James and Jonathan have climbed back in and Connal is observing everything in sullen bewilderment.

'Look,' says Jonathan.

The aeroplane is sinking. The top wing settles below the surface and it's only possible to see it in the dip between the waves. Then it tilts slightly, so the tip of the wing emerges again, points to the sky with a last moment of defiance before it sinks. Doody's dreams have just submerged with it. Now there are other things that concern her more. She starts coughing again, spitting out more water.

Jonathan looks wet, but unflustered and in control as if he does this sort of thing every day of his life. Straker is lying across the back seat, gasping for breath. One of his legs is bent backwards in an awkward position as if it's broken.

'Straker,' says Doody, between coughs, 'you weren't meant to wreck the plane, you know. You weren't even meant to fly it. When I said run, I meant run, not fly.'

He tries to open his eyes and the whites appear before the oil starts to drip down into them. He closes them quickly.

'I only wanted a short trip with my girlfriend,' says Connal miserably, as he starts to row back to the shore. 'I'm not really one for death and glory.'

'Well, now you're a hero,' says James.

As if to agree with him, a ragged cheer goes up from the shore. They can hear it rolling across the water towards them.

Doody climbs on to a seat. 'They didn't want you dead after all, then,' she says to Straker.

'I'm not going to make my meeting,' says Jonathan. 'I might have known everything would go wrong.'

'You never told me you'd learned to swim,' says Doody.

Carmen stirs in the bottom of the boat. 'Can I sit up?' she says.

Doody studies her for a second. She looks different, subdued, as if a light has gone out inside her. 'Depends if you're going to try to kill him again.'

'No,' she says. 'It's finished. I had to try – for Robbie.'

'Come on then.' Doody helps to pull her up.

Straker's head turns towards Doody again. His mouth opens and she can see his white teeth and pink mouth. 'Doody,' he says and smiles, shutting his mouth before the oil gets in.

Suddenly she feels good, although she's soaking wet and her Tiger Moth has gone.

The water slaps against the side of the boat. Connal's rowing seems more efficient as they head back for the harbour, cutting easily through the sea. The red cliffs are glowing in the afternoon light and their reflection glimmers on the water. It's just possible to see the stripes of the lighthouse on the next headland as it catches the sun.

Epilogue

Harry has been walking for three hours. He caught the train to Exeter and a bus, but then, rather than wait for a second bus, decided to walk – because he likes walking. He has a sleeping-bag with him, there's no hurry. You don't have any control over natural processes. He might have to wait several days.

He thinks of Alison at home, the welcoming atmosphere of her kitchen, people dropping in regularly, knowing that there's always food available. He thought at first that he would resent this sharing of Alison, the way she has so many friends. They tell her their secrets, ask her advice, want her approval. But what he actually feels is pride that, of all the people who like and need her, he's the one she chose. She took him in and offered him her home, so he's different and that's the only thing that matters in the end.

And she has never questioned it when he says he doesn't want to go abroad because he can't get a passport. He could be a criminal for all she knows, or an illegal immigrant.

'Harry Stanwick,' she said once. 'Whatever you want, we do it. No questions, no prying. We live together, we share, we're happy. That's it.'

One day he will tell her.

Harry adjusts his step to cope with a niggling nerve above his left knee that has bothered him ever since the accident. The extra weight he has gained in the last few years hasn't helped. He rolls towards the right leg until it feels more comfortable, then continues to walk, enjoying the comfortable rhythm of his stride.

'I want to see it go,' he said to her yesterday. 'I don't know why.'

'There'll be lots of other people there. You don't like people.'

'I know. But I want to see it go.'

She grinned at him, with the lopsided, knowing smile he loved. 'Go, then,' she said.

'Will you come with me?'

'What? Hang around in the cold? No way. I'll be here when you get back. Hotpot, I think, with some fresh lamb from the farm.'

'It may take a few days.'

'Don't worry. You can ring me. Then I'll start cooking.'

His stomach moves as he walks, and he knows he should stop eating so much, but he doesn't really care. He has come to believe that food is the path to happiness, and wonders why he never understood this before.

He walks across the uneven grass towards the lighthouse, passing more and more people, cars, motorbikes, television vans. There are men with cameras, professionals with tripods, and amateurs, media people, all of them talking to locals, tourists, visitors, observers like him who have travelled to witness the event. He stops a little way short and watches them all. He doesn't want to be noticed or interviewed. He puts up his hood and pulls the drawstring so that it covers his mouth. Once he feels secure he walks further on.

There's a police cordon well short of the lighthouse.

'Sorry, sir,' says a policeman, as he approaches it. 'You can't go any further. Not safe.'

'Any idea how much longer it will take?'

The policeman smiles. 'Any time now, the experts say. There again, they've been saying that for the last week.'

The lighthouse is leaning at a precarious angle, unbelievably still in one piece. The edge of the cliff is so close that it looks as if a child could push it over with a single finger. Harry stands for a long time, studying it. He's seen the pictures in the papers, and it's exactly as he imagined. He's not quite sure why it's so important to him to see it go into the sea. Something to do with his childhood, when he came here with his family, all his brothers, when his life was uncomplicated before he met Imogen. They owned a cottage further along the coast and they came every Easter, running along the clifftop every morning, until they reached the lighthouse. Then home for breakfast. It was a fundamental ritual of their life together until he went off to university and met Imogen. He used to have a photograph in his room – his family when young, posing, with the sea behind them. Happy, innocent.

The lighthouse is a symbol of all that's gone before, of the life he abandoned. When it falls into the sea, he hopes it will take his past with it, and demolish some of the burden that he has carried around with him for so many years. Once the cliff starts to crumble, you can't put it back together again, however much you want to. In the end, the whole thing collapses. Some things just can't be saved.

'I told you Magnificent would still come back if you didn't shut him in.'

He half turns, the voices quite close to him. He sees a tall, wiry man with a dark beard, streaked with grey, leaning on a walking-stick, and a short, sturdy woman next to him, picking up a Siamese cat. She has neatly cut grey-blonde hair, and her face is sharp and animated. As she talks to the man, her eyes are darting around, strong and intelligent. There's something about the way she stands there, her face cross, that makes him turn away quickly.

Surely not. He must be mistaken.

'He'll be all right. Cats are survivors.'

'Nonsense. Cats are not familiar with lighthouses collapsing.'

'Suleiman knows. We passed him on the way up here. Sitting up a tree, watching.'

'You didn't tell me. Why didn't you tell me?'

'You didn't ask.'

Harry remains still, his heart pounding. It's Imogen. He knows it's Imogen. The expression, the voice, the manner. But it's impossible. His mind whirls, he tries to remember how she looked when he last saw her, the physical details, and he can't remember. The more he tries to produce a picture, the more vague it all becomes. He has felt the responsibility of his abandonment of her for most of his adult life. More than the worry about his family. The day he stepped out of the crashed train and walked away, the guilt settled down over him like a blanket and it has never left him. He has always known that he should have gone back and identified himself, but when he turned away from the train he became someone else. He was being offered a new life. A new name, a chance to go the way he wanted to go, and although he sometimes wakes at night, almost suffocated by that blanket of guilt, he has never seriously considered giving up his accidentally acquired freedom.

She laughs. He doesn't hear what the man says that is funny, or what she says, but the sudden burst of hilarity is something he remembers right from the beginning, the laugh that fizzled and died quietly after they married. And he sees that she's all right. All his years of worry have been wasted because here she is, happy, married presumably, watching a lighthouse collapse with the same degree of interest as himself. She's survived. They have both survived and flourished away from each other.

The pile on the blanket of guilt is wearing thin, becoming threadbare. Maybe only his mother now prevents him tearing it into holes and discarding it completely.

People start to shout, and there's a loud roar, a rumbling vibration beneath his feet, like an earthquake.

'It's going!'

Huge cracks in the side widen and somehow slide apart, the top leans over at an impossible angle, and breaks off, disintegrating as it flies over the cliff, the violent crash mingling with the wind and waves. It collapses in slow motion, an enormous explosion, bricks spitting out and flying through the air. It's like an oversized Lego tower weakened by loose joints, pushed by a child-giant, rolling over, tumbling down into the ever-ready, waiting sea.

Acknowledgements

I would like to thank the following:

Chris, Pauline, Gina, Jeff and Dorothy for their energy, generosity and willingness to argue with me.

The Gateley family for not minding my presence on their upstairs floor while they get on with their lives.

Laura Longrigg for all her help, criticism and support. I didn't realise that having an agent would be such a pleasant experience.

Tony Podmore for an enlightening three hours going round the Shuttleworth collection of old aircraft at Old Warden, and for persuading me that a Tiger Moth would be more realistic than a Sopwith Camel. They do have a beautiful Sopwith Pup there, however. I was greatly tempted.

Mark Webb for teaching me how to fly without ever leaving the ground.

The charming retired lighthouse-keeper, whose name I don't know, who showed me and my daughter around the lighthouse on the Lizard on a very wet and windy day. I don't think he will remember us.

Carole Welch, Amber Burlinson and Hazel Orme, whose rigorous editing was much appreciated, and everyone else at Sceptre, who gave me such a good time when I first met them.

Ellen Seligman for her midnight telephone call that gave me some interesting new thoughts.

All those Biggles books from my past. The references to Biggles are the result of my respect and gratitude for a misspent childhood.

Alex and Heather for sharing my earlier success with such enthusiasm.